CIA agent William Danner had tried to leave the game. But
now a clever *mole* is sabotaging covert operations, threatening the survival of the CIA itself.

Danner will have to play the game one more time . . . will
have to outmaneuver the KGB, the mysterious group of
"old boys" fired by the CIA, and his own agency.

Playing alone, Danner must stop a frightening plot from unfolding at the highest levels of government.

If he wins, he only gets to keep on playing.

If he loses, he loses his lover, his daughter, and his own life.

The Children's Game

David Wise

PINNACLE BOOKS NEW YORK

THE CHILDREN'S GAME

Copyright © 1983 by David Wise

Pinnacle Books edition, published by special arrangement with
St. Martin's Press, Inc.

St. Martin's edition published 1983
Pinnacle edition/December 1984

ISBN: 0-523-42310-1

Can. ISBN: 0-523-43318-2

Printed in the United States of America

PINNACLE BOOKS, INC.
1430 Broadway
New York, New York 10018

9 8 7 6 5 4 3 2 1

To Joan

The Children's Game

CHAPTER
ONE

The bears, as expected, had been excellent. The lead bear came gliding into the ring on roller skates, pirouetting gracefully to the music. Another followed him, riding on a bicycle. Then more bears, roaring in on motorcycles as the crowd began to clap rhythmically. Filatov, their trainer, was a genius; the bears were the true stars of the Moscow Circus.

Seated in the first row, in the place of honor, Yuri Vladimirovich Kalin, general secretary of the Communist Party and president of the Soviet Union, joined in the applause. He loved the circus and enjoyed all the acts. The bears, the monkeys, the leopard that rode a horse. He had especially liked Tamara Krasnilova, the blond aerialist, who had appeared near the start of the show, working high above the arena without a net, in her little red tights. She had a nice ass.

Kalin looked at his watch. The moment he was waiting for was almost at hand. His favorite act of all. He turned to his right and patted his pudgy married daughter Galina on the knee. "*Milaya*," he said, grinning like a child, "my dear. *Seychas budut klouny*. Time for the clowns."

It was cold and gray in Vienna and the cobblestones glistened in the early morning rain. Stein leaned into the chill wind whipping across the Kernstockplatz and pulled the collar of his raincoat tighter around him.

The dampness went right through him anyway. He held the paper bag closer to his side to protect it from the misting rain.

1

He turned into the Haslingergasse, made his way along to an apartment house in the middle of the block, and pushed open the door.

The ancient building, now badly in need of repair, stood as a shabby reminder that Hernals had once been an upper-middle-class neighborhood. The glass-sided elevator, which required a coin to operate, was not in the parterre. Peering up the stair-well, Stein saw that someone had forgotten to return it from the top floor. He shrugged. He would walk, and it would save a schilling.

Very slowly, he mounted the stairs. He was a short man, al-most thirty pounds overweight. His flat was on the fourth floor, and it occurred to him as he climbed that it had been getting harder of late to walk up.

At the top landing he paused for a moment to catch his breath. He fumbled for his key, opened the door, and entered the apartment. Carefully, he took the *Kipferl* he had bought at Lainer's out of the sodden bag and put them on a plate. He lit the pilot light of the gas stove with a wooden match and turned on the burner under the espresso pot. From a wheezing refriger-ator, he removed half a stick of butter and put it on the plate next to the two croissants. Only then did he take off his wet raincoat, which was fraying at the sleeves, and sit down to wait for the water to boil.

It wasn't just the stairs, Stein reflected; everything was getting harder. It was not like the old days. During the four-power occupation, one could see the agents for each side sitting at adjoining tables at the Gartenbau and the other cafés along the Ringstrasse. In those days, he was prosperous; he had col-lected from everybody for the same secrets.

It was different now. The Americans were paying him only 1,200 schillings a month, less than $80. His wife, Lili, worked as a waitress in the Café Europe on Graben, and with tips, she made far more in a week than he made in a month. It was humiliating.

The coffee was ready; he fixed himself an *Einspänner*, add-ing a dollop of thick cream but no sugar. He sat down again heavily and sighed. The business wasn't fun any more and his health was not good. Yet, if all went well, this day could be a turning point. His life could change.

It depended on Vlasa, in her office only a few kilometers away on the Penzinger Strasse. This morning she would be changing the printed circuit board, a little four-by-six-inch plastic card. All she had to do was run it through her copying machine. In three seconds, the pattern of the delicate little ridges of metal would be captured. If she didn't lose her nerve.

He looked at his watch. It was still early. He would take the tram to the U-bahn and meet her in the gardens of the Schönbrunn at noon. In the meantime there was nothing he could do but wait.

As he ate his breakfast, he thought back over the past six weeks. Not without pride; he had handled the operation perfectly. He had shown her all of the city he loved so well. Vlasa was crazy about the Prater, so he even took her there, feeling conspicuous as they rode the ferris wheel, like a spy in a book. Afterwards, they rode to the top of the Donauturm and had drinks and looked out across the Danube to the Stephansdom and the Votivkirche.

They made love, when they did, at a flat the Americans had provided in Gersthof. He never told Lili, of course. Business is business and women would never understand.

He was jarred from his reverie by the doorbell. He was not expecting anyone; Lili was not due back from work until late in the afternoon. He went to the window, pulled aside the curtain, and looked down into the street. It was still raining. A yellow-and-blue moped was parked by the curb in front of the building.

He moved close to the door but did not open it. *"Ja, bitte?"* he asked.

"Postman," a voice answered cheerily. "Express letter for Herr Stein."

Stein opened the latch on the peephole, looked through, and relaxed. It was a postman in the familiar blue uniform and braided blue-and-white cap.

"Einen Moment, bitte," Stein grumbled, as he took off the chain and fussed with the lock. If Frau Kubic, the watchful *Hausbesorgerin*, permitted the mailman upstairs, it meant that a signature was needed. This morning he could not even enjoy his *Einspänner* in peace.

The postman, a heavyset middle-aged man, smiled and handed him a clipboard and a pen. "Sign here please."

As Stein wrote his name on the form, the postman reached into the leather pouch that hung by a shoulder strap on his left hip. He removed a .22 caliber automatic.

When Stein looked up, it was pointed straight at him. Instinctively, he stepped back and tried to slam the door, but he was not quick enough. The man fired twice. Stein heard no sound but felt the unspeakable pain explode within him as the bullets tore into his flesh, and then he fell to the floor. The postman stepped over Stein's inert figure, careful to avoid getting blood on his shoes, and picked up the clipboard and the pen. He calmly replaced the pistol in his leather pouch, closed the door, and left.

The helicopter dipped low over the river and the pilot gestured toward the scattering of houses set among the trees along the far bank. His only passenger, a big, blond man in a green business suit and aviator sunglasses, had to shout to make himself heard over the noise of the engine.

"Blackville?"

"Right. Won't be long now."

The pilot, a thin, weatherbeaten man, wondered about his passenger. He was an American, clear enough, nothing so unusual about that. But almost every outsider who flew in to this part of New Brunswick came to fish the Miramichi for salmon. His passenger wasn't even carrying a fly rod.

Moreover, the blond man had refused to land at the airstrip in Upper Blackville. He had demanded to be taken to a clearing in the wilderness, across the river and several miles from the town. Still, his money was good. When the blond man had chartered the Bell Jet Ranger at Fredericton, he had peeled off five $100 bills, U.S., from a fat roll.

The pilot swung the chopper south and followed the river upstream. Within a few moments he found the clearing the American had described and zoomed down at a steep angle toward the treeline. In the passenger seat, the blond man felt as though his stomach were floating. He took a deep breath. No matter how often he flew on these things, the landings always gave him the sensation of being trapped in an elevator that was falling too fast.

A few seconds later, the helicopter had decelerated to zero

airspeed and was hovering over the clearing, its whirling blades spewing grass, pine needles, and dirt in every direction. Off to one side, in a shadow of the fir trees, the pilot could see a man waiting beside a jeep. He had his arm up to shield his face from the flying debris. The helicopter set down in its skids, but the pilot did not cut the engine. The blond man stepped out, ducked his head to clear the blades, and ran over toward the jeep as the helicopter roared aloft.

The blond man, whose name was Larry Gates, got into the jeep beside the driver, a young Canadian in his early twenties. They rode in silence for a time along a bumpy dirt road. The grass and weeds were two feet high along the center line.

Gates looked at his watch. "How far to the camp?" he asked.

"Ten kilometers, sir." Like the pilot, the driver wondered why his passenger carried no fishing rod or other gear and wore a business suit. But he was not paid to ask questions. He said nothing.

Gates glanced at his watch continually. It was a nervous habit, since he knew the time. He was uneasy about the mission that had brought him from Washington to the remote Canadian wilderness. He was under great pressure from his superiors to succeed in his task. Moreover, the Canadians were touchy, and he knew that his presence on their soil had not been cleared with Ottawa. Officially, he wasn't even here.

They had been driving south, parallel to the river, which Gates knew was somewhere off to his right, although he couldn't see it. The road soon became deeply rutted and muddy, and the ride bumpier. They had driven about half an hour when he was able to make out some buildings through the trees ahead. In another moment, the driver slowed down and stopped.

Gates climbed out. He didn't bother to say goodbye. Before him were half a dozen rough-hewn log cabins set among the firs and maples, and a larger building that served as a combined lodge, dining room, and cookhouse. A terraced lawn dropped steeply toward the river below, and a long flight of wooden steps led down from the buildings to the water. The camp appeared empty, but Gates had expected that. It was mid-morning; the fishermen and their guides would long since be out on the river.

Gates headed down the steps. Two long, V-stern canoes were moored below along the bank, and a man, who looked to be a guide, was bent over one of them, tinkering with a small outboard motor. He straightened up as Gates drew near. He was short, but powerfully built, and wore chest-high rubber waders over blue jeans and a plaid shirt. His hat was made of black felt, with a broad, flat brim and a white headband into which he had hooked a dozen large salmon flies. The band was a kaleidoscope of red, blue, yellow, green, and gold hairs and feathers that danced in the sunlight as the man looked up. He had an open face, wide, simple features, blue eyes, and a ready grin for the stranger.

Gates was unsmiling. "Where's Danner?" he asked.

"Upriver a ways, by the mouth of the Cains," the guide replied. He spoke with a distinctive brogue.

"How do I get there?"

"I can take you."

He indicated the second canoe and Gates got into the bow. The guide sat in the stern and started up a little six-horsepower Mercury motor. Looking around, Gates for the first time realized how wide the river was. He guessed it might be five hundred feet to the opposite shore. The canoe moved along rapidly even though they were traveling against the current.

"I'm Johnny," the man volunteered. Gates grunted in acknowledgment.

They had gone about a quarter of a mile when Gates saw a man standing in waders about five feet offshore. The canoe veered toward him. As they approached, the man snapped his rod back, then forward, in a practiced motion, shooting out what Gates estimated to be sixty or seventy feet of line toward the opposite shore. The guide hugged the bank, careful to keep well clear of the line.

The canoe touched the shore, and Gates jumped out awkwardly, spattering mud on his shoes and trouser cuffs. The guide swung the boat around, waved, and headed back toward camp.

The angler in the water appeared to pay no attention to his visitor. He had his back to the shore, and was wearing an old khaki rain hat that partially hid his face. He was a handsome man, with even features and dark hair just beginning to be flecked with gray. He was a shade under six feet, with the muscular, athletic frame of a man who kept himself in good physical shape. As his line floated downstream, he slowly followed it with the tip of his rod. Then he began reeling in.

"Danner?" Gates peered forward, trying to catch a glimpse of the man's face. "I need to talk to you."

The man in the water turned for the first time and looked at his visitor.

"No shit," he said.

Gates licked his lips. He had known this wasn't going to be easy. "Can we talk?" he asked.

"You'll catch a hook standing there."

Gates moved to his left several feet. Danner twitched the rod and the line flew behind him. It stretched straight back thirty feet over the bank in a smooth arc. A split second before the fly could drop low enough to snag the bushes, he brought the rod forward gracefully and the line shot out over the river again.

"It's important," Gates pleaded.

"Not to me."

"For Chrissakes, Bill."

Danner did not reply. He seemed intent on watching the fly as it floated downstream just under the surface.

It was late June and the sun was hot. Gates was beginning to perspire in his city clothes. He loosened his tie, took out a handkerchief and mopped his brow.

"I thought—" Gates broke off and began again. "We thought you still cared about your country. Enough to listen."

Danner turned angrily. "I care," he said. "And I love my country. You and your friends damn well know that." His voice became calm again. "It's the agency I don't love."

Gates removed his jacket and laid it down carefully on the bank. "The agency's part of the country," he said. "We need your help."

Danner wondered why they had sent Gates as their messenger boy. He had worked with him on occasion, and considered him a mediocre officer. He wasn't dumb, just unimaginative. He was about the last person Danner would have chosen to send into the Canadian wilderness on a sensitive mission. A mission that was futile to begin with. Another misjudgment by the company. Not that it mattered. It had been seven years, and there was no way he was ever going back.

Danner whipped the line over his shoulder and cast forward again. He was using an 8.5-foot English fiberglass rod, a Hardy, which he preferred to the more expensive graphite models. To the end of the leader he had fixed a white Butterfly with a golden peacock herl and a Number 6 hook. On his reel, he had 100 feet of line and more than 300 feet of 20-pound test backing. If a salmon took, he knew, he might need every bit of that.

"You do any fishing?" Danner asked.

"Naw. Not really."

"There's nothing like it. I get out here on the river and I don't have a care in the world." He was reeling in again. "But I don't have much time for it these days. Camp's filling up now, and running it is a full-time job."

"You could hire someone else to run it for a while," Gates said. He mopped his forehead again. He was longing for a cold beer. "If you came back to Langley, I mean."

Danner continued as though he hadn't even heard Gates. "The Atlantic salmon isn't like any other fish. I mean we're talking about a fish that can run three feet long and weigh twenty-five pounds. When he strikes—well, an old-timer once said to me, 'It was like the first time she ever put her hand on it.' "

Gates laughed appreciatively. If Danner wanted to talk fish, he'd go along for a while.

"Nobody can really explain their migration," Danner said. "How they find their way thousands of miles from the North Atlantic to the tiny stream where they were born."

Gates eased himself down and sat on the bank. "Instinct, I guess."

Danner said, "One theory is that the salmon have an internal guidance system and use the earth's magnetic field to find their way."

"Maybe we should look into it," Gates said. "The Office of Technical Service has been experimenting with fish. They've been working with dolphins, seals, and otters, too."

"Why fish?" Danner asked.

"To see if they could be used as weapons."

"What kind of fish?"

"Electric eels, piranhas. They had the idea you could use the eels, for example, to stun people. Or kill them."

Danner cast again. The line made a whooshing noise as it shot overhead and flew out over the water. "My own guess is that the salmon go mostly by their sense of smell. But maybe they use the sun, and even celestial navigation. The truth is, nobody knows."

Gates tried again. "I've brought a message from Dixon Hadley."

Danner smiled. "It's a nice day. Why don't you just enjoy the scenery? When you get back to headquarters you can say you did your best, but I wouldn't listen. You'll earn points for trying."

Gates mopped his brow with his handkerchief. "Hadley wants you back. There's something wrong at the agency."

"There's a lot wrong. That's why I got out."

Gates took out a cigarette, lit it, and inhaled deeply. "You don't understand," he said. "This is recent. Just the last few months. The whole DDO side is tied up in a knot. Hadley's a wreck. I don't think he's getting more than four hours sleep a night. His hands are starting to shake."

Danner reeled in. He had decided to change the fly. He cut off the Butterfly, and from a little plastic box in his jacket pocket, he took out a Black Bear Cosseboom with a hook one size larger that would sink faster. The river was slightly high from the rain. It meant the fish would be moving along at a good clip, not lingering in the pools as long as they did normally, and the heavier hook might help. He tied the red-and-black fly on the line.

Gates lowered his voice, even though there was no other soul in sight except Danner. "I'm not authorized to give you any of the details," he continued. "But our operations are going bad all over the place. Agents are being blown right and left. The Sovs seem to know what we're doing even before we do it."

"In case you haven't noticed," Danner replied, whipping the new fly far out into the river, "I'm out of the business."

"Some of our people may get killed."

Danner made no reply. Some fat blue jays were scolding in a

stand of maples nearby. There was no other sound except the quiet murmur of the river.

"The pattern is clear," Gates went on. "Somebody high up with access to our operations is deliberately sabotaging them." He paused. "There's a mole in the agency. We want you to find him."

Danner had started to reply when the fish struck. Gently, he lifted the rod to set the hook and then he immediately released the knob of the reel as the fish began its run. The fiberglass rod was bent double.

"Jesus!" Gates jumped to his feet.

Danner fought to keep the rod up. The salmon was taking the line downstream. As the two men watched, the great fish leaped two feet out of the water, a shining flash of silver in the sunlight.

Gates gasped at its size. "I'll be damned," he exclaimed.

Danner was grinning. "He's a big one," he shouted. "Twenty-two pounds easy."

With enormous strength, the fish was still making its run downstream toward the ocean. It had taken the entire line and about half the backing, jumping several more times as it went. Each time the salmon leaped, Danner lowered the tip of his rod slightly to create a little slack. He watched the line intently, hoping the fish would stay downstream. That way, when he reeled in, the fish would be fighting the current as well as the line and it would tire faster.

Typically, Danner knew, a hooked salmon would make its run toward the ocean, just as this one was doing. Perhaps it was some ancient instinct that drove the fish toward the safety of the open sea. For the moment, Danner was upstream, where he wanted to be. But there was no way to control where the fish would go. Even as he watched, the salmon turned, creating a bell in the line, and headed back upriver. Danner reeled in fast to take up the slack.

Not even the drama of the struggle between man and fish discouraged Larry Gates. "You wouldn't have to come back for long," he pleaded. "Maybe only six months. A temporary assignment."

Danner had his hands full. He wished Gates would shut up.

"You don't need me," he said, reeling in steadily, keeping his rod up and his line taut. "It's a job for CI."

Gates snorted. "Counterintelligence, as you may have heard, is now under Al Dobbins, the celebrated plastic kitchenware manufacturer from Dayton. As near as I can see his head is made of plastic, too. He's totally useless."

Danner knew about Dobbins, a political appointee who had been a prominent figure in President Lansing Forbes' presidential campaign in Ohio. After the election, Forbes had allowed Brooks Jordan, a career man, to remain on as director of Central Intelligence. But, as part of the price, he had forced him to take Dobbins as his deputy. There had been a hue and cry in the press, but, predictably, it had died down and been largely forgotten.

Gates made no effort to hide his contempt. "He makes plastic cups, plastic spoons, plastic knives, plastic forks, plastic everything. He also makes an adjustable plastic bottle cap for soft drinks. One size fits all. 'Why lose the fizz?' Al's very proud of that one. But he couldn't find a KGB agent in Dzerzhinsky Square."

Danner was playing the fish confidently, easily, as Gates talked on. The salmon was still leaping, which was good, because it would tire more rapidly that way. Landing the fish would take about twenty minutes, Danner knew; the rule of thumb was a minute a pound for the Atlantic salmon.

"We need you," Gates said. "You were the best."

Gates was not exaggerating. In his twenty years with the Directorate of Operations, William Danner had become a legendary figure inside the Central Intelligence Agency. He was known, quite simply, as the best agent in the Clandestine Services. Until seven years ago when, without warning, he quit.

He walked out of his office at Langley, Virginia, headquarters one April morning, drove his car from the parking lot, and never went back. Not even to clean out his desk. His detractors in the Clandestine Services whispered that he was a burnt-out case. Danner knew better. He understood the reasons for his disillusionment. Some of those reasons were private and seared indelibly on his soul.

The salmon, on its upstream run, had reached a point about eighty feet away and almost opposite where Danner stood in the shallow water. Suddenly, the fish turned and rocketed down-river once more. Danner released the handle of the reel.

On the bank, Gates was still pleading. "We need a professional," he said. "And it's got to be an outsider."

"Fine. But not me."

"We can't trust anyone in the agency for this job," Gates explained. "He might turn out to be the mole. And you've been down this track before, with Nosenko. You know where the bodies are buried."

Danner shrugged. Yuri Nosenko, an intelligence officer assigned to the Soviet disarmament delegation in Geneva, had contacted the agency there late in January 1964, claiming to be a defector from the Komitet Gosudarstvennoi Bezopasnosti, the KGB. He was brought in by Arne Morefield, the base chief in Geneva. Fifteen days after Nosenko signaled the CIA from a pay phone, he was whisked over the Swiss border by car to Frankfurt and then flown to Washington. His interrogation, sometimes brutal, went on for years and in the end split the agency open like a machete slicing through an overripe melon. There were those who believed in Nosenko, and those who did not. The agency's counterintelligence staff had microscopically examined a tangled mosaic of old cases in an effort to prove or disprove Nosenko's bona fides. But the cases were an interlocking puzzle that led nowhere.

Danner wished Larry Gates would go away. He was trying to concentrate on the fish. Suddenly, it happened: the huge salmon turned and came directly at him. This was the hardest run to handle, because there was the greatest danger that the fish would move faster than the angler could reel in. With only a little bit of slack, the fish might throw the hook. Danner held the rod straight up and reeled in as fast as he could. He was lucky. After a few moments, the fish veered off toward the opposite bank. He appeared to be slowing down now, but just a little.

On the shore, Gates' tone changed from supplication to a kind of oily bonhomie. "You and I go way back, Bill. I suppose we could take a chance and give the job to one of our younger officers. But you know them. They're a whole new breed. They buy their clothes at Britches and hang around the singles bars in Georgetown. They'd rather play with computers than run agents.''

Danner grunted. He knew what Gates was talking about. But it made no difference. The fish was tiring, and he began reeling in again. It was hard work.

"There's not many of us left any more," Gates said. "Come back on temporary assignment. You can have whatever resources you need to do the job."

"No."

"Do it for your country."

"Horseshit. I've put in my time."

"We'll pay you whatever you want. The sky's the limit. There's an open budget for this one."

"Fuck off."

Danner was still reeling in, and now the fish, exhausted, turned over and for the first time showed its side. It was the moment to bring him into the net.

Gates continued to press his argument. "At least think about it."

"No."

Danner glanced over his shoulder at Gates and pointed toward shore. "Here, make yourself useful. Hand me that net."

Gates picked the net up and walked over to the water's edge. He stepped out onto a flat rock a couple of feet from shore and passed the net to Danner, who hooked it to his belt.

Gates remained on the rock. This was the part he dreaded. Danner was unpredictable. There was no telling how he might react. Gates spoke, but his tone was no longer friendly. "If that's your answer," he said abruptly, "then we'll poison the river and kill the fish. No more hotshot New York business executives will come here to fish at a thousand a week."

Danner, still playing the salmon, turned to stare in disbelief at the big man.

"We won't kill you," Gates went on, "but we'll ruin you. If you move somewhere else, we'll find you there, too, and do the same thing. Even if you give up and go into some other line of work, we'll find you and screw it up. It's simple. Either come back, or William Danner won't be able to earn a living—here, or anywhere else." Gates smiled. "You'll starve."

Twenty years. He had given them twenty years and it wasn't

enough. They couldn't let him live his own life. They had to track him down here in the wilderness, after seven years. With a threat to crush him. And he was supposed to be grateful that they weren't going to kill him.

The anger that had been building inside Danner broke with full force. "You dirty sons of bitches! What makes you think I won't go public and expose your threats? I'll go to the press if I have to."

Gates looked unperturbed. "Who would believe you?" he asked. "An ex-spy with a grudge against the agency and a wild story about killing fish. Acid rain kills a lot of fish up here; you won't be able to prove anything." Privately, Gates doubted that Danner, a lifelong covert operator, would go public in any event. But Gates drove the threat home: no matter what Danner did, or where he went, the agency would find him and destroy his ability to make a living. And Danner knew they could.

The salmon was only a few feet from shore now. Despite his fury, Danner was determined to land him. He would not let himself be distracted by Larry Gates, Dixon Hadley, or the whole damn agency. He unhooked the net and slipped it just below the surface of the water with his left hand. Holding the rod high in his right hand, he maneuvered the thrashing fish, head first, toward the webbing. It was a critical point at which many a salmon broke free. Danner dipped the tip of the rod down to give some slack to the line. Otherwise, he knew, the leader might whip the fish right back into the water. In another moment, the enormous salmon, bright silver and red, gills heaving, was landed.

"There," Danner said. "He's in the net."

Gates flicked his cigarette into the river. "Yes," he replied. "So he is."

CHAPTER
TWO

For three days after Larry Gates' visit, Danner tried to deal with it by putting it out of his mind, like a nightmare half-remembered on awakening. He busied himself with the routine of running the fishing camp. He played the genial host to his guests, drinking with them in the lodge after supper, swapping fish stories. He made sure that the more finicky guests were assigned the guides they had requested. He worked in the office. He took advance reservations over the telephone, answered the mail, and checked the food shipments and supplies as they came in from Fredericton.

And he spent as much time as he could with Carrie, his eleven-year-old daughter, who had come to spend the last half of June and all of July with him before returning to her mother in California. He took her fishing twice, and the second time she landed a respectable eight-pound grilse, a young salmon.

When Danner had walked out of the CIA seven years earlier, he was not sure what he would do. He knew only that he wanted it to be something far removed from the agency, both spiritually and geographically. He had always loved the outdoors, and his thoughts turned to Canada's maritime provinces, where he had worked at odd jobs during his summers at college.

With his savings, and a bank loan, he had been able to buy an old fishing camp near Blackville. It had been owned by a Minnesota corporation for the use of its executives, but it had been closed for several years. With his own hands, and local labor that he recruited, he had remodeled the cabins and slowly gotten the place back into shape. He had put in kerosene stoves, baseboard heaters, and running water. He lost money at first, but by the third year of operation he broke even, and now he was doing well.

Up until three days ago, the main economic threat to his livelihood had come from poachers, who were sporadically active along the river, and from the commercial fishermen laying their nets near Chatham, sixty kilometers to the northeast, where the river flowed into the sea. But he could live with those problems. They were serious, but not crippling. Now, out of his past, the agency threatened to destroy all that he had struggled to build for his future.

And the worst of it was they could. He knew that. Gates had not voiced an idle threat. In the middle of the night, Danner remembered a report he had read and sat bolt upright in his bed. The document had crossed his desk when he had worked at headquarters in the mid-sixties. The agency's laboratories had been secretly experimenting with drugs. One of the scientists involved had also been working on survival aids for CIA agents who might find themselves in a hostile environment—a jungle or a wilderness area. Almost by accident, the scientist discovered that LSD killed fish. He had dropped some in a stream; the fish acted erratically and were soon belly up in the water. The scientist enthusiastically proposed that from then on agents carry a little packet of LSD in their survival kits. There was one small hitch, Danner remembered—volunteers who ate the drugged fish were soon tripping out, seeing vivid colors and bizarre shapes, or screaming in terror. But the agency's scientists, whether they used LSD or some other drug or poison, could easily kill the salmon as they moved upstream through the half a dozen pools that Danner owned. And Gates was right—it probably *would* be blamed on acid rain, which had already destroyed the fish in nine salmon rivers in neighboring Nova Scotia.

Danner had told no one of Gates' visit, not even Carrie. The guide, Johnny Miller, asked no questions. He was a simple man, and once he had taken Gates to Danner, he had given not a moment's thought to the visitor, who he was or what he wanted.

But this morning, Danner knew, he would have to talk to

Carrie. It could be postponed no longer. She had breakfasted in the kitchen with Danner and the guides and then skipped off somewhere. It was a beautiful summer morning; there was not a cloud in the azure sky, and although it was still early, it was already warm.

Perhaps she had gone to play with her cat, Mr. O'Malley. He liked to hang around in front of their cabin, where, by this hour, a warming patch of sunlight would have filtered through the trees.

He found the gray-and-white cat, licking his paws and luxuriating in the sunshine. There was no sign of Carrie. He walked completely around the cabin and peered over the hill toward the canoes below, but she was not down at the landing, either. Then from above him, he heard a giggle.

He looked up and spotted Carrie, grinning at him from twenty feet overhead in the branches of a maple. "I should have known," he said, smiling back. "The monkey banana girl."

Carrie made a face. Danner could see she had split a green maple bud and had pressed it against the bridge of her nose. She was a pretty girl, with blond hair and light freckles under her blue eyes. But she was saved from looks that were ordinary by her perfectly straight, chiseled nose. She had gotten that from Francesca. She wore faded blue jeans, a cotton polo shirt, and old sneakers. By contrast, her hair was held in place by a barrette made of beads in the colors of the rainbow. She was still half tomboy, but fast growing out of that, Danner thought. In a few months she would be twelve.

"Planning to spend the morning up there?"

"It depends."

"On what?"

"On what we're doing today."

"Come on down," Danner said craftily, "and I'll tell you."

Carrie scrambled out of the tree, jumping the last four feet to the ground. "I wish you wouldn't call me the monkey banana girl," she complained, "I'm too old for that."

"Well, as long as you live in the trees, you might be mistaken for a monkey," he said, ruffling her hair. "If you'd rather, I could call you coconut head."

"*Dad.*" She picked up Mr. O'Malley and cradled him like a

baby, stomach up. He would not let anyone else hold him that way. She kissed the cat on the nose, and rubbed her cheek against his. "Okay," she said. "What's the plan for the day?"

"I'm taking you fishing," he said. "And you can pick the spot."

"Terrific!" Carrie ran to get her rod from the rack on the outside of the cabin.

Carrie knew the river almost as well as Danner, and over the years she had learned to cast a wet fly with almost as much accuracy as her father, although not as far. Danner was proud of her skill as an angler. More than that, the fishing was something that brought them together.

Danner got his rod, and they walked down to the landing. Johnny had left a canoe for him. Carrie climbed into the bow and Danner got in the stern. "Where to?" he asked, knowing what the answer would be.

"The Cains. Let's go beyond the little island, to the ledge."

It was Carrie's favorite spot on the river. The Cains was a tributary of the Miramichi, and there was a long, flat ledge of rock about two miles upriver where one could fish, and talk, and catch the sun. It was their special place.

He started the outboard and they were quickly under way. "Dad?" Carrie asked. "I heard the guides talking the other day. Are Cains river fish *really* different from the others?"

"Sure. Look close the next time you catch one and you'll see. They're more red, and more spotted."

It was, in fact, extraordinary. The adult salmon, after spending two to four years in the Atlantic, entered the Miramichi from the Gulf of St. Lawrence in the spring, moving upriver on their mysterious journey to the spawning grounds where they were born. At the mouth of the Cains, just beyond Danner's camp, some of them took a left turn, like commuters streaming off the Pomona freeway in the evening rush hour. Somehow they knew they were Cains river fish, and they continued on up to the headwaters to spawn. When fall came, the female salmon, using their tails, would begin to scoop out their long nests or "redds" in the gravel of the remote streams that fed the rivers of the province. The females would lay their thousands of eggs and the males would release their milt. The adults would spend the winter in the river, growing lean and dark under the ice, and the ones that lived would swim back to the sea in April. The eggs would hatch at about 68 degrees, a month later. The rivermen called the young salmon parr when they were min- nows. Those that survived the attacks of the kingfishers, mer- gansers, and ospreys would turn silver near the end of their second year and become smolts. By that time they were ready to make the journey to the open ocean, where they would grow into adults and migrate thousands of miles, beyond Greenland. Then, when it was time, they would find their way back to the Miramichi, and the cycle would begin anew.

At the ledge, Danner moored the canoe. For half an hour they fished, saying little. They were enjoying the morning to- gether, the warmth of the sun, and the summer sounds, the birds chattering in the branches and the cicadas somewhere high above them. Danner put his rod aside and sat down on the rock just watching Carrie fish.

"Dad?"

"Yes?"

"You know what I was thinking?"

"What?"

"I was thinking that summer is like a scoop of chocolate ice cream."

"How do you mean?"

"Well, it's delicious, but you have to remember to enjoy each mouthful. Otherwise, before you know it, it's over."

Danner nodded. "Life's like a summer, too."

She thought about that a moment, and said, "I really love it here so much. And the best part is I've still got five whole weeks before I have to go back to California."

"Carrie." Something about his voice, perhaps a little catch in it, made her turn and look at him sharply. "Carrie, come and sit down with me for a minute." She reeled in and came over.

"Carrie, you remember what I used to do, a long time ago."

"Sure. You were a spook."

"I was an intelligence officer."

"Same thing."

Carrie tossed a pebble into the river. It made a little ripple that soon vanished in the current. She asked, "Why did you stop being a spy?"

"I didn't like it any more."

"Was it because it was too dangerous?"

"No. That wasn't it."

Carrie scuffed the heel of her sneaker against the rock. "Were you a spy for a long time?"

"Yes, for a long time. Even before I knew your mother."

"I wish you would call her Mom, or Francesca. I don't know why you always say 'your mother.' "

"I'm sorry. You're right. I'll call her Francesca."

"You've never said much about it. Being a spy, I mean."

"No, I haven't." Danner hesitated. "There's something I have to tell you."

She tossed a stick into the water and watched it float away, but did not reply.

"A man came to see me on Monday. From Washington. I have to go back there for a while."

"To be a spy again?"

"Sort of."

"But you don't like that any more. You said so."

"Carrie, what do you like the least, or hate the most?"

She brushed a strand of hair out of her eyes, and thought for a moment.

"School. School sucks."

"I wish you wouldn't talk that way. You could just say you don't like it."

"It sucks," she said stubbornly. "That's why I don't like it."

"Your mother—Francesca, I mean—says you're doing well in school. She says you really do like it."

"Maybe once I'm there, with my friends, especially Jessica. It's the going back at the end of the summer I don't like. And I hate school because of Harvey Vogelmeyer. He's so gross."

"I don't think I know him."

"He's such a dip. I *hate* Harvey Vogelmeyer. He waits under the little wooden bridge on Olive Mill Road and when I walk by after school, on the way to Jessica's house, he jumps out and throws rocks at me."

"But in September you'll go back to school."

Carrie sighed, a long sigh. "Yes. I suppose so."

"Well, it's the same with me. I have to go back. I don't want to, but I have to."

"How long?"

"I don't know. A while. And that's the point. You can't stay here."

The blue eyes were suddenly red with tears. Danner put his arm around her, gently letting her head fall on his shoulder. "I can stay here," she pleaded. "I can take care of myself and just wait here until you come back."

"It might be weeks or months. I can't leave you alone in the care of a bunch of guides. They don't know anything about kids."

"Cookie can take care of me. And I can play with her daughter. She's my age."

"Mrs. Anderson has her own family over in Blackville. She's only here during the day to cook for the guests. You know that."

"But I don't want to go back to Santa Barbara now. I've only been here for two weeks."

"It's nice there in the summer. You can go horseback riding with Jessica. Maybe Richard will take you sailing."

"Richard's okay. But he's not my real father. And he doesn't like me climbing trees. He says I might hurt myself. It's not the same as being with you."

"I know."

"Then let me stay."

"I can't. We'll have to fly to Montreal the day after tomorrow. I'll put you on a flight to Los Angeles, and I'll go on to Washington. I'll call your mother this afternoon so she can meet your plane."

"Francesca."

"Sorry. I goofed again."

He wiped away her tears, and she recovered her composure. Suddenly, she broke out into a grin. She took the maple bud from her nose, leaned over, and stuck it on Danner's nose. Then she pushed back to admire the effect, and started giggling. "I'll bet James Bond never wore a maple bud on his nose," she said.

Danner laughed and took her in his arms and hugged her for a long time. "I love you, Carrie."

She held onto him tightly. "I love you, too, Daddy." In their embrace, the maple bud brushed loose and fell to the rock. Danner picked it up and stuck it in his shirt pocket.

"Why'd you do that?" she asked.

"It might bring me luck," he said.

CHAPTER
THREE

As he drove in from Dulles in his rental car, Danner's mood alternated between rage and resignation. One moment he was pounding the steering wheel with his hand, furious to find himself capitulating to the agency's threat. The next moment he was calm, assuring himself that he had thought through his options and alternatives. He didn't have any.

The rolling hills of northern Virginia swept by, luxuriant and green in the early summer. They were a bittersweet reminder of all he thought he had put behind him forever, no less painful for their beauty.

He turned on the radio and tried to get some classical music, but the announcer on WGMS was talking, as usual. At least that much hadn't changed in seven years. He flipped it off. He left the airport access road and swung onto the Capital Beltway, heading east.

They had, he realized, attacked him in his most vulnerable spot. Had they chosen to threaten him with physical harm, he would have brushed them off. It was not that he had any personal security in Canada; he did not, aside from an old Winchester Model 94 hunting rifle that he kept over the mantelpiece. But it was not in Danner's nature to yield to a physical threat.

His decision had been hard on Carrie. He thought, with a sudden surge of tenderness, of the scene at the Montreal Airport when he had put her on the plane to L.A. She had made him swear to take good care of Mr. O'Malley and to visit her in California in the fall. Then they had hugged, and kissed goodbye, and she had gone off through the gate with her flight bag, her tape recorder, a box of cassettes of the Beatles, several paperback books, a camera, her favorite Teddy bear, whose name was Edward, and a large chocolate ice cream cone in her right hand that had started to drip down the sides. He smiled at the memory.

But the present intruded. They were clever; they had threatened him not with physical harm but economic destruction. Unlike so many other veterans of the Directorate of Operations, he did not come from a moneyed Eastern family. He had grown up in the East, all right, in a little town in New England, but there was no money. He had always lived on his agency salary, and as a retired intelligence officer he received a monthly check from the government. But he depended on his income from the fishing camp. Even that was seasonal—the camp, under the strict fishing laws of the province, could only operate in April, and again in June through September. He had no independent means to fall back on.

And he had to live. There was the mortgage on the fishing camp each month, a payroll and other expenses to meet, and child support payments to Francesca for Carrie. If the agency waged all-out economic warfare against William Danner, he realized, it would win, and he would lose.

He was on the George Washington Memorial Parkway now, driving south along the Potomac. He let his mind wander back to the very beginning, when he had first arrived at the CIA as a Junior Officer Trainee. It was 1958, after Korea and before Vietnam. He was a gung-ho JOT, fresh out of Dartmouth. He had gone through the usual training period, including several weeks on "The Farm," at Camp Peary, Virginia. Every year, thousands of tourists drove by the gates of The Farm as they traveled the main road to Williamsburg, unaware that they were passing the CIA's secret training base for its agents. There, he had learned the tradecraft of a spy—bugging, wiretapping, microdots, dead drops, safe houses, brush contacts, cutouts, codes, invisible writing, lockpicking, letter opening, and all the rest. He had gone through rugged paramilitary training at Camp Peary as well. He had learned to shoot pistols, rifles, and submachine guns. He had loved it all.

He looked in the rear view. A girl in a red MG was tailgating him, impatiently trying to nudge him over into the right lane. Smiling a little, he slowed down slightly and made her go around on the right. He got a glimpse of her as she zoomed by, noting that she was dark-haired, pretty, and driving too fast.

Camp Peary seemed a million years ago. Danner wondered whether he could be the same man who had come off The Farm ready to save the Western world. It hardly seemed possible. His disillusionment had not come about suddenly, he realized; there had been no blinding light on the road to Damascus. Rather, it had been a gradual process, like aging. The changes were incremental and imperceptible.

In the beginning, he had thought he was protecting and serving his country, a Cold Warrior in the secret service of the United States. What could be more glamorous, noble, and exciting, and above all secret?

The first doubts had come with the trauma of Lisa's death in Berlin. He had been in charge of the operation. The damage assessment committee had officially absolved him of any blame. None of that would bring her back. He shook off thoughts of Lisa. But the ache, and the sense of loss, would not go away, ever.

Without even thinking about it, he had left the parkway at the CIA exit. In a moment, he was at the chain link fence and the guard booth. It felt strange to be stopping there, instead of flashing his badge at the guard and driving through, but he no longer had any agency identification.

"William Danner," he told the guard. "I'm expected." He handed over his driver's license without being asked.

The guard checked his manifest, gave him a little buff-colored map of the grounds, and directed him to the visitors' parking lot, explaining that it was a quarter of a mile up the road. "I know where it is," Danner said.

He turned left and in a moment or two the grayish-white concrete headquarters building came into view on the right through the trees. He passed the north lot, then turned right and drove around the green quadrangle in front of the main entrance. He parked in the visitors' lot and got out. The building looked dirtier than he had remembered it; even in the countryside, the pollution was taking its toll. He walked up the front steps and under the vaulted concrete portico.

To his right, the domed headquarters auditorium lent a Martian atmosphere to the grounds; it always reminded him of a white beehive from outer space. He looked at the bronzed statue of Nathan Hale tucked discreetly in the corner just north of the entrance. He noticed the pavement was crumbling around the base. Headquarters was getting a little seedy.

He opened the door and went inside the lobby, crossing the big gray-and-white seal of the Central Intelligence Agency inlaid in the marble floor. He glanced at the inscription carved in the stark, white Georgia marble on the wall to his left: "And ye shall know the truth and the truth shall make you free." He smiled inwardly at the irony.

Danner glanced at a display panel just beyond the seal to see what was playing that night. The CIA had its own movies for the entertainment of its employees. A placard announced that *The KGB Connection* was showing at 9:00 P.M. in the headquarters auditorium.

At the guard desk, he was stopped by a woman in a blue uniform. That was new; the guards were all male when he left seven years ago. Also new were the four white-and-red computerized badge-reading machines beside the little gates that barred his way. The guard examined his driver's license, checked a list of names, made a phone call, and finally waved him up a short flight of stairs to the reception lounge. There, he signed in and a clerk handed him a V badge, which he clipped to his lapel like any visitor.

A blond woman was waiting for him. "Mr. Danner?" she asked. "My name's Melinda."

They walked through a small anteroom and into a second room hidden behind it, where they waited for the director's private elevator. They got on and she punched seven. Senior staff were allowed to use the private elevator, Danner knew, except when the director was aboard; then his security man turned a key so that the elevator went only to seven and would not stop at intermediate floors.

They got out. The elevator opened into the director's outer office, but they walked down the hall to a door that said: "Deputy Director for Operations." Despite the innocuous-sounding title, the DDO was the man in charge of all covert operations and espionage for the CIA around the globe. He was one of the most powerful men in the world; yet his name was virtually unknown outside these sterile, guarded corridors.

As Danner entered the office, Dixon Hadley was rising from his desk, smiling broadly.

"Danner," he said. "Good to see you."

The DDO extended a moist hand, and Danner shook it. He immediately wished he hadn't. Hadley waved him to a walnut chair with orange Naugahyde padding, came around the desk, and sat down opposite him. The DDO was a somewhat heavyset man in his fifties, with thick, horn-rimmed glasses that accentuated his fussy, academic manner. He had, many years earlier, taught philosophy at Yale, but he had given up the good, the true, and the beautiful for the darker ambiguities of the Clandestine Services. He was stoop-shouldered, and beneath his sandy hair, his face was permanently pink and flushed, as though he were a heavy drinker, which he was not.

The DDO's penthouse office was furnished in executive modern, with a lot of dark woods and chrome. The east wall was entirely glass, and the morning sunlight poured in. Sitting and squinting in the same office years ago, Danner remembered, it had struck him that the darkest place in the agency was incongruously bright.

"Well," Hadley began with a satisfied air, "we were so very pleased that you've thought things through and agreed to come back."

Same old Dixon, Danner thought. Always so polite, with his commons-room manner, even when he was ordering an agent terminated, a prime minister blackmailed, or a government overthrown.

"I'm here," Danner said simply.

"Aaarwk! Wanna eat?" It was Hadley's blue-and-gold macaw, in a cage by the picture window.

"Be quiet, Socrates," Hadley ordered. To Danner, he said, "You know, he's always perfectly calm—a model bird—until we get a visitor. Then he fusses."

"You could try leaving him home."

"Oh my, no. This is a lonely job." Hadley smiled and surveyed Danner. "I must say you look wonderful. You've apparently been thriving in the outdoor life."

"I'm okay."

"And your family is well? The little girl would be about fourteen now?"

"Eleven."

"Yes, in any case, you haven't remarried?"

"No."

"Fine, fine. Well, I suppose in some ways that will make your task here easier. No encumbrances, as it were."

Danner was silent, waiting for the DDO to get on with it. A nervous man, Hadley had a habit of chewing on a pencil, holding it sideways in his mouth. Danner thought it made him look a little like a golden retriever showing off his favorite stick.

The deputy director cleared his throat. "Well, as Larry has undoubtedly told you, we've been having a bit of trouble."

"More than a bit, according to Gates."

Hadley sighed. "In point of fact, a great deal of trouble, I'm afraid." He chewed on the pencil furiously. "We thought that perhaps you could help." Danner noticed that Hadley's hands really were shaking. Gates had been right about that.

"To come directly to the point," Hadley went on, shifting forward in his chair, "our operations are being blown."

"Where?"

"Everywhere. In the past ten months, we've had ops go bad in Vienna, Madrid, Tokyo, Bujumbura, Buenos Aires, and several other places."

"With what result?"

The DDO shook his head miserably. "Different in each case. Sometimes the Soviets have been tipped off. Sometimes our agents have been rolled up. We had one shot in Vienna."

Socrates was scratching noisily in his cage. Danner waited for Hadley to continue.

"In Tokyo, the first secretary of the Soviet Embassy, who was actually a KGB man, was all set to defect to us. McIlhenny was handling the operation, a good man."

"Yes, I know Steve."

"Well, at the last moment, just when everything was ready, the Soviets whisked the target into an ambulance that had pulled up in back of their embassy. He was seen strapped to a stretcher, and not moving. Drugged, of course. They drove straight to Narita Airport and put him on an Aeroflot jet for Moscow.''

"With a connecting flight to the Gulag,'' Danner observed.

"No doubt. Sometimes, the operations aren't blown to the Sovs, but to the press. That happened in Madrid.''

"Same difference.''

"Yes.'' Hadley was gnawing on his pencil, hesitating. Then he leaned forward and lowered his voice. "There's a peculiar and extremely awkward aspect to the whole thing.''

Danner raised his eyebrows questioningly.

"In each city where an operation has been blown, a former agency officer has been seen. Or his personal trademark has been evident.''

Danner could not suppress a faint smile. He was not a man who was easily surprised. But he had not expected this. "You mean a DDO officer, of course? An old boy.''

"Yes. Yes. Exactly. One of our own.'' Hadley looked really distraught. The pencil was clenched immobile between his teeth; he wasn't even chewing it.

Danner was becoming intrigued, in spite of himself. "What sort of trademark?''

"I was coming to that.'' Hadley was at his most professorial. Conducting a seminar for one, Danner thought.

"Vienna station has been running an agent for several years, code name MS/SKYLARK, true name Max Stein. He's a low-level agent, long past his prime. We keep him on because he still has some contacts in the eastern European community, going back to the days of the four-power occupation. What he provides now is mostly chicken feed. You know—the third secretary of the Hungarian Embassy is bouncing a nightclub dancer on the Zirkusgasse and has a wife and three kids back in Budapest. That sort of thing.''

"Ho hum.''

"Yes, most of the time. But about three months ago, he stumbled into something. He was trolling for secretaries from the Czech Embassy. The embassy is on the Penzinger Strasse, two blocks from the Schönbrunn Palace. He figured that when the weather was nice, some of the secretaries might eat their lunch in the palace gardens. They're very beautiful, you know. The gardens, I mean.''

"So that's where MS/SKYLARK brought *his* lunch.''

"Precisely. Stein showed up with his brown bag every day for two weeks, and nothing happened. Then, just as he was about to give up, bingo.''

"He got one?''

"A beauty. A homely, thirty-five-year-old woman named Vlasa Radek, a butcher's daughter from Bratislava. Unmarried, and no prospects.'' Hadley paused for effect. "And she worked in the code room.''

Danner whistled. The macaw, thinking it was meant for him, whistled back.

"Shutup, Socrates,'' Hadley said.

"Aaarwk!'' the bird screeched. "Top Secret! Top Secret!''

"The woman actually sat down on Stein's bench,'' Hadley continued. "Talk about incredible luck.''

"It was love at first sight,'' Danner offered.

"Just about. Stein struck up a conversation and gave her one of his cards. The card said he was in the import-export business. Naturally, he started romancing the girl.''

"Naturally.''

"They met again the next day and went on the tour of the palace together. She was looking for a father figure, the companionship of an older man who would take her to dinner, take her to bed, flatter her, and most of all, pay attention to her. It was all very *gemütlich*.''

"Who was handling him?''

"Tyler Ashford. He's under consular cover in the embassy. He told Stein not to rush the girl, but Stein knew that. He took her to concerts, museums, dinner, to the opera, the cinema, and the Prater. There were assignations in one of our safe houses. An apartment actually. He told her it belonged to him.''

"He's married, then?''

"Oh yes, his place would have been out of the question. His wife's a waitress, Lili, I think is her name. No children, or they've long since grown and gone.''

"When did he make his move?''

"Tyler made him wait a month. But you don't want to wait *too* long, either. You know how these things are.''

"Yes," said Danner, "I know."

"Stein waited until the right moment. Then he told her he wanted the circuitry on the code machine."

"How did she react?"

"She was shocked, of course, and scared to death. But he told her he had a partner who was manufacturing code machines for commercial use. He gave her some double talk about how diplomatic codes were so much more sophisticated, and if only he knew the wiring on the Czech machine, they could get the edge on their competitors."

Danner looked skeptical. "And she believed that?"

"She wanted to," Hadley said. "It took a while, but in the end, she agreed. The Czech machines don't have microchips. They still use printed circuit boards; they're probably cast-off Soviet equipment. Once a month, they change the circuit board."

Danner could visualize the board, a little plastic card about one sixteenth of an inch thick, laced with strips of metal forming slightly raised ridges. Its circuitry formed the heart of the code machine. Even one board would provide invaluable clues to the workings of the machine.

"What did Stein tell her?" Danner asked.

"It was her job to change the circuit board on the twelfth of each month," Hadley explained. "All she had to do was get it to a Xerox machine."

"Didn't they change the keys for each message as well?"

"Of course. But he asked her to bring out a few plaintext messages. To help him understand the machine, he told her. Once we had the copy of the circuit board, NSA could have cracked the code by comparing the plaintext messages to our intercepts."

"How was she going to get the stuff out of the embassy?"

"On her lunch hour, in a brown bag. She would meet Stein in the gardens at noon. They didn't go there often after their first chance meeting, for fear of arousing suspicion. But they would eat lunch there again this time, and MS/SKYLARK would gather up the trash afterward to dispose of it."

"And we'd have our copy of the circuit board, covered with mayonnaise."

"Yes, only it didn't work out that way. On the morning it

was supposed to happen, our Austrian friend was alone in his apartment. He answered the doorbell, signed for a special delivery letter, and was shot in the genitals.''

''Ugh.'' Danner involuntarily covered his vitals with his hand. ''Did he live?''

''Yes, just barely. His balls were completey shattered, of course. And one of the bullets severed the nerves in his leg. It was hours before his wife found him, lying unconscious on the floor, bleeding. He's permanently crippled now. Gets around in a motorized wheelchair. We bought it for him.''

''That was generous.''

''We thought so. At any rate, the point is that the fake postman used a .22 caliber pistol, the weapon of choice for professional hit men. The impersonation of a mailman, the caliber of the gun, and the, ah, area of the body chosen as the target are all quite familiar to us.''

''I see.''

The DDO leaned forward. ''The hit had Nick Rossi's signature.''

Danner bit his lower lip. He mentally pulled Rossi's file. Nicholas Aldrich Rossi, age about fifty. Skilled marksman. Princeton graduate. Mother American, of Eastern establishment family. Father, Giovanni Rossi, Italian aristocrat and heir to a Milanese automotive fortune. Out of the agency now, but for his last several years at CIA, used when it was necessary, as it sometimes was, to ''terminate with extreme prejudice.'' A gentleman killer who wore white gloves and drove a Ferrari.

''So that was the trademark?''

''Yes. There's no question it was Rossi.''

''And who was seen in Tokyo?'' Danner asked.

''Tracy Thatcher. Thirty-six hours before the defector was set to come out, Tracy checked into the Okura Hotel, registering as the representative of an American business firm, Eklund Consultants International of San Francisco. There's no such company, of course.''

''When did Tracy retire?''

''He didn't. He was fired by Admiral Turner in the Halloween Massacre in nineteen seventy-seven, a few months after you left us.''

''And someone was spotted in Madrid, too?''

"Yes. Kermit Gardner. He came through as a tourist the week before a very embarrassing story about our operations surfaced in *Mundo Obrero*, the Communist Party weekly. Gardner was put over the side in seventy-seven, at the same time as Thatcher.''

It had become apparent to Danner, as he listened, that the old boys were loose. These were the now-aging spies who formed the heart and soul of the agency during the 1950s and 1960s, the high-WASP, often wealthy graduates of the best Eastern prep schools and the Ivy League. Many of them had served under General William J. ''Wild Bill'' Donovan in the Office of Strategic Services during World War II. After the war, they had gone to work for Allen Dulles at CIA.

Others, Danner knew, had been recruited during the postwar years on the campuses of Harvard, Yale, and Princeton. There had been an enormous attraction and great glamour in secret work in those days. And the CIA appealed as well to the puritan heritage of these scions of the Protestant establishment, to the sense of service and duty that had been inculcated into them since childhood.

It was this group of men, bound together by their class values, old school ties, and supreme self-confidence, who formed the core of the Directorate of Operations, or Clandestine Services, as the agency's dirty tricks department was also known. Aside from their common backgrounds, they shared a belief that the ordinary rules of morality, the rules that governed society as a whole, could be set aside by them in the higher interest of the state.

By 1977, however, the old boys had fallen upon hard times. Congressional investigations, news stories, and a presidential commission had focused the unpleasant spotlight of publicity on abuses by the CIA and the intelligence community—drug testing on innocent Americans, wiretapping, and plots to assassinate world leaders, some involving the Mafia.

In the shakeout that followed, more than eight hundred old boys were said to have been dismissed, forced to retire, or otherwise booted out of the Clandestine Services. The action had been swift, unexpected, and somewhat mysterious, Danner remembered. He had left Langley five months before it happened. The firings took place on October 31, and so became known as the "Halloween Massacre."

To the outside world, it was not much of a story. But within the secret confines of the CIA, the results were cataclysmic. Some of the most powerful secret agents in the world had been swept away in the tidal wave of dismissals. Men who had run important divisions and bureaus at headquarters, experienced agency hands who had been station chiefs, who had lived like royalty in remote corners of the globe, were suddenly unemployed, reduced to sitting around the Metropolitan Club, drinking too much, and railing at the injustice of the world.

Against that background, the implications of what Hadley had been telling him were mind-boggling. Danner asked, "What do they want?"

"We don't know."

"Who's running them?"

"We have our suspicions, but again, we don't know. I'm afraid that's one of the things we want you to find out."

"But not the most important thing."

"No. Quite obviously, someone inside the agency—someone with access to our plans for covert operations—is betraying them. We have to find him."

"Or her."

"Yes. I suppose, these days, it could be a woman."

"There are still some old boys inside the agency. They weren't all fired, were they?"

Hadley turned an even darker shade of pink than usual. "Well, I suppose I would qualify as one," he said with an awkward laugh. "No, not all of them walked the plank. But we've already fluttered two dozen people." Hadley spread his hands in a gesture of helplessness. "The polygraphs say they're all innocent. Including me, I might add."

Danner looked out the window at the thick cover of trees that surrounded the headquarters. He wondered why the agency bothered to rely so heavily on lie detectors, since anyone who took a Miltown could beat the machine. The polygraph was no match for a 400-milligram dose of meprobomate. He wished like hell he were out on the Miramichi.

"I'll come back for a while," he said. "But only on my own terms."

Hadley brightened. "Name them," he said.

"One, a free hand to poke anywhere inside the agency and get anything I want. Two, complete independence to do the job; I'll be taking orders from no one. Three, the director must agree to my terms. And I want to hear it from him."

"Done." Hadley arose. "I'll take you in to see him right now." He led the way down the hall to the director's office next door.

"As far as money is concerned," Danner said on the way, "whatever my old job pays now will be okay."

"Fine, fine."

They walked into the director's reception area. In the glass booth on the left, a plainclothes bodyguard from the Office of Security watched them and nodded to Hadley. In a moment, they were ushered into the director's office.

The office was huge, fifty feet long and twenty-five feet wide, with floor-to-ceiling picture windows covered by white metal venetian blinds, which Jordan had drawn. It was furnished in bright colors, and the walls were paneled in blond wood. A three-dimensional ceramic seal of the CIA hung on the wall to the left of the director's antique mahogany desk. Two sofas were set at right angles in the corner, with a pair of apricot-colored armchairs in front of them. At the far end of the room there was a large conference table with blue padded leather chairs, and an American flag.

Danner had not seen Brooks Jordan since President Forbes had named him director of Central Intelligence. As they entered, he arose from the black leather swivel chair behind his desk. He was tall and white-haired with cold gray eyes that looked at the world through rimless glasses. Jordan was heavier than Danner had remembered him, and his hair seemed whiter. But it had been seven years.

"Hello, Bill," the director greeted him, shaking hands. "It's really good to have you aboard again."

"You didn't give me much choice."

The director looked pained. "I'm sorry about that," he said. "I do apologize. But as Dixon's undoubtedly told you, we have rather a large problem." He sat down and motioned them into chairs by the desk.

"He's consented to come back," Hadley explained quickly,

"but he wants your personal writ to delve anywhere in the house, and to operate independently."

"Agreed," Jordan said immediately. He swiveled in his chair and gazed at the CIA seal on the wall, hands clasped in front of his chest. "Your job, put simply, is to find the mole."

"And when I do?" Danner asked.

The director turned back and smiled. "Leave that to us."

CHAPTER
FOUR

A week later, Danner had settled in. He rented a one-bedroom apartment in Alexandria near Shirley Highway, about twenty minutes from the agency. The apartment was furnished in nondescript modern, with a couch and matching chairs covered in aquamarine stripes. Danner thought it looked like the waiting room of a moderately successful dentist.

The agency provided him with a car, a gray Skylark, for the duration, which he parked in a space behind the apartment building. He had a telephone installed with an unlisted number. At a shopping mall nearby, he bought an answering machine, made a trip to the Safeway, and filled a shopping cart with food and household supplies. He bought a lot of frozen dinners. At the liquor store next to the supermarket, he got a liter of J&B Scotch.

At headquarters, he was given a small office in an obscure DDO subsection on the fifth floor, off the C corridor. He was issued a new identity badge, which showed his photograph against a blue background, and he was assigned a parking space on the VIP/visitors' lot, a privilege he had demanded and gotten from Hadley. He was also issued a set of formal agency credentials, which came in a leatherette folder with a gold CIA seal on the cover. It opened up like a card case and contained his picture inside in color, his physical description—height, weight, hair and eye color—and Brooks Jordan's signature. It was called a Permanent Contact Credential and could be flashed to outsiders when strictly necessary. It was accompa-

nied by a memo from the Director of Security warning of dire
penalties if it was lost.

In the halls, and in the cafeteria, Danner ran into a few of his
old colleagues. To those who asked, he said simply that he was
back on TDY doing some consulting. Several people he passed
in the corridors nodded absently at him, seemingly unaware
that he had been gone for seven years.

He missed the Miramichi, and he worried about the fishing
camp. He had left Andy, his head guide, in charge. He telephoned him in mid-week to see how he was doing and to ask
him to forward any personal mail to the address in Alexandria.
He also gave Andy his phone number but instructed him not to
give it, or his address, to anyone.

He missed Carrie a lot. On Tuesday night, he picked up the
telephone in the apartment and started to call her, but then put
the receiver down again. It would be better to allow her a little
more time to readjust to being back with Francesca and her
stepfather.

On Thursday, after leaving headquarters, he drove to
Georgetown and bought three T-shirts for Carrie at Com-
mander Salamander on Wisconsin Avenue. He also bought her
a new fishing pole at a shop in Bethesda and had everything
mailed to California for her birthday.

By Friday, he was feeling lonely and at loose ends. It was
pouring outside; a summer cloudburst, accompanied by thun-
der and lightning, drenched the capital. Instead of driving
home, he got off the parkway at Arlington and pulled up in
front of the Jefferson Davis Towers, a red-brick apartment
building that looked like all the others in the neighborhood.

There was a desk in the lobby, tended by an elderly blue-
haired woman wearing rhinestone glasses. A small sign on the
counter said: "Visitors Must Be Announced."

"Would you ring Mr. Green, please?" Danner asked.

The woman peered at him over the top of her glasses, a look
of disapproval that Danner decided she reserved for all strang-
ers. "Name?"

"Danner. William Danner."

She announced him, and he took the elevator to the sixth
floor. Sam had the door open and was standing halfway out in
the hall before he reached the apartment.

"Bill," he said, his pudgy face beaming. "I can't believe it. Come on in. Have a drink, a piece of cheese." He gestured toward the cocktail table, where some cheddar and crackers sat next to a half-finished bottle of beer.

"Hello, Sam," Danner said. "Nice of you to let me come in out of the rain." He surveyed his friend, a short, thickset man with dark hair, bushy eyebrows, and the beginnings of a pot belly. Danner shook his head, disappointedly. "You gained a little weight, Sam?"

"No way, I'm losing," Green remonstrated. Then, remembering that this was Danner's standard play, he said, "You *mamzer*. Wandering for seven years in the wilderness and you come back still peddling the same old bullshit."

Danner laughed. He was very glad to see Sam, who was perhaps his closest friend in the agency. Yet in those seven years he had not even sent him a postcard. It was Danner's way.

"Sit down, sit down," Green said, indicating an armchair across from the couch. "You still mainlining Scotch?"

"On the rocks, with a twist of lemon," Danner said, ignoring the insult. Actually, he did not drink a lot, except when his leg bothered him. He had twisted his knee badly in Berlin, more than twenty years before, and found that Scotch was the best way to ease the pain. Or so he told himself.

Green bustled about in the kitchen, getting the ice. Then he joined Danner in the living room and handed him the drink. He poured out some more of his beer and raised his glass. "Cheers, you bum," he said.

"Cheers."

"Now, tell me, what in the world blasted you out of the north woods?"

"I was called back in for a little consulting." Danner rattled the ice cubes in his glass. "There are some problems in my old shop. More I cannot say, and even that's too much."

Green waved the subject aside. "I've already forgotten it. But I'd give anything to know how they got you back."

Danner took a sip of his drink. The damp weather wasn't good for his leg, and the Scotch felt good going down. He forced a smile. "Gentle persuasion," he said. "Tell me, how are things at Mother K?" Danner used the insiders' jargon for the CIA, originally derived from KUBARK, the cryptonym for the agency.

"Very interesting," Green said. "We've got some birds up there now that are shooting incredible stuff. Even I have trouble believing what they're bringing back." Sam was a photo interpreter for the agency and one of the best. His job was to analyze the pictures, magnified many times, that were taken by U.S. spy satellites whirling overhead in outer space. His specialty was the Soviet Union. If the Russians changed the location or configuration of any of their nuclear missiles, Sam Green would know about it within twenty-four hours.

Sam said, "We're getting fantastic detail of Kalin's dacha, outside Moscow near Zhukovka." Yuri Kalin, at age seventy, was still firmly entrenched as the leader of the Soviet Union. "The photos show him cavorting with his mistress, who wears a purple bikini, or nothing at all." Sam giggled. "She's really stacked."

"I didn't know you guys were shooting X-rated stuff these days."

Green laughed. "You don't know how right you are," he responded. "There's a solarium on the roof, and that's where they get it on." Sam paused for effect. "Using micrometry," he said triumphantly, "we've been able to calculate the exact size of Kalin's dong."

Danner smiled indulgently. "Sam old Sam. Always something new."

"Keeps the job interesting. But what about you? Do you ever miss the business?"

"Never, Sam. I put it behind me. At least I thought I had until now."

Green said mildly, "I was never sure that a fishing camp would be enough to hold you after the company."

"I like it," Danner said. "It's what I want."

"And Carrie, how is she?"

Danner smiled. "She's eleven, almost twelve, and a terrific kid. She loves fish and horses. Boys will come next, I think."

"Do you see her often?"

"Not as much as I'd like. She lives with her mother in California. She visits me every summer, and I try to get out there as much as I can."

"You got her picture?"

Danner took a snapshot from his wallet and handed it to his friend. "A real nice kid," Green said, studying it professionally. "Real nice. Fortunately, she looks more like her mother."

"Thanks a lot," Danner said. "Francesca's remarried, by the way. To a man named Richard White, a lawyer who owns avocado ranches. They live very nicely, in a house up in the hills in Montecito. It's a little fancy for my taste. But Carrie seems to be happy there."

The rain was still coming down, pelting slantwise against the windows of the living room. Danner held up his glass. "I need a refill."

In a moment, Green returned from the kitchen with the drink. "I know how you felt," he said. "But I don't think I'd ever have the guts to up and quit, like you did."

"I'm forty-seven, Sam. The age when you begin to realize that a lot of your life is behind you. I put in twenty years with the agency, my best years. What have I got to show for it? A broken marriage and a background that no corporation would want, even if I could tell them about it."

"You're not blaming the agency for the divorce?"

Danner took a slug of his drink before he replied. "Look, you're a bachelor. Marriage is a little out of your orbit. I'm not saying Francesca left me because of the agency. But it was all connected."

"I know there was trouble when you were posted to Madrid," Sam recalled.

"There was trouble before that," Danner reminded him. "She hated the secrecy. There was a lot I couldn't tell her about my work. She resented it, bitterly. She said I couldn't really share my life with her."

Sam nodded. "That's true of so many agency marriages."

"Living with someone is the most difficult thing any human being can do," Danner said. "And when you're in this business, it's twice as difficult."

"Maybe that's why I've never tried it."

"No, I know you. You just like the variety."

"There's nothing wrong with a little strange," Sam said defensively. "At least you don't get bored."

"We were never bored," Danner said. "But there were times when I had to leave for weeks, even months, and I couldn't tell her why. It was like the agency was my mistress, and she was always jealous."

"Well, you can see why a woman might be suspicious."

"And sometimes with good reason. You remember Skip Murphy? He was on a trip to Jakarta one time and they arrested him in the park. He was drunk as a skunk and balls-ass naked with three girls from a local cathouse. He'd paid them to go skinny dipping with him in a lily pond. The ambassador was not amused."

"What happened to him?"

"The chief of station intervened with the local cops, who were on his payroll anyway, and got him off."

Sam laughed. "No wonder Francesca didn't like your trips."

"Especially Bangkok, in sixty-eight. We had reports that some of our guys were using agency aircraft to smuggle heroin out of the Golden Triangle. I was sent out to investigate. I was gone for two months."

"And when you got back?"

"Francesca was totally pissed. She put me in the deep freeze for six weeks."

"Skip Murphy probably got six months when he got home."

Danner grinned. "But he deserved it." He cut a slice of cheese and nibbled at it. "Things settled down for a while after that," he said. "Until the summer of seventy-two, when I was made COS in Madrid. Francesca was pregnant with Carrie and I could only give her three weeks notice of the move."

"That's when you had the house on Lorcum Lane?"

"Yeah. It was hot as hell that summer. We were trying to leave in a hurry and everyone's nerves were frayed."

"I remember how hot it was," Sam said. "I came over to help you pack."

"But you didn't know how tense things were below the surface. One night we had a fight and Francesca was screaming at me about the secrecy. She said the CIA was compartmented for secrecy. She said I had compartmented my soul."

Sam was silent. He stared at his shoes.

"Maybe she was right," Danner said. "Anway, we hung in

there until seventy-six. The divorce decree came through the day that Jimmy Carter got the nomination.''

"I remember," Sam said. "You and I went out that night and did a lot of drinking.''

"We sure did.'' Danner got up, walked into the kitchen, and wrestled some more ice from a tray. He refilled his drink.

He rejoined Green and sat down again. "I don't blame the agency for Francesca. On the other hand, maybe it wouldn't have happened if I'd been working for IBM.''

"You'd have been bored to death.''

"Maybe, but when I left the agency, I tried the corporations. Some of the guys I went to college with are at the top of the corporate world now. A lot of them, anyway. Earning big salaries, living normal lives.''

"You went around to see some of them?''

"Sure. They were friendly enough. But they weren't able to do anything for me. I couldn't put a damn thing down on my job application. I could say I had worked for the agency, and that was about it. From college to the time I quit was a twenty-year blank. It never happened.''

Sam looked sympathetic. "You have no past.''

"Let's face it. I spent twenty years in this place, working for the government while my contemporaries got rich. I missed the brass ring. So I got off the merry-go-round.'' He paused and took a drink. "I like it up in Canada,'' he said. "No one bothers me.''

"It's different for me,'' Sam explained. "When you're a specialist, a technical expert, they leave you alone. Merriwether, my section chief, is an asshole. But, basically, nobody bothers me either.''

"I understand. But I couldn't have stayed. I came to feel more and more that all of us in the agency were just children playing secret games. It didn't seem like work for grownups.''

"Some of it has to be done.''

"A lot of it would be better left undone. Most of our covert ops, for starters.''

Sam's eyebrows went up. "Are you trying to put Dixon Hadley out of business?''

"Let me tell you a story about Dixon Hadley. Nobody

knows this, and I found out about it purely by accident. From a friend who knew his family in Philadelphia.''

"He grew up there?"

"Yes, in St. David's. When Dixon was ten, he killed his brother."

"Jesus."

"They were playing soldiers. His brother was six and he was down behind a couch, using it as a fortress. He popped up and Dixon blew his head off with a shotgun. He didn't know it was loaded."

"My God," Sam said.

"Dixon really loved his kid brother," Danner said. "He's never gotten over it. But I think, after that, he never had a problem with anything he had to do for the agency."

"What do you mean?"

"Well, you know they say that for a Mafia hit man, after the first one the rest are easy. Dixon handled the assassination planning for Executive Action."

"I didn't realize he was with Executive Action."

"There were some things in Nam, too. Dixon was out there with Operation Phoenix and some of the people under him were running one-way interrogations."

"How do you mean?"

"You know. They'd take a captured Viet Cong up in a chopper and start asking him questions at ten thousand feet. If he didn't have the right answers, he got pushed out."

Sam shook his head. "And he looks like a college professor."

"He was. At Yale."

"That explains it. We had no killers at NYU."

Danner smiled. "You think only the Ivy League breeds killers?"

"Especially Yale. Where else would you find a secret society that called itself Skull and Bones?"

Danner laughed. He got up and walked over to the window. The rain was still coming down. He turned to Sam.

"Maybe you can help me catch up on a little history."

"Sure. Ancient or modern?"

"Modern. What do you know about the Halloween Massacre? It happened six months after I left."

Sam smiled broadly. "The Halloween Massacre," he said, "was the only pogrom in history where the Jews were safe."

Danner grinned. He came back and sat down again.

Sam continued, "Only the WASPs were shot."

"I know it was targeted at the old boys. No ethnics. Did they really fire eight hundred DDO people?"

"The press overplayed it. Only two hundred forty-three were canned. The rest was attrition. You know, a guy retires and they eliminate his job. But it was bloody."

"What was the reason for it?"

"Some of them were just getting old. Living off their OSS reputations and their Metropolitan Club connections."

"But it wasn't just a geriatric problem?"

Sam shrugged. "You hear different rumors. There may have been more to it than that. I'm really not the best person to ask. You ought to talk to some of the DDO types."

"I'll do that. Brooks Jordan was the deputy director of the agency then, wasn't he?"

"Yeah," Sam replied.

"But he survived."

"That's right," Sam said thoughtfully, "he survived and now he's number one."

"Interesting," Danner said.

"Very."

Outside, the rain seemed to be letting up a little. Green looked at his watch. "Listen," he said, "it's almost eight o'clock and I'm invited to a party at Sandy Berens' place. Why don't you come along?"

"Oh, I don't know. I thought I'd head home, maybe watch a little television."

"Come on, you might as well enjoy yourself now that you're back in the big city. Sandy's nice. She works with me in Imagery. There'll be a lot of people there, and plenty of food. What do you say?"

Danner shrugged. "Okay. What the hell."

"Great. We'll take my car. It's not far."

In Sam's blue Mercedes, they drove along Lee Highway to Rosslyn. The 450 SEL was Sam's favorite toy, a luxury he could afford as a bachelor. Sandy Berens, Sam explained on the way, lived in Harbor Towers, a luxury high-rise overlooking the Potomac.

In a few moments, Sam pulled up at the building. Harbor Towers advertised panoramic views, twenty-four hour secretarial service, color-coordinated kitchens with microwave ovens, two swimming pools, full security, and a marina nearby on the Potomac where some of the residents kept their boats. It was a place that a lot of the swinging singles at the agency aspired to, but few could afford. Sandy could, Sam explained, because she came from a rich family in Chicago.

"She gives great parties," Sam added as they walked through the gilded lobby. The stereo was turned up high and the apartment already crowded with people when they arrived. They stood for a moment, looking around, when a pretty, brown-haired woman in tight designer jeans and a knit top spotted Green and threaded her way through the crowd.

"Sam!" She threw her arms around him and gave him a kiss.

"I brought a friend. This is Bill Danner. Hope you don't mind."

"Are you kidding?" she asked. "He's handsome." To Danner she said, "I'm Sandy. The bar's on the terrace if you can fight your way there." She pointed out toward the balcony.

They threaded their way through the living room. The Rolling Stones thumped from the speakers. Several people were dancing in the center of the room. Danner sought a path around them. An athletic-looking man with an open shirt, a gold chain, and a lot of black, curly chest hair, bumped into him, spilling some of his drink on Danner's jacket. "Hey, sorry pal," he said. "Some party, huh?"

"He agency?" Danner asked Sam.

"Yeah. A hood from OS." Like a lot of agency employees, Sam was not fond of the Office of Security or its staff. They administered the periodic lie detector tests that all CIA workers had to take, and they constantly nitpicked about open file cabinets, burn bags, and other regulations.

"A gate-crasher?"

"No," Sam answered. "He's Vicky Robinson's current boyfriend, and she's Sandy's best friend. Everyone here is agency."

Danner had assumed that. Employees of the company were

encouraged to socialize among themselves as much as possible. He looked around the room and saw no familiar faces. Most of the people were younger than Danner, in their early thirties, he guessed.

They were skirting the dance floor when Danner's eye was drawn toward a strikingly beautiful woman dancing with a blond, mustached man in a blue blazer. It was the girl in the red MG. She wore white pants, leather sandals, a purple silk shirt, and gold loops for earrings. She was deeply tanned and her hair was jet black.

It was her bright green eyes under dark lashes that Danner noticed first, and only then the full, sensual lips. She danced effortlessly to the music, her whole body caught up in the rhythm, enjoying her own beauty, knowing that a lot of people were watching her move. Danner figured she was anywhere between twenty-eight and thirty-three.

"Who's *that*?" he asked.

"Julie Nichols," Sam replied. "She's taken, I think. The cool-looking guy she's dancing with is Turk Wilcox. He's DDO, Soviet Russia division."

They made it to the terrace, and Danner asked the bartender for a Scotch and water. Sam had a gin and tonic.

The music drifted out onto the balcony. Steely Dan was playing "Do It Again." The rain had finally stopped. The night was cool for early July, and the trees along the river smelled fresh.

They were breathing it in and enjoying the air when Danner smelled the odor of pot drifting across the terrace. He was mildly surprised, since the OS hood with the gold chain was there at the party and might report it. Then he looked across the terrace and saw that was who was smoking the joint.

A voluptuous red-haired woman linked her arm through Sam's and pulled him off toward the dance floor. There were several people crowded around the table that served as a bar, and Danner stepped back out of the way and maneuvered over to the railing in the corner. He stood by himself and looked out at the Potomac.

To his right he could see the Lincoln and Jefferson memorials, the Washington Monument, and in the distance, the Capitol. All were floodlit and stark white, etched against the dark summer sky. Whenever he saw the monuments at night, he was struck by their beauty. They were symbols, he thought, of what was best about the country.

Below him, there were a few boats moving on the river. It was clearing up rapidly now and the stars were coming out. The cheerful sounds of the party, the music, clinking glasses, animated conversation, laughter, and an occassional shriek drifted out onto the terrace. He had forgotten for the moment that his leg hurt.

"Are you counting the stars?"

The husky, pleasant voice came from behind his right shoulder. He turned and saw it was the woman he had admired on the dance floor.

"No," Danner said, "The years."

She laughed. "There can't be that many."

"Then I'll stop counting. My name's Bill Danner. I'm a friend of Sam's." Out of the corner of his eye, he could see Turk Wilcox waiting to get her a drink at the crowded bar.

She smiled, and her teeth were white against the tan face and the black hair. She was even prettier close up.

"I'm Julie Nichols." She extended a hand. It was soft, yet firm and Danner held it a fraction of a second longer than necessary. "Are you *the* William Danner?"

He laughed. "I haven't checked lately. I was this morning."

"I've heard of you. Everyone has. But I thought you'd left us."

"I did. But I'm back for a while." Danner smiled. "Do you drive a red MG?"

The green eyes widened.

"How did you know?"

"You shouldn't tailgate," Danner said. "It's dangerous to get too close."

Julie looked puzzled. "Where—"

"About a week ago," he said, "on the George Washington Parkway. I made you go around."

She laughed. "Oh, I remember now. I was annoyed with you. But I'm quick to anger, quick to forgive." The radiant smile again.

Danner couldn't help looking at her body. Her breasts were full under the purple silk blouse, and the tight pants revealed trim hips and legs, and no extra weight. Danner guessed she jogged.

"You dance very well," he said.

"Is that an invitation?"

"If you like," Danner found himself saying.

"Let's." She led the way back inside to the crowded dance floor. Turk was eyeing them now, but he was still stuck at the bar with three people on line ahead of him.

They squeezed through the crush and started to dance. The Rolling Stones were singing "Let's Spend the Night Together." Danner was out of practice, but he managed reasonably well. She was moving sensually, gracefully, as she had before. She was very near him now, their bodies almost touching. Danner realized how long it had been.

She looked up at him challengingly and smiled. "Is it dangerous to get too close?"

In Canada, Danner had lived the life of a loner. There had been some casual contacts with women in New Brunswick, but not often. His energies had gone into rebuilding and operating the camp. Now, unexpectedly, he found himself enormously attracted to this dark and sensual younger woman.

He started to reply when Turk came up to them with two drinks. "Vodka and tonic," he said, handing one to Julie.

"Oh, thanks, darling," she said. "Turk, this is Bill Danner." The blond man with the mustache nodded, did not offer to shake hands, and gently steered her away. She smiled a goodbye smile at Danner.

Danner headed for a corner of the room that looked slightly less crowded. He tried to edge around behind a hulking, redhaired man who was deep in conversation with a short, blond woman. The man turned suddenly and Danner realized, too late, that it was Frank "The Artist" Gibbons.

Gibbons was a cowboy, a tough paramilitary type who had led the mercenary force recruited by the agency in Angola. He had gotten his nickname several years earlier in Frankfurt. Interrogating suspected KGB plants among a group of refugees from the Baltic states, he had painted their testicles with turpentine. Eventually the director heard about it, and ordered it stopped. Gibbons was ordered back to Langley and for a time had to walk the halls. It was a punishment reserved for DDO

officers who had fallen into disfavor. The walkers were transferred to headquarters but given no office or assignment. They
literally had nowhere to sit down, except the cafeteria. But after
six months, Gibbons had been rehabilitated.

"Danner!" Gibbons exclaimed, grabbing his arm. "Where
the fuck have you been?"

"Wish I could tell you," Danner replied without breaking
stride. "It's classified." He finally made it to the corner, where
a slim, owlish-looking man with thick horn-rimmed glasses
was chatting with an intense, dark-haired woman in a beige
suit.

"I'm Winckelmann," the man said, extending a hand to
Danner. "Office of Medical Services. And this is Dr. Quimby
from Psychiatry."

"Bill Danner."

"I've heard of you," the owlish-looking man said. "But I
thought you were gone."

"I am," Danner said. "I'm just back temporarily. Doing
some consulting." He smiled. "You a shrink, too?"

"Other end," Winckelmann said. "I'm a urologist."

"Ah," said Danner, not knowing how to make small talk
with a urologist, and not particularly wanting to. The agency
had physicians of all kinds who were cleared to treat CIA personnel. In particular, the agency had its own psychiatric staff. It
would not do to have covert operators spilling secrets to outsiders.

Dr. Quimby broke in. "Murray was just saying how he'd
give anything to get a specimen from Kalin."

"Why Kalin?" Danner asked.

"We could tell a lot," Winckelmann replied. "I'm not just
medical staff," he explained. "I work a lot with your shop. My
speciality is urinalysis of major world leaders."

"I see," Danner said.

"My biggest coup was Khrushchev. It was back in sixty-
one. I had just started with the agency. When Kennedy met
Khrushchev at the summit meeting in Vienna, I went over a
week early to supervise the set-up."

Danner nodded.

"The first meeting took place at the American ambassador's
residence in Hietzing. You can see the opportunity."

"I think so," Danner said.

"We rigged the bathroom," Winckelmann explained. "When Khrushchev peed, it went directly into a special trap in the basement. That's where I was, standing by in the basement. We used an Air Force jet to fly the specimen back to Langley."

"What did it show?" Danner asked.

"He had diabetes," Winckelmann said triumphantly. "Four-plus sugar and traces of acetone."

"Well, so what?"

The doctor's face fell. "That kind of information can be very important to the policymakers. A president might need an estimate from us of how long a Soviet leader will live."

"But Khrushchev was thrown out. He didn't die until much later."

"Even so," Winckelmann insisted, "it was important. I got a promotion."

"Psychiatry branch does the same sort of thing," Dr. Quimby said. "Of course we can't be expected to go skulking around in men's rooms."

"Naturally," Danner said.

"But we prepare the psychological profiles. Before that summit meeting, Kennedy had been given our psychiatric report on Khrushchev. We advised the president not to back him into a corner. We did similar profiles on Brezhnev for Nixon, Ford, and Reagan. And on Andropov."

"You don't do only Russians, I suppose," Danner ventured.

"Heavens, no," she said. "A couple of years ago I did a very interesting study on Margaret Thatcher."

"What did you conclude?" Danner asked.

"Penis envy. She sent the fleet to the Falklands to try to prove she was a man."

"Marvelous, Barbara," Winckelmann said.

Danner wished he had picked another corner to stand in.

"What about Kalin?" he asked.

Dr. Quimby looked grave. "I think something serious is going on," she said. "We're watching him carefully. His behavior has been increasingly erratic. I think he's decompensating."

"Meaning what?" Danner asked.

"He's becoming withdrawn, canceling Politburo meetings.

That behavior alternates with periods of hyperactivity and enormous energy.''

''What about his megalomania?'' Winckelmann asked.

''That goes with the job,'' she said. ''But according to the reports I read, it's increasing. He believes more and more in his own infallibility, and brushes aside the views of his advisers. He may be a borderline psychotic.''

Well, Danner thought, she might be right about that, anyway. It was the prevailing wisdom inside the agency that the Soviet leader had been acting dangerously flaky. Although, Danner reflected, he seemed to be behaving normally enough in the solarium.

Winckelmann was shaking his head. ''That's why it's so important to get a specimen from Kalin.'' He turned to Danner. ''A lot of people think we analyze urine only for physical conditions—you know, we look for sugar for diabetes, protein as evidence of nephritis, or red or white cells for kidney or bladder trouble. Or to see if someone's on drugs. But we can detect mental illness, too.''

Danner looked skeptical. ''From urine?''

''It's a new frontier of research, very controversial. But there's no question. For example, the level of the metabolite MHPG is low in the urine of depressed patients.''

''I see.''

''It's a substance produced by neurotransmitters, the chemical messengers between the brain cells. Or take cortisol, which the adrenal gland produces. The level in the urine is elevated for persons under stress. A high level of melatonin, the hormone of the pineal gland, can mean the subject is manic.'' Winckelmann was just warming to his subject.

''Been nice talking to both of you,'' Danner said, edging away. Five minutes with Winckelmann was enough to remind him why he had left the agency. He practically collided with Sam, who had his arm around a young and tipsy secretary from Computer Services. The girl, giggling, said her name was Cheryl.

''Time to go,'' Sam said. ''We'll drive you back to my place, so you can pick up your car.''

''Fine with me,'' Danner said. The Rolling Stones were singing ''Honky Tonk Woman.'' He looked around and saw

Julie Nichols talking to someone a few feet away. He smiled as he brushed by her, then realized she had slipped something in his hand. He put it in his pocket.

Sam and Cheryl dropped him off at his car. Driving home, he reached into his jacket and took out the matchbook. He flipped open the cover and saw the phone number written inside. He put the matches back in his pocket and wondered whether he would call her.

He thought about the party, and about Julie. He was surprised to find that he had enjoyed the evening. Meeting her had been exciting. He realized he was still aroused from talking to her, dancing with her, and touching her. It disturbed him, because he had not expected to enjoy anything about being back.

He swung off the Shirley Highway and turned right toward his apartment building. He knew that he was gradually being drawn once more into the life he had left seven years ago. He was not sure he liked that. What frightened him was that part of him did.

CHAPTER
FIVE

Danner was in his fifth-floor office at headquarters, studying the Damage Assessment Reports on the operations that had been sabotaged. There was a knock on his door.

He opened it. A skinny young man in a dark, pin-stripe business suit stood there holding a black attaché case. "I'm from the Office of Technical Service," he said. "Come to fix your typewriter."

"There's nothing wrong with it," Danner said. He wondered why, even in the agency, typewriter repairmen dressed like corporate executives.

The young man eyed Danner appraisingly. "You're new," he said in a tone of mild reproof. "Your typewriter hasn't been deactivated." From his attaché case, he removed a five-pound metal flywheel. He took the cover off Danner's Selectric III.

Danner shook his head resignedly. OTS was always coming up with new devices.

"Won't take but a minute," the technician said. Using two screws, he attached the flywheel to the end of the electric motor. He tested it to make sure it worked. Then he snapped the cover back on the typewriter. "There," he said. "Except for the added weight, you wouldn't even know it was there."

"What's it for?" Danner inquired.

"Security. Most people don't realize it, but a typewriter can be bugged. Whoever does it can tell what you're typing. The reason is that the typewriter motor gives off electrical impulses that are slightly different for each letter."

54

Danner nodded.

"The difference is only in microvolts, but it's measurable. You've got a series of little latches on the bottom of the typewriter. The motor operates different ones for each letter. If you underline a word, for example, there's a big increase in voltage, because all the latches are used."

"And the flywheel?"

"It smooths out the impulses for each letter. Makes them uniform. So if anyone is listening electronically, it will sound like you're hitting the same letter over and over again."

"There are days when I feel like doing that."

The technician looked concerned. "Have you tried talking to Dr. Quimby? She's real nice."

"I've already done that," Danner said. "It didn't help."

"Well, thank you, sir," the OTS man said, backing out of the office. "Sorry to have disturbed you."

"It was no trouble." Danner went back to his reports. When he had finished reading, he picked up the telephone on his desk. It was an ordinary phone, one of the agency's Black System telephones, and it could not be used for discussing classified information. By pushing a red button, however, it became a Red System phone, an internal secure line for calls within the building. There were two other phones on his desk; a Green System phone for secure calls to other intelligence agencies in Washington, and a Gold System phone connected to a small steel box containing a scrambler, for calls to all other government offices.

Danner pushed the red button and dialed Dixon Hadley's office. Melinda answered and he asked to see the DDO. She gave him an appointment for 11:00 A.M.

He had time to kill and decided to go downstairs for a cup of coffee, his third of the morning. He took the elevator to the cafeteria for covert employees. It was separated by a wall from a second cafeteria that was for the use of overt employees and visitors. He went through the line, got his coffee, and found an unoccupied table. He used the time to finish reading *The Washington Post*.

The world had not progressed very much while he had been off fishing the Miramichi, Danner decided. President Lansing Forbes, in a speech in Indianapolis, had attacked the Soviet

Union for meddling in Central America. The Secretary of State, in a follow-up press conference, charged that the Russians were supplying arms to Marxist guerrillas in Costa Rica. According to the Secretary, the CIA had collected extensive documentation to prove the Soviet involvement beyond doubt, but the material could not be released to the American public without revealing intelligence sources and methods. There was more trouble along the Soviet-Chinese border. A twenty-year-old college student, alone in her car when it broke down on a rural road, had been gang-raped, beaten with tire chains, and murdered in Hyattsville, police said. They were looking for four men in a beige van with Maryland plates. Charlie Brown had pitched another losing ball game.

Danner dawdled over his coffee until it was almost time for his appointment with Dixon Hadley. At four minutes before the hour, he left and took the elevator up to the seventh floor.

As he walked down the corridor toward the DDO's office, he saw a blind man coming toward him with a guide dog, a brown akita in a leather harness. The man was prematurely gray and wore dark glasses. Danner realized it was Roger Jellison.

Jellison had been brought in by the Clandestine Services to solve a problem peculiar to CIA. Despite the complex, four-color phone system used by the agency, when anyone at headquarters placed a long-distance call to someone outside the government, it was handled by the telephone company like any other call. A record of the call was automatically registered on a tape that was fed into a computer at the Chesapeake and Potomac Telephone Company's billing office on Hungary Springs Road in Greendale, a suburb of Richmond, Virginia. And every month, the CIA was billed just like any other customer. If the phone company or its billing computer in Greendale were penetrated, the records of long-distance calls could be obtained and the people whom the agency had called could be traced by their numbers and identified.

In fact, Danner knew, it had actually happened. Security was difficult; thousands of telephone company employees had access to long-distance records. And even without inside help, there was always the danger that the KGB, or some other hostile intelligence service, could find a way to tap into the telephone company's long-distance billing computers. There seemed no way around the problem, until someone discovered Jellison. The blind man had perfect pitch, and he was used to whistle ultra-confidential long-distance and overseas calls illegally. He could exactly match the tones that activated the calls. The calls were "sterile" and could not be traced.

Jellison had explained the technology once to Danner. Long-distance calls are completed by the use of multi-frequency tones, the hi-pitched musical beeps that one often hears when placing a call to another city. Actually the beeps are paired tones in the 700 to 1700 Hz range, with each pair representing a digit of the number called.

To place a long-distance call that bypassed the telephone company's automatic billing computers, Jellison would first gain access to a long-distance line by dialing any toll-free 800 number. Just before the party answered, he would whistle a 2600 Hz single-frequency signal that switched the call to a tandem, an open intercity circuit. Then he would whistle the desired area code and number.

Some years earlier, an agency technician had discovered that a little whistle enclosed in the Captain Crunch cereal boxes was perfectly tuned to 2600 Hz. For a time, some of the more electronically-minded agency employees were using the cereal box whistles to place their calls. The director decided it was undignified for CIA to use kiddie whistles, and he ordered the search for an expert that eventually resulted in Jellison's recruitment.

Circumventing the telephone company was not a new idea. College students and phone phreaks had often tried the same thing, using illicit devices called blue boxes. They made the mistake of leaving the gadgets attached to their phones for long periods of time, and were often caught. Jellison was used sparingly and the telephone company's detectives would never catch him. He was a living blue box.

Jellison halted as he drew near, listening to the footsteps. "Danner, is that you? I thought you had retired, years ago."

"Hello, Roger," Danner said. "I'm just back on temporary duty." He was not surprised that Jellison knew him, even after seven years. The blind man could do things like that.

"Well, nice to see you."

Danner remembered that Jellison had a disconcerting habit of using that phrase. "Nice to see you, too, Roger," he said.

Melinda was waiting for him in Dixon Hadley's outer office. He had to cool his heels for five minutes. Then a buzzer sounded and Melinda flashed her best smile and said he could go in.

"Danner." Hadley arose and shook hands. Danner sat in one of the orange-padded chairs, squinting because there was, as usual, too much sunlight streaming into the room. He looked around and noted with relief that Socrates seemed to be asleep. Or dead, Danner hoped.

The DDO was gnawing on a pencil. "How are you getting along?" he asked.

"Just easing back in. Been a while, you know."

"Of course."

"The flywheels are new. What's that all about?"

"We started putting them in a few years ago. We discovered that the Soviets were circling headquarters in vans disguised as catering trucks. They're actually mobile ELINT units, packed with electronic equipment. They were trying to pick up signals intelligence from typewriters, code machines, telephones, anything they can get."

"They still out there?"

Hadley nodded. "Rain or shine, all day long. And sometimes at night." He took his glasses off and rubbed the bridge of his nose. "You making any progress?"

"I've been reading the reports."

"And?"

"I guess for openers I need to know more about the Halloween Massacre. Who got fired, and why."

Hadley sighed. "It's a long story," he said. "You remember Farrell and Griffin?"

"The Libya connection."

"Right. They quit the agency and peddled what they'd learned as DDO officers to the highest bidder."

"And the highest bidder turned out to be Qaddafi."

"Unfortunately. They became millionaires by selling him explosives disguised as ashtrays, coat hangers, even teakettles. They also got a fat contract to train his people as terrorists.

Griffin was living like a king on an estate in Middleburg. He used the oil money to join the horsey set.''

"What's that got to do with the Halloween Massacre?"

"Everything. The director found out that six of our people, then currently employed by the agency, were working with Farrell and Griffin. Even helping them make the teakettles.''

"Shit."

"Exactly. The director went off the pad. He decided the old boys were to blame.''

"Were they?"

"I suppose to some extent. After all they'd been running the DDO from the start. A lot of them came in with Allen Dulles. And plenty of others were in the woodwork even before that.''

"So he drew up a little list."

Hadley picked up a fresh pencil and began chewing it. "Oh, the director didn't. Not personally. He turned it over to Brooks Jordan, who was deputy director then. It was Brooks who drew up the list.''

Danner leaned forward. "And Jordan fired the old boys?"

Hadley smiled faintly. "No, he had his assistant Miles Osborn do that.''

Danner nodded.

"The director turned around and fired the executioner.''

"Osborn?"

"Yes. Miles was quite bitter about it. Of course, Jordan was in the background, pulling the strings the whole time. And when the dust settled, he ended up on top. The director resigned, and Jordan was appointed to succeed him.''

"When President Forbes was elected, why did he decide to keep Jordan on?''

"I'm not sure. Maybe he felt we'd been through enough.'' Hadley lowered his voice. "The truth is, I don't know how secure Jordan's position is with the president.''

Danner asked, "How did you and Jordan survive? After all, you're both card-carrying old boys, as much as any of those who were fired.''

"Brooks really masterminded the whole coup. He was in control. He made sure it didn't touch him.''

"And you?"

"Brooks and I were in Bones together at Yale.''

"I see." Danner looked out the window at the trees lining the George Washington Memorial Parkway. "I guess I should know who was shaken out."

Hadley shrugged. "Well, Osborn of course. Tracy Thatcher. Kermit Gardner. Those names you know. Talbot Braswell, Wade Seabrook, Huntington Trowbridge, Wellington Lloyd. The list goes on."

"I'd like a copy."

The DDO looked dubious. "Of *all* names?"

"I suppose so," Danner said. "I have to start somewhere." The list, Danner knew, was vital. One or more of the names on it could be the key to what was going on.

Hadley sighed and made a little note on a pad. "All right, I'll talk to Personnel and see what I can do."

"I'll also need Nick Rossi's 201 file."

Hadley made another note on his pad.

"Aaarwk!" The deputy director's macaw had awakened and was preening in his cage.

"How long do those things live?" Danner asked.

"Seventy-five years. Sometimes even a hundred."

Danner tried to conceal his disappointment with a smile. He got up to leave.

"There's one other thing," Hadley said after a slight hesitation.

"Yes?"

The deputy director walked over to the birdcage and dropped in some sunflower seeds. "It was indiscreet of Sam Green to discuss Kalin's, ah, recreational activities with you. The source of that information is highly sensitive. And I don't appreciate your discussing my personal life, either."

Danner, stone-faced, made no reply. He left, routinely returning Melinda's smile as he passed her desk, but he was furious.

So he was under surveillance. He might have expected it. Knowing that sooner or later he would call on his old friend, they had even bugged Sam. He *had* been away from the business, Danner realized. He had almost forgotten what nice folks he worked for.

CHAPTER
SIX

Charlie's was tucked under the Whitehurst Freeway in Georgetown, along the Potomac River. It had low ceilings with discreet spotlights overhead, brown walls, and a soothing decor. It was the place to go for jazz and supper.

Danner had chosen it, and Julie was pleased. They ordered a bottle of white wine; it was cold and dry, which felt good, because outside it was typical Washington weather for late August, very hot and muggy. Charlie's was the sort of place where you weren't supposed to talk during the music, and that suited Danner fine because it gave him a chance to look at Julie.

She was wearing a white summer dress decorated with splashes of bright colors; it set off her black hair and her tan dramatically. She wore a couple of gold bracelets on her left wrist, and no other jewelry or makeup. She didn't need any.

The set ended, and the musicians took a break. Julie sipped her wine and said, "It took you a while to open the matchbook."

Danner laughed. "I don't smoke." He had waited several weeks before he called her, persuading himself it was because he was busy; besides, he remembered Sam's remark that she was taken. "Your tan's gotten deeper since the party," he observed.

"It's the weekends. I share a house in Rehoboth with Sandy Berens and two other women. We're out on the beach a lot. And sometimes I jog at the agency, on my lunch hour." She smiled. Danner thought she looked terrific.

61

A waitress came and asked if they were ready to order. She looked like a clean-cut college student, probably from Georgetown, Danner guessed. Julie decided on the lobster bisque, a salad, and the poached salmon. Danner ordered a swordfish steak.

Julie asked, "Do you like being back?"

"I'd rather be fishing."

She laughed. "You say that like you mean it."

"I do."

Her green eyes searched his. "Then why did you come back?"

"They made me an offer I couldn't refuse."

"I see." She studied his expression for a clue to his meaning, but found none. She took a sip of her wine. "You haven't told me what you're doing."

Danner looked around. They had a corner table, well out of earshot of the other diners. "A little consulting for the DDO," he replied. "They're having some problems and thought I could help. And you?"

"I'm in SO," she said.

"That must be new," Danner said. "I don't know it."

"Special Operations," she explained. "We're covert, but we're not really part of the DDO."

The food came, and they stopped talking while the waitress put it on the table. When she had gone, Danner asked, "What do you do in SO?"

Julie hesitated for a second before answering. "Research," she said.

"From the name of the unit," Danner said, trying to sound casual, "I thought it might handle terminations."

Julie took a bite of her poached salmon. "It's delicious," she said. She shook her head. "We don't do any now."

"What's the 'now' mean?"

"Well," Julie said carefully, "we have to maintain the capability."

Danner recoiled. Did this beautiful and intelligent woman really believe the agency should kill people? It was easy to talk about. But he wondered if Julie herself could carry out such an order.

"I don't agree," Danner responded. "Look what happened

when we hired the Mafia button men to try to kill Castro. It didn't work, and when it leaked out it caused the agency all kinds of grief. We're still recovering from it."

"Suppose a termination could prevent World War Three?" Julie countered. "Wouldn't you favor it then?"

"There are exceptions to every rule. But as a general proposition, I'm against it."

"Why? In a war people get killed. Espionage is a kind of war."

Danner was becoming irritated. "I don't think anyone appointed us God," he said. Dropping the subject, he asked, "What sort of research do you do?"

"I work a lot with the Central Cover Staff. We're trying to build up our commercial cover."

"It's overdue," Danner agreed. "We've relied too much on embassy cover."

"And it doesn't take the opposition very long to know who our people are in an embassy."

Danner nodded. "Sure. In tropical posts, you can always tell who's agency by the cars. They're the biggest ones, with the air conditioning."

She laughed. Danner removed the wine bottle from the ice bucket alongside the table and poured another glass for each of them. He didn't know whether to believe her. Special Operations didn't sound like a place that would need a researcher.

Julie sensed his doubts. "I try to locate and analyze mid-size American companies that do a lot of business in the Middle East and Africa," she said.

"And if SO finds them suitable?"

"Then I try to develop contacts within the companies and persuade them to hire some of our people. We pay their salaries, of course, and no one in the company except our cutout knows they work for us."

"But SO runs operations as well?"

"Some."

Danner decided not to press further. "Where are you from?" he asked.

"Everywhere," she answered. "I was a foreign service brat. Wherever my father was posted, we went with him. I grew up in half a dozen countries. English is almost my second language.''

''So it was a natural background for the agency.''

''Yes. I was recruited in my senior year at Bryn Mawr. By my English professor.''

They listened to the guitar doing an intricate jazz solo with a lot of riffs and improvisations. Then Julie asked, ''And what about you? How did William Danner become a legend?''

''I'm not feeling much like a legend. I've been out of it for seven years.'' Julie looked beautiful by candlelight.

''Tell me more,'' she said. ''I want to know it all.''

''There's not much to tell. I grew up in a little town in New England. My father was a railroad engineer for the Boston and Maine.''

''What was the town?''

''White River Junction.''

She looked wistful. ''It must be nice to grow up in one place.''

''It was. But my father was away a lot, because of his job.''

''What was your mother like?''

''Irish, with a temper to match. She was wonderful, though. Raised three children on very little money and taught us to fight for what we wanted.''

''And you know what you want?''

''I thought I did a long time ago. I'm not so sure now.''

''When did you join the agency?'' she asked.

''Right out of college, like you did. My father set great store in education, although he never went beyond the eighth grade himself. He encouraged me to read a lot as a kid. I ended up at Dartmouth, on a scholarship.''

''I guess, in those days, you almost had to be Ivy League to get hired by the agency.''

''Just about. Of course, being a Dartmouth man, I had the Ivy League credentials. But I'm also a townie. I've never been entirely accepted by Dixon Hadley and his friends.''

''You're sort of half a member of the club.''

Danner laughed. ''You could put it that way. I signed on in 1958. After my JOT training, I was posted to Berlin. I was in the station there for two years. Then I worked with the Cuban exiles in Trax Base, Guatemala, before the Bay of Pigs.''

"That must have been hard, later on."

"It was. I was offshore on the *Boxer* while the brigade was being chewed up on the beaches."

"And after that?"

"A series of posts in Latin America, Africa, and Europe. In between I worked at headquarters and did some special assignments. I got lucky on some of them."

The musicians were playing a Chet Baker arrangement of "You Better Go Now." Danner liked the song, and they paused to listen to it.

"Why did you quit?" Julie asked.

"Lots of reasons. My marriage had broken up, for one."

"Were there children?"

"Just one, my daughter, Carrie. She's almost twelve."

"Do you see her often?"

"As much as I can. She's a great kid."

"But there were other reasons for leaving."

"Sure. I'd changed. I just didn't believe in it any more."

"Why?"

"I guess it began in Berlin. There was an opération. We lost someone. I don't think it was worth it."

Julie nodded, but said nothing.

Danner continued. "Guatemala, Iran, and Indonesia all took place before I came on board. But I saw firsthand what happened at the Bay of Pigs. And from a distance, I watched our performance in Laos, Vietnam, and Angola."

"We had to try, didn't we?"

"In the long run, I don't think a single one of those operations advanced U.S. interests."

Julie shook her head. "You're wrong. We won in Guatemala."

"But the people lost. Look what's happened since. They've had a series of military juntas, terrifying violence, and the peasants are still earning forty cents an hour on the coffee *fincas*."

"What about Iran? We put the Shah back on the throne and bought some time for the West."

"At enormous cost. The country turned so bitterly anti-American that they booted out the Shah, took over our embassy, grabbed the hostages, and humiliated the president."

"You really have lost faith."

"Not in the country. Just in some of our assumptions. I don't think we can manipulate the whole world from Langley."

"You sound like a State Department fink." She laughed. "Maybe you should have been a foreign service officer."

"Like your father?"

She blushed. "He never lost faith."

Danner ran his finger around the rim of his wineglass. After a moment, he said, "It wasn't just the big operations."

"What do you mean?"

"So much of what we do began to seem pointless to me. For example, in the Third World we spent an incredible amount of our energies trying to recruit Soviet defectors. People on the outside don't know how much time and money we squandered."

"But the objective was worthwhile."

"Yes and no. Suppose we get a KGB defector or agent in place. Is he real or a plant? We can never be sure. Because the more he tells us, the greater the possibility that Moscow Center is building him, giving away real secrets to establish his bona fides. To make us believe."

"Then you've worked in counterintelligence?"

"Some of the time."

"It must be interesting."

"It's a little crazy. Like a permanent job in a carnival fun house. The mirrors are all distorted. You end up trusting no one, suspecting everyone."

"But surely the Russians have tried to plant a mole in the agency. Do you think they've succeeded?"

Danner grew silent. Julie was edging into areas he wasn't supposed to talk about.

She sensed his mood. "Am I getting too close again?" she asked.

"No," he lied. "I just can't answer the question." She was smart, he realized, as well as beautiful.

The waitress came and they ordered dessert and coffee. They lingered for a long time over the coffee, listening to the music. The group was playing "You Don't Know What Love Is."

It was getting late and Danner asked for a check. He hated to leave. He had been enjoying the evening at Charlie's, the music, Julie.

They walked out into the warm night but neither of them felt like going home. "Let's go to the kite store," Julie said impulsively. He took her hand; it seemed natural enough. They strolled up toward M Street, crossing the canal. They found the store and Danner bought her a Japanese dragon kite with a fifty-foot tail.

"First windy day, we'll go down to the Monument and fly it," she said.

"It's a date," Danner found himself agreeing. "Provided you bring the picnic."

"If you'll bring the wine."

"I'll have to sneak it in," he said. "They don't allow booze on the Monument grounds. Park Service rules."

"You see? You're not really against covert operations, after all."

Danner laughed. *"Touché."*

Julie bought them each a balloon, the silvery, helium-filled kind that stay up for days. She tied one by the string to Danner's finger. "That's so you don't forget our date," she said.

"I won't forget."

"Good." She smiled at him.

Danner looked at her, putting his arm around her waist. He hadn't felt this good about a woman in a long time, and it scared him. All kinds of warning lights were going off in his head. Julie was a lot younger than he was, and he was breaking his rule. He had decided, after Berlin, never to become involved with anyone who worked for the agency. It was a difficult rule to adhere to; the agency was a closed group, and the people who worked there tended to form friendships among themselves. It was safer that way. It was possible for someone who did not work for CIA to live in Washington for years, to go to parties frequently, and never meet anyone from the agency. The circle was tight.

"A nickel for your thoughts," she said.

He corrected her. "The expression is a penny."

"Inflation."

He laughed. "You win." He checked his watch. "I guess it's getting to be time to take you home," he said.

They walked back toward the canal, where he had parked on a side street. Danner tried to stuff the balloons into the car, but it was difficult, because they kept popping out. Julie started laughing and tried to help him and soon they were both laughing. Danner solved the problem by tying the balloons to the belts on the rear seat.

There were a lot of people crowding the sidewalks and the bars along M Street, and traffic was heavy, even at that hour. They finally made it across Key Bridge, and drove south along the river to Alexandria.

Julie had the downstairs apartment in a lovely, weathered-brick house on St. Asaph Street in Old Town. There was a pretty garden along the side of the house, with its own entrance through a brick archway with a wooden gate. They parked nearby, and he accepted when she invited him inside for a brandy. Julie collected the balloons; Danner brought in the kite.

They went through to the kitchen in the back. It had a fireplace, and Julie had hung a lot of copper pots and plants, including an enormous spider plant suspended over the table in the center of the room. She found a bottle of Courvoisier in the cupboard and poured some into two crystal brandy snifters. The kitchen opened up into the garden, but it was still too hot, even after midnight, to sit outside.

They walked back into the living room. The house was air-conditioned and the apartment comfortable. The living room was furnished in Danish modern, with a lot of teakwood and more plants. Julie put a record on; they sat down together on a white couch across from the hearth.

They sipped their brandy slowly, and she drifted closer and rested her head on his shoulder. In a moment, he had his arms around her and they were kissing, their lips searching and exploring each other. The smell of her perfume mingled with her breath and Danner kissed her again. She was lightly moving her fingers up and down his back.

He wanted her and sensed she felt the same. But she disengaged and kissed him quickly on the neck. "Not now," she murmured. "Not yet."

The words were full of promise. When Danner left, he wanted to break into a dance. Walking toward his car along the cobbled streets of Old Town he realized he felt happier than he had in a long time. Even though he knew it probably wouldn't last. It never had.

CHAPTER
SEVEN

ENTER DEVICE INSERT BADGE FACE UP

Danner stepped onto the rubberized mat and stood sideways in the narrow stall. There were four in a row in the middle of the CIA lobby, like the starting gates at a racetrack. A narrow black bar with slanted yellow stripes blocked his way at the front of the stall.

Facing him, mounted chest high, was a machine about the size of a typewriter. It had a white outer casing and a bright red inner face on which the letters TRW identified the manufacturer. Obeying the instructions printed above the keyboard, he inserted his badge face up, holding it by the large metal clip at one end. The machine made a whirring noise as it read his name and digested the information.

REMOVE BADGE AND KEY IN FOUR DIGITS

Under the watchful eyes of the guards, Danner entered his code number, 3941, and the machine, satisfied now, raised the barrier. In the event of trouble—if a KGB agent attempted to enter CIA headquarters with an imperfectly forged badge, for example—a second yellow-striped barrier would snap down behind the person in the stall. He would then be trapped there while he tried to explain himself to the guards.

Danner clipped the badge to his jacket, crossed the lobby, and took the elevator up. He got off and walked down a corridor toward the rear of the building. His leg hurt and he wondered whether the hot, humid weather made it worse. In the hall, he recognized the pot-smoking hood from OS who had

70

bumped into him at Sandy Berens' party. The open shirt, chest hair, and gold chains were nowhere to be seen; the security man was wearing a light gray suit and a conservative tie. He did not recognize Danner.

After turning left and right again, Danner came to Imagery. He pushed open a door marked: "Restricted Area: Do Not Enter." The code letters on his badge permitted him to go almost anywhere in the building.

He found Sam sitting in a darkened room in front of a huge screen that cast an eerie green light on his face and body. A photograph, blown up many times its original size, filled the screen. Sam was peering intently at the image and entering numbers into a computer keyboard in front of him. Danner watched silently for a moment until Sam became aware of his presence and turned.

The bushy eyebrows jumped. "Sneak up on a guy, will you?"

"I didn't want to interrupt."

"It's okay. Pull up a chair and sit down."

Danner did. "What have you got?" he asked.

"Silos," Green replied. He picked up what looked like a metal pen but turned out to be a pointer with collapsible sections. He extended it and indicated an area near the center of the screen. "They're camouflaged," he said, "but you can just see the faint outlines. There."

"What are they?"

"SS-18s, Mod 4. Kalin's biggest. Range, 6,800 miles, from a cold launch."

"Fifty megatons?"

"Yes. Maximum yield. It would only take one of these to vaporize Washington—and Langley."

"You've really brightened my day, Sam. It makes you wonder about all those airheads in the Pentagon, writing their strategy papers about 'protracted nuclear war.' "

"We estimate a nuclear exchange between us and the Soviets would last no more than twenty-four hours."

"Try twenty-four minutes."

Sam laughed. "You're probably right."

"What are you keying in?" Danner asked.

"Data for image enhancement and microanalysis," Sam

said. "The computer improves the picture, gives us the precise measurements of the objects in the photograph, and tells us whether anything's changed since the last time the satellite passed overhead." He moved his pointer. "These latrines over here, for example. They've added a new one. That means they're bringing in more people. We're trying to figure out why."

"Where are they located?"

"Just east of the Urals, near Chelyabinsk."

Danner hesitated. "Sam."

"Yeah?"

"I dropped by because there's something you ought to know."

"Such as?"

"They're bugging your apartment."

Sam looked at him. "Jesus Christ. Who's doing it?"

Danner shrugged. "Either OS or Division D, I suppose."

"Goddamn shit-kicking wiremen. How'd you find out?"

"Hadley's reading the traffic. He said you shouldn't have told me about Kalin fucking the girl in the solarium."

"Oh, Christ, this place really is Disneyland, with all the Mickey Mouse that goes on." Sam shook his head dolefully. "I should have listened to my mother and gone into business."

"You wouldn't have liked it."

"Says who? I could be cutting velvets on Seventh Avenue and living in a nice house in Great Neck. Golf every weekend and a condo in Miami in the winter. It would be a lot better than sitting around here trying to measure a Russian shithouse."

Danner laughed. "I'm sorry. The bug is my fault. But I thought you should know."

"Well, thanks." Green sighed. "I guess Hadley got an earful the other night. When I brought Cheryl back from the party."

"Oh?"

"Things got a little kinky. She was bombed to begin with. She found an old hat of mine and was parading around with it in her garter belt, stockings, and high-heeled shoes. She insisted she was Liza Minelli. You know, in *Cabaret*."

"Well," Danner asked innocently, "what's wrong with that?"

"Nothing. But Hadley's so square, he probably put a mark on my record. I had to call her 'Liza' all night. It was the only way I could get to screw her."

"Sorry," Danner repeated. "But I thought you ought to know you're on the air and all America is listening."

"Thanks a million."

Danner arose, said goodbye, and walked back along the corridor. He took the elevator down to the cafeteria, bought a cup of coffee to go, and carried it up to his office on the fifth floor. He read *The Washington Post*, and spent what was left of the morning flipping through some reports from the counterintelligence staff that Dixon Hadley had sent to him. The files dealt with past investigations of suspected moles inside the agency.

Danner was surprised at how many such investigations had taken place; it seemed as though the search for double agents inside headquarters was almost constant. The files included a couple of well-publicized cases of CIA officers who had sold secrets to Russians for money; they had been tried, convicted, and sent to prison. The reports summarized several other cases that had never become public. A base chief in Milan had been dismissed by the agency for peddling agency documents to the Albanians. It was decided not to prosecute, because the director concluded that release of the secrets in open court would be too damaging. In a lot of such cases, the company decided that the price of prosecution was too high. Defense lawyers for the suspects knew how to play the game of "graymail" against the agency. If their clients were brought to trial, they warned, the documents they sold might become Exhibit A.

It made for mildly interesting reading, but the files were no help to him, Danner realized. The provided no leads to the mole who was currently burrowing away inside headquarters and giving Dixon Hadley the shakes. It was all small potatoes, a waste of time.

"Albanians," Danner said aloud. "Shit." He gathered the reports together, attached a routing slip, and put them in his out-basket.

He was staring out the window, wondering whether he had been given an impossible assignment, when the telephone rang. It was Melinda.

"He'd like to see you for lunch. Can you come up now?"

Anything was better than the Albanians, Danner decided. "Sure," he replied.

He went upstairs to the seventh floor. Hadley kept him waiting the usual five minutes before Melinda ushered him into the office. "I've got a few things for you," Hadley said. "We can stop by here again after lunch and you can pick them up."

They walked down the corridor to the executive dining room. It was a lot nicer than the cafeteria. The members, all senior CIA officials, were billed monthly.

Hadley found a table near the window. He was full of himself because he had accompanied Brooks Jordan to the White House that morning to brief President Forbes on the Persian Gulf. The president, he informed Danner, was looking well. "Remarkable man," he said, "amazingly well preserved, when you consider his age."

"It's the pancake makeup," Danner said.

"He only wears that on television," Hadley replied with irritation. He did not want Danner to take away from his White House glow. Over the years, Danner had noticed that otherwise intelligent men came away from the Oval Office on a sort of high; they seemed to be tingling for several hours. He decided it was the political equivalent of Chinese restaurant syndrome.

"I have a question for you," Danner said.

They were both eating the chef's salad, but Hadley was attacking the rolls and butter as well. The deputy director had a weight problem.

"Fire away," Hadley said.

"I'd like to know what Special Operations does."

Hadley looked quizzically at Danner. "I'm not sure you need to know that," he said.

Danner reminded him of their arrangement. "I'm cleared for everything," he said. "Even the crown jewels."

Hadley cleared his throat. "Special Operations was established six years ago," he said. "It was a follow-up to Executive Action."

Danner understood. Executive Action had been set up during the Kennedy administration to handle assassination planning. It was EA, for example, that had hired the Mafia to try to kill Castro. For a while, Hadley had run the unit.

"We told Congress that EA had been shut down," Hadley

explained. "And it was. We wouldn't want to mislead the intelligence committees."

"Of course not," Danner said.

"But SO is broader than that," Hadley continued.

"In what way?"

"It can handle terminations. But it also carries out special operations that are assigned to it, and controlled, by the director."

Danner could see why the deputy director had been reluctant to talk about SO. The unit was outside his turf.

"That's an odd arrangement," Danner said.

Hadley nodded. "It's the way the director wanted it. The unit is tightly compartmented from the rest of the house." They talked further, and Hadley made it clear that even as chief of the agency's clandestine activities, he was either told nothing about SO's work or was advised of it only in vague terms.

"Do they do any research?" Danner asked.

Hadley shrugged. "I suppose so. They're pretty much self-contained."

The waiter brought them coffee. Hadley took his with two creams and a teaspoon of sugar.

"What's the material you have for me?" Danner asked.

"I've got the list of old boys you wanted. Everyone fired in the Halloween Massacre."

"Good."

"Also, Nick Rossi's 201 file."

Danner nodded.

Hadley leaned forward. "I'm afraid our troubles are continuing," he said. He lowered his voice. "There's been an anomaly in London."

"Bad?"

"Bad enough. Several of our people were blown. Their names were published in *Private Eye*."

"How are the Brits reacting?"

"M16 is being sympathetic, but obviously we'll have to pull them out. In fact, I've already seen to it."

"Same business?"

"I'm afraid so." The DDO shook his head. He stirred his coffee for a moment, in silence.

"Who was seen?"

"Trowbridge. He checked into the Connaught about two weeks before the names surfaced."

Hadley's coffee cup was too full and he had trouble getting it to his lips. A little of the coffee spilled on the white tablecloth.

"Sorry to hear it," Danner sympathized.

The deputy director put his cup down. It rattled against the saucer. "What we need to know," he said, "is where you plan to start."

Danner could understand why Hadley was getting edgy. The calendar had slipped into September and he wasn't making much progress. But then, the job hadn't been his idea to begin with. He drummed his fingers on the table for a moment. "Vienna," he finally replied.

The DDO nodded approvingly.

"I want to retrace the operation. Find out everything possible about it. I can stop off in London and Madrid on the way in."

"Excellent." Hadley seemed buoyed by the fact that Danner was ready to move.

"I'll want to see MS/SKYLARK, of course."

Hadley hesitated. "That may be difficult. He's rather bitter. And his wife extremely so. But I'll see what I can do."

"Good."

They left the executive dining room and walked back to Hadley's office. Socrates greeted them with a squawk. The DDO went over to his cage and talked to him soothingly.

"Tell me, Dixon," Danner said. "Since you're spending time at the White House, does the president know about me?"

"Good heavens, no," Hadley replied, a look of alarm crossing his face.

"Then I take it he doesn't know about any of the blown operations, either?"

"Of course not. We try to settle our problems in the house. You know that."

Hadley handed over two file folders, both labeled "Top Secret" in red letters. Danner took his leave and went back to his office. He closed the door and flipped through the list of dismissed CIA men.

Then he opened the 201 file. It was headed ROSSI, NICHOLAS ALDRICH. Its contents were like a Michelin Guide through the darker pages of the agency's past. According to the file, Rossi had been the agency's contact with the Mafia in the Castro assassination attempt and the case officer for the operation against Lumumba in the Congo. He had provided the gun used to kill General Schneider in Chile. He had fired a shot that nicked Qaddafi in the jaw, although the Libyans hushed up the incident.

But what interested Danner the most was the notation near the end of the file. Rossi had left the CIA four years ago. But for the last two years of his agency service, he had been assigned to Special Operations.

CHAPTER
EIGHT

The telephone was ringing insistently on the table next to the bed, and Danner, vaguely aware of the noise, wondered if he'd overslept. He'd been out late with Julie the evening before. They were seeing each other almost every night now. He half-opened his eyes, looked at his clock radio, and saw that it was only a little after 6:00 A.M. The alarm hadn't gone off yet.

He turned on his left side and pulled the covers up over his head. The telephone had stopped ringing. Just as he dozed off, it began again. This time he groped for the receiver. He propped himself up on one elbow.

" 'Lo," he croaked.

The voice sounded far away. "Mr. Danner? I'm glad I got you. I must have dialed wrong the first time."

"Andy, how are you? How's everybody?" It was the head guide whom Danner had left in charge of the camp. He was delighted to hear Andy's voice, despite the early hour.

"I'm fine. We've been busy."

"Are you catching any?"

"Yes. Yesterday, Doctor Harris' wife, she caught a twenty-pound hookbill. She was real excited. Doc, he wasn't too happy."

Danner chuckled. Doc Harris was one of his regulars. He came to camp every summer with three dozen little metal boxes full of salmon flies and an array of expensive graphite rods. He fished with the fierce intensity, bordering on obsession, that typified the Atlantic salmon addict. His wife hardly knew how to cast.

"Tell Doc his turn will come," Danner said.

"I did," Andy responded, laughing, "but he didn't invite me in for a drink." It was customary to ask the guide to come to the cabin for a friendly libation after a day on the river. If Doc Harris had neglected to do so, he must have been truly furious at his wife's luck, Danner realized.

"He'll get over it," Danner said. "Now what's up that couldn't wait until I've had my coffee?"

Andy hesitated. "It's your wife, Mr. Danner. Your ex. I hope I did the right thing. She called a little while ago and asked to talk to you. I wouldn't give her your number. You said not to give it out to anybody."

Danner was sitting up, alert now, a little stab of fear in his belly. "Did you say a little while ago? It's only three o'clock in the morning in California."

"She called just a few minutes ago, sir. She sounded kind of upset. Said she had to talk to you right away. So I said I would get a message to you."

"Okay, thanks, Andy. You did the right thing. I'll take care of it."

He hung up and dialed Francesca. She answered on the second ring. She was a continent away but her voice sounded like it was next door. The same throaty, normally confident voice he knew too well. Only this time, she was crying.

"Bill, thank God. Maybe you can do something."

He always had mixed feelings when he heard that voice. Part of him still loved her, in spite of himself. And now she sounded so damn vulnerable. It wasn't like her.

"Take it easy. What's the matter?"

"Carrie's gone. Disappeared. I'm sure she's been kidnapped."

"Oh, no." Danner felt like someone had kicked him in the stomach. His hands were cold and he was having trouble breathing. This couldn't be happening, and yet it was. Carrie gone! Even as he heard the words he knew what it meant.

If Carrie had been kidnapped, he was the reason.

Francesca was sobbing. Finally she managed to stop. "I

don't know what to do," she said. "I thought maybe you had a friend in the FBI."

"Tell me what happened."

"Yesterday afternoon, Carrie didn't come home from school. Usually she goes over to Jessica's for a while, so I didn't start to worry until it got to be six o'clock."

"What did you do then?"

"I called Jessica's house. I talked to her mother. Carrie hadn't been there."

"Damn, damn, damn." He felt an enormous pressure in his chest, like a deep-sea diver who'd come up too fast.

"So I checked some other friends' houses, and Carrie hadn't been to any of them. So then I called the police." She started to cry again.

"Take it easy," Danner said again. "Were the cops any help?"

She blew her nose. "They came to the house and talked to me. They wrote everything down. Then they called a few hours later to say that some kids had found Carrie's bike in Toro Canyon Park, covered with brush. They just happened to stumble on it."

"Toro Canyon? That's almost four miles out of her way." It was not a good sign.

"I know. I tried to tell them."

Danner drew a mental map of Santa Barbara. Normally, he knew, Carrie rode her bike from Montecito Union School to Jessica's house on Olive Mill Road. From there she took Hot Springs up to East Valley Road and then turned left on San Ysidro to her house on Mountain Drive. If her bike was found in Toro Canyon Park, someone else had put it there.

"Has anyone called?" Danner asked. "Has there been a ransom note?"

"No." She sounded terribly tired. "The detectives who came to the house are treating it as a missing person case. Just another runaway kid."

"What did they say?"

"There were two of them. The younger one was nicer. He said, 'She's probably gone to visit a friend, or she's on her way to see her father.' He said it happens all the time."

"Assholes."

"They said because there was no ransom demand, they couldn't treat it as a kidnapping and they couldn't call in the FBI. They said they couldn't rule out homicide, but there was no evidence of that, either. They said she's probably hitchhiking to LA."

"She's a happy kid," Danner said. "She'd have no reason to run away."

"That's what Richard said. He's been very good. He's making me some coffee right now."

At least Francesca had someone to share the pain. "She didn't leave a note or anything?" he asked.

"No. Nothing. She didn't take any extra clothes with her to school. I checked her room."

"What about her bear?"

"Edward is sitting in his usual place on her bookcase. You know she wouldn't go anywhere without Edward." She cried again, and Danner waited for her to stop.

He was terrified by the news, because he recognized it for what it must be—a kidnapping by professionals who were sending him a message. He knew that, but Carrie didn't. He thought of her wrenching fear when she was kidnapped, of the awful terror, made even worse by the fact that she did not know why it was happening. Other dreadful thoughts crowded in. First Lisa in Berlin; and now Carrie?

But they were professionals. He clutched at the hope. It would almost certainly take two people to snatch a twelve-year-old child on a bicycle. A driver to cut her off, and a second person to jump out of the car and drag her in. They probably used a van so they could hide both Carrie and the bicycle. That was great, Danner thought. Go find a van in California.

If Carrie had been running away, he reasoned, her bike would never have been found in Toro Canyon, south of Montecito. She would have pedaled in the opposite direction, to State Street. The traffic along Highway 101, the main north-south artery, had to stop there for a light. It was by far the best place to hitch a ride in Santa Barbara, either north toward San Francisco or south to Los Angeles. College students, and sometimes younger kids, would wait there on the corner with hand-lettered cardboard signs announcing their destination. It wasn't too hard to get a ride.

But Carrie hadn't done that. He traced her route in his mind again. They had probably jumped her on San Ysidro Road, just after she crossed Las Tunas. It was an isolated, shady stretch, with very few houses, screened by thick foliage. She would have slowed down because it was uphill.

He tried to think of other possibilities. Carrie might be the victim of a sex crime, in which case, God help her, she could be dead by now. But even as he thought that, he knew it wasn't true. Child molesters seldom worked in pairs. The most telling sign of all was that there was no ransom demand. That meant that Carrie had not been kidnapped for money, by ordinary criminals. Her disappearance bore all the earmarks of an operation, the work of a team of trained intelligence agents.

"I'm afraid it was done by someone trying to send me a signal," Danner said.

"What do you mean?" Francesca asked sharply.

"Someone is trying to get me to stop something I'm doing."

"My God, Bill, this is Carrie. What are you talking about?" He could hear Richard in the background trying to calm her.

"I can't tell you any more."

Francesca exploded. "It's the same old shit," she screamed. "It's all a big secret. Agency business. Well, this time its our *daughter*, dammit!" She broke down and cried uncontrollably.

Danner felt the knot growing in his chest. Her accusation had roiled up all the old emotions and antagonisms that had led to their divorce in the first place. He loved Carrie more than anyone in the whole world, and he was scared and horrified by what had happened because she was in terrible danger. And now on top of everything, Francesca was doing her old numbers, trying to paint him as a heartless monster who put the agency ahead of his family.

He took a deep breath. It would only make matters worse to argue with her now. "Look," he said, "I love Carrie. I'll do everything I can to find out who has her."

"Then tell me what's going on."

"I can't."

"I don't believe you." She was infuriated, her voice whipping out the words like razor blades.

"I'll fly out there. I'll talk to the police." Even as he said it,

Danner knew it wouldn't do any good. Whoever had Carrie wasn't going to be caught by the county sheriff's department.

"Don't bother," she snapped.

"Francesca—" But he got no reply. She had hung up.

Danner put down the phone and realized his left hand was white from gripping the receiver. He had never felt worse in his life, not even in the morgue in Berlin. He was overcome by remorse, guilt, and fear. His whole body shook. William Danner, who in his day had been known as the toughest, most glamorous agent in the CIA, was crying.

CHAPTER
NINE

Danner showered, shaved, and had a quick breakfast of orange juice, toast, and coffee. He ate mechanically, his mind racing as he thought back over the phone call.

He dressed hurriedly, reviewing the details again. He found it very hard to get beyond three overwhelming facts: Carrie had been kidnapped. Her life was in danger. And it was his fault.

He closed the door to the apartment and literally ran down the carpeted hall to the elevator. It was slow coming and stopped three times on the way down to let people on. He got off at the ground level and dashed out the back of the building to his parking space.

Driving east along the Shirley Highway, he pushed the Skylark as fast as he could, weaving in and out of the morning rush-hour traffic. He cut off a yellow Volkswagen beetle, and the bearded driver, who looked like a college student, glared and gave him the finger.

As he drove, Danner concentrated on who would have a motive to abduct Carrie. The most likely kidnapper was whoever was betraying the agency's secrets. The mole. And perhaps his confederates inside CIA, if there were others.

That would also mean that the mole knew that Danner had been brought back into the agency and why. But any number of people had access to that information. The heads of both the Counterintelligence Staff and the Office of Security had, of necessity, been advised of Danner's mission. That meant that some of the secretaries and support staff for the director, for

Dixon Hadley, and in CI and OS also knew. And of course there was Larry Gates.

He sped past Arlington Cemetery and the Pentagon and swung onto the George Washington Parkway. If the mole had kidnapped Carrie, the purpose was to signal him to stop his investigation. But there were other possibilities, he realized. The agency itself, perhaps on orders from Brooks Jordan or Dixon Hadley, could have engineered the kidnapping as insurance. To make certain he pressed ahead vigorously with the investigation. The agency's motive would be the exact opposite of the mole's.

He swerved around a thin, gray-haired man creeping along in a vintage Pontiac. But it was at least equally possible that the old boys had snatched Carrie. They were working with the mole, perhaps taking orders from him. If the mole knew about Danner, so did the old boys. They, too, would want Danner to stop his investigation. He left the parkway at the CIA turnoff.

One other organization would have an interest in acquiring leverage over him, Danner knew—the KGB. The Russians were reaping the benefits of the blown operations. If the mole had warned them that he was in danger, the Soviets might well risk a covert operation on U.S. soil. It would not be the first.

One, the mole. Two, the agency. Three, the old boys. Four, the Russians. And there was no way to know which of them had his daughter. Dear, sweet Carrie, what have I done? Danner thought. Will you ever forgive me? Will I ever forgive myself? He was at the guard booth. He held up his badge and swept through the gate onto the CIA grounds. It was 8:30 A.M. and traffic was streaming into headquarters.

He parked, trotted into the lobby, and got in line to go through the badge machines. He chafed while he waited; it was like a goddamn supermarket checkout line, he thought. He imagined that the agency's recruiters downplayed this part when they talked about the glamorous life of a secret agent.

He crowded onto the elevator and took it directly to the seventh floor. Walking rapidly, he made his way along the corridor to Dixon Hadley's office.

Melinda frowned when she saw him. He was not expected. "I'm afraid he's in the morning staff meeting with the director," she said.

"Pull him out," Danner ordered.

"I don't think—"

"Get him now."

From Danner's grim expression, she realized he meant it. She got up, looking uncertain. "I'll tell him you're here," she said noncommittally.

Danner paced up and down the reception area as Melinda went off to Brooks Jordan's office. The meeting was in progress, and she let herself in discreetly. Hadley was sitting at the conference table on the director's right. She tiptoed over to him and whispered something in his ear. The DDO scribbled a note and slid it across the table to the director. He got up and left the room with Melinda.

He hurried back to his office. Danner was still pacing, his hands shoved deep into his pockets. Hadley noticed that he hadn't combed his hair very well and his tie was askew.

"Hello, Bill," he said calmly. "Where's the fire?" He held open the door to his office for Danner and motioned him inside. Danner chose one of the padded chairs across from Hadley's desk. He stared balefully at the deputy director, who put a pencil in his mouth and began chewing it.

"What the hell is going on?" Danner demanded, his voice rising with anger.

Hadley removed the pencil. "You tell me," he countered. "I thought by now you'd be on your way to Vienna."

"You're going to say you don't know why I'm here."

"That's right," Hadley said. "I don't know why you're here."

"Fuck!" Danner got up and slammed his fist down hard on Hadley's desk.

"Would you like a cup of coffee? You look like you could use it."

Danner exhaled. There was no sense antagonizing Hadley until he knew more. For Carrie's sake. "Okay. I'll have some. Thanks."

Hadley pressed a buzzer. Melinda appeared and he asked for the coffee.

In a kindly voice, Hadley said, "Why don't you tell me what's happened?"

"Carrie's disappeared."

"Your daughter?" Hadley sounded genuinely surprised. "No wonder you're upset. That's distressing news."

"She didn't come home after school yesterday."

"And the police?"

"There's been no ransom demand, so they're treating it as a runaway kid case. But it's clear to me she's been kidnapped. By professionals."

The deputy director removed his horn-rimmed glasses and slowly massaged his eyes and forehead. "I'm sorry," he said. "This is a—complication."

"The timing isn't coincidental," Danner declared.

Hadley put his glasses back on. "I'm afraid you're right," he said.

"I thought you might know something about it."

The DDO looked shocked. But that didn't mean a damn thing, Danner knew. In the agency you were trained to lie, with facial expression as well as words. They began teaching you how in the dramatics classes at The Farm.

"It wasn't us," Hadley said. "Why in heaven's name would we? You're back."

"Maybe for insurance."

"No, no. We made one threat, and only one. And I've apologized for that."

"How can I be sure?"

Hadley sighed. "You can't. But if it was us, we'd tell you. There wouldn't be much point otherwise, would there?"

"Perhaps you wouldn't tell me. You might prefer to keep me wondering."

The DDO threw up his hands. "We don't kidnap children," he said. "Very rarely, anyhow."

"Well, someone has," Danner said.

"The mole," Hadley suggested.

"Or the old boys. Or the Russians."

"All of those are possible, I'm afraid."

"It doesn't matter. I'm quitting."

Hadley looked stricken. "That's the very worst thing you could do," he warned.

"I'm going back to New Brunswick," Danner insisted. "It's the best chance I have of getting Carrie out of this mess alive."

Melinda arrived with the coffee. Hadley waited until she had left.

"You're wrong," he declared. "Quite wrong."

"It's fairly simple," Danner replied. "Whoever has Carrie wants me to stop what I'm doing. So, I'm going to stop. And hope they let her go."

"They might let her go," Hadley said. "Or they might kill her."

Danner put his coffee cup down, "Okay. You have any better ideas?"

"Yes," Hadley said. "Keep going. It's the best chance you have."

Danner shook his head. Hadley wasn't making any sense.

"Look," Hadley continued, "let's assume you're right. This was done by professionals, and their purpose is to get you to stop. The only leverage you have over the kidnappers is to keep going."

"It's too risky. For God sakes, she's my daughter!"

"If you keep after the mole, you may smoke them out. They may show their hand and make contact with you or your wife."

"And if they do?"

"If they do, there's a chance of finding them. If they don't, there's no chance at all. We'll start by putting tracing equipment on your phone, and on your wife's, if she agrees."

Danner thought it over. Despite his anguish, he must think clearly. He knew that Hadley's argument was self-serving; the DDO desperately wanted him to stay. But it also made a kind of sense.

Hadley said, "You'll have the full resources of the agency behind you. You know we have the best technology. If there's any contact, we'll move fast. We'll do everything we can to get Carrie back."

Danner got up and walked over to the window. He looked out at the lush, green Virginia hills. Even in early September, some of the leaves were beginning to turn.

He had walked straight into a maze, he realized. Ahead of him lay a complex matrix of tunnels and byways, false leads, and dead ends. But at the end of the maze, if he could somehow get through, he might find Carrie. He might, and he might not. That was the damnable part of it.

He turned away from the window. "All right," he said.

Hadley looked enormously relieved. "You've made the right decision," he declared. He grasped Danner's hand and shook it.

"I'm flying to Santa Barbara today," Danner said. "I promised her mother. Francesca," he corrected himself.

"Of course," Hadley said.

"I don't expect to find anything. But I owe it to Carrie to have a look around."

"Naturally. It might be best if you didn't tell the police you work for us."

"I hadn't planned to."

"Get one of the pool secretaries to book your flight and arrange for a rental car and a hotel." It was Hadley's way of saying that the trip was company business.

"I'll be there for a day. Then I'll fly back here and leave immediately for London, on Friday. I'll spend two days there, and two days in Madrid. I should be in Vienna on Tuesday, one week from today."

"Good. I'll notify the stations. I've already cabled Ashford to expect you. And I've instructed him to pave the way with MS/SKYLARK."

"Fine."

Hadley smiled encouragingly. "Keep your chin up."

"I'll check in with you before I leave for London," Danner said. He left and walked down the corridor, his mind churning, wondering whether he had done the right thing. If he had not, if his decision was a mistake, the cost was too horrible to contemplate. He took the elevator to the fifth floor. All the way to his office, he continued thinking about Carrie.

Back at his desk, he telephoned Nancy Baker in the secretarial pool and asked her to book him on the midday United Airlines flight to Los Angeles and a connecting flight to Santa Barbara. He told her to arrange a motel room and to have a midsize rental car waiting for him at the airport.

Then he telephoned Julie at her office. He said he had to go out of town unexpectedly, but planned to be back Thursday and asked her to keep the evening free. She said she would and he promised to call her about 8:00 P.M.

He left and drove out to Dulles on the airport road. He was

scarcely conscious of where he was driving. He thought only of
Carrie. He had received a letter from her just four days earlier,
forwarded from New Brunswick by Andy. She had sounded
very happy, and thanked him for the birthday presents. She also
relayed what she called fantastic news. Harvey Vogelmeyer
was no longer at Montecito Union; he and his family had
moved to Thousand Oaks.

She had gone sailing a couple of weekends ago with Richard
and Francesca, and they had taken Jessica. It had been a spar-
kling day and they had sailed out beyond the oil rigs halfway to
the islands. She had been riding in the hills near Sycamore Canyon Road on her favorite horse, Major. The previous Saturday,
she and Jessica had rented roller skates and spent the whole day
eating pizza and skating along Cabrillo Boulevard by the water.
They had gone all the way to the bird refuge and back four
times. With the letter, she enclosed a single strand of purple
wool, three feet long. It was for Mr. O'Malley.

CHAPTER
TEN

"Captain Blanchard has turned off the seat-belt sign," the flight attendant announced. "You are now free to move about the cabin if you wish. However, we do recommend that you keep your seat belt fastened while seated."

Danner stretched out and eased his seat back, glad to have the California trip behind him. It had been even harder than he had expected. The most painful moment had come when he stood alone in Carrie's room, looking at Edward Bear sitting forlornly on the bookcase. Francesca had shown the good grace to remain downstairs in the living room with Richard.

The flight attendant asked if he would like a drink and he said he very much would. He ordered a Scotch and she brought it with a package of stale peanuts. He had decided to drive down to Los Angeles from Santa Barbara. LAX had been a zoo as usual, and it had been a scramble to turn in the car and make the flight. He was tired, physically and emotionally, from the trip.

Francesca had been much more composed than in her initial, grief-stricken phone conversation. She agreed to let the agency put the tracing equipment in. But she was still bitterly angry at Danner, and blamed him in so many words for Carrie's disappearance. He couldn't argue with her. He knew she was right.

So he had confined himself for the most part to filling her in on his meeting with Detective Radley Walker, who was handling the case for the Santa Barbara sheriff's department. He had gone straight from the airport to the sheriff's headquarters on Calle Real, a one-story, cream-colored building with a

Spanish-style tile roof. After signing in, he was given a visitor's tag and escorted to the detectives bureau off the front lobby.

Walker, a broad-shouldered young man with a droopy mustache, called him sir. He was in shirtsleeves and had a Smith and Wesson 9 millimeter automatic tucked in his shoulder holster. The call from Mrs. White had come in to the watch officer shortly after 6:00 P.M., he said, and two uniformed sheriff's deputies had been dispatched to the home. The case fell under the jurisdiction of the county sheriff's department, rather than the city police, he explained, because the family lived in Montecito, outside the city limits of Santa Barbara.

The deputies had interviewed the mother and taken an incident report. They had determined the usual route that Carrie took from the school to her house, the name of her teacher, and who her friends were. They had ascertained what telephone calls Mrs. White had already made to try to locate her daughter.

Although they felt it was probably a case of a runaway, they were concerned because twelve was a little young for a runaway, although "they do occur." Walker added, "If the child was fourteen or fifteen, we wouldn't worry as much." The search and rescue team had been called out immediately and had retraced Carrie's customary way home, checking off-road areas as well. Later in the evening, when the bicycle had been found, the crime lab had been dispatched to Toro Canyon Park and, under floodlights, had processed the scene for trace evidence—footprints, fingerprints, bloodstains. Nothing of value had been found, however. It was entirely possible, Walker noted, that Carrie had left the bicycle there herself.

The detective pointed out that, at any given time, the department had ten to fifteen cases of missing juveniles. Usually, he said, they turned out to be runaways.

Although homicide was a possibility, Walker said, there was no evidence of foul play, no eyewitnesses, and of course, no body. He explained carefully that in the absence of any kidnap evidence, such as a demand for ransom, the department could only treat Carrie's disappearance as a missing person case. And without a ransom demand—a note, or a phone call, for example—they could not bring in the FBI.

Walker conceded that there were some cases where a kidnapper wanted a child, rather than money, but he said those abductions almost always involved babies or toddlers. A twelve-year-old taken against her will could not be watched every moment of the day and night, and would presumably attempt to escape, or telephone the police or her parents, at the first opportunity.

So Carrie was officially listed as a missing person. Detective Walker was very sympathetic but said no leads had been developed as to her whereabouts. Danner asked whether a teletype or all-points bulletin had been distributed nationally to police jurisdictions around the country, giving Carrie's name and physical description.

Walker said he was sorry, but no formal system existed for notifying police agencies in routine missing persons cases. Of course, they had put out a BOL, a "be on the lookout," for Carrie that night on the orange channel, their primary working channel, and on the red channel, which went to every police cruiser in both Santa Barbara and San Luis Obispo counties. And, he added, there was a monthly bulletin, published privately, in which parents of missing children were free to place ads.

Danner was appalled. Apparently, when kids disappeared in America, nobody much cared. No system for notifying police in other states. He could take out an ad.

The detective said he thought Danner should know one thing more. After thirty days, Santa Barbara would notify the California Department of Justice. The coroner's office would send Carrie's description, fingerprints—if they could be obtained from her room—and dental charts to Sacramento. So that if her body were found in the state, sir, it could be identified.

Danner thanked Detective Walker. He told him that he was a civilian employee of the Department of the Army based in the Pentagon. He gave him a telephone number with the Pentagon's exchange that rang in his office at CIA headquarters; it was a standard arrangement for the agency's clandestine employees. Detective Walker promised to call the minute he heard anything.

Afterward, Danner had driven up Gibraltar Road, high into the foothills of the Santa Ynez Mountains. He had parked on a turnoff, as he had often done with Carrie, and looked out over the Pacific toward Santa Rosa, Santa Cruz, and Anacapa, the channel islands. The water was bright blue shading into emerald and the air was so clear that the islands looked deceptively closer than they were. All of Santa Barbara was spread out below him, green hills, dotted with rust-colored terra-cotta roofs, plunging steeply down to the palm-fringed beaches and the sea. To the right he could see the airport and far to his left, Carpinteria Beach, Carrie's favorite, where she loved to run free, swim, and climb the eucalyptus trees.

He thought about Detective Walker's report. A child was gone and no one seemed upset. It was all so damned casual. Usually they turned out to be runaways, sir. But perhaps he had no right to be angry with the cops. There was a lot he hadn't told them. And couldn't.

That evening at dusk, after visiting Francesca and Richard, he had walked down San Ysidro Road to the isolated stretch where he thought it likely the kidnapping had taken place. At the corner of Las Tunas, across from a fragrant lemon grove, he stood for a long time looking across the open meadow and listening to the insistent chorus of the tree frogs. A chestnut stallion roaming the field had come over to inspect him, and remained to chew the tender shoots of grass along the fence. He knew instinctively that the horse was Carrie's friend.

He had paced the roads in the area until it was dark. Then he walked along Mountain Drive under the stars, which were incredibly bright against the black sky, since there were no street lights. Even now, on the jetliner streaking east, he could still smell the musky odor of eucalyptus trees.

He ordered another Scotch and the flight attendant brought dinner. Danner occupied the window seat; during dinner the friendly young couple on his right introduced themselves. Their names were Bob and Jane, and they talked with Danner about jogging.

Danner told them he liked to run, too, but didn't have much time because of his job. He said he was a crop inspector for the Agriculture Department. The woman asked him what he specialized in.

"Soybeans," he said. "Soybeans and lentils." He explained that he also worked some with alfalfa but didn't like it nearly as much.

Afterwards, Danner snoozed and it seemed only a moment later that the plane was descending for its approach to Dulles.

He found a telephone in the terminal and called Julie. She answered on the second ring and sounded glad to hear his voice.

"I'll be there in about forty-five minutes," Danner said. "We'll have dinner in Old Town and go somewhere afterwards for a drink."

"Sounds perfect," Julie said. "I'll get ready."

Danner said goodbye and hung up. His bag seemed to take forever to get off the plane, but finally it appeared on the conveyor belt, and he grabbed it and walked out to the taxis. Half an hour later, he pulled up in front of Julie's house in Alexandria.

They kissed in the hallway after she had closed the door. She rubbed her fingers along the muscles of his back and could feel the tension in his shoulders. He was holding her tightly in his arms.

She looked up at him, brushing her cheek against his. "What's wrong?" she asked.

"Tell you later," he promised. "Let's get some dinner first."

They drove in her MG to the Fish Market. The restaurant was crowded. They ordered the soft shell crabs and Danner asked for a schooner of beer.

"Where've you been?" Julie asked when the waiter had gone.

"California."

"To see your daughter?"

Quietly, Danner explained that Carrie was missing. He sketched in the facts, but said nothing about his belief that she had been kidnapped. Julie took his hand; it felt very smooth and good against his. "Why didn't you tell me?"

"It isn't your problem."

"It is now. I care about you."

He smiled and caressed her hand. "I know," he said. "I know you do." He took a sip of his beer. "I'm only here overnight. I leave for Europe tomorrow. Agency business."

"How long will you be gone?"

"Maybe two weeks. Of course, I'll be back right away if there's any news of Carrie."

She fell silent and ate her dinner for a while. Finally she asked, "Do you think Carrie's disappearance has anything to do with your work for the agency?"

Now he was right on it. Poised on the edge. He wanted to tell her. But Julie worked for SO, and so had Nick Rossi. He could either deflect the probe or take Julie into his confidence.

He nodded.

"Oh, God." She touched his hand again. "Oh, Bill."

He signaled the waiter for a check and paid. They left and wandered up King Street past the big, floodlit fountain at Market Square. Danner was debating how much to tell her. "Let's get a drink," he said suddenly.

They went into Henry Africa's, an attractive restaurant with a piano bar in the front. They sat down at a table in the bar and Julie ordered a green crème de menthe over crushed ice. Danner had a brandy. Tucked into a quiet corner, he broke all the rules. He didn't really care. He felt under tremendous pressure. There was no one he could talk to. Not Sam, not Hadley, certainly not Francesca. The words came in a torrent. He began at the beginning, with Larry Gates. He told her how he had been coerced into coming back, how DDO operations had been blown in half a dozen places, and of the traces that had been picked up of the old boys in each case. He shared his fears that Carrie had been abducted and went over the list of those with a possible motive. He explained why he had decided to press ahead with the hunt for the mole, beginning in London the next day.

When he had finished, she sat for a long time without saying anything. Finally she spoke. "If I can, I'd like to help."

"That's the answer I was hoping for."

"Tell me how."

"All right." Relief and happiness flooded through him. He leaned close and spoke quietly. "Hadley swears the agency had nothing to do with Carrie."

"But you're not sure you believe him."

"Even if he's telling the truth, the one unit that could carry out a sensitive domestic operation is outside his control. Your shop. Special Operations."

"All of our operations are in the SO computer," Julie said. "As a researcher, I have access to it."

"That's a break."

"There's a problem. Each operation has a code name, of course. But it's all compartmented on a need-to-know basis. The access lists are kept very small and they're tightly held."

Danner had been playing with a matchbook; now he crushed it in his fist.

Julie went on, "Without the code name, there's no way to call up an operation in the computer. Even to tell whether it exists or not."

"See what you can do," Danner said. "Maybe you can figure out a way."

"I'll try."

"There's one other thing. A top hit man for SO, Nick Rossi, retired from the agency about four years ago. I'd like to know where he is now. And anything else you can find out about him."

"I've heard the name. I'll check it out."

"Thanks." He paused. She was offering more than he had any right to expect. "You're sticking your neck way out for me. You're sure you want to?"

"I'm sure."

"I'll call you in a few days, maybe from London or Madrid. I'll ask about a missing package and an old friend."

"All right." She finished her drink. "Take me home now."

"I was thinking the same thing."

He paid the check and they drove back to Julie's house. They were lucky and found a parking spot nearby. In the living room, Danner took off his jacket and stretched out on the couch while Julie put on a Carly Simon record. It had been a long forty-eight hours.

She came over and sat down by him. They listened to the music and talked quietly for a time. She leaned over and gave him a light kiss. "I'm going to miss you," she said.

"I'll miss you, too," Danner replied.

"No you won't. You'll be too busy." She traced the outline of his lips with her finger. "London is so exciting. But I think of all the cities in Europe, Vienna is my favorite. I lived there for a while, you know."

"I didn't know."

"When I was ten. My father was second secretary in the embassy. We had a house in Döbling. It's a beautiful section."

"So you learned to speak German."

"Yes. I still can."

Danner stretched and rubbed the back of his neck. Julie reached inside his collar and began kneading his neck and shoulders.

"Mmmm," Danner said. "That feels good."

Julie smiled. "Would you like me to rub your back?"

"Yes." He got up, took her hand, and they walked into the bedroom. Danner removed his shirt and tie and Julie pulled back the blankets to expose the sheets.

"You might as well take everything off," she said. "I'm going to."

Danner smiled. He removed the rest of his clothes and stood before her naked. She came over and put her arms around him. He helped unbutton her dress.

She looked down at his loins. "You're going to have a lot of trouble lying on your stomach," she said, laughing.

"I'll manage somehow," he said.

She unhooked her bra, let it fall, and took off her panties. She disappeared into the bathroom and emerged with some sort of white cream in a bottle. She sat on the bed and began slowly rubbing the cream into his back and shoulders, and then into his buttocks and the back of his legs.

"Turn over," she said. He did and she caressed him, her hands slippery from the cream. He was hard and wanted her and in a swift motion she parted her thighs and sat on him. "Julie," he murmured as he entered her. "Julie."

He was thrusting upward and suddenly he pulled her down to him and rolled over on top of her, staying in her all the while, and loving her and wanting her and she was whispering his name, and then they came together, exploded together, belonged together.

"Again," she whispered. "It's happening again." And she came to him once more and he held her tightly and forgot about anything else.

Afterward, Danner lay back with Julie's head cradled against his shoulder, her dark hair spilling out over his chest, and he told her he loved her, which were words he had not expected to say again.

"I love you," she said. "I love you. I love *you*." Then she laughed, and rubbed her nose against his cheek like a large, green-eyed cat and kissed him gently on the lips.

They talked for a long time and then drifted off to sleep in each other's arms, enjoying the sensation of their nakedness, yet clothed in the warmth of their love.

In the morning, they showered together and Julie made coffee, orange juice, and English muffins. She dropped Danner off at his apartment, where he packed a bag and drove to headquarters. He checked in briefly with Dixon Hadley, who said the telephone tracing equipment was already in place both at Danner's apartment and Francesca's house. Hadley wished him luck.

He picked up his airline tickets and hotel reservations from the pool secretary and drove out to Dulles again. The airport was getting familiar, Danner reflected.

He checked in with British Airways and boarded the Concorde flight for London. They took off promptly and the supersonic jet climbed at a steep angle to its cruising altitude of 53,000 feet. There was no noticeable change inside the narrow cabin when the plane broke through the sound barrier. The flight was very smooth. For most of it, Danner leaned back, alone with his thoughts. It had been an extraordinary seventy-two hours. He had gone through a crazy quilt of experience and emotions. Edward Bear. Detective Walker and his police jargon. Francesca. Then Julie, warm and sensual and loving. And now, streaking across the Atlantic ten miles high at Mach 2, twice the speed of sound.

His thoughts returned to their night together. There was something that kept nagging at him, something that was wrong. What the hell was it? Yes, it was something she had said. In the apartment when they had returned from Henry Africa's and she had put on the Carly Simon record, Julie had said she loved Vienna, and that she had lived in Döbling. *But he hadn't mentioned Vienna to her.*

Danner pushed a call button and asked the flight attendant for a Scotch on the rocks. She brought it in a moment and he thanked her. He looked out the tiny cabin window. It was getting dark now and the clouds below were gradually turning into a blanket of gray as the Concorde raced away from the sun.

Could he have been mistaken? He went back over the evening in his mind. At the Fish Market he had told her he was going to Europe, but he hadn't said where. They had taken a walk after that and gone to the piano bar and there he had said he would call her in a few days, perhaps from London or Madrid. He wasn't wrong. He had never said Vienna.

Perhaps it was simply a coincidence. They had been talking about Europe, and she loved Vienna; it would have been natural enough for her to say so. Or it could mean that she already knew where he was going. He sipped his Scotch slowly. The lemon peel was tart against his tongue. It could mean that SO was, in some fashion, monitoring his movements. And Julie, if not directly involved, at the very least had access to the traffic about him.

If so, was it a slip on her part, or was she trying to tip him off that he was being watched? Whose side was she on? There was no way to tell, just now. He had shared his anguish over Carrie with this woman, and told her that he loved her. He wondered now whether her "I love you" had been real. He berated himself for having opened up to her so easily.

His mission was proving to be more of a puzzle than he had realized. He had to force himself to consider the next question, but it could not be avoided. Had he really met Julie by chance, or had it all been carefully arranged?

He tried to reconstruct the party at Sandy Berens' apartment that rainy summer night. He had noticed Julie dancing, but then later, it was Julie who approached him on the terrace. But that would mean that Sam—he rejected the idea before it was fully formed in his mind. It was the road to paranoia. His meeting Julie had to be accidental. But SO might be tracking him. That was about as far as he could take it for now.

And Carrie. He could only pray that she was not being mistreated. She was strong and independent-minded; if any twelve-year-old girl could survive and keep her spirits up in the worst of circumstances, he knew it would be Carrie.

His thoughts wandered to the Miramichi, and he longed to be back in that peaceful, uncomplicated world. He remembered one night in June, before Larry Gates' visit, when he and Carrie

had sat out in front of the cabin on the high bluff overlooking
the river. It was utterly silent except for a faint splashing noise
below. In the moonlight, they could see it was a muskrat, digging for clams as he made his way along the shore. The water
was calm, mirroring the dark reflections of the spruce and pine
on the opposite bank. They had sat there together for a long
time, sharing the tranquillity.

His reverie was interrupted by the steep descent of the
Concorde. Below him in the night he could see the blue runway
lights of Heathrow.

CHAPTER
ELEVEN

There were deep shadows in the twisting, narrow streets around the Judenplatz. Danner took two false turns before he found the Parisergasse, and there, at the end of the street, a cobblestoned courtyard and a gray four-story building.

He entered, walked up a narrow spiral staircase to the second floor, and rang the bell. A wizened old man in a worn dark blue suit opened the door. Very few people visited Vienna's clock museum on weekday mornings, and the old man seemed glad to see him. There was no one else there.

Danner started to glance at his watch, and then realized he didn't have to. All the clocks in the rooms were ticking and they told him he was ten minutes early. He began to browse among the exhibits. The floors in the 300-year-old building creaked with each step.

He stopped before a nineteenth-century figure clock by Jakob Streicher of Graz. Made of brass, with a short pendulum, it was set in the porcelain figure of a jolly little man wearing a red jacket and striped pants. Danner glanced out the window; he could see the courtyard and the Choir of Angels Church, but no one was approaching the building.

He wandered into another room and stopped to admire a cobalt blue case clock, an elaborate pastiche of gilt and bronze topped by two smiling and garlanded gold cherubs. Seeing Danner studying it, the old man shuffled over and flashed him a gap-toothed grin.

''The mistress of Franz-Josef once owned this clock,'' he

confided in heavily accented English. "She was a famous actress, Katharina Schratt. The clock was in her villa at Bad Ischl."

"I guess it helped him to know when it was time to hot-foot it back to the palace," Danner said. The elfin guard leered his agreement.

The doorbell buzzed, and he went off to answer it. In a moment, a tall, young man stepped into the room and moved toward Danner, his hand extended in greeting.

"Tyler Ashford," he said, smiling. "Sorry to drag you to the Uhrenmuseum, but the KGB does a rather efficient job of bugging the embassy."

The guard remained in the front room, out of earshot. Ashford had a neatly trimmed blond mustache and wore a gray Brooks Brothers suit, a blue button-down Oxford shirt, and a blue-and-red silk rep tie. Danner decided he did not like him.

"I've been catching up on the sex life of the Hapsburgs," Danner said. "Did you know they paid for their pussy with clocks?"

Ashford looked nonplussed. He glanced around nervously to make sure no one had heard Danner, but the ancient guard was still in the front room. Ashford decided it was best to ignore Danner's question. "Headquarters has asked me to pull together the complete file for you on the operation," he said briskly. "You can come to the Boltzmanngasse any time it's convenient to read it."

"I'll do that," Danner said. "Probably later today." The CIA station operated out of the U.S. Embassy, at Boltzmanngasse 16.

"That's the good news," Ashford said.

"What's the bad news?"

"I'm afraid the Skylark won't sing."

Danner was alarmed. "You don't mean someone got to him? He's not dead?"

"No. Just uncooperative."

"But he'll see me?"

"Yes. We're paying him disability. And we gave him a wheelchair. It's just that he isn't in a mood to be very helpful."

"Where do I find him?"

"He lives in Hernals. The address is in the file."

"All right."

The museum guard came into the room and they broke off. "You gentlemen may be interested in these clocks over here," he said. "They are clocks for the blind. See, the faces are all in Braille."

"Very interesting," Danner said.

"Yes, indeed," Ashford chimed in.

"And over here," the guard said, pointing to another display case, "is the world's smallest pendulum clock. It's so small it can fit in a thimble."

"I see," Danner said.

"We have another floor above," the guard went on enthusiastically. "There you find clocks with beautiful birds."

"Do they sing?" Danner asked.

The guard lowered his voice and spoke in reverential tones. "*Ja*. But only the Führer is allowed to wind them up. The big boss. He has a special key. He comes on Sonntag, in the morning, and he winds them, and then all the birdies sing." He rolled his eyes heavenward. "It's beautiful."

That's what I need, Danner thought. A key to wind up the Skylark.

When the old man had wandered off, Ashford said, "Let me know if I can be of any help." He looked uncomfortable. "I hope the DDO isn't too upset. This kind of thing has never happened to me before."

"It's time it did."

Ashford looked puzzled, but let it pass. "I think I should leave first," he said. "No point in our being seen together."

"Good tradecraft," Danner said drily.

Ashford left and Danner decided to go up to the third floor to see the birds. Bidding the guard goodbye, he climbed the narrow, winding staircase again. He rang the bell and was admitted. There were several elaborate cuckoo clocks, and he stopped to admire a cage containing two mechanical but very lifelike birds with real feathers, undoubtedly the ones the guard had described. He wished Carrie were with him now. She would like the birds, and the story about the man with the special key who allowed them to sing on Sunday.

The hot water coming out of the shower in sharp needles felt good against his back. Danner had chosen a small hotel in the Annagasse; it was centrally located but on a quiet side street, and everything worked.

He got out, dried himself with a bath towel, and stretched out naked for a few moments on the featherbed. He had been going nonstop in London and Madrid for the past four days. He hadn't learned very much; he hoped Vienna would be better.

He got dressed and phoned the desk for a taxi; it was waiting for him by the time he got downstairs. Fifteen minutes later he pulled up outside the American Embassy, an imposing rococo building in a quiet residential area. On the front of the embassy, the statues of four enormous cherubs kept watch over the colonnaded entrance. Danner paid the driver 55 schillings and got out. A lone Austrian policeman guarded the entrance.

A buzzer opened the front door, and he showed his credentials to a receptionist in a glass booth in the lobby. The archway at the top of the great central staircase was barred by a white metal grill. There were armed guards positioned behind it.

A secretary came and got him after a few moments. They took an elevator upstairs and she escorted him through wide halls to an empty office with brown leather couches and pea green carpets.

The secretary said her name was Sheila and she was from Paterson, New Jersey. She was overweight; Danner guessed she had been eating too much pastry in Vienna. She sat him down at a polished mahogany table and said she would be right back.

She returned in a few minutes with a thick file folder, which she set down in front of him. There was a telephone on the desk. "Call me when you're through," she said. "I'm on extension 26."

The file was labeled MS/SKYLARK and stamped "Top Secret." The first item was an Intel from Tyler Ashford to Dixon Hadley summarizing the case. After that the file ran chronologically, beginning with Ashford's approval, as Max Stein's case officer, of the initial effort by MS/SKYLARK to make contact with employees of the Czech Embassy in the gardens of the Schönbrunn Palace. On April 2, there was a brief memo to the files from Ashford reporting the successful contact earlier that day with Vlasa Radek. There was a memo giving details of her background, as learned from her by Stein, and a cable from Prague station reporting that a discreet check in Bratislava had located a butcher named Radek who had a daughter whose age, name, and description matched that of the woman in Vienna.

There was a message from Hadley's deputy, dated April 7, giving approval for MS/SKYLARK to proceed with the operation but cautioning the case officer, Tyler Ashford, to monitor it closely. There followed a series of memos from Ashford summarizing the progress of Stein's romance. There were several expense vouchers for dinners at the White Chimney Sweep Restaurant, apparently one of Vlasa's favorite spots, because, Stein dutifully reported, she liked the piano player.

The file also contained an Intel from Ashford to Hadley that Danner examined closely. It was dated April 15 and proposed that on May 5, MS/SKYLARK make his move and request that Vlasa Radek copy the circuit board of the code machine, with the actual copying to be carried out one week later, at noon on May 12.

A return message—this time signed by Hadley himself— approved the timetable, provided that in the case officer's judgment, "the relationship between MS/SKYLARK and the subject Radek had progressed to the point where the request that she become operational could be made with minimal risk."

"Cover your ass," Danner murmured to himself. Well, he thought, that's how you become the DDO.

The file then described how Stein had been shot in the genitals on the morning of May 12 by someone in a postman's uniform. There was a medical report from the attending physician at the hospital to which he had been taken that afternoon. The report found that one of the two bullets had entered the leg at an angle, severing the sciatic nerve and causing severe trauma to other nerves in the area of the sacral plexus. A subsequent medical report said the victim's wounds had resulted in atrophy of the gluteus maximus and the biceps femoris, resulting in numbness and chronic pain. Stein, the doctors, concluded, was permanently disabled and would require a wheelchair.

There was also a memorandum, dated May 12, of a report telephoned in by an immigration clerk at Vienna's Schwechat Airport who worked for the agency. The report said a woman using a passport in the name of Vlasa Radek and matching her description had been put aboard a nonstop Czechoslovakian Airlines flight to Prague at ten o'clock that morning. And an Intel, Ashford to Hadley, informed the DDO that the Austrian police had agreed to assist Vienna station in doing everything possible to keep the shooting out of the papers.

Finally, the file contained a pretext interview with the concierge of Stein's apartment on the Haslingergasse which added little to what was known. The *Hausbesorgerin* had permitted the postman to take the elevator up because he had an express letter for Herr Stein that required his signature, and for that reason the letter was not left in the lobby box as would normally have been the case. She knew Herr Stein was home because she had seen him come in a few moments earlier from the baker, as was his custom each morning. She also provided a somewhat better description of the gunman than did MS/SKYLARK, which, Danner reflected, only proved that concierges were, in most cases, better observers than spies. A few *Hausbesorgerinnen*, Danner thought, could probably do better than the whole damn Clandestine Services.

The rest of the file consisted of nervous cables from Tyler Ashford to headquarters reporting negotiations with MS/SKYLARK over the size of his disability pension, the "unreasonable financial demands" of Lili Stein, and the arrangements for purchase of the wheelchair out of the Vienna station's contingency fund.

Danner closed the file and stared out the high windows of the embassy for several minutes, drumming his fingers on the polished table. Then he wrote down some dates and MS/SKYLARK's address and telephone number on a little slip of paper that he put in his wallet. He dialed extension 26 and told Sheila she could come and get the file.

She walked in a couple of minutes later. Danner looked at her ample hips. "Who has the best pastry in town?"

Her eyes lit up. "Oh, Heiner's on the Kärntner Strasse," she said. "Try the schokoletti. It's cream-filled with rolls of yummy chocolate on the top for forty schillings."

"Thanks for the tip," Danner said.

He left the embassy and walked down to the Währinger Strasse, where he got a taxi back to the hotel. He decided to spend the rest of the afternoon catching up on his sleep. He hadn't had much in the past week.

Back at the hotel, he threw off his clothes and rolled gratefully into the featherbed. When his wristwatch alarm woke him up, it was 8:00 P.M. He took a quick shower, dressed, and found a little café on the next street where he had a holsteiner schnitzel, a beer, and a very good cup of coffee. He topped off the meal with a Slivovitz.

Then he walked up to the Kärntner Strasse, with its brightly lit, expensive-looking store windows and the crowds promenading in the street, which was closed to traffic. At the corner of the Johannesgasse, a group of young musicians was playing superb Dixieland jazz. A crowd had gathered and Danner stood there while the band played "Muskrat Ramble" and "When the Saints Go Marching In."

He followed the Kärntner Strasse to St. Stephan's. A blind man was playing the accordion outside the floodlit cathedral; Danner dropped a schilling in his cup. He went into the cathedral and stood in the rear for a few moments listening to a priest celebrating mass in German.

Then he walked back out into the chill night air and continued north along the Kärntner Strasse. The streets were less well lit now and the stores no longer prosperous-looking. There were fewer people around. He crossed the trolley tracks and stood alone in the darkness on the bridge over the Donau Kanal, looking east toward the Czech border.

Max Stein had only lost his balls, Danner thought. God knows what the Czechs did to Vlasa Radek. It was cold on the bridge and, shivering, he turned up the collar of his jacket. It was a rotten business in which people, lives, were expendable. No, he thought, disposable. They were used and thrown away.

He hoped to hell that Carrie was all right, wherever she was. He left the bridge and began walking back toward his hotel. Tomorrow, he would pay a call on MS/SKYLARK.

CHAPTER
TWELVE

The wristwatch alarm went off at 5:30 A.M. Danner rolled out of bed and felt his way into the bathroom. He splashed cold water on his face, went back into the bedroom, and turned on the light on the night table.

He picked up the telephone and got a sleepy clerk on the front desk. He gave him Julie's number in Alexandria. It was 11:30 P.M. in Virginia, and she would probably still be up. In a couple of minutes, the overseas operator had Julie on the line. She sounded far away.

"Bill? Is that you? Where are you?"

"Vienna." But perhaps she already knew that, he thought.

"Darling, I've missed you. It's only been six days, and it seems like six weeks."

It felt good to hear her voice, and he longed to hold her and touch her. Some of his suspicions melted away. He had to force himself to bring them back. "I'll be home soon," he said.

"Oh, I hope so," she said. "I'm in bed. It's very lonely here without you."

"I'll remedy that."

"Soon."

"Yes, soon. But tell me, did you hear anything about the missing package?"

"I've checked, and it wasn't ours, I promise you."

"Was the access a problem?"

"No, I found a way. I'll explain when I see you."

"Okay, good."

109

"And you've heard nothing?"

"No," Danner replied. "Nothing. My office hasn't called with any news."

"I'm sorry. I wish I could help."

"You have. What about my old friend?"

"Better luck there," Julie said. "I found him. He's retired now. I have an address and a phone number."

"All right, hang onto them."

"I love you."

He hesitated for a fraction of a second. "Same here. Goodbye, darling."

He lay back on the bed for several moments, enveloped by the warmth of her being, surrounded by Julie, feeling her presence. Perhaps she really did love him. He wondered if he was a damn fool, then decided he wasn't. He got up and took a long shower. He dressed and went downstairs to the pleasant little breakfast room off the lobby where he had coffee and *semmerl*, little hard rolls, with marmalade. He took a copy of the *International Herald Tribune* from the rack on the wall and dawdled over it while he had a second cup of coffee. It was still early.

A little after eight thirty, he went out the back entrance of the hotel. There was a post office next door, and he found an unoccupied phone booth inside. He dialed MS/SKYLARK's number.

It rang several times before a man answered. *"Ja, bitte?"*

"Herr Stein? This is William Danner. I'd like to come by and see you this morning."

There was no reply, but Danner could hear a woman's voice arguing loudly in the background. Finally, the old man spoke again. "There is nothing I can tell you."

"I'll be there at nine o'clock."

There was a click and the line went dead. Stein had hung up.

Danner hailed a cab and gave the driver the address in Hernals. He was not looking forward to the interview, but it had to be done.

The taxi dropped him at the old apartment building on the Haslingergasse. Danner noticed a curtain being pulled back on a ground-floor window as he got out of the cab. That would no doubt be Frau Kubic, the concierge, checking him out. Stein must have told her he was coming.

He went into the lobby, and opened the metal outer doors to

the glass-sided elevator. He got in and closed the wooden inner doors of the cage, and the lights went on. He put a schilling in the slot and pushed the button for the top floor. As Rossi must have done, he thought. The elevator lurched slowly and noisily upward.

He got off at Stein's floor, pushed the button to return the elevator to the ground floor, and rang the doorbell. He could hear the latch swinging away from the peephole and felt someone staring out at him. "William Danner," he announced.

The door opened; a squat, broad-shouldered woman of about fifty-five confronted him. Her eyes were too small for her large, coarse features. It was not likely, Danner thought, that Lili Stein had ever been pretty. Right now, she looked angry.

"My husband is a sick man," she snapped. "There is nothing he can tell you."

"May I come in?"

She hesitated.

"I won't tire him. It shouldn't take long."

Grudgingly, she stepped aside and let him in. He followed her into the living room. It was stuffy in the little apartment, and there were cooking smells even in the living room. Cabbage, he thought.

There was a gray-haired man sitting in a wheelchair by the window, his back to Danner. He turned slowly, pushing the wheels with his hands. His eyes were hollow and defeated.

"You have come all the way from Washington," he said haltingly, with a trace of a smile. "But I cannot be that important." Stein lit a cigarette with shaking hands. He blew out the match and put it in an ashtray on the little table beside him.

"I'm sorry for your trouble," Danner said. "I wanted to talk to you in person. We're trying to find out what happened."

Lili Stein started screaming. "What happened! You want to know what happened! You already know. They shot him and crippled him and ruined our life, and you want to know what happened!"

"Please, Lili," Stein remonstrated.

"Fool, don't interrupt me," she shouted. To Danner she said, "My Max was nearly killed, and you pay us in a month less than a whore on the Krugerstrasse earns in a single night. We are not whores!" She stomped out of the room.

"I apologize for my wife," Stein said. "She is very upset. Please," he gestured to a sofa, "please sit down, Mr. Danner."

Danner did. Max was being polite. Apparently it was Lili Stein who, out of anger at the agency, did not want her husband interviewed. The stuffing was coming out of the pillows on the couch, but he pretended not to notice. "I have just a few questions," he said.

"And I have only one."

"What's that?"

"What went wrong?"

"That's what we're trying to determine."

"I can't understand it," Stein said, shaking his head. "Everything was going well. And then, this. . . ." His voice trailed off and he started coughing. Danner could see he was still in pain.

"Herr Stein," Danner began, "you first met Vlasa Radek early in April, correct?"

"Yes, in the gardens of the Schönbrunn." A flicker of pride crossed the haggard face. "It was my concept. The Czech Embassy is just two blocks away. I guessed that in the spring, when the weather turned nice, some of the secretaries would bring their lunch there. Have you ever been in Vienna in the spring, Mr. Danner?"

"No."

"It is beautiful."

"I'm sure it must be." Danner cleared his throat. "During the period that you were seeing Radek, did you ever detect any surveillance?"

"Of course not. If there had been anything unusual, I would have reported it to Mr. Ashford. I am a professional, Mr. Danner."

"She was to copy the circuit board of the code machine on May 12, the same morning you were shot?"

"That is correct."

"But you first made the suggestion to her a week earlier?"

"Yes. She was nervous, as I knew she would be. I needed a week to build up her confidence, to work on her. And of course I needed time for Mr. Ashford to get operational approval from headquarters. I know how these things work. I have been in the business for many years.''

"I understand. But that last week, after you had put the question to her, was the period of highest risk. Wasn't there any countersurveillance?''

"The last week, yes. On three nights when we went out to dinner, your people were in the restaurant. Mr. Ashford told me to expect them.'' He smiled. "I am afraid they were somewhat conspicuous.''

"Could Vlasa have noticed them?''

Stein shook his head. "No. She was only a secretary, she was not an agent. She saw nothing.''

"One of those nights was the last night?''

"Yes.''

"How did she seem?''

"Like always. A little more nervous, perhaps, but that would be quite normal.''

"But she didn't try to back out, or to warn you in any way?''

"No. We hardly talked about it. It was understood she would copy the board in the morning. After dinner, I took her to the safe house and we made love. Then I took her home, about one in the morning. It was the last time I saw her.''

Danner said sympathetically, "I'm sorry it ended this way.''

Stein ground out the stub of his cigarette. "She betrayed me. She must have told them.''

Danner shrugged.

Stein said, "Unless they caught her that morning, saw her copying the circuit board, and forced her to talk.'' Stein looked almost hopeful. He would have preferred it that way.

"I'm afraid not,'' Danner replied. "They put her on a ten A.M. flight to Prague. She never made it to the embassy that morning. There wouldn't have been time.''

Stein nodded, his features sagging. "It was my fault,'' he said. "At my age, to make the mistake of trusting a woman.'' He shook his head.

"I'm almost through,'' Danner said. "But I wanted to ask you about the postman. You told our people who interviewed you at the hospital that you didn't hear the gun go off.''

Stein nodded. "*Ja.* It was very strange. There was no sound at all.''

"You're sure?"

"Yes. It is not that often I am shot."

"And the gun. Did it have a silencer?"

"No."

"All right." Danner paused. "Did you tell your wife about Vlasa?"

"Of course not," Stein said quickly. He leaned forward in the wheelchair and lowered his voice. "She has taken a lover, Mr. Danner. A man I thought was my friend."

"Sorry to hear it," Danner said, getting up to leave.

"I can't really blame her," Stein said. "I am useless to her now."

"Thanks for seeing me," Danner said.

"I had no choice."

"Neither did I."

Danner let himself out of the apartment, and walked down the stairs. He had already found out most of what he wanted to know, but there were some locations he wanted to check out before he left Vienna.

He hailed a taxi and asked the driver to let him off on the Linke Wienzeile, by Auer-Welsbach Park. He cut north across the park on one of the wide gravel paths that ran beneath the trees, and emerged on Mariahilfer Strasse in front of the Technical Museum. He stopped to admire a modernistic Victor Kaplan sculpture of a blue turbine that stood in front of the entrance. He glanced back at the park. No one had followed him.

He strolled down the block to the corner, waited for the light because of the heavy traffic, and crossed the broad Schlossalle. Then he entered the Penzinger Strasse, a quiet residential street. From the corner, he could see the three-story, yellow Czech Embassy, with its castle-like ramparts. He crossed to the north side of the Penzinger Strasse and walked down the street past the building. The single policeman guarding the embassy paid no attention to him.

He walked for another block, then doubled back to the Schlossalle and turned right toward the Schönbrunn. He crossed the bridge over the Wien River, which was very low in its streambed, and, dodging cars, made his way to the cobblestoned courtyard of the palace. He walked the length of the courtyard, passed through the archway beneath the building, and emerged in the formal gardens in the rear.

The Baroque gardens were intersected by gravel paths that formed a series of rectangles. Within them, other paths radiated outward, like spokes in a wheel, from two large fountains of Roman water nymphs. The gravel paths were very wide, with comfortable green park benches, and they were lined with stately trees on both sides. He walked for a while, then sat down on one of the benches, wondering if this might be the same one where Vlasa Radek had chanced upon MS/SKYLARK.

Danner was a great believer in shoe leather. It was not the first time he had investigated a failed operation, and he always made it a point to visit the scene when he could. It was a habit he had picked up in his days in counterintelligence. He liked to get the feel of a city, the places, the buildings, and the people, to see where they had walked, and sat, and laughed, and loved, and lied to each other. Sometimes he learned nothing that way; sometimes he learned everything.

Even in the last half hour he had confirmed two small details of Stein's story. It had taken him twelve minutes to walk from the Czech Embassy to the gardens, which meant that employees of the embassy would have ample time to go there, eat their lunch, and return to the office. And from the contents of the wire trash baskets along the gravel paths, it was clear that people customarily brought their lunch to the gardens.

So they had met in the spring, as the trees were turning green, and the aging spy, trying to impress his quarry, had pretended to be a successful businessman. The homely butcher's daughter from Bratislava had responded to him eagerly, probably because she was terribly lonely, and there had been, for a few sad months, some kind of love between them, for reasons that were probably no more artificial than in many other cases. Now she was undoubtedly dead and Stein was finished. He would go to his grave thinking she had betrayed him. And Danner could not tell him the truth.

He got up and walked back toward the Schönbrunn. He kicked at the gravel, taking stock of his own situation. It wasn't a hell of a lot better than Stein's, he thought. Forced back into the agency, he was caught up again in a world of deception he thought he had finally shed. He had been obliged to entrust his business to a guide with a sixth-grade education. His daughter, an innocent, was in the hands of his enemies, in mortal danger because of his own actions. Julie, the woman he had begun to love, who had gotten past his automatic defenses—his Berlin Wall—might be working against him. It was even possible that his employer, the CIA, was lying to him about Carrie. And while he had learned a good deal in Vienna, he was no closer to unmasking the mole, who seemed to be holding all the strings to which he, the puppet, danced.

He would find him, Danner vowed. He would find him. He had come to the broad central plaza of the gardens, and he turned right, toward the back of the palace. What was it Stein and Vlasa had done at their second meeting? They had toured the Schönbrunn. He went inside, bought a ticket, and joined a crowd of tourists.

The enormous palace, the playground of the Hapsburgs for almost two hundred years, was a melange of gilded rooms, inlaid floors, crystal chandeliers, scrolled frescoes, and elaborate tapestries. The tour guide, a short, little man with thick glasses, talked, in the manner of all tour guides, like a robot for whom the words, by endless repetition, had long since lost all meaning.

"Meine Damen und Herren," he intoned, "we are now in the chambers of the empress Maria-Theresa, whose daughter, Marie-Antoinette, the future queen of France, spent her childhood here in the magnificent palace of the Schönbrunn." They passed through the room where Franz-Josef had died, and Danner wondered irreverently whether the emperor's demise had been hastened by all those strenuous visits to Katharina Schratt. In several of the rooms there were enormous white-and-gold porcelain stoves; the palace, with its 1,200 drafty rooms and high ceilings, must have been difficult to heat in the cold Viennese winters.

In the concert room, the guide explained that here the young Mozart, at the age of six, had astonished the empress Maria-Theresa with his musical genius. They went through two Chinese rooms, decorated with beautiful lacquers and porcelain. Near the end of the tour, Danner and the rest of his group crowded into a chamber that contained two enormous mirrors, with rococo gilded frames, facing each other at opposite ends of the room. The effect, as the guide pointed out, was to create an endless hall of mirrors, stretching as far as the eye could see.

A group of German children who were with their parents on the tour, jostled each other to get a better look, and as the crowd milled about, a fat woman awkwardly brushed by Danner. It was a full minute before he felt the crumpled piece of paper in the right-hand pocket of his jacket. He knew if he stopped to read it, he would never catch her.

He bolted after her, but the woman had disappeared. He ran through the empty rooms, beneath bright chandeliers, past more gilded mirrors, shouldering his way through groups of tourists, drawing annoyed looks and some angry muttering. But the woman had a good head start and was nowhere to be seen.

Danner realized that the route of the tour ran in a circle through the apartments, and he was almost back at the starting point. He dashed down the stairway that led to the ground floor. As he did so, he caught a glimpse through a window of the fat woman running across the gravel toward the front gates.

Only the fat woman had become a fat man. Somewhere along the way he had shed a wig and a skirt. Danner ran out into the courtyard dodging through the crowds of tourists streaming toward the palace.

Danner could see where the man was heading. Just outside the gates on the Schönbrunner Schlosstrasse, a car waited, its engine running. Danner was fast, but the fat man had too big a lead. He jumped in beside the driver, and the car peeled out. As Danner reached the street, he could see it was a black Peugeot sedan. He was barely able to catch the last three digits of the license plate. He quickly wrote them down.

Then he reached into his jacket pocket and uncrumpled the note. When he saw the handwriting, it was as though someone had shoved a knife in the middle of his chest.

"Dear Daddy," the note said, "Please do whatever they say. I want to come home. Love, Carrie."

At the bottom of the piece of white airmail paper, someone had scrawled a warning in black ink: "Mr. Danner—if you want to see your daughter alive, you will leave Vienna immediately and drop your investigation."

CHAPTER
THIRTEEN

Dixon Hadley lived in Cleveland Park, a neighborhood of Victorian homes, stately oaks, and liberal lawyers with swimming pools whose wives drove Volvo station wagons. Most of the agency's senior executives found the politics and proximity of suburban McLean, Virginia, more compatible, but a few, like Hadley, ventured across the river into Washington to live in Georgetown or Cleveland Park. Hadley told his neighbors he worked for the State Department.

It was early Saturday morning. Danner eased his Skylark into Newark Street and slowed down. He had been there once, years ago, at a cocktail party and he remembered a big frame house painted white with red shutters. He found it, pulled into the driveway, and parked.

It had been after 10:00 P.M. by the time he finally cleared customs at Dulles. He had called Hadley at home from a phone booth at the airport. The deputy director had not been thrilled at the prospect of a Saturday morning meeting, but Danner had insisted. He walked up a flight of wooden steps to the wide, shady porch and rang the bell.

The door was answered by one of Hadley's teenage sons and a rambunctious golden retriever. Danner shook hands with both of them. They led him through the kitchen, which had been remodeled with spacious picture windows, to a broad redwood deck at the rear of the house.

Hadley was sitting at a wrought-iron table, reading the morning papers over coffee. He was wearing Bermuda shorts and a green alligator shirt.

He got up when he saw Danner. "Elizabeth is still asleep," he said apologetically. "But I can manage a cup of coffee if you'd like one."

"Thanks," Danner said. "I would."

Hadley went into the kitchen for a moment, and emerged with a cup for Danner. They sat down at the table and Danner noticed that the deck overlooked a steep ravine that plunged downward from the edge of Hadley's small backyard. At least there was no lawn to be mowed. It was a perfect September morning; the sun warmed the deck pleasantly even though the air was cool.

"Got some news for you," Hadley said.

"Good or bad?"

"Mixed," the deputy director replied. "But at least we know who we're dealing with."

A yellow jacket had landed on the rim of Danner's cup. He brushed it away and waited for Hadley to continue.

"I got a call from the watch officer at seven thirty this morning," the DDO said. "Elizabeth didn't appreciate it. After all these years, she's still not used to it." He shook his head. "Ashford gave the three digits you got to our liaison with the Austrian police. It took them a while, since you didn't have all the numbers, but they traced the car." Hadley allowed himself a broad smile.

Danner could feel his adrenalin working. "What did they find?"

"It was a hired car. Rented earlier that day from one of the large commercial agencies on the Schwedenplatz."

"Rented by whom?" Hadley could be maddeningly slow in getting to the point.

"Officially, the police wouldn't take it any further than that." Hadley paused for a sip of his coffee. "Austria is neutral, after all."

"And unofficially?"

The DDO smiled again. "Vienna station has certain contacts in the police, at a high level. They were useful to us in keeping the denouement of the MS/SKYLARK affair out of the press. Late yesterday, Ashford got a telephone call from one of his contacts. It seems the car was hired by a woman named Grete Wolf.''

"Who is she?"

"An Austrian national. She was merely a cutout, of course. But her sister, according to our police friend, is married to one Otto Bauer, also an Austrian.''

"What do we know about him?"

"Otto Hans Bauer is a small-time support agent employed by Pavel Kurozev, the KGB *rezident* in Vienna.''

So it wasn't the old boys or the agency, after all. Somehow, Danner had hoped it would be. The danger might be as great but they seemed less alien. He looked out over the ravine at the oaks and maples that would soon be losing their leaves. "I guess I owe you an apology," he said at last.

Hadley dismissed the thought with a wave of his hand. "What will you do?" he asked.

"There's nothing to do," Danner replied gloomily, "except keep going. You deal with the Russians from strength. Moscow Center took a risk in kidnapping Carrie. It means they're desperate to protect the mole. My only leverage with the KGB is to keep looking for him."

"It's your decision," Hadley said. "But I agree."

Danner wondered where they were holding her. Perhaps in San Francisco, where they had a consulate. Or at the other end of the country in Riverdale, where their UN delegates lived. Or on Maryland's eastern shore, where the Soviet Embassy in Washington had a summer enclave at Pioneer Point, on the Chesapeake Bay. But Carrie could be anywhere by now, perhaps even behind the Iron Curtain. He felt sick.

Hadley interrupted his thoughts. "I'm anxious to hear what you learned on your trip," he said.

"Not very much in London. I talked to Chandler Hamilton. He's still pretty upset." Danner had understated the case. The London station chief was frightened to death that Hadley would reassign him to some place like Mogadishu.

"He wasn't at fault," Hadley said. "It was the usual pattern, as far as I've been able to determine. Someone tipped off the old boys. Trowbridge turns up, and two weeks later six names are published in *Private Eye*. And their job descriptions."

"Is MI 6 still flapping?"

"They've settled down a little. But C isn't returning Chandler's phone calls."

"That will pass."

"Yes, but GCHQ has let it be known that they prefer to deal with NSA from now on. They say our people are too hot." It hadn't taken Danner long to size up the situation in London. GCHQ, or Government Communications Headquarters, was the British equivalent of the National Security Agency. It handled all electronic spying and code breaking for the United Kingdom from its main facilities in Cheltenham. For several years, the Brits had also been closely involved with NSA's secret listening center at Menwith Hill, in the Yorkshire Moors. The center tapped telephone and telex communications throughout all of Europe. The CIA officers whose names had been published in London were assigned to liaison with Cheltenham and Menwith Hill. But the publicity had focused attention on the massive wiretap operation, and Fleet Street had pounced on the story. Despite the Official Secrets Act, a lot of embarrassing information had seeped out.

"We can't let NSA have the whole pie," Hadley insisted. "It may take a while, but we'll get our people back in at Menwith Hill. We've got a few inside NSA, for that matter." Hadley grinned. "Although you'd better forget I said that."

"I'm not surprised," Danner replied.

"What about Madrid?"

"Same story. Kermit Gardner pops up with a Nikon over his shoulder and a guidebook, and makes a big show of wandering around the Prado like Joe tourist. Ten days later, *Mundo Obrero* has a pretty detailed account of our contacts with the Basques."

"I know. I read it."

"It was very damaging, because the story claimed we were funneling money into ETA." The fiercely independent Basques lived in three provinces in the north of Spain. ETA, the Basque terrorist group, had killed hundreds of people; it wanted a completely independent Socialist state. The agency had its lines into the Basque movement, but it worked mostly with elements of the Partida Nationalista Vasco, the more moderate nationalist party. The relationship went back to World War II, when a lot of the PNV people had cooperated with the OSS.

Hadley shrugged. "It's fairly predictable. They're trying to tie us in with the terrorists."

Danner nodded. "The station is in touch with ETA's two political fronts, on a discreet basis, of course. That much is true. But now that the story is out, every time another officer of the Guardia Civil is shot, it will look like we pulled the trigger."

"And there's not a great deal we can do about it." Hadley went inside to the kitchen, brought out the coffeepot, and refilled their cups. He shooed away the dog, who had been hanging around hoping someone would drop some food on the deck.

"That brings us to Vienna," the DDO said.

"I had better luck there."

"How so?"

"Well, to begin with, you're almost certainly right about Rossi. The shooting had to be done by someone who works for the agency, or used to."

"Why?"

"Stein never heard a shot. Yet he's positive the gun had no silencer. That means the hit man used silent ammo."

Hadley nodded. "Of course. A low-signature bullet."

"It's the only explanation." The silent ammunition, Danner knew, had been developed for the agency, and its very existence was highly classified. Yet it worked on a simple principle. There were two reasons why a shot made noise: the gas escaping from the shell under enormous pressure and the sonic boom of the bullet breaking the sound barrier. The silent ammo contained a tiny piston inside each cartridge that accelerated 18,000 feet per second, forced the bullet out, then sealed the end of the shell so no gas could escape. Since the bullet left the barrel at subsonic speed, there was no sonic boom either.

The deputy director wore an expression of dismay. "Rossi must have kept some of the ammo when he left us. It would be easy enough to do." He paused. "What else did you find out?"

"A lot. It was all there in the file. But no one had put it together."

"What do you mean?"

"Okay, you know the outlines. MS/SKYLARK meets Vlasa Radek on April 2. Five days later, your deputy approves the operation. On April 15, Ashford sends you an Intel proposing that Stein put his requirements to Radek on May 5. On May 12, the

day it was all supposed to happen, Nick Rossi shoots the Skylark and Radek is hustled aboard a plane to Prague.'' .

Hadley looked puzzled. ''I'm not sure I get your drift.''

Danner leaned forward. ''We're assuming the mole has access to the traffic. That means he—or she—must have known
that something was going on as early as the first week in April.
By the fifteenth, the mole knew the precise target—the Czech
code. Yet almost a full month goes by before anything happens.''

The light began to dawn on the DDO. ''In other words—''

''It's obvious,'' Danner interjected. ''If the STB had known
about the operation all along, they could have pulled Radek out
of Vienna at any time. But they didn't. What it means is, *the
Czechs didn't know.*''

''The evidence does suggest that,'' Hadley said cautiously.
''Of course, they may have wanted to catch her in the act.''

Danner shook his head. ''No. Our side does that to obtain
legal evidence. The Czechs don't need to bother.''

''I suppose you're right. They would have pulled her out.''

''Of course they would. No fuss, no muss, just a quiet transfer of a secretary back to Prague and oblivion.''

''But the STB found out at some point,'' Hadley observed.
''Perhaps she told them during that last week. She may have
lost her nerve.''

''I don't think so. I questioned MS/SKYLARK closely on that
point. He saw nothing unusual in her behavior that week. The
station had countersurveillance, and they didn't pick up anything, either.''

''If you're right,'' Hadley said, ''it means the old boys never
told the Czechs. Not until the very end.''

''That's the point,'' Danner continued. ''Vienna means that
the mole is working primarily through the old boys. Not directly with the Soviets or their friends. He's a very odd mole indeed.''

Hadley got up and began pacing the desk. ''And it also
means the old boys control whether and when the Soviets or
some other service are clued in.''

''Exactly. And there's one thing more. It's obvious the old
boys weren't interested simply in blowing the operation. If that

was their motive, all they had to do was tip off the STB and Radek would have been sent packing.''

"Then what were they after?''

"A high-visibility scandal to embarrass the agency. With trumpets and crashing cymbals. They must be hoping that sooner or later the press will hear about it.''

"If it doesn't, they can always help it along.''

"They may. In the meantime, there's sure to be gossip at headquarters. Some of it might even reach the ears of the White House.''

Hadley shuddered. "We try to shield the president from details of that sort.''

"I can believe it,'' Danner said.

"They want the director's scalp,'' Hadley said slowly. "His and mine.''

Danner stepped on a yellow jacket and crushed it underfoot. "It looks that way.''

CHAPTER
FOURTEEN

In the middle of the night, Danner woke up to Julie's kisses. She started on his lips and then moved to his neck, his chest, and his belly, while at the same time she caressed him with her long, cool fingers.

"Again," she said.

"Sleeping," he protested.

She laughed and pulled him against her. They made love again in the dark, silently, fiercely, then joyously. Danner wasn't complaining any more.

Afterward, she lit a candle by their bedside. "I want to see you," she explained.

"There's nothing to see, now."

"That's *not* what I meant." She giggled, then leaned over and kissed him.

He had not told her yet about the note from Carrie, or about MS/SKYLARK. They had just wanted to be with each other, away from the pressures of the real world.

After a while, they grew sleepy and Julie blew out the candle and they drifted off. When Danner awoke, the sunlight was streaming through the white curtains of the bedroom windows. Julie was already up.

He found her in the kitchen, sipping orange juice, deep in the Sunday comics.

"You're sure that's not too heavy for you?" he asked.

"I like Snoopy," she said. "If you don't like Snoopy, you can't sleep in my bed."

125

"I like Snoopy."

"Have some orange juice." She handed him a glass and the pitcher.

He poured some, got ice out of the refrigerator for his glass, and scanned the headlines. "President Forbes is at Camp David for the weekend," he said in a newscaster's voice. "The chief executive is meeting with his top foreign policy advisers, including the Secretary of State and Brooks Jordan, the director of the CIA."

"That means that Felicity Jordan has been complaining she never gets invited to Camp David."

"It also says that President Forbes was saddened to learn upon arrival at his Catoctin mountain retreat that one of his favorite horses had died."

"Another one? Do you think he abuses them?"

"We could start a rumor."

Julie put two English muffins in the toaster and pushed the lever down. "What are we going to do today?" she asked.

"What would you like to do?"

"Sit out in the garden and read the papers for a while," she said. "Then go on that date you owe me."

"Where?"

"To the Monument grounds, to fly the kite. Remember? I'll pack a picnic."

"You're on. It's a perfect day for it. Just enough breeze." He recalled something and looked worried. "But I was supposed to bring the wine." She laughed. "It's all right. I've got some."

They ate the muffins with strawberry jam and had coffee in stoneware mugs. Then they lazed about the garden for most of the morning. Julie found some cold chicken and a bottle of chilled Soave and packed them in a straw basket with a few apples, a tomato, a loaf of French bread, and two wineglasses. They drove over the Memorial Bridge and found a place to park on Constitution Avenue near the Monument grounds.

They spread a blanket on the grass at the top of the hill and lay in the sun for a while, listening to the flags flapping in the breeze on the poles that ringed the Monument. Then Danner got out the kite and tied it securely to the end of a ball of nylon string.

Julie held the kite and Danner let out about twenty feet of string to get it started. The breeze lifted it quickly and the kite sailed aloft, its long, tapered tail of green, orange, and yellow trailing behind the purple dragon head. It flew with an undulating, serpentine motion so that it almost looked alive. A dozen other kites, flown by both children and adults, filled the sky.

When the dragon had reached a satisfactory height, they sat down on the blanket and Danner tied the string to the handle of the picnic basket. Julie poured them each an illegal glass of wine. Danner lay back and watched the kite dancing and the puffy white clouds rolling by.

Julie lay down beside him. "Do you mind if I ask you something?"

"No. Go ahead."

"At Charlie's that night, you talked about an operation in Berlin. What happened?"

Danner shook his head. "It was all a long time ago. Light years. It doesn't matter."

"But it does. You said that was the beginning. When you began to lose faith."

Danner looked at her. "I've never really talked about it before." He gazed at the kite for a moment. "There was a girl. Her name was Lisa Hallam. She worked with me."

"Were you in love with her?"

"Yes."

"And still are, in a way?"

"I still think of her, sometimes. She's dead."

"What happened?"

"The Soviets operated from Karlshorst, in East Berlin. It was a huge compound across the Spree near the Trabrennbahn, the trotting racetrack. Their military headquarters was based there, and other branches, including the KGB, of course. The whole place was surrounded by an iron fence and barbed wire and guarded by German police with dogs, and Soviet sentries."

"The KGB had their own building?"

"Oh, yes. At the eastern end. Three stories high, a former hospital, and crawling with armed guards."

"Where did Lisa fit in?"

"Lisa was fluent in German. She worked for the station but

under deep cover, posing as a German national. That made her a high-priority target. Beside that, she was very beautiful. It was an old story, a honey trap, and a KGB colonel fell into it.''

"And you were running the operation?"

"Yes," Danner said. "It was my operation."

"And something went wrong?"

"Yes. We were building her, of course, giving her material to pass along. It had to be good enough to be of real interest to their First Chief Directorate, but not damaging enough to do us any lasting harm."

She nodded. "How long did it go on?"

"About four months. Then, when the time looked right, she made her move and tried to recruit him. It was very risky, of course. They were having dinner at a restaurant near the Kurfürstendamm. He was in civilian clothes. I was riding shotgun in a car with two other officers parked across the street and down the block about fifty feet. When they came out and started walking toward his car, she shifted her purse from her right to her left shoulder—the danger signal."

"It meant the colonel wasn't buying it."

"Yes. We started up the car and cut him off. But he was very quick. Instead of getting into his car, he ducked into an alley, pushing her ahead of him. He had a gun in her back. We jumped out and ran after them. There were loose bricks and rubble in the alley. I twisted my leg and went down hard. I yelled to the others to keep going. But it was pitch dark and we lost them."

"You never saw her again?"

Danner looked away. "Only once. In the morgue. They fished her body out of the Havel weeks later. It was badly decomposed."

Julie touched his hand. "I'm sorry. I shouldn't have asked."

Danner shrugged. "You wanted to know about me. That's part of me."

"There's another part of you I want to know about. What was it like growing up New England?"

Danner smiled thinly. "White River Junction was a tough mill town. And a railroad town, of course. We used to see the Dartmouth students arriving at the depot every September in their white bucks and expensive clothes. I envied them. They looked down on us.''

"That still bothers you, doesn't it?''

"Of course. But I've learned not to show it. If you asked a Dartmouth man what White River was, he'd say, 'That's where the whores are.' The whores and the railroad station. They called us Emmetts.''

"Why Emmetts?''

"It was their idea of a hick New England name.''

"And yet you went to Dartmouth.''

"On the back of the bus. I got a scholarship. I didn't join a fraternity. The Psi U's didn't want a kid from White River. I worked in a greasy spoon on Main Street, earning seventy-five cents an hour.''

"But you must have had fun some of the time.''

"There was a lot of drinking, a lot of parties. I made some friends. I avoided the really sophomoric stuff, like the spring 'wet down.' The freshmen had to run the gauntlet across the green and the sophs would whip them with their belts as they ran through.''

"Yuk. Did you do a lot of skiing?''

"Oh sure, everyone did. And Winter Carnival was fun. We'd build a huge snowman in the middle of the campus. Girls would come in for the weekend from other colleges. There'd be an ice show at night. One year we flooded the football field and turned it into an ice rink.''

"Where was the nearest girls' school?''

"Smith. But it was a three-hour drive to Northampton. The guys with cars used to take road trips. Then there was Green Mountain Junior College. The girls there were very friendly. It was known as 'Groin Mountain.' ''

"Sounds like a typical Ivy League environment. Did anybody ever study?''

"Not a lot.''

A sudden down draft sent the kite into a dive and Danner quickly untied the string from the basket. The dragon was spiralling toward the ground in tight little circles. He leaped up and started running down the hill, into the wind, holding the string high. Julie laughed and cheered him on. The tail came perilously close to the ground, but Danner managed to save it and the kite soared aloft again.

He came back to the blanket, only a little out of breath; Julie applauded. "You looked like Baryshnikov going down that hill."

"Milady's kite," he said, with a mock bow, handing her the string. She tied it back on the basket.

"How about lunch?" Danner asked.

"Fine with me." Julie opened the basket and spread out the chicken, the bread, and the apples. He poured another glass of wine for each of them.

He looked around. There was no one within earshot. "You were going to tell me about the computer," he said.

Julie nodded. "I had no trouble logging on. My password for the computer is 8L6D4Z. As a researcher, I have access to the terminals. But there's no way to call up a specific operation unless you know the password for that operation. Without it, you can't get into the data base. But before you have to give the password, the program requires you to select a category. You enter the word HOMETOWN for domestic operations or STRANGER for foreign. I entered HOMETOWN and a line of zeros came up on the screen. What it meant was, there were no domestic operations in the computer. That's how I was able to tell you it wasn't us."

"I know that now. They've made contact."

He told her then about the warning he had received in Vienna, the note from Carrie, and the traces the station had picked up from the Austrian police that led straight to the KGB. He also told her of his decision to keep going, despite the risks.

She took his hand and held it tightly in both of hers. "If the Soviets are trying to stop you," Julie said, "they won't harm Carrie. She's no good to them dead."

He wanted desperately to believe she was right. "That's the gamble I'm taking."

"You'll get her back. I know you will." She spoke with a passionate intensity.

It was getting late. People were beginning to drift away to their cars. They packed up the remains of the lunch and Danner started to pull in the kite.

"Let's let it go free," Julie said suddenly. "Maybe some child in Montana will find it. Or China."

"Okay with me," Danner said.

Julie took a paring knife from the basket and cut the string. The kite took wing, soaring straight up, its long tail dancing crazily in the wind, until after a few moments, it was only a distant speck in the afternoon sky.

CHAPTER
FIFTEEN

Sailor Cummins was sitting at the downstairs bar in the Holiday Inn at Tyson's Corner, which was exactly where Danner expected to find him. He was a big, red-faced man in his late fifties, with a large pockmarked nose, a thatch of brown hair, and the watery eyes of an alcoholic. He was wearing a hounds'-tooth jacket, maroon slacks, and a yellow sports shirt open at the neck.

Danner eased into the bar stool next to him, and waited for the Sailor to recognize him. After a few moments, Cummins turned and stared. "Jesus Christ," he said. "Danner."

"Hello, Sailor," Danner said. "What are you drinking?"

"Jack Daniels and water. Same as always."

Danner caught the bartender's eye. "Scotch on the rocks," he said. "And a refill for my friend." He surveyed the older man. Time had not improved his appearance. He was called Sailor because years before, as a young agency officer, he had kept a boat in Annapolis. He and a group of his friends would go down there on weekends for legendary drinking parties. Sometimes, the boat never left the marina. There were others who believed that Sailor got his name because when he was drunk, which was most of the time, he swore like one.

"Where the hell you been?" Cummins demanded.

"Fishing," Danner replied. "Up in Canada. And you?"

"Drinking," Sailor said. "In northern Virginia."

Danner looked at his watch. "I guess the meeting's due to start in a little while."

"They won't miss us. It's all bullshit, anyway."

The Retired Intelligence Officers Association was holding its annual convention at the motel, which was a favorite rendezvous for agency employees. A few years earlier, the motel, in possible deference to its clientele, had named the bar the Secrets Lounge. Now it had been done over as an Irish pub. On the convention agenda was a resolution calling on Congress to investigate the news media for publishing intelligence leaks, and another urging that the CIA be given power to wiretap suspected foreign agents without a court warrant. The association liked to pass resolutions.

"S'all bullshit," Sailor repeated.

"Never a truer word was spoke," Danner said, raising his glass. "Cheers."

"Down the hatch," Sailor said. Abruptly, his mood changed. He eyed Danner suspiciously. "If you're in Canada," he said, slurring his words, "how come you're here?"

"Trying to get a piece of the action," Danner confided. "No reason the beltway bandits should get it all."

"You're tellin' me," Cummins said. He leaned his puffy face close to Danner. "But you're wasting your time."

The beltway bandits were the dozens of research and development firms scattered around Washington in northern Virginia and Maryland. Staffed mostly by former government officials, the bandits lived off government contracts, performing research on weapons, electronic warfare, anti-terrorism, and similar subjects for the Pentagon, the CIA, NSA, and other agencies. In an era of high defense budgets, the bandits were prospering.

Danner ordered another round of drinks. The bartender, finally convinced he had a couple of live ones, put out a little bowl of peanuts.

"I'm here to make some contacts," he said. "The convention's a good place to make contacts."

A couple of portly, middle-aged men in Western hats came up to the bar, and one of them slapped Cummins on the back. The newcomer wore a plaid shirt, and a turquoise stone hung from his neck on a leather throng. Sailor grunted a greeting; the man put out his hand and introduced himself to Danner.

"Herbie Allen," he said. "President of the Santa Fe chapter."

"Harry Pringle," Danner replied, shaking the man's hand. "Des Moines chapter. Nice to meet you."

The two conventioneers moved on and Sailor asked, "Why'd you do that?"

"Just keeping in practice," Danner said with a smile.

Sailor shook his head. "Like I said, you're wasting your time."

"How so?"

Sailor leered at him. "We're nothin'," he said. "You and me and the Herbie Allens. We're nothin'. We can come to some crummy convention, and we get the association newsletter every month, and that's about it. *They* have the real power, same as always."

"You're right," Danner agreed.

"You're fuckin'-A right I'm right," Sailor said. "They have the power."

"The old boys," Danner said. It was more of a statement than a question.

Sailor shrugged. "Gotta know the right ones. You want to get cut in on the cushy consulting deals, the fat contracts, they decide. They don't like you, forget it."

"How do I get inside?" Danner asked.

"You don't. They come to you."

"Who does?"

Sailor smiled enigmatically. "You're wasting your time, good buddy. Gotta be able to yodel the right tune."

"What do you mean?"

"Gotta be able to talk to the gnomes."

Sailor wasn't making much sense. His head was beginning to droop to his chest.

"You're right," Danner said.

"Fuckin'-A."

Danner called for the check and paid it. "So long," he said. "Good to see you again."

The Sailor waved goodbye. "S'all bullshit," he said.

Danner drove out the Leesburg Pike into the Virginia countryside, glancing once in a while at the rough map he had drawn from Will Lamont's directions. The road he followed was the old market route to Georgetown, now a highway slicing through the congested northern Virginia suburbs, past the bedroom community of Reston, and across Loudoun County. Not far to the south, some of the Civil War's bloodiest battles had been fought. The only reminder now was an occasional Confederate flag flying from the front porch of a wooden frame house, usually one that needed paint. He drove almost to the Blue Ridge, but turned just after Purcellville and followed a series of back roads to the farm.

He hadn't seen Will Lamont in almost ten years, and he was looking forward to it. Will and his wife, Ann, had bought the place in the early seventies. He had retired there a few years ago to write poetry on a glass table top that rested on an enormous brass rhinoceros he had brought back from Africa. Lamont was a sort of renegade WASP; he had the money and the social credentials to be accepted in circles that would always remain partially closed to Danner, but he had turned his back on the worlds of Middleburg, Newport, and Jupiter Island, and instead chose to live in splendid rural isolation. His wife, a warm and earthy woman with strawberry-blond hair, was a Berkeley graduate and former hippie who was now a vegetarian and deep into organic farming.

He found the blue mailbox where Will said it would be, and turned the Skylark into the dirt road that led to the house. He was just getting out of the car when Ann appeared on the porch, wiping her hands on an apron and smiling.

Danner bounded up the steps and gave her a hug. It was hard not to hug Ann. ''Will's out back in the barn,'' she said. ''He'll be along in a minute. Come in and sit down.''

She led Danner in through the kitchen; he stopped to admire the herbs growing in the window pot.

''How's your garden?'' he asked.

''We've had a good summer. Lettuce was the best ever. I still have some late corn, squash, cucumbers, and tomatoes. You can take some back with you, if you'd like.''

''I wasn't hinting. But I'd love to.''

An offered him coffee and he accepted a cup. They sat at the kitchen table.

''How's Carrie?'' she asked. ''She must be a big girl by now.'' Danner hesitated. Then he smiled. ''She's fine,'' he said.

Will came in the back door of the kitchen and greeted Danner. He had the sort of aristocratic, chiseled face that seemed to improve with age. After ten years there were more wrinkles around the blue eyes, which were set over flat, high cheekbones, and the creases in his forehead were deeper, but he was still an extremely handsome man.

"You haven't seen the farm," he said. "We have six acres. Let me show you around."

He took Danner on a tour of the barn, the stable, Ann's vegetable garden, and the pond at the bottom of the meadow. At one time it had been a working dairy farm. Now the cows were gone but Will kept chickens, and there was hay in the barn that Ann used as mulch in the garden.

Will led him back around to the front driveway and over to a cool, clear brook covered by a small stone house. "All our water comes from this spring," he explained. "The first owner of the farm covered the spring to protect the water supply and keep it from freezing over in winter. Then he lived here while he built the main house. The spring house is two stories, which is common in Loudoun County but not elsewhere. A lot of folks around say they were born over the spring house."

"Who settled this area?" Danner asked.

"Quakers. They came down from Bucks County two hundred years ago. This is the only part of Virginia that sent a regiment to the Union Army. The houses the Quakers built, like ours, were very simple and symmetrical, door opposite door, window opposite window."

"Beautiful place," Danner said. "How's the writing going?"

Lamont smiled. "The muse visits me intermittently. The farm is a little hard to find. But a few of my poems were published last spring."

"Glad to hear it."

"But you didn't come to talk about my poetry."

They sat down on the boulders near the spring house. "No," Danner said. "I'm back in the agency, temporarily."

Will's eyebrows arched but he said nothing.

"It's a long story," Danner said. "I won't bore you with the details. But we're having some alumni problems."

"Ah. The worst sort."

"Yes. Apparently some of the people shaken out in the Halloween Massacre haven't forgiven the company."

"That's not surprising. When you take a stick to a wasps' nest, they tend to get angry."

Danner laughed. "I've been led to believe that some of the old boys are more equal than others."

Will nodded. "True enough."

"And that the insiders control who gets the consulting jobs and the fat contracts."

"Yes. That's true too."

"I was hoping you could tell me who they are."

Will looked out across the brook to the cornfields beyond. He turned to Danner. "I've been out for half a dozen years. I live a nice, quiet life here with Ann."

Danner understood. "I won't use your name," he promised.

"They made a pass at me, you know," Will said. "I told them I wasn't interested."

"I didn't know."

"They call themselves the Group."

"I need names, Will."

"Go see Talbot Braswell. He lives on O Street, in Georgetown. He's in the book."

"He's high up?"

"He's more or less the screening committee for the Group."

"But not their leader."

"No. The real power is Wellington Lloyd."

"Lloyd!" Hadley had mentioned him. And Danner knew him; Lloyd had been high up in the covert bureaucracy. "He was fired in the Halloween Massacre."

"Yes."

"Where does he live now?"

"I don't know. He keeps a very low profile. Perhaps Binky will know, although I doubt he'll tell you."

"Binky?"

"Braswell. That's what everyone calls him."

"You've been a great help," Danner said. "I really appreciate it."

"Be sure to leave me out of it," Will said. He looked worried.

Danner put his hand on Will's shoulder. "I haven't even been here," he said.

CHAPTER
SIXTEEN

Georgetown was a self-contained world. Its quiet, tree-shaded streets and Federal-style brick homes were the domain of senators, diplomats, Supreme Court justices, senior law partners, and syndicated columnists. Beneath the surface charm, everything about the neighborhood bespoke wealth and power.

It was also a very difficult place to park. But Danner had chosen mid-morning for his cold call on Binky Braswell, and at that hour here and there a space could still be found. He squeezed the Skylark in between a van and a BMW on 28th Street, and walked around the corner to O Street.

Lamont was right; finding Braswell had not been difficult. The problem would be getting in to see him. Danner came to the number he was looking for. It proved to be an elegant red-brick three-story house with black shutters. The front door had an expensive brass knocker. Danner wondered why it hadn't been stolen. Along the west side of the house, a wrought-iron gate led into what was probably a garden in the rear.

Danner tried the knocker. After a long wait, a black-haired woman in a white uniform opened the door. Danner guessed she was from Guatemala.

"Good morning," Danner said, flashing his best smile. "I'm from the telephone company. Is Mr. Braswell in?"

She looked him over doubtfully. "Maybe he is in the garden, I think," she said, with a heavy Spanish accent. She pointed to the gate. "You can go here, *señor*."

Danner thanked her, opened the gate, and walked along the

side of the house toward the back. He got a glimpse of the living room through the windows. It was expensively furnished with antiques. There was a lot of dark, polished wood, a grand piano, and a huge Oriental rug.

He found Braswell down on his knees, digging in the topsoil with a trowel. He was wearing a broad-brimmed panama hat with a red band, a blue button-down work shirt, the fancy kind with epaulets, and a pair of dirty khaki pants. He straightened up at Danner's approach.

"Mr. Braswell?"

"Yes?" He drew the word out so that it almost had two syllables. He made no move to get up.

"I'm William Danner. We met once. Bucharest, I think."

Braswell slowly got to his feet. "Did we? I'm afraid I don't remember." His voice was nasal, cultivated, and faintly disdainful. He kept his work gloves on and did not offer to shake hands. He was a gray-haired man, in his late sixties Danner judged, and he wore horn-rimmed glasses. He was tanned, but his skin was blotchy and freckled.

"Mind if we talk?"

"We seem to be," Braswell said. "But the truth is, I'm rather busy just now. I'm setting out my tree peonies. This one"—he pointed—"is a white Godaishu. And this is a Shirotae. A white semi-double with a yellow center. Charming flower. Of course, the trick is to use enough compost and bone meal. And shelter them from the wind. They're rather temperamental, you know."

"I won't take up much of your time."

"Well," Braswell said, "I generally prefer it if my visitors telephone first. But since you're here." He led Danner over to the flagstone patio behind the kitchen, and they sat down in Salterini chairs.

"Would you care for some iced tea?" Braswell asked.

"Yes, thank you." Danner marveled at the patrician mind. It was important to display good manners in the most awkward circumstances, and especially to one's enemy. Binky Braswell was being elaborately polite.

Braswell called through the screen door. "Maria? Would you bring two iced teas? With lemon, *por favor*."

"Marvelous woman," he said to Danner. "Been with me

since I was station chief in Guatemala. I found her barefoot in a little Indian village near Quezaltenango.''

"You're fortunate," Danner said.

"Yes, well, you know what it is to get help these days." Braswell smiled. "She wears Guccis now."

Danner said, "I've come to you for some advice."

"Why me, my dear fellow?"

"I've been told you're influential. In the Group."

Braswell's eyes clouded over. He peeled off his work gloves and tossed them on a table. "I've never heard that term," he said. "And as for my being influential, I'm just a retired government official digging and planting in my garden, as you can see. I lunch at the Metropolitan Club occasionally, and buy a book or two at Francis Scott Key. Otherwise I scarcely venture out. I've been a widower for two years now."

"When did you leave the agency?"

"In October seventy-seven, when it was suggested that I retire. Mine is just another unmarked grave in the Halloween Massacre, one might say."

"I left that spring," Danner said. "Before it all happened."

"And now?"

"I run a fishing camp in New Brunswick. It's not very profitable. So, recently, I came back to do some consulting for the agency."

Braswell nodded. Danner had the distinct impression that he already knew all of that.

The maid appeared with the tea. She was carrying a silver tray with the drinks, which were in tall glasses. Alongside them, slices of lemon had been arranged to form a perfect circle on a Wedgwood plate. She put the tray down on the little side table between their chairs. "*Gracias*, Maria," Braswell said.

"Frankly, I'd like to broaden my options," Danner continued. "Move into a field with more opportunity." He didn't know if it would work. But perhaps the old boys would get the idea that if they could not scare him off, they could buy him off.

"A new career," Braswell said. "Difficult to do with an agency background. It's rather limiting."

"I know," Danner said. "But some of our former colleagues seem to be doing extremely well. Advising major corporations on anti-terrorism and security. Or they've set up as private consultants, with fat government contracts.''

"I don't doubt that some have been fortunate," Braswell replied.

"Perhaps you can give me a few leads. I was hoping you might suggest some people I could see.''

Braswell stirred his tea with a long thin silver spoon that tinkled against the glass. "I'm most sympathetic, Mr. Danner. But I wouldn't really know whom to suggest.'' His tone was polite but cold. "And of course you weren't asked to leave with the rest of us.''

"I see," Danner said.

"Well, it's not only that. If you're presently working for the agency, some of my friends might find it awkward to meet with you. I'm sure you understand.''

Danner had finished most of his tea. "There was one person in particular I thought I should see," he said. "Wellington Lloyd.''

"Wellington?'' Binky Braswell looked up at the trees and seemed to search his memory. "He and I share an interest in gardening; we're both fond of flowers. He's out of the business, of course. Forced to walk the plank by the admiral. But I haven't the faintest idea where he is.''

Outwardly Braswell appeared calm. But Danner thought he detected a tremor in his voice. "I was hoping you would know,'' he said.

"I'm afraid not. Haven't seen him for years.''

"Well, thanks anyway.''

Braswell arose. "I'm afraid I really can't be of much help to you, much as I might like to.''

Danner said goodbye and left the way he had come, along the side of the house. He had struck out again. He thought back over the past two weeks. He had learned a lot in Vienna, but he was no closer to finding the identity of the mole. As for the list of old boys, it was too long to go through one by one. He had shortcut that process by seeking out Sailor Cummins and Will. Now he had to find Wellington Lloyd, but where? So far, Danner thought ruefully, the mole is pitching a no-hitter.

Braswell did not go back to his gardening. He waited a moment to be sure that Danner had gone, then slipped into the house. He walked to the front hall and mounted the steps to his study on the second floor. He went inside, closed the door, and picked up the telephone.

Dixon Hadley's office was too warm. The sun was pouring in and overwhelming the air conditioning. The deputy director never drew the blinds.

"The old boys," Danner said. "They're organized. They call themselves the Group."

"I'm not surprised," Hadley said. "Our operations have been cleverly and systematically blown. There had to be an intelligence behind it, staff work." He cleared his throat. "Have you been able to find out who's running them?"

"One of the high-level victims of the Halloween Massacre. Wellington Lloyd."

Hadley's eyebrows went up. "I'm not really surprised at that, either. Wellington was staff assistant to the DDO. He knows how everything works. I mean everything. He's independently wealthy, so he has the social connections with the old boys as well."

"I want you to help me find him," Danner said. "Fast."

"We don't keep track of our ex-employees," Hadley explained. "That's the problem."

"Wellington Lloyd worked for the agency for twenty-five years," Danner replied. "You must have some way of finding him. We've got to track him down. He's the key to everything—the blown ops, the mole, my daughter."

Hadley had been chewing on a pencil. He removed it. "This agency has been around since 1947," he said. "We lose about twenty percent a year through retirement, resignations, dismissals, and death. That's normal attrition. That means that more than a hundred thousand people have left us. Actuarially, even if half of them are dead by now, there are still more than fifty thousand former employees out there."

"What about his retirement check?" Danner asked. "You must be sending it somewhere."

Hadley smiled. "Of course. And the number of people drawing retirement pay would be smaller. But if he's keeping a low profile, you don't think an old fox like Wellington Lloyd would have his check sent to his real address, do you?"

"No, it's probably going to an accommodation address. A lawyer's office in Tulsa, or some such. But maybe we can trace it from there."

"I doubt you'll have any luck. But you're welcome to try."

"Whom should I see?"

"You might start with Wilbur Ogleby in Personnel. He heads the retirement section."

Danner thanked him and left. He took the elevator down to Personnel, talked his way past a secretary, and was ushered into Ogleby's office. The chief of the retirement section had apparently managed to postpone his own retirement. He looked to be a man in his mid-sixties, with silver hair, a precise manner, and rimless glasses. He reminded Danner of a loan officer at a bank.

"I'm trying to find a former employee," Danner said. "I figure you must be sending him a check."

"If he qualifies under the CIA Retirement and Disability System, he would be receiving a monthly payment," Ogleby agreed. "Although it would not necessarily be a check."

"What do you mean?"

"A lot of our annuity payments are made by electronic funds transfer. For convenience. In that case, there's a direct deposit into the retiree's bank account."

"If the man I'm looking for is paid that way, knowing the name of the bank could be very helpful," Danner explained.

"Yes. But on the other hand, many of our retirees do receive monthly checks," Ogleby went on in his meticulous way. "Of course, we don't handle any of it."

"Who does?"

"The Treasury Department. We simply certify to them that a check should be sent to an individual at the address he or she provided upon retirement. Alternatively, an EFT payment can be made to an account number at a given bank, if the employee requests it."

"How do you certify the payments to Treasury?"

"On a magnetic tape. So they can put it right in their computers."

"The man I'm trying to locate is named Wellington Lloyd."

Ogleby took off his rimless glasses and rubbed the bridge of his nose. "Mr. Danner," he said, "at the present time, we have 9,046 former employees receiving retirement pay. I'm quite willing to describe the system to you in a general way, as I've done. But to provide you with information on a specific individual would violate the Privacy Act. I'm afraid I can't help you there."

"I'm on special assignment for the director," Danner said. "I'm authorized to get any information I need. You can check with the seventh floor."

Ogleby coughed slightly. "I see," he said. "Well, there's really no need to involve the director. He's a busy man. We'll run our copy of the tape through the computer and see if we have a record of your Mr. Lloyd. I'll have my secretary call you if we find anything. You'll understand, of course, that we're doing this confidentially and unofficially."

Danner rose. "I'd like the information as soon as possible," he said. "Within the hour."

"I'll do my best," Ogleby promised. He seemed a lot friendlier.

Danner went down to the cafeteria and had a chicken sandwich, coffee, and apple pie. Sam Green spotted him, waved, and came over to his table. They talked briefly. Sam complained of eyestrain. "A few more years in this job," he said, "and I'll have to borrow Jellison's dog to get around the halls."

After listening in further detail to Sam's problems, Danner said goodbye and took the elevator up to his office on the fifth floor to wait for Wilbur Ogleby's phone call. It came within ten minutes.

"Mr. Danner? I have that information you requested. I can't help you with the name of a bank, because it's not an electronic funds transfer. The gentleman in question gets a Treasury check. It's sent to him on the first of every month at P.O. Box 46, Hobe Sound, Florida 33455."

Danner thanked him and hung up. He banged his fist hard on the desk. "Shit," he said.

It had been worth trying, but Hadley was right. Lloyd was too smart to leave any traces. A P.O. box. What it undoubtedly meant was that a friend or confederate picked the checks up and forwarded them to Lloyd, wherever he was. It was almost impossible to put surveillance on a post office box. There was no way to know what day the friend would come and his visits to the box were probably deliberately irregular. The agency could hardly have someone standing around the Hobe Sound post office all month. Even if the friend were spotted, it would do no good; he would simply pick up the check and remail it later from another location. It might be sent anywhere in the world.

He thought for a moment, then dialed Ogleby back. "What happens to the canceled checks?" he asked. "Do they come back here?"

"No. We don't write them, so they don't come back to us."

"Well, where do they go? Treasury?"

"I suppose so. You'd have to ask them."

Danner's next call was to Jack Stanford, a Secret Service agent he had worked with on a sensitive currency case a decade earlier. After some preliminaries, Danner explained what he wanted: "I need to know what happens to a government retirement check after it's cashed."

"I dunno. I suppose they put them in boxes somewhere."

"I need to find one."

Stanford laughed. "Last year, for all purposes, the federal government issued approximately seven hundred million checks. Good luck."

"That sounds like a lot of boxes to go through."

"The guy you want to see is Al Kelly," Stanford said. "Head of the check claims division. They're squirreled away in the Liberty Loan Building. It's the funny-looking little building with the tunnel going through it, on the left-hand side just as you come over the Fourteenth Street bridge from Virginia."

"Thanks, Jack."

Danner dialed Kelly. His secretary said he was in a meeting. Danner left a message, and in about forty minutes the Treasury official called back.

Danner identified himself. "I'd like to come over and see you this afternoon," he said. "It's about a canceled check." Kelly sounded friendly and said he was free at three o'clock.

Danner drove south along the Potomac, crossed the river on the Fourteenth Street bridge, and found the L-shaped, gray concrete building tucked in next to the Bureau of Engraving and Printing. He took the elevator to the fifth floor.

Kelly was a thin, red-haired man, younger than Danner had expected from his voice, with a rawboned Irish face and clear blue eyes. Danner showed him his credentials.

"A retirement check looks like any other Treasury check," Kelly explained. "It's a computer card with holes in it, green on the front, buff on the back. We have almost two million former federal employees drawing pension checks, not counting the military. That's twenty-four million retirement checks a year."

"Do they come back to you after they're cashed?"

"No. We get the microfilms. The actual checks are stored in federal records centers around the country."

"Is there any way to find one canceled check?"

"With certain information it can be done, yes. Where did your man work?"

"CIA."

Kelly looked surprised. "CIA has its own retirement system. So does the Postal Service and Congress. But it all works about the same. In most cases when you retire, the agency you work for tells the Office of Personnel Management the size of your monthly check and OPM certifies that information to one of our disbursing offices. There are eight of them scattered around the country. Since CIA has its own pension system, they don't need to go through OPM. They send the information directly to a Treasury disbursing office on a magnetic tape. That way it can go straight into the computers that write the checks."

That jibed with what Ogleby had said. "What happens after the checks are deposited or cashed by the people who get them?" Danner asked.

"The bank sends the check along to the nearest Federal Reserve bank. The Fed does three things. It sprays a locator number on each check, makes a microfilm copy of the front and back, and creates a mag tape of the transaction. The actual checks go in numbered boxes and get shipped to the federal records centers for storage. The microfilm cartridges and the mag tapes are sent to us, here in this building."

"So the locator number is the key?"

"Exactly." Kelly was obviously proud of his system. Finding Wellington Lloyd's canceled check was shaping up as a personal challenge, which was what Danner had been hoping would happen. Kelly continued: "The mag tape is sent over to the central computer in the General Accounting Office. It tells the computer that the check has been paid and credits the Fed. At that point, the money is finally taken out of Treasury's pocket, as it were."

"But how can you match a name to the locator number?"

"To do that, I need a check number and a symbol number. Without them I can't help you."

Danner was trying to follow the complex procedure. "Okay, where do I get those numbers?"

"Remember I said there were eight disbursing offices? The retirement checks are issued serially, each with a check number, and the symbol number tells us which disbursing office issued a particular check."

"How do we know which disbursing office to call?"

"Chicago writes the retirement checks for almost all federal agencies in Washington. Don't ask me why. But CIA's pension checks are written by the Washington disbursing office. If you'd like, I'll make the call for you. It will save time."

"I'd appreciate it." Danner handed Kelly a slip of paper. "That's the man's name."

Kelly buzzed for his secretary and handed her the slip. "Call Herman in the Washington DO," he said. "I need a check and symbol number." To Danner he added, "The symbol number for Washington is in the three thousand range, but it changes as new series of checks are written. We need to know the exact numbers."

While she telephoned, Kelly explained the next step. "Since we know the name on the check and the agency he worked for, it won't take them long to retrieve the numbers. Once we have that information, I'll query our main computer and it should kick out the locator number. Then we're home free. Unless you need the actual check."

"No. The microfilm will be fine."

The secretary was back in a few moments with the data. "Follow me," Kelly said confidently. They walked down the hall, and he led Danner into a room with a small computer terminal. Kelly sat down at the keyboard and entered the information.

In less than a minute, the Treasury's main computer responded with fifteen digits. "The locator number," Kelly said with satisfaction. He printed it out and showed it to Danner: B52572641298470.

"What does it tell you?"

Kelly was studying the number. "The B means the check cleared through the New York Fed," he said. "The five tells us the fiscal year—1985. The next three numbers are the Julian date. Two hundred fifty-seven means the check cleared through the New York Fed on September 13. The three numbers after that identify the New York bank. I'd have to look it up to see which bank it is. Now go back a bit. The first eight digits also give us the number of the microfilm cartridge and the number of the box it's in. And the last seven digits tell us the sequence number on the cartridge."

They walked out to the elevator and rode down to the first floor. Kelly led the way into a huge vault, with a heavy steel door and time locks.

On the metal shelving were row upon row of cardboard boxes containing microfilm reels. Kelly strode among them like a king in his realm, with Danner at his heels. He stopped at last, pushed a rolling stepladder into place, and climbed up to where he could reach the top shelf. He opened one of the boxes and removed a single reel of film.

He got down and they left the vault. "All checks cleared through the New York Fed go to the federal records center in Bayonne, New Jersey," Kelly explained on the way out. "Your check is physically sitting there, in Building Twenty-two. But the picture of it is right on this roll."

In the room across the hall from the vault entrance were several microfilm readers. Kelly went to one of the machines, threaded the end of the reel through the rollers, and sat down. He advanced the reel until he reached the correct sequence number.

The he stopped. He peered into the screen and adjusted the focus. "Got it!" he said triumphantly. "I'll print it out for you." He pushed a button, and a piece of paper slid slowly from the machine. He handed it to Danner with a broad smile.

Danner studied the printout of the check. After state and federal taxes, Wellington Lloyd received $1,810.37 a month. On the bottom of the check, the letters CIARDSANNU were printed, which meant "CIA Retirement and Disability System Annuity."

But it was the microfilm picture of the back of the check that interested Danner. It had cleared through the Manufacturers Hanover Trust Company in New York; however, the bank in Manhattan had simply acted as a correspondent for an overseas bank.

The stamp of the foreign bank where the check had originally been deposited was slightly blurred on the printout, but Danner could read it: "Schweizerische Kreditanstalt, Zürich."

Talk to the gnomes. Now Danner understood. The Sailor had been right all along.

CHAPTER
SEVENTEEN

Danner asked the flight attendant for a cup of coffee; she brought it with cream and sugar and a smile. Through the cabin window of the Swissair 747 he watched the dawn come up over the Atlantic.

He had managed to sleep fitfully for a few hours after the plane left Kennedy, but his mind was racing too fast for him to relax. He felt he was closing in on his target now, and it was as though all of his senses were heightened and sharpened.

The sky grew lighter outside, and other passengers began to stir. Before long, the flight attendants served breakfast—orange juice, scrambled eggs, croissants, and thin slices of ham and Emmentaler cheese. After breakfast, Danner leafed through a copy of *Newsweek* to pass the time. At 10:30 A.M., the jet began its descent into Zürich's Kloten Airport. Danner had a good view of the Alps, towering in the distance to the south.

The landing was smooth, and in a few moments, he was riding in a small bus to the terminal building. Inside, he chose the "Nothing to Declare" gate and a customs officer waved him through. At the change window, he bought $100 worth of Swiss francs. He took an escalator down to the train platform and boarded one of the green coaches for Zürich. In twelve minutes he was at the Haupt-Bahnhof, the central railroad station, with its big, arched skylights, long rows of tracks, and teeming crowds. Out front he hailed a taxi and told the driver to drop him at the Ammann, a small hotel in the Kirchgasse.

The room on the fourth floor was plain but clean. He tossed

151

his bag on the bed, undressed, and took a long, hot shower. He shaved, changed his clothes, and went downstairs feeling much refreshed.

It was clear and cool in Zürich, a good day for walking. He crossed the street and made his way along the Limmat to the Bellevue Platz. He continued along the quay, then cut over past the Opernhaus to the Kreuzplatz. The flower shop was still there.

So was Felix Tobler, the proprietor, a huge man who greeted Danner with a hug and a crushing handshake. Well over six feet, Tobler looked more like an ex-linebacker for a pro football team than a florist to Zürich's high society.

"What a wonderful surprise," Tobler boomed out. "Erich did not tell me you were coming."

"Erich doesn't know I'm here," Danner said. "I haven't had a chance to call him." Erich Hoffman was Swiss, a college classmate of Danner's who had returned home to become a professor of English literature at the University of Zürich. It was through Erich that he had met Felix Tobler fifteen years before.

Danner surveyed the shop admiringly. "The roses," he asked. "Are they local?"

"Yes, from Dietikon. The chrysanthemums are from Mönchaltorf. Beauties, yes? The yellow roses, the begonias, the red gerbera, all are from the Zürich area. Everything you see is Swiss. In November, we get carnations from Italy, and in January roses from Colombia—yes, from South America. Our customers like them."

It was Felix's customers that interested Danner. The Blumenhaus Kreuzplatz catered to the city's Gold Coast, the millionaire bankers, financiers, and businessmen who lived in their mansions in Zollikon, Küsnacht, Herrliberg, and the other cloistered communities that stretched along the north side of the Zürichsee. In the hills above the lake, the city's wealthiest families dwelled in majestic privacy among their vineyards and Jaguars.

Tobler himself was a Zunftmeister, the former head of one of the twenty-five powerful guilds that still thrived in Zürich. Originally formed by various crafts and professions, they were now tight little social organizations of about one hundred members each. His stature in the guild nurtured his business success;

when the Gold Coast needed flowers to adorn its tables, it called Tobler.

While the two men talked, a salesgirl waited on a stout matron who was fussing about some begonias. Another customer, a well-dressed elderly man, entered the shop. Felix greeted him, then motioned Danner into a large, sunny back room with big windows and a huge work table, on which the flower arrangements were prepared. "Here we have some privacy," Felix said. "How can I help you, my friend?"

"I'm looking for a man," Danner said quietly. "An American."

"There are many Americans in Zürich."

"This one is wealthy. He's just the sort of person who would buy a house on the Gold Coast. Your turf. And he likes flowers. I thought you might have heard something."

"The lake houses do not change hands very often. Many of them stay in the same family for generations."

"I understand. But occasionally a mansion will be sold to a newcomer."

"Yes, sometimes. What is your gentleman's name?"

"Lloyd. Wellington Lloyd. He'd be in his late fifties."

Tobler spread out his hands and shrugged. "The name is not familiar to me. I know of only one American who has bought on the Gold Coast. A Mr. Kramer."

"When was that?"

"About two years ago. He purchased the von Bruhler estate in Herrliberg. A beautiful place, right on the Zürichsee."

Danner moved aside some yellow roses and sat down on the edge of the work table. "Tell me more about Mr. Kramer. You've met him?"

"Not personally. But he is a good customer. He entertains a lot, small dinner parties. Usually on Saturday morning, his housekeeper calls and orders an arrangement for the table."

"I might like to check him out. Can you give me his address and telephone?"

"Certainly." Felix lumbered over to a metal card file sitting atop the desk in the corner. He searched through the cards. "Seestrasse seven," he said. "Here, I'll write it down for you, with the telephone number." He scribbled the information on an index card and handed it to Danner.

Danner tried to reign in his mounting sense of excitement. There was no point in jumping to conclusions about Kramer. Yet he knew this could be it. "Thanks," he told Felix. "Can I use your phone? I want to call Erich."

"Of course, of course," Felix replied, indicating the telephone on the desk. "I will be out front, taking care of the customers. The room is yours."

Danner dialed the university and asked for Professor Hoffman. A secretary who answered said he was in class just now, but would be back in his office in a half an hour.

"Ask him to wait there for me. I am an old friend. My name is Danner."

"Very well, Herr Danner. I will give Professor Hoffman your message."

"Danke schön."

"Bitte."

Danner said goodbye to Felix, then hailed a taxi and took it to the university, a cluster of ancient brown buildings mixed in with a few modern ones, on a hill overlooking the Limmat. He was sitting in Erich's office when he returned from class.

Erich stared in surprise at Danner over the top of his half glasses, and then broke into a broad grin. "Dartmouth's in town again, run girls run. How are you, Bill?"

"Fine, Erich. It's good to see you." Hoffman was a lanky man, with an unruly shock of straight, sandy hair, a rumpled tweed sports jacket, and a pipe. He looked every inch the academic. Seeing him again brought back a host of memories.

Erich fussed with his pipe, tamping in some tobacco and lighting it. "So," he said, shaking out the match. "And what brings you to Zürich?"

"Business. I was hoping you could help."

Hoffman closed the door to the office so that they were alone. "If I can, naturally. I never believed you were really running a fishing camp. It was cover, yes?"

"No," Danner said. "It wasn't. But I've come back to the company on a special assignment. Not for long, I hope."

"I see." Erich struck another match and sucked in on the pipe. Finally satisfied that it was well lit, he asked, "How can a scholar of Chaucer and the English poets possibly be of help to an international, let us say, businessman?'' He smiled mischievously.

"It isn't your scholarship I need," Danner said. "It's your contacts. In particular, your friend, Colonel Zeiss.'' Walter Zeiss, as Danner knew, was high up in UNA, the Swiss military intelligence agency. He was also Erich's childhood friend.

Hoffman shook his head in mock sadness. "And I thought you had come to talk about John Donne. The seventeenth century is so much more pleasant than our own.''

"But I'm trapped in our own.'' Danner smiled ruefully. "Perhaps one night at dinner we can talk about poetry. But today at lunch I'd like to see Colonel Zeiss. Do you think you can arrange a table at Chez Max?''

A look of alarm crossed Erich's countenance. "Rather steep for a mere academic,'' he said. "For Walter, too, I imagine.''

"I'm on an expense account. My treat.''

"In that case, Chez Max. But let me see if Walter is free.'' Erich dialed his friend and a brief conversation took place in Swiss German. He hung up and turned to Danner. "You're in luck,'' he said. "Walter will be delighted to join us.'' Erich had his secretary make the reservation, and they drove along the shore in his green Volkswagen to the restaurant in Zollikon. The sky was bright blue over the lake and the sailboats were out in force.

They were already seated at their table when Colonel Zeiss arrived. Erich made the introductions. The colonel looked to be in his mid-forties. He was in mufti, wearing a dark blue suit and a conservative tie. He had jet black hair and piercing eyes, and might have been handsome except for a low hairline that, Danner thought irreverently, made him look faintly prehistoric.

They ordered aperitifs and chatted amiably, luxuriating in the elegant atmosphere. The restaurant had dark brown walls hung with modern paintings, and there were flowers everywhere. Danner wondered if they were from Felix's shop.

When the ice had been well broken, Danner showed Zeiss his agency credentials. The Swiss intelligence officer opened the leatherette folder, studied the picture inside carefully, nodded, and handed it back. "I was hoping you could give me some unofficial, back-channel help,'' Danner said. "As one professional to another.''

"That is not so easily done in Switzerland," Zeiss said. "Even for an old friend of Erich's. Why are you not working through your Bern station? They have liaison both with the Bundespolizei and with us."

"My mission is extremely sensitive. I'm operating as a singleton."

The sommelier brought a bottle of Pouilly-Fuissé and the colonel, after inhaling the bouquet and taking a sip, pronounced it charming. The wine seemed to improve his mood. "Tell me what you need," he said, "and we shall see."

"There is an American named Wellington Lloyd," Danner said. "I believe he's here in Zürich. He banks at the Schweizerische Kreditanstalt. He probably has a secret numbered account. I need to know as much about him as possible. Including his address, for openers."

Walter Zeiss chuckled. "You expect me to get information on a numbered account from Credit Suisse? Perhaps you would also like me to climb the Matterhorn barefoot? Or fly to the moon like your astronauts?"

Erich looked embarrassed. Danner smiled and said, "I know all about your strict Swiss banking laws. I also know that what I'm asking is not impossible."

"Under Article 47 of the Banking Act," Zeiss recited, "any bank officer or employee who reveals a secret confided to him is liable to six months in prison or a fine of fifty thousand Swiss francs. That's a great deal of money, Mr. Danner. More than twenty-five thousand dollars."

"I'm aware of that. I also know that Swiss Intelligence has its sources inside the banks."

The waiter arrived with their lunch. "In any event," Zeiss said when he had gone, "I doubt that your man has a numbered account. Since about seventy-eight, the major Swiss banks have been very cautious about opening numbered accounts for U.S. citizens. There's been too much pressure from Washington about Mafia money flowing into Zürich."

"Lloyd would have opened his account in 1977. When he left us."

The colonel's eyes widened. "Ah," he said. "Now I understand the delicacy. One of your own."

"Yes."

Zeiss's expression became more sympathetic. "It is still a difficult request," he said. "Very difficult." He sighed and shook his head. "But, as I said, we shall see."

"I did some research in our files," Danner said. "The numbered accounts are handled on the third floor, in the trust department. When a customer goes there to open a secret account, the bank assigns a number, two to eight digits. The monthly statements are computerized, like any other account, but there are no names in the computer. Four senior people in the trust department know the name that matches the number. But there are about one hundred people who work in the trust department, and all of them have access to the files containing the names. All you need is one of those people."

Zeiss raised his wineglass. "I salute you, Mr. Danner. You are remarkably well informed about the internal workings of the Schweizerische Kreditanstalt. The bank's officers would be appalled if they could hear you."

"I'm at the Ammann," Danner said. "Room 418." He raised his glass in turn. "To Swiss banking secrecy."

It was disconcerting to hear Lorne Green speaking German as he rode through the sagebrush, but the dubbed western was the best thing Danner could find on his television set. He had gone downstairs for breakfast, and now he was stretched out on the bed in his hotel room, waiting. He had never liked the waiting, but it came with the territory, he told himself. He tried not to think about Carrie.

Just before 11:00 A.M., the telephone next to the bed jangled. A voice he recognized as Walter's said abruptly, "Meet me at the Lindenhof in fifteen minutes." Then the caller hung up.

Danner grabbed his jacket, dropped his key at the desk, and walked across the Münster Bridge. He turned at the quay and walked along the Limmat to the park. Near the fountain, he found Zeiss.

They strolled along under the plane trees, like two old friends. "Your Mr. Lloyd does have a numbered account," Zeiss said. "And it's very active. It has several million dollars in it. Most of the money is invested in the Euromarket. That way he earns five times as much interest as if he kept the money in the bank. And he avoids paying thirty-five percent of his interest income to the Swiss government in withholding taxes.''

"When was the account opened?" Danner asked.

"Just as you said, nineteen seventy-seven. In December."

"Where's the money coming from?"

"Various countries. A lot of it is flowing in from Libya in petro-dollars. Mr. Lloyd seems to have high-level oil connections. And there are several large payments from two of your more notorious alumni—Edward Farrell and Richard Griffin.''

They walked over to the edge of the terrace and gazed out over the Old Town and the spires of St. Peter's and the Fraumünster. "Where does the money go to?" Danner inquired.

"It's disbursed to dozens of people all over the world. I did not attempt to write down the names. There were too many."

"I'm very grateful for this much. And curious about your leverage.''

The colonel smiled. "Do you remember the Chiasso affair?"

"I'm afraid not."

"Well, there's no reason you would. But it rocked our banking community to the core. It was the largest bank scandal in Swiss history, involving hundreds of million of dollars. And Credit Suisse was right in the middle of it.''

"Why was it called the Chiasso affair?"

"Chiasso is a small town in southern Switzerland, on the border with Italy, near Lake Como. The manager of the Credit Suisse bank in Chiasso had funneled almost nine hundred million dollars into a holding company in Lichtenstein in which he had a secret interest. They were investing in wine, plastics, hotels. Most of the money was in Italian lire, smuggled across the border illegally. When the bubble burst, the branch manager went to jail. And a lot of the top executives in Zürich were shaken out.''

"But not everybody."

"You are very shrewd, Mr. Danner. No, not everybody. Certain arrangements were made, certain charges quietly dropped. Some of those who remained in the top echelons of our Zürich banks are, shall we say, under a continuing obligation to us." Zeiss smiled broadly.

"So the Chiasso affair turned out to be very useful to Swiss Intelligence. Did you arrange the scandal to begin with?"

The colonel chuckled. "I like the way your mind works, Mr. Danner. No, I am afraid we were not that inventive. Ordinary avarice explained Chiasso. Or perhaps it was proximity to the Italians."

"I am greatly indebted to you, Colonel."

"We can't afford renegades in our profession, Mr. Danner. I am pleased to have been able to help."

Danner could feel his adrenalin flowing. "There is one more thing. I need Lloyd's address. It would be in the bank's confidential records."

"Yes, I have it for you." Zeiss reached into his breast pocket and removed a small, black notebook. He wet one finger and began turning the pages. "Here it is," he said. "Your Mr. Wellington Lloyd lives in Herrliberg. At Seestrasse seven."

CHAPTER
EIGHTEEN

As he drove south along the lakefront toward Herrliberg, Danner was surprised by the seagulls. He had not expected to find them in a landlocked, Alpine country, far from any ocean. Yet there they were, fat-breasted, sleek birds, wheeling over the Zürichsee and swooping low to dive for fish.

Like the other residents of the Gold Coast, Danner thought, the gulls looked prosperous and well fed. A Mercedes flashed by, the sixth one he had counted in the last ten minutes. He felt a little out of place in his rented Fiat.

According to his Michelin map, he had already passed through Zollikon, Küsnacht, and Erlenbach. The Zürichsee, like most of the Swiss lakes, was long and skinny. He could clearly see the houses of Thalwil on the opposite shore.

In a few moments, he was in Herrliberg. From the description Felix had given him, he had no trouble finding the house. The Seestrasse was a narrow, busy road paralleling the shore. Most of the houses were on the terraced hillsides across the road from the lake. But the von Bruhler estate, as Felix had said, was right on the water. He pulled off onto the shoulder and parked.

A whitewashed stone wall, nine feet high, protected the estate. The front of the house was set well back from the road, inside a wide, cobblestoned courtyard fringed with flower beds. The entrance to the courtyard was secured by two large wrought-iron gates topped with spikes.

Danner assumed that the rear of the house overlooked a lawn

that sloped perhaps 150 feet to the lake. Almost certainly, there would be a private dock or marina as well. Because of the high wall, he could not see toward the back of the house from his vantage point on the road.

There was a garage inside the courtyard, to the right. The house itself had three stories and what appeared to be an attic level above them. It was built of stone, whitewashed like the wall, and the windows had black shutters. The window frames and mullions were bright red, and there were large carved wooden crosses, also red, tucked under the eaves.

He got out, approached the iron gates, and rang the bell. A metallic voice crackled out of the box mounted on the pillar next to the gate. Danner did not understand all of the Swiss German, but the meaning was clear. The voice wanted to know who he was and what he wanted.

"William Danner," he said. "To see Mr. Kramer."

There was a long silence. Then the voice crackled again. "Herr Kramer is not at home."

"Fine. I'll speak to Mr. Lloyd."

There was another silence, longer this time. Then a buzzer sounded. Danner pushed open the gate. He walked across the courtyard. The house was bigger than he thought. Twenty feet to his right, two enormous Doberman pinschers growled at him. Danner noted with relief that they were safely behind a chain link gate between the garage and the house. At night the gate was probably opened so the dogs had the run of the grounds. He noticed there were floodlights mounted on the front and sides of the house.

He rang the doorbell and waited. It was opened by a toughlooking manservant in his twenties. The voice in the box, Danner guessed.

He motioned Danner to go up the stairs and followed a few paces behind. At the top of the stairs, he slipped past Danner and turned left, beckoning him to follow. Danner caught a glimpse of a large living room and a dining room fronting on the lake. Just beyond them, on the same side of the hall, was a corner study paneled in light, finely oiled wood.

By the desk in the study, framed in the large windows, with the light streaming in and the Zürichsee behind him, stood Wellington Lloyd.

"Danner," he said. "It's been rather a long time."

It was typical of Lloyd, Danner thought. No explanation of why he was living in Switzerland under an alias, no questions about how Danner had tracked him down. Just a polite, casual greeting, as though he had unexpectedly bumped into an old acquaintance at the club.

"Seven years," Danner said. He studied Lloyd. The man was remarkably unchanged. His hair was as white as an albino's, as it had been for years. His face and nose were thin, almost effeminate, but the lips were full and sensual. The soft brown eyes were masked by gray-tinted glasses. He reminded Danner somehow of a large laboratory rat.

"You've come back," Lloyd said. "Or so I hear."

"You keep in touch, then?"

"Not really. I'm a businessman now. I've put the agency behind me. I hear stray bits of gossip sometimes, but nothing more."

They sat down in armchairs facing each other. Lloyd still had his back to the window, so that his face was in shadow. Danner had to squint to look at him.

"I should explain straightway why I've come to see you," Danner said. "I'm in financial difficulty. I have a fishing camp in Canada, but it's not doing well. The company brought me back on a temporary assignment, against my will. Perhaps you've heard something about it."

Lloyd shook his head. "No, only that you were back."

"What I'd like to do is what you're doing. Become a consultant for the multinationals, the oil companies."

Lloyd didn't nibble. "An admirable ambition," he said. "I wish you luck with it."

"From what I hear, it takes more than luck." Danner spoke deliberately, watching Lloyd's face. "It's my understanding that you control a well-financed network of old boys that calls itself the Group."

Lloyd's eyes flickered, but his expression did not change.

"I've been told that without your approval, no former agency people can get any major contracts, either from the government or private industry."

"Absolute rubbish," Lloyd said. "It sounds like one of Dixon Hadley's fantasies." He smiled. It made him look even more sinister behind the tinted glasses. "But if you've come all the way from Washington, the least I can do is offer you a drink."

Danner returned the smile. "I wouldn't mind a Scotch on the rocks."

Lloyd went over to a bar by the window. While he fixed the drinks, Danner looked around the room. A couch and two side chairs filled the far end. Floor-to-ceiling bookcases lined the walls, except on the window side. A heavy oaken desk dominated the area to Danner's left. To his right, in the center of the room, an expensive-looking Bertoia sculpture, about twenty flexible brass rods pointing straight up in a circular cluster, was mounted on a wooden base. There were no paintings, because the bookcases occupied most of the wall space.

Lloyd handed him the drink. "I see you've been admiring the house. It's three hundred and fifty years old. The previous owners used the downstairs largely for formal entertaining. The rooms on the ground floor are huge, really ceremonial. So the living room, dining room, and kitchen are on this floor." He waved a hand toward the window. "With a better view of the lake, as you can see."

"You're well protected," Danner said. "Those are fierce-looking dogs. But I noticed they didn't bark at me."

Lloyd smiled. "They're trained to attack silently."

"I also saw some wine casks in the courtyard," Danner said.

"We produce our own. There are grapes fermenting right now in the vats in the cellar. There's quite a lot of wine grown along the Zürichsee. Those hills directly across the road are all my vineyards."

"You lead a pleasant life here."

"A quiet one. I congratulate you on finding me. I am not easy to find."

"I know."

"But I'm afraid you have gone to a great deal of trouble for nothing. There is no Group, as you call it, and while I'm sympathetic to your financial plight, there is really nothing I can do to help."

You're going to help, Danner thought. You just don't know it yet. "I'm disappointed."

They both got up. Lloyd walked over to Danner and stood

very close to him. "I might add that I greatly value my privacy. Interfering with it can prove to be a dangerous occupation."

Danner wondered whether it was Lloyd who had tipped off the Soviets about him. Whether this man standing a foot away from him was the cause of his daughter's disappearance and his own anguish. Lloyd might even know where Carrie was being held at this very moment. He resisted a strong impulse to reach out and throttle him, to see the impassive white face turn red and the soft eyes fill with terror, the terror Carrie must have felt when they dragged her into the van. But killing Lloyd would defeat his purpose.

"Thanks for the drink," he said evenly. He turned on his heel and left. The manservant was waiting silently in the hall downstairs and opened the front door for him. Danner crossed the courtyard to the gate. The two Dobermans, now joined by a third, were still there, growling and salivating. They clearly don't appreciate my finer qualities, Danner thought. The buzzer sounded as he approached the gate, and he let himself out.

Seestrasse 7 was not a very friendly place. But he felt exhilarated. He had not only found Wellington Lloyd. He had just cased his house.

Danner drove back into Zürich directly to the Kreuzplatz. He parked and went into the Blumenhaus. Felix was out, so he crossed the street to an outdoor café. He sat down at a table, ordered a Feldschlösschen beer, and drank it slowly, watching the entrance to the shop.

After fifteen minutes, he saw Felix return. He finished his beer. *"Zahlen bitte,"* he called to the waiter. He paid the check and walked across to the shop.

Tobler was delighted to see him, and gave him another bear hug. "I was afraid you had left Zürich," he said.

"No. Just doing a little sightseeing in the suburbs this morning."

"In Herrliberg, perhaps?"

"Yes. You said that Mr. Kramer usually orders flowers on Saturday morning?"

"Yes. Almost every week."

"So he should call tomorrow morning. How do you make delivery?"

"In the white van. You can see it parked just outside."

Danner glanced through the front window. The van was pulled up partly onto the sidewalk at an angle because there wasn't enough room to parallel park.

"I'd like to go along with the driver."

"That can be arranged." He called into the back room. "Karl."

A young man in blue jeans and a T-shirt appeared. Felix told him, "Tomorrow you will have a new helper, just for the day. Please do what he says. He will leave with you at eleven, for the regular route."

Danner shook hands with the driver. "Thanks," he said. "I appreciate it."

"It will be good that you come," Karl said. "I have visited in Chicago my aunt. I can practice my English with you."

Danner smiled. "You do a lot better than I do in Swiss German. I'll see you tomorrow, then. A little before eleven."

It was drizzling the next morning when Danner ducked into the flower shop. The van was parked out front with its back doors open. Karl was loading in the morning's orders, which had been prepared in the back room and were ready to go out. One of the orders was for Kramer, Karl told him.

Danner was dressed in work clothes that he had bought at Jelmoli the previous afternoon—blue jeans, a denim shirt, and a khaki cap. Felix looked him over with an amused expression. "Not bad," he said. "Perhaps you would like a permanent job?"

"Don't call me," Danner said. "I'll call you."

Felix patted him on the shoulder and looked serious. "Good luck."

Outside in the light rain, Danner conferred for a moment with Karl. "I'll follow you in the Fiat," he said. "You go ahead and make your regular deliveries along the way. When you get to Herrliberg, there's a side street going off to the right, toward the water, a block before you reach the Kramer estate. Pull in there, go halfway to the lake, and wait for me. I'll be right behind you."

They drove through Zollikon and Küsnacht, sometimes on the shore road, sometimes inland, as Karl made his deliveries. Danner followed at a discreet distance in the Fiat. It was past noon when the white van turned into the side street in Herrliberg. A moment later, Danner pulled up. He got out and walked over to the van.

"The flowers for Kramer," Danner said. "I'll need them." Karl opened the back of the van. There were two dozen red roses arranged in a straw basket and covered with white butcher paper to protect them from the rain.

"You can get back behind the wheel," Danner said. "I'll join you in a minute."

Karl shrugged. Clearly Herr Tobler and the American were up to something, but it wasn't his job to worry about it. "Is cool," he said, grinning.

Danner got in the back of the van and carefully opened the butcher paper without tearing it. From his pocket, he removed a clear plastic box containing two squares of foam rubber. He opened the box and gently pulled apart the squares. From between them he removed what appeared to be a tiny black beetle, about one eighth of an inch long. It was made of plastic but was extraordinarily lifelike, with arms and legs, a tiny head and eyes.

Danner took a tweezer from his pocket and used it to peel off a little adhesive strip on the bottom of the insect. Then, using the tweezer to hold the beetle by the midsection, he gently inserted it deep into one of the roses. Satisfied that it was adhering to the bottom of the petals, he carefully withdrew the tweezer and rearranged the paper so the flowers appeared undisturbed.

Danner had brought the beetle with him from Langley. It was the latest, most sophisticated creation of the Office of Technical Service—a powerful transmitter that would broadcast for up to thirty hours to the voice-activated tape recorder locked in the trunk of the Fiat. OTS had come up with the ultimate to meet Danner's needs—a bug that looked like a bug.

He climbed out, closed the door, and got into the passenger seat next to Karl. "Okay," he said. "Let's go. When we get to Kramer's do whatever you normally do. I'll stay in the van. If anybody asks about me, just say I'm your new helper."

Karl nodded and started up the van. The rain was coming down harder now. He turned around, went back out to the Seestrasse, and drove the short distance to the house. At the gate, he got out, rang the bell, and said "Blumenhaus Kreuzplatz" into the squawk box. The buzzer sounded. He opened the gate, got back in, and drove into the courtyard. Danner, slouching in the passenger seat, pulled his cap down low over his forehead.

The thuggish-looking manservant opened the door, and Karl handed him the basket. The man did not even appear to notice anyone in the van. But while he was busy signing for the roses, Danner had a chance to observe the house again. The three Dobermans were in their usual place at the side gate, watching. Apparently there were only three. He studied the roof and noted that the portion over the north wing was flat.

Karl got into the van and backed out of the courtyard. The servant ran out in the rain to close the gate, then hurried back inside.

"To your car?" Karl asked when they were away from the house.

"No. I'll ride back into town with you."

"Okay. No charge is extra."

"No extra charge," Danner corrected him.

Karl shook his head disappointedly. "I am needing more practice," he said. "To learn, one must listen carefully."

"You're doing fine," Danner said in a kindly tone. "You listen very well."

He hoped the OTS bug would do the same. Everything depended on it.

CHAPTER
NINETEEN

Danner spent the rest of Saturday waiting. The rain had ended. He wandered the narrow, twisting streets of the Old Town and browsed among the eighteenth-century ceramics at the Landesmuseum. He walked the length of the Bahnhof Strasse and wondered how many billions of Swiss francs were sitting in the banks that lined the avenue.

When he passed Credit Suisse on the Paradeplatz, he could not resist glancing up at the third floor. He looked in the glittering store windows at the expensive gold watches resting in their cases of black velvet. He watched the shoppers streaming by. But mostly, he waited.

On Sunday, he was expected for dinner at the Hoffmans. At 5:00 P.M. Erich was waiting for him in front of the Ammann. They drove out to Herrliberg to pick up the Fiat. Danner followed Erich back into town to his apartment on the Steinbruchelstrasse. They parked in front. Danner unlocked the trunk of his car and slipped the microrecorder in his pocket.

They walked up the stairs together. Erich's wife, Anna, a woman of dark hair and a quiet beauty, was waiting with a cold bottle of Fendant from the Valais. She ran the Hoffman household with Swiss efficiency and worked full time as well as a research scientist at the university.

"The children have eaten," Anna told them. "Erica, come and say hello to Mr. Danner." The Hoffmans' teenage daughter appeared and shook hands. She had her mother's good looks and reminded him of Carrie.

"I have a daughter almost your age," he said. The words did not come easily.

"Peter is watching television in his room," Anna said. She called to him to come and greet their guest, and a dark-haired boy of about ten came bouncing out of the bedroom. "Do you play Ping-Pong?" he asked Danner.

"I was very good once."

"I can beat you."

"Peter," his mother remonstrated.

"I can. I challenge you to a match after dinner."

"Deal," Danner said.

The children drifted off, and the three adults sat down in the living room. They sipped the wine and talked about their lives. Anna wanted to hear all about the Miramichi.

During dinner, Danner found it hard to concentrate on the chit-chat about schools, the children, and politics. He was impatient, anxious to go off by himself to Erich's study and listen to the tape. He had told Erich he needed some private time after dinner. Anna served dessert and coffee and he thought the moment had arrived when he could gracefully excuse himself and slip into the study.

Just as he was about to, Peter appeared with two Ping-Pong racquets and a ball. "The table's downstairs," he said. "In the storage room. You better be good."

Danner, smiling, gestured helplessly to Erich and Anna. "One game," he said.

The boy was good. Danner showed off a few slams and tricky serves but let him win by two points.

"I told you I could beat you," Peter said proudly as they went back upstairs.

"I'm going into training. Next time you won't have a chance."

"I'll be ready."

Danner envied the Hoffmans. They had managed to stay together and raise two nice kids. It was no small accomplishment. It was the one thing you could never have in the agency. A normal life. Erich took him into his book-lined study. "No one will disturb you here," he said. "Take as long as you want."

"Thanks."

Danner removed the battery-powered microrecorder from his

jacket pocket and settled himself in a comfortable brown leather chair. It was safer to listen to the tape here, rather than in his hotel room. As an added precaution, he used an earphone. The ultra-thin tape, developed in the OTS laboratories, could hold three hours of conversation. Danner figured it was more than enough to pick up anything said at the dinner table.

He rewound the tape to the beginning. Since the bug was voice-activated, there would be nothing on the tape until Lloyd and his guests went into the dining room. The roses would have been put on the table as a centerpiece, Danner assumed.

The device worked. The first sound Danner heard was a voice that he recognized as Lloyd's saying he much preferred a French wine to the best the Swiss could offer. There was a scraping of chairs and some clinking of glasses and the sound of liquid pouring into a glass.

"A Clos Vougeot Grand Maupertuis," Lloyd said. "By any measure, one of the great wines of Burgundy."

"It *is* excellent," a second, slightly nasal voice agreed. "An uncompromising vintage. One wonders how the monks of the Vouge ever managed any ecclesiastical pursuits."

Danner backed up the tape and played the remark again. It was maddening. He knew the second voice, yet he could not place it immediately.

He advanced the tape again. "How are things in Washington?" Lloyd asked.

"Jordan still has the president's backing," the nasal voice said. "But it's bound to be wearing thin now. Too much has gone wrong."

"But he's been able to contain it?"

"So far, but there's beginning to be some talk. Stray bits and pieces. Stirrings on the Hill. I've even had a question or two at the club. Of course, I deny any knowledge of trouble."

Danner pushed the rewind button and listened to the last part again: "How are things in Washington? . . . I've even had a question or two at the club. Of course, I deny any knowledge of trouble." Suddenly Danner knew whose voice it was he was hearing. The second man was Binky Braswell!

There was the sound of a door opening, and a woman's voice, a maid serving dinner. "Would you care for some more Rösti, Herr Kramer?"

Footsteps, the woman leaving the dining room. More clinking of glasses and silverware. A cough. Then Lloyd's voice again: "I tend to agree with you. We've accomplished a great deal in the last few months. I think our friend Jordan's days are numbered."

"It would be poetic justice if he were fired by the president." Braswell answering.

"How did things go with Janney?"

Danner played the sentence over to be sure he had heard the name right. There was no question of it, he had. Richard Janney was President Forbes' chief of staff, a smooth southerner who had managed the presidential primary campaign of Vice President Prentiss Brock. Brock had lost his presidential bid, but Forbes had selected him as his running mate. And now Janney was the most powerful man in the White House. To everyone's surprise, he had eclipsed and outmaneuvered the president's own aides, emerging within the Forbes inner circle as first among equals.

"Very well," Braswell replied.

"You actually met in the White House?"

"I didn't think that would be discreet. Some reporter might have spotted me coming in. No, we had drinks at Wade Seabrook's house on Dumbarton."

"Janney's thoroughly briefed?"

"There wasn't time to go into a lot of detail. But the general outlines, yes. He's aware that a series of ops have gone awry, and he's very disturbed that Jordan has concealed them from the president."

"Excellent. Is he going to talk to Brock?"

There were some interfering noises, the cover of a dish being removed and replaced, perhaps; Danner could not hear all of Braswell's reply. But he could make out the words "the best channel."

Then he heard Lloyd boasting that he had kept up his contacts "with Prentiss." They had worked well together on "the seventh floor."

Brock was the best channel. To whom? To the president, of course. And Lloyd had remained close to the vice president. Now the old boys' political objectives were clear.

Danner stopped the tape and thought it through. Prentiss

Brock was a former director of CIA. Word of the agency's fiascos had been deliberately leaked to Richard Janney, who promised to pass them along to the vice president. Brock, in turn, would tell the president. And because of Brock's own background as CIA chief, President Forbes undoubtedly leaned heavily on him for advice on agency matters. If the president decided to replace Brooks Jordan, he would ask Prentiss Brock and Richard Janney for their recommendations. And they would recommend Brock's friend, Wellington Lloyd, an experienced CIA officer whom Brock had relied on during his own tenure as director.

Suddenly it all made sense: Tokyo, Madrid, London, Vienna, Nick Rossi shooting MS/SKYLARK. It was all part of a well-organized plot by the old boys to destroy the top leadership of the CIA and take over the agency.

And now it was clear that Wellington Lloyd and the old boys had a channel directly into the White House. The Soviets were on the sidelines reaping the benefits. No wonder they wanted to stop Danner.

The agency had brought him in too late, Danner thought bitterly. There was no way to prevent what was happening. It had already gone too far and reached too high. And Carrie was the innocent victim.

He pressed the "start" button on the tape recorder again. Lloyd was still playing lord of the manor, extolling the beauties of the von Bruhler estate to Braswell, going on about his vineyards. The first growth wine and the second growth.

Dessert was brought in and Braswell complimented Lloyd on the fresh fruit tart. Lloyd asked if he would like a little more whipped cream. Braswell said he would. Spoon rattling in the whipped cream bowl.

They were swapping agency war stories now, anecdotes about former colleagues. Predictable stuff. Danner listened, but impatiently. Then he heard his own name.

"Danner was here." Lloyd's voice.

"I warned you he was rooting around at the edges." Braswell cleared his throat. "Same story he was peddling in my garden?"

"Yes. Offering himself as bait. Claiming he needed money."

"He knows nothing." Braswell's voice was smug.

"Perhaps. But I didn't like the fact that he found me. He's a dangerous man."

"There's nothing he can do. We're close to the end now. Danner's of no consequence."

"Pricks," Danner said aloud. "We'll see."

Over coffee, the talk between the two men turned to money. Lloyd was assuring Braswell there was no problem. "It's flowing in from Libya," he said. "Like oil. Farrell and Griffin are the key."

"They're cowboys," Braswell said distastefully. "Why are they paying us?"

"For God's sakes, Binky, how do you think they've been able to operate openly all this time, with a chain of federal indictments around their necks?"

"We've helped them?"

"The Group still has lines into Langley. You know that. We've brokered their protection by the agency. In exchange for a percentage of the take."

"I've tried to be generous with my own support."

"And so you have." Lloyd talking. "We're grateful for that as well." Danner knew that Talbot Braswell was a millionaire; he was married to Marsha Meadows, whose father owned the biggest department store in Chicago.

Some more anecdotes and small talk. Lloyd offering Braswell a Cuban cigar. A joke about Castro. And then Braswell's voice: "And we still don't know our benefactor's identity?"

"I haven't a clue. All I know is that the information is pure gold."

"It's not a voice you recognize?"

"No. And I was warned, when the first one arrived, months ago, not to try to find out. Or they would stop coming."

Danner ran the tape back and with mounting excitement listened again: "Our benefactor's identity . . . not a voice you recognize . . . when the first one arrived, months ago." Danner realized what it meant. The mole had not risked direct contact. *Wellington Lloyd was getting tapes.*

"This is an excellent Havana." Braswell's voice again. "We used to have to get them for Kennedy, you know. He smoked H. Upmann's. He was smoking Cuban cigars at the height of the missile crisis." Laughter on the tape.

Lloyd spoke again. "You'll be interested to know that another one came in two days ago. Right on schedule. Would you like to hear it?"

"Yes, indeed."

Sound of scraping chairs and footsteps, gradually fading away. Danner cursed. He could hear them walking down the hall, probably toward Lloyd's study. The voices were muffled and the words indistinct. Then silence.

He listened for two minutes but there was nothing on the tape. He was about to shut off the recorder and give up when he heard, quite faintly, a weird, unearthly sound. It was unlike anything he had ever heard before. There was some resemblance to church bells, or chimes, but it was not quite either of those.

Maybe Wellington Lloyd is picking up music from outer space, Danner thought. He listened for another ten minutes but the sound did not recur. There was nothing more on the tape. He clicked off the recorder and sat quietly in Erich's study for a long time.

And then he knew.

CHAPTER
TWENTY

The Shanghai restaurant out on Lee Highway was crowded at lunchtime, as usual. It was a favorite hangout for agency people.

Sam Green was having trouble with his Moo Shu pork. He'd rolled the pancake well enough, but he forgot to close one end, and when he tried to lift it to his mouth, all the bamboo shoots and the meat fell out onto his plate. He finally gave up and used a knife and fork.

Danner, eating shrimp and snow peas with his chopsticks, tried not to laugh but couldn't help himself. "You're being punished," he said. "For eating pork."

"Chinese pork is allowed," Sam replied. "Because an hour later, you're hungry."

"You missed your calling," Danner said. "You should have been a nightclub comic."

Sam grinned, pleased at the compliment. "You have to have a sense of humor in this business. Have you heard the latest?"

"No. What?"

"The Office of Security has been putting classified trash in bags labeled 'Frisky Dog Food.'"

"You're kidding. I thought the stuff was all destroyed in the pit."

Deep inside the headquarters building was a destruction area for secret trash. At CIA, copies of classified documents that were no longer needed could not simply be thrown out. The regulations required that they be placed inside clear plastic cylinders labeled "Burn" that were collected daily from each office. The classified trash was then taken to the destruction area, known as the pit. There, the papers were pulverized in a Disintegrator. The grayish-white pulp that remained was shipped to West Virginia, to be used for landfill.

Sam shook his head. "Apparently we're producing more classified trash than the pit can handle. So they're trucking the overflow to another location to be burned. Some genius in OS got the idea they should disguise it as dog food, in case it fell into the wrong hands en route. It's called Operation Rover."

Danner was incredulous. "But that's insane. Suppose a bag did fall off a truck, and somebody found it. If it looks like trash, they'd throw it away. But if it's labeled dog food, they'd open it up to give to their dog."

Sam nodded. "And if the dog ate the stuff, he'd be hungry an hour later."

Danner broke up. "Cut it out, Sam. I can't eat if you keep me laughing. Besides, I'm buying lunch for a reason."

"I should have known."

Danner leaned forward and spoke quietly, so he could not be overheard. "I need a photograph."

Sam held open his jacket. "Feelthy pictures," he said in an exaggerated French accent. "Goat fucking girl. You like?"

"Sam, be serious. I want to know if you can program one of your birds to take a picture of a particular house. I want to check out what the roof looks like."

Sam dug into his bowl and spooned some more rice onto his plate. "It can be done," he said. "But I'll need higher authority."

"I can get you that. Is Dixon Hadley good enough?"

"Yep. The flight patterns for the KH-14 are set by the National Reconnaissance Office on the basis of intelligence requirements they get either from the DDO, the intelligence side, or the Pentagon. Occasionally from State or NSA. Any one of them can put in a STAR."

"What the hell does that mean?"

"Special Target Acquisition Request. That's what you should ask for. Where's the house?"

"A suburb of Zürich called Herrliberg, on the north side of

the lake. I can give you enough of a description so you can figure out the coordinates."

"That's no problem. Our computers can pinpoint the house
once you give us the rough data."

"How long will it take to get the picture to me?"

"We have a satellite that covers western Europe. We can re-
route it over Zürich for one pass. Film capsule recovery in the
Pacific. That's where your time factor comes in. You're looking at forty-eight to seventy-two hours, unless its a priority
One, which you won't get."

"Okay, that gives me three days. I've got some preparations
to make, anyway. Thanks, Sam."

Danner asked the waiter for a check and paid for lunch. They
drove back to the agency in Sam's Mercedes, walked into the
building together from the north lot, and then parted company.
Danner took the elevator to seven and walked down to Dixon
Hadley's office.

Melinda was a little friendlier than usual, perhaps because
he'd been away. She got him in to see Hadley in four minutes
instead of the usual five.

Danner thought the office smelled of macaw. But Hadley
didn't seem to notice. He got up and greeted Danner effusively.

"I've found Lloyd," Danner told him. "In Zürich." He
sketched in for the DDO what he had learned about Lloyd, the
Group, and the money flow in and out of Switzerland.

When he had finished, Hadley looked pleased. "You've
done well," the deputy director said.

"There's more. He's getting tapes. From someone in the
building."

"Aaarwk! Polly Graph!" Socrates was in full throat. Hadley
scowled at the bird.

"So that's it."

"Yes. That's it."

The deputy director cleared his throat. "Under the circumstances, I suppose some appropriate counteraction should be
taken. It would be of enormous interest if the material could be
examined directly, as it were."

"If you want me to steal a tape, Dixon, why the fuck don't
you say so?"

The DDO looked alarmed. "I can't approve anything like

that," he said. "But if you were to act on your own, it would be in the highest national interest. Provided it's not traceable to us, of course."

"I'll need you to sign off on a STAR. I want a picture of—"

Hadley put up his hand, palm out. "Don't tell me any more than you already have. I'll sign the request in blank. You can fill in the particulars."

"I'll also need some special equipment from OTS," Danner said, turning the screw.

"You've already got authority for that," Hadley interjected. "There's no need to burden me with unnecessary details." His tone became warmer. "I don't want to leave you with the wrong impression. You've done an excellent job thus far. I wish you every success with the next step. But if anything should go wrong, well, you understand my position. The operation has not been authorized."

"That's the kind of support I know I can always count on," Danner said.

"On another matter," Hadley continued, ignoring the remark, "I'm afraid the monitors have nothing to report from Santa Barbara. There's been absolutely no contact with your former wife by the Soviets. Routine phone calls, that's all. And one from the sheriff's office yesterday to tell her there was nothing new. A Detective Walker."

Danner's heart sank. "All I can do is hope. And keep going."

Hadley shook his head sympathetically. "I'm sorry."

"All right," Danner said. "Thanks for staying on it. I'll be flying back to Zürich in a couple of days. Nancy in the secretarial pool will know where to reach me."

"Good luck."

"I'll need it. He's got three Dobermans."

Back in his office, he dialed Sam and told him that Hadley had agreed to the STAR request. He gave him a detailed description of the house and its location on the Seestrasse. Sam promised to let him know the minute the picture came in.

Danner left headquarters in mid-afternoon. He drove out the main gate onto Route 123, ahead of the rush-hour traffic. At his apartment, he changed to a polo shirt and slacks, took a can of

cold beer from the refrigerator, and sat down in the living room
by the telephone. He checked his answering machine for any
messages, but there were none.

He started to call Francesca, but then thought the better of it.
There was nothing he could tell her.

He reached Andy in Canada. The fishing season was over
and the guides were busy storing the canoes for winter, re-
painting the rooms in the cabins, and carrying out other mainte-
nance work. Andy had shot a moose during the three-day
season late in September. It was almost 1,000 pounds, so there
was enough meat in the freezer for the entire winter.

He called Julie at her office, and told her he would pick her
up at her house at 6:00 P.M. Then he showered, changed for
dinner, and drove to Alexandria.

She answered the door, and he stepped into the front hall.
She looked terrific; she was wearing a cream-colored silk
blouse and a brown tweed skirt, with a beige cardigan sweater
thrown over her shoulders. He nuzzled her neck, smelling her
perfume, and kissed her lightly on the lips.

"Where are we going?" she asked.

"L'Auberge Chez François. We have a reservation for six-
thirty."

"Fantastic."

They drove north on the capital beltway and got off at the
Georgetown Pike. For the last few miles, they followed a country lane across the rolling farmland to the restaurant.

It was a cozy place, with dark wooden beams on the ceiling,
stained-glass windows, and white tablecloths with prints of
flowers and birds. Danner asked the waitress to bring a bottle of
Trimbach, an Alsatian Riesling.

They sipped the wine, and Danner realized how much he had
missed her. "I'm making some progress," he said.

She touched his hand. "I'm glad. Where have you been?"

"Switzerland." He did not offer more. He felt very close to
her, sitting there in the restaurant, but ambivalent, too. He had
never asked why she had talked about Vienna—he saw little
point in confronting her, she would only deny any advance
knowledge—but he could not forget it, either. His love was
tempered with caution.

"And no word about Carrie?"

"Nothing. No further contact."

"It's so frustrating, and frightening. Aren't you scared?"

"For Carrie. Not for myself."

Her voice softened. "I know."

"I've never worried very much about the physical danger in our work. It's a risk that goes with the job. Like a movie stuntman, or a window washer."

Julie laughed. "I guess that's as good a way as any of looking at it." She picked up her green-stemmed wineglass and twirled it in her hand. Then she looked at him. "I'm going on a trip," she said. "I'll be gone for three weeks."

He wanted to tell her he would be away, too, but didn't. "Where to?"

"The Mideast and Africa. I get to go about once a year, to check out our commercial cover arrangements. I make sure there are no rough edges."

"Stay away from the sheiks."

"Don't worry. I mostly talk to financial officers for American corporations. Bookkeepers can be pretty boring."

He raised his wineglass. "To bookkeepers."

She clinked her glass against his. "I do believe you're jealous."

"You're damn right I'm jealous, wouldn't you be?"

It was much later in the evening, after they had made love in Julie's bed, that she looked at him with her big, green eyes and challenged what he had said.

"There is something you're afraid of," she said.

He kissed her gently. "Meaning what?"

"You don't give all of yourself when me make love. I think you're afraid to."

Danner wondered if she sensed his hidden reservoir of doubt about her loyalties. She had helped him, she had taken risks on his behalf, yet he could not be sure of her.

"I give as much of myself as I can," he answered honestly. It was a hell of a way to run a love affair, he thought. But Danner wondered whether two people ever trusted each other completely. Or was it only a problem for spies, who were trained to mistrust? Danner didn't know the answer.

It was two days later when Sam Green turned up in Danner's

office with a large manila envelope stamped "Top Secret—
UMBRA." He was whistling.

"Got what you wanted," he said, after he had closed the
door behind him. "A beautiful picture. There was no cloud
cover over the Alps."

He removed an eight-by-ten glossy print from the envelope
and laid it down on the desk. Danner was startled by the clarity
of the photo, which had been taken from more than two hundred miles in outer space. The roof of Wellington Lloyd's
Swiss villa practically leaped out at him. He could even see the
texture of the shingles.

The roof over the main part of the house was peaked, but it
was the flat section over the north wing that interested Danner.
He studied it more closely. There were two high-gain direc-
tional communications antennae arrayed on either side of a skylight.

Danner pointed to the skylight. "How big would you say that
is?"

"Maybe six feet by three feet," Sam replied. "We can tell
you exactly if it's important."

"It isn't. But I'm interested in the lock. I can't read the name
on the cylinder."

"We're having a special on enlargements this week," Sam
said, grinning. "Can I interest you in one?"

"Yes. Just the portion around the lock on the skylight."

"Okay," Sam said. "I'll be back."

He returned in less than an hour with another print. He
handed it to Danner, along with a Bausch & Lomb magnifying
glass. "With the reading glass, you can make out the name
now," Sam said. "It's a BKS, a high-security German lock,
pin tumbler type. It's a deadbolt, of course. If someone
smashed the glass, they still couldn't open the skylight without
a key."

"The pictures are a big help. I really appreciate it."

"No problem." He smiled as he let himself out the door.
"Just don't get any glass in your ass."

For the next forty-five minutes, Danner wrote out a list of
equipment on a yellow pad. Then he took a scissors and cut a
little circle out of the enlargement. He took the circle and the
list with him to the Office of Technical Service.

OTS, the successor to the old Technical Services Division, was part of the agency's Directorate of Science and Technology. Down these corridors were the laboratories and offices where agency scientists and technicians developed the CIA's most sophisticated weapons, drugs, and espionage equipment.

Danner came to a door marked "Director" and went in. In a moment, a secretary ushered him into the office of Dr. Louis Weinberg, the wizard of OTS, a legendary—some preferred the word sinister—figure within the CIA. It was Weinberg, a scientist now in his sixties, who had been responsible for developing many of the drugs, poisons, and biological weapons that the agency had used in its assassination plots during the 1960s.

And it was Weinberg, Danner knew, who tried to introduce deadly bacteria onto the toothbrush of Patrice Lumumba when the CIA was attempting to kill the Congolese leader more than two decades ago. Weinberg himself had visited the Congo to explore the feasibility of the operation.

Dr. Louis Weinberg did not get up when Danner appeared in his office. He was confined to a wheelchair, paralyzed from the waist down by an illness he had contracted in Africa. It was whispered around the agency that the CIA scientist might have accidentally ingested some of the disease-bearing bacteria meant for Lumumba. "I think he used the wrong toothbrush," Sam Green had once remarked to Danner.

"I've got a shopping list, Lou," Danner said. "I'll need your help to get the stuff together as soon as possible."

"If it's special weapons or equipment, we're running four to six weeks on delivery," Weinberg responded. "Of course, if we have it in stock, there's no problem." He peered over his thick glasses in their heavy black frames. The refraction made his eyes look unnaturally small, an effect that was exaggerated by his round, heavyset face, which was topped by a shock of unruly white hair.

"There are only one or two unusual items," Danner said smoothly. "I'm sure you can have them made up quickly."

"On whose authority?" Weinberg looked doubtful.

"The director and the DDO. You can check with them."

"You might have said so to begin with." He lit a fat cigar and gave it a puff or two to get it well started. "What do you need, my boy?"

"For openers, a skeleton key for a BKS lock. I've got a picture of the lock, if that's any help." He put the cut-out portion of the enlargement on Weinberg's desk.

The OTS chief studied it. "On this type of BKS, normally the keys can only be duplicated by the manufacturer. They're in Velbert, in the Ruhr near Dusseldorf. But we have the capability of reproducing any key in the world right here in this building."

"Good. Is there anyone I should see about it?"

"There's no need. I'll give the photo to Roudebush in Lockpicking. Unless we run into a snag, he should have the key for you tomorrow. Where's the target, by the way?"

"I haven't said."

Weinberg glared at him. Several puffs of smoke rose from his cigar. Danner thought he looked like Mount St. Helens.

"I'll also need scuba gear—mask, hood, flippers, wet suit, night compass, and buoyancy compensator."

"And the air tank?"

"I'll pick that up when I get where I'm going."

Weinberg was taking notes. "What else?" he asked.

"I need a thirty-foot ladder of lightweight nylon rope with grappling hooks at one end. The hooks have to be rubberized."

"That will have to be made up specially."

"Okay. Also, a dart gun and six incapacitating darts."

"Human or animal targets?"

"Dogs."

"Body weight?"

"You figure it out. They're Dobermans."

Weinberg wheeled his chair around and took a book down from behind his desk. "Let me check the chart." He studied a page in the book. "All right, seventy-five pounds. What's your required incapacitation time?"

"I need an hour."

"I'd recommend etorphine. It's our most effective immobilizer, a thousand times more powerful than morphine."

"Will it work on a dog?"

"Oh yes. It's designed for animals."

"And the dosage?"

Weinberg leafed through his book. "Let me see, species Canidae. Yes, here it is: 3.2 milligrams should do it. I'll have

Weapons Research Branch prepare the gun and the projectiles.''

"Good. Will the darts be visible?''

"Yes. We can't use nondiscernible microbioinoculators with etorphine, unfortunately. The darts will be very small—the dosage we're talking about is a little over half a teaspoon—but you'll have to remove them when you're done. Assuming, of course, that you don't want your visit to be known.''

"All right.''

"Be careful how you handle the darts, by the way. Etorphine is a paralytic that attacks the central nervous system. A drop of it on the skin can kill a human.''

"I'll be careful.''

"We'll provide you with some vials of the antidote, diprenorphine, just in case. But you might not have time to use it.'' Weinberg smiled. "Risks of the game.''

"Since it's a paralytic agent, the dogs won't actually be unconscious?''

"No, they'll be wide awake, eyes open, watching you. But they won't be able to move. Fortunately, dogs can't talk. They won't be able to tell anybody what they saw.''

"Lucky for me.'' Danner checked off the items on his list. "Also, a small burst tape recorder for high-speed copying. I'll be making a duplicate of a cassette and I want to do it as fast as possible.''

"We have burst transmitters, of course. I'm not sure about burst copiers. You'd better talk to Kerwin in Electronic Services. Three doors down on the right. Then check back with me.''

Mike Kerwin was a slight, stoop-shouldered man with graying hair, steel-rimmed glasses, and a professorial air. His large laboratory was jammed, floor to ceiling, with electronic equipment, much of it designed for the agency's exclusive use and not available on the open market. It was Kerwin's shop that had furnished the beetle-shaped bug Danner had dropped into Wellington Lloyd's roses.

Kerwin shook his head when Danner explained what he wanted. "When you record at high speed," he said, "you decrease the band width at the upper end. You lose the fricatives.''

"Meaning what?"

"Your 'f's and 'v's, for example. You're going to lose quality."

"But it can be done?"

"Sure. Anything can be done. Doubling the speed when you dub tapes is fairly common. I can kick it up to about sixteen times faster than usual. The trick will be to copy it at the identical speed. Then when you listen to the tape on a conventional recorder, it will sound normal."

"Fine. Go ahead and make up a miniature recorder for me. It will have to have dual capacity—two compartments, one for the cassette being dubbed, one for the copy. Set the speed as fast as you can without losing intelligibility. Oh, and I'll need it in two days."

"That's impossible. There's a four- to six-week wait on special-order equipment."

"Lou Weinberg has authorized it."

Kerwin sighed. "All right. I'll put it ahead of our back orders. But I wish Weinberg would tell me when he does these things."

Danner thanked him and went back down the hall. Weinberg was finishing up a phone call but waved him into a chair. "I don't care how big your contract is with the LAPD," Weinberg was saying into the receiver. "You promised me five gallons by the middle of the month, and I expect delivery on time. Right." He slammed down the receiver.

"One of our suppliers in the Middle West," Weinberg said, relighting his cigar. "He makes conductive paint. Great stuff."

"How do you use it?" Danner asked.

"It's the latest wrinkle for wiretapping," the scientist explained. "No more alligator clips, or cutting into wires. Now all we do is locate the board for the target house or building. We find the pair—the terminals—for the number we're interested in, then use the conductive paint to take it from the terminal to a wire concealed behind the board. When the paint dries, it blends in with the board. What you've got is an invisible 'wire'—made of paint—that can't be detected." He puffed on his cigar. "How'd you make out with Kerwin?"

"He'll do it."

"Good. What else do you need?"

"A waterproof flashlight, a set of lock picks, and waterproof pouches for the dart gun, the darts, and the tape recorder. Also a knife to strap to my leg over the wet suit."

"That it?" Weinberg asked hopefully.

"No. There's one final item. I need a sheet of rubber an eighth of an inch thick cut in a circle, diameter eighteen inches. Around the rim of the circle, two inches in from the edge, I want holes the size of quarters spaced a quarter of an inch apart."

Weinberg looked puzzled. "What the hell is that for?"

"It's a survival kit," Danner said.

"A survival kit? That thing?" Weinberg was fairly sputtering. "For whom?"

"For me."

CHAPTER
TWENTY-ONE

Danner checked into the Helmhaus, a small hotel *garni* on the Schiffländeplatz, near the Limmat. He did not contact Felix or Erich; if anything went wrong, there was no sense involving them. This time, he was on his own.

He spent a day and a half getting ready. On the afternoon he arrived, he rented an Audi, but not at the same agency where he had hired the Fiat. After that, he found a diving store on the Stampfenbachstrasse and purchased an aluminum scuba tank, which he had them fill with compressed air under 3,000 pounds of pressure.

He locked the tank and the special gear prepared by OTS in the trunk of the car. The next morning, he drove around the south side of the Zürichsee to Thalwil. He parked by the lake, and with a pair of binoculars reconnoitered the opposite shore.

He was able to pick out the house easily. As he had thought, there was a small wooden dock, and the lawn, which sloped gently toward the water, was not fenced or walled along the water. Wellington Lloyd's fortress was protected only on three sides.

He judged the distance across the Zürichsee at that point to be two kilometers. It would take over an hour to swim in rather cold water that reached a depth of 470 feet. There was no point in starting from that side. He got back in the car and drove back around the lake past Rüschlikon and Kilchberg, through Zürich again, then south to Herrliberg. About a quarter of a mile beyond the house, he came to a wooded stretch where there were no homes. He pulled off the road and parked.

He got out and cut through the trees a short distance to the lake. The spot was ideal; it was screened from the road by the foliage. He returned to the car, started it up, and headed back to Zürich. He spent the afternoon waiting in his hotel room, went out for a light supper at a nearby restaurant, and turned in early, at 9:00 P.M. He set the alarm for 1:00 A.M.

He need not have bothered; he couldn't sleep. He was half dozing when the alarm went off. He showered, dressed, and went downstairs. The streets near the hotel were quiet at that hour. It was a cool, clear night and the moon and stars were out. It meant he would have good visibility, Danner thought, but so would anyone in the house who happened to look out the window toward the lake. He breathed in the crisp night air and it brought him fully awake.

Behind the wheel of the Audi, driving the now-familiar route along the Gold Coast, Danner felt a mixture of conflicting emotions. He still resented how he had been dragooned back into the agency. Now he was undertaking a risky operation without official authority; Hadley, ever the bureaucrat, had made that clear enough. If he got in trouble, he could look for no help from Langley. At the same time, Danner was honest enough to recognize his own sense of excitement at the mission that lay before him; he had tracked down his quarry and was about to enter the lion's den. His pulse was beating fast and his mind alert.

He thought of Carrie and knew that he had no choice but to go on. Somewhere in the house on the lake was a tape that might be the key to her freedom.

He was in Herrliberg. He cruised slowly past Seestrasse 7. Looking through the wrought-iron gates, he was relieved to see that there was no light in the windows. He checked his watch; it was just after 2:00 A.M.

A quarter of a mile beyond the house, at the place he had selected on his reconnaissance during the afternoon, he parked and got out. He opened the trunk and removed his gear. The only heavy equipment was the air tank, which he slung over one shoulder. He made his way through the trees to the Zürichsee. The water was shimmering in the moonlight, and it looked cold. He dipped in his hand; it was.

He stripped down to a T-shirt and a pair of swimming trunks and got into the black wet suit. It covered him from the neck to the ankles. He slipped the buoyancy compensator over his head, and stowed his flashlight in its pouch. He put on the luminous wrist compass, strapped the knife to his ankle, and buckled six pounds of weights around his waist. He clipped the waterproof pouch containing the dart gun to his belt, along with a smaller, separate pouch that held the skeleton key, the miniature tape recorder, the lock picks, and the odd-looking sheet of rubber. He carried the rope ladder and the air tank to the water's edge, sat down, and stretched a pair of thin, skin-tight rubber boots over his feet. He fitted the flippers over the boots and checked to see that the pouches were secure and watertight. He rubbed blacking on his face and pulled the hood over his head and ears, so that only his darkened eyes, nose, and mouth were visible. He adjusted the mask so that it was tight. Then he strapped the tank to his back, picked up the nylon ladder, and slipped silently into the lake.

He dove to a depth of twelve feet, just enough so that he could not be seen from the shore, and deep enough so that there would be no surface turbulence, only bubbles, to mark his progress. Despite the bright moon, it was like swimming in a pool of black ink. After he had gone about fifty yards straight out, he turned to the right, and using his compass, steered a course parallel to the shore. He kicked steadily, letting the fins on his feet, rather than his hands, do the work.

When he thought he had swum far enough, he surfaced, remembering to breathe normally as he ascended. Even at that shallow depth, he knew, if he held his breath coming up, he might blow out his lungs and instantly die.

When his head bobbed above the water, he checked his position and realized he had misjudged the distance slightly. He had been swimming parallel to the shore, but he had not gone far enough. He dove down and silently swam another fifty feet. It was tough going, because the rope ladder was awkward and created drag. The water was cold, even through the wet suit, and his leg was beginning to ache.

He surfaced again; this time, he was directly opposite the

house. He slipped back into the murky water and made for shore. He came up under the wooden dock, and worked his way quietly forward. The house was completely dark; there was no sign of anyone, or of the dogs.

He came up out of the water like some dark, amphibious creature and removed the regulator from his mouth. He tossed the rope ladder on the grass and unsealed the pouch containing the dart gun. Even as he reached for the weapon, he could see them coming, three blue-black shapes racing swiftly and silently toward him in the moonlight.

There was no time to take off the heavy tank. The dogs were almost upon him and he could see the gleaming eyes and sharp, jagged teeth and even the flecks of saliva in the jaws of the lead Doberman as it leaped for his face. Danner fired; the dart embedded itself noiselessly in the dog's deep chest. The animal crashed into Danner, slid off the front of his wet suit, and collapsed at his feet.

He was jolted back into the lake by the impact, almost losing his footing in the slime. He hoped the water would act as a barrier, but the second dog was splashing in after him, water or no. Quickly, Danner reloaded. He darted the attacker a fraction of a second before the dog, his jaws open, would have torn away a large chunk of his leg.

The third Doberman stood on the shore, a few feet away, growling menacingly, challenging Danner to come any closer. He reloaded again and edged in nearer to the beast. The dog's eyes were following Danner's movements and he was poised to spring when Danner fired the third dart and caught the animal in the shoulder. The dog collapsed like a rag doll.

Quickly, Danner pulled out the dog that had fallen in the water. The animal was heavy, and he had trouble getting him up on the grass. Then, exhausted, Danner sat down at the edge of the lake to catch his breath. He prayed that Dr. Weinberg had not provided too heavy a dose of the incapacitant. He did not want the dogs to die. If all went well, Wellington Lloyd would never know that anyone had paid him a visit in the night. He looked down. The Dobermans were breathing normally, fully conscious but paralyzed.

Danner slipped off the air tank and left it on the grass. He took off his fins. Underneath, he was wearing the rubber boots that would have to do as shoes. He unbuckled his weights and wriggled out of the wet suit. He extracted the flashlight from the pouch of the buoyancy compensator and picked up the nylon ladder and the pouch containing the rest of his gear. He reloaded the dart gun and kept it at the ready, in case there was another guard dog somewhere.

Keeping low, he ran toward the north wing of the house, the section with the flat roof. He was an easy target in the moonlight; there was no cover between the shore and the house, and he had to traverse some fifty yards of lawn. He made it, and looked at his watch. It was just after 3:00 A.M. He would have a little less than an hour before the dogs shook off the effects of the etorphine.

He untied the rope ladder, and stepped back about fifteen feet from the house. Holding the rope ten feet down from the grappling hooks, he swung the ladder back and forth until he felt he had enough momentum, then let it fly toward the roof. It fell far short and dropped to the ground. But the rubberized hooks were almost silent, even as they hit the side of the house. Danner tried again, swinging the rope ladder back and forth like a gaucho. This time, his aim was better: the hooks caught the edge of the roof and held. He tested the ladder gingerly to make sure it would take his weight. Then he stashed the dart gun back in its pouch and climbed up the ladder.

At the top, he hauled himself silently onto the roof. There were a few clouds now, racing across the moon. He looked around. It was utterly quiet, except for the sound of the wind in the trees. Quickly, he pulled the rope ladder up after him. It was cold on the roof in his T-shirt and swim trunks, and he started to shiver. Directly in front of him, just as they looked in Sam Green's satellite photo, were the skylight and the communications antennae. He crept across the roof to the front side of the skylight, where the lock should be. The clouds were making it harder to see, but he did not dare risk using the flashlight on the roof, where someone might see the light from the road or from one of the neighboring estates.

He opened the smaller waterproof pouch and reached in for the key, praying that OTS had done its work well. It would be no fun trying to use his lockpicking tools in the dark and the cold on a windy rooftop.

He eased the key into the lock, and tried to turn it to the right. It would not budge. He pulled the key back a fraction and tried again. No luck. Danner swore. He jammed it in as far as it would go and still the lock would not give. He reached into the pouch and removed a tiny can of aerosol spray that the agency's technicians had packed with the key. He sprayed the graphite into the lock, and tried once more. He jiggled the key up and down; suddenly, it turned. He realized he was sweating despite the chill night air, and he wiped his forehead with the back of his hand.

Gently, he lifted up the skylight. The hinges creaked noisily. Danner drew in his breath and listened. Only the wind answered him. There was no sound from inside the house.

He peered down through the frame of the open skylight but could see nothing. It was like staring into the Grand Canyon at night; he had no idea how big a drop it was to the floor. He walked back to the edge of the roof, retrieved the rope ladder, and hooked the grapnels to the frame of the skylight. He lowered the rungs until he felt the ropes go slack against the floor. Then he climbed down into the house.

He waited a moment for his eyes to adjust to the dim light. The high-ceilinged room in which he found himself would have been perfect for an artist's studio, and Danner assumed the von Bruhlers might have built it for that purpose. There were no easels in the room, however; just some boxes, a couple of chairs, a desk, and a lot of electronic equipment that he could make out in the shelves that lined one wall.

The electronic gear explained the antennae on the roof. Danner assumed that Lloyd had his own communications system for contacting his people around the globe; coded radio transmissions from anywhere in the world could be plucked from the airwaves by the roof antennae and fed right into this room in Herrliberg. He moved to the door and tried to open it. Locked. He checked his watch. It was 3:15 A.M.

He decided to risk the flashlight and turned it on, but dimmed the light by putting his fingers over it. He studied the lock. It was a Dictator-Technik, another German make. His BKS key would be useless.

He reached into the pouch and removed his lockpicking tools, which were inside a plastic case. He took out a tension wrench, a thin, flat band of tempered steel, and a diamond pick, so named for the shape of the point. He inserted the wrench in the keyhole and twisted it to the right, to create turning pressure on the plug, the small cylinder that turns with the key to operate the lock. He slipped the diamond pick into the keyhole and felt for the tumblers, the five pins, varying in length, housed in the hollow shafts inside the cylinder. If he could push them up exactly the right amount—which was what the serrated edge of a key normally did—the plug would turn.

He first felt for the pin with the most spring tension on it, and eased it up, then worked the other pins. The tension wrench was designed to turn the plug a thousandth of an inch, just enough to keep the pins from falling back down as he eased each one up the shear line. But it was a difficult lock. There was one short tumbler between two long ones, which, from the lockpicker's point of view, was the worst possible arrangement. In trying to reach the short pin, Danner was afraid he had shoved the one in front of it up too far. The lock did not give.

He released the tumblers and began over. Still, the lock would not yield. It was well machined, and difficult to pick. It took ten minutes, and several more tries, before he succeeded. Exhilarated, he put away the tools in the little case. He turned off the flashlight and eased the door open.

He stepped into the hallway. The wooden floor was old and it creaked. The door was ajar to the bedroom off to his right. He moved down the hall a step at a time. He took a step, then listened. Then another step and he listened again. All he heard was the steady breathing of someone asleep in the bedroom.

He was almost at the head of the stairs when he bumped into a chair that scraped hard against the wall. He thought he heard someone stirring in the bedroom and froze. Whoever was there—and Danner assumed it was Lloyd—was coughing and turning in his sleep. After a couple of minutes, the rhythmic breathing resumed. Warily, Danner crept down the stairs to the second floor.

He moved quietly past the open dining room and the living room to the study in the corner. The door was open and he slipped inside. As he had hoped, the moonlight shining through the large windows overlooking the lake gave him good visibility.

He checked his watch. It was 3:30 A.M. Getting through the skylight and picking the lock had eaten up time. He had only half an hour until the dogs recovered—if the paralytic agent worked exactly as OTS said it would. There was always the possibility that the drug would wear off sooner than it was supposed to.

He looked around for a wall safe, but as he had expected, he did not find one. He moved to the Bertoia sculpture in the center of the room. Opening the pouch again, he took out the miniature tape recorder and the circular sheet of rubber with the peculiar pattern of holes cut in it.

He studied the sculpture for a moment. The thin brass rods, clustered in their wooden base, were almost four feet high. The top of each rod formed a cylinder, much wider than the rods themselves and about two and a half inches in length, so that the sculpture looked a little like a cluster of metal cattails. The cylinders were almost touching, barely a quarter of an inch apart.

Bertoia, Danner had learned from his research, had been born in Italy, but moved to the United States in the 1930s and grew up in Detroit. He became a successful sculptor, his works commissioned by cities, banks, and universities all over the country. But he was best known for his "sounding sculpture." Harry Bertoia's sculptures played music.

If he so much as brushed accidentally against the sculpture, Danner knew, the delicately balanced rods would go into motion, swaying crazily against each other and chiming loudly enough to wake up the entire household. Wellington Lloyd has chosen an ingenious place to hide his tapes. The Bertoia was an artistic burglar alarm.

Moving with extreme care, Danner held the rubber circle above the sculpture. Gently and slowly, he lowered the sheet until it was resting on the flat tops of the metal cylinders. He exhaled. The rods had not touched.

Gingerly, he began the delicate task of working the holes over the tops of the cylinders. He did one at a time, relying on the weight of the rubber to hold the other rods steady as he slipped each cylinder in turn into the disc-shaped holes. The job took eight minutes.

When it was done, Danner stepped back and admired his

handiwork. It was probably the first time in history, he reflected, that anyone had used a silencer on a sculpture.

He got down on his knees and checked the wooden base of the Bertoia. It was round and apparently one piece. There were no knobs or drawers visible. He tapped lightly on the base. It sounded hollow. He examined it more closely and saw that the base was actually built in panels very smoothly and tightly joined.

He pushed in on each panel, but none of them gave way. There was a small kickspace where the base rested on the carpet, and he ran his fingers around underneath the edge of the wood, hoping to find a release lever. There was nothing.

He wondered if he had made it all the way to Wellington Lloyd's study only to be stymied inches from his goal. Then he had an idea; he began pressing on the panels in tandem, with two hands, on opposite sides. Nothing happened. He tried different combinations, applying pressure here and there, moving both hands around the base systematically. Several minutes went by, and then, suddenly, the front section of the base fell open. As he had suspected, the flap operated on a spring-released mechanism that was pressure-sensitive.

He reached inside. There was a single cassette in the hollow base, inside an ordinary plastic holder. He opened it up, removed the tape, and put it in the recorder. He needed to know how much of the tape to copy. He inserted an earphone in the jack and ran the machine forward at high speed, stopping twice to make sure that there was still someone talking on the tape. Only a little way through the first side, the voice stopped and the rest of the side was blank. He turned over the cassette and listened. There was nothing recorded on the other side. He flipped the cassette back to the first side and pushed the rewind button until the tape stopped.

The recorder was especially designed for dubbing, as Danner had requested. It had two compartments on opposite sides. The side he had just used was for playing only, so a tape could not be erased by mistake. A blank cassette was already in place in the recording compartment on the other side, ready to roll. He pushed the "record" button. His watch said 3:45 A.M.

At high speed it took only an instant to copy the tape. When it was done, he remembered to rewind the original. He put it back in its plastic box and returned it to the same position in which he had found it inside the base. He closed the flap, and the base was sealed once again.

He stood up and eased the rubber sheet off the Bertoia, releasing each cylinder separately. It was excruciatingly slow work and it took all of his self-discipline not to hurry. Finally, he freed the last cylinder. The brass rods of the sculpture were vibrating slightly, but the cylinders were not touching.

He stowed the rubber sheet and the tape recorder back inside the waterproof pouch and sealed it. He looked around to make sure he hadn't left anything. The room was clean. He looked at his watch: 4:00 A.M. He had run out of time.

Slipping back into the hall, he moved as quickly as he dared back up the stairs to the third floor. The bedrooms were quiet. He crept along the upstairs hall to the room with the skylight, stepped inside, and softly closed the door behind him. It clicked shut. He tried it; it was locked. The rope ladder was just as he had left it, hanging down from the skylight. He hoisted himself up, and clambered out onto the roof.

He pulled up the ladder and closed the skylight, which locked behind him. He secured the grapnels to the edge of the roof and lowered the ladder. The clouds had grown thicker and completely obscured the moon.

He peered out toward the water, but he could not see the dogs in the darkness. He took out the dart gun and checked it to make sure it was loaded. Then he went over the edge of the roof and climbed down to the lawn. He jiggled the ropes to free the grappling hooks, and they tumbled down. He gathered up the ladder and ran toward the water.

At least he could not be seen from the house now. The problem was the dogs. Where were they?

He reached the lake and looked around. He was relieved to find the Dobermans right where he had left them. One was not moving, but the other two were beginning to stir. When they saw Danner, their awkward, uncoordinated movements became more agitated. Quickly, he pulled the darts from their bodies, dropped them in the pouch, and sealed it.

Danner guessed he had no more than a minute or two before the drug wore off and the dogs were upon him. He jammed his legs into the wet suit, then his arms, zipped it up, and pulled the buoyancy compensator over his head. He strapped the compass to his wrist, the knife to his leg, and the weights around his waist. He clipped the pouches to his belt.

One of the Dobermans, the biggest and fiercest-looking of the three, was trying to get to his feet now. He was growling, enraged at seeing his enemy again, his powerful jaws flecked with foam.

Danner sat down at the water's edge and slipped on his fins. The dog was moving toward him now, stumbling groggily but still coming on fast, a lethal blue shadow in the night.

"Good boy," Danner said, "good boy."

He strapped the air tank on his back, and fell backward into the water at the same instant that the dog leaped. As he sank to safety in the frigid waters of the lake, he could see the yellow eyes of the Doberman staring down at him from the surface of the Zürichsee.

CHAPTER
TWENTY-TWO

The loft in SoHo was secluded in a three-story building that in an earlier life had been a paint factory. Pete Vanucci had converted it into a sound studio.

His business seemed creative enough to blend in with the surroundings. The lower Manhattan neighborhood, once an industrial area, had gradually been taken over by art galleries, restaurants, and little shops that sold antiques, ceramics, handmade jewelry, and hanging ferns.

Danner punched the elevator bell, but nothing happened. He shrugged, walked up to the top floor, and rang the bell.

"Your elevator doesn't work," he said when Vanucci answered the door.

"I got tired of paying off the inspectors."

Danner stepped inside. Vanucci was a short man, slender but wiry, with jet-black hair. Although he was clean-shaven, his beard was so dark that his jaw looked almost blue even in mid-morning. He might more easily have been taken for a Sicilian bandit than for what he was, one of the top experts in the country on tape recordings. Now in his early forties, he had left the agency several years earlier to set up his own sound lab. The loft was crowded with electronic equipment.

"How you been, Pete? How are Rosa and the kids?"

"I'm doin' okay, and the family's fine. The older boy's finishing college." He smiled. "We still live in the same place." Vanucci took the PATH train home to Jersey City every night by choice. He was successful now, and he didn't have to commute across the Hudson. But he had grown up on the other side of the river, his roots were there, and so was his wife's large family.

Danner took the cassette out of his jacket pocket and put it down on a table. "This is it."

Vanucci picked it up and examined it. "I got a question first. You want me to analyze this for you. How come you didn't take it right to the OTS lab? Some of those fellows are as good as you'd find anywhere."

"You're supposed to be better than anyone else at voice identification."

Pete grinned in acknowledgment. "I won't say no." Operating from his modest loft, Vanucci made a lot of money working for corporations that were trying to protect their trade secrets, and for lawyers in domestic cases. He did no wiretapping or bugging himself. But tapping a line was only the beginning. Often it was essential to identify the voice at the other end. Who was buying secrets from the disloyal lab technician in a drug company? Who was calling an adulterous spouse to arrange an assignation? Identification was the key. Pete Vanucci offered a complete range of such highly sophisticated audio services.

"The material on the tape is extremely sensitive," Danner cautioned. "But since you're an alumnus, the DDO felt you would be discreet."

"Shit, in my line of work, I'd be at the bottom of the river by now if I talked about what I hear. You can leave all that national security bullshit back in Washington. You're in the Big Apple."

Danner nodded. "I knew I could trust you."

"Well, why don't we listen to it?" Vanucci moved over to a work table, put the cassette in a Sony tape recorder, and pushed the "play" button. A woman's voice boomed out of two huge speakers in the corner. They both sat down to listen.

"This is your friend again. The information contained on this tape should be of p-p-p-particular interest to the G-G-Group. Rome station is r-r-reviving the secret Masonic lodge known as P-P-Propaganda Due, or P-2, under a new d-d-designation. As you know, the most p-powerful members of the Italian establishment in all walks of life b-b-belonged to P-2. The operational objective of the f-f-ounding of the new lodge, which will be known as Milano Uno, will b-be to increase the station's penetration of the Christian Democratic P-P-Party and through them, the agency's control over, or influence within, the Italian government. The DDO officer responsible for creating the M-1 lodge is Kendall Cameron. F-F-Funding will be handled by Rome station via M-M-Milan base.''

There was a crackling noise, as though a microphone had been switched off, and then silence.

''That's it?'' Vanucci asked.

''That's it.''

Vanucci hit the ''rewind'' button and wound the tape back part way. He played a portion of the tape again. ''As you know, the most p-powerful members of the Italian establishment in all walks of life b-b-belonged to P-2.''

Vanucci turned off the recorder. ''I remember that business,'' he said. ''It was a few years ago. All the generals, and bankers, and judges, and members of Parliament belonged to Propaganda Due. There was a lot of crooked stuff going on. It brought down the government, didn't it?''

Danner nodded. ''Yes. Forlani had to resign.''

''The world changes. But not Mother K.''

''Uh-huh,'' Danner agreed.

''And you don't have any idea of whose voice it is?''

''No. Some of her inflections are familiar, but I would remember anyone who stuttered like that. I don't know her.''

Vanucci furrowed his brow. ''I can't be sure yet,'' he said, ''but my guess is that the voice on the tape has been altered. It sounds a little mechanical to me in places. The harmonics aren't quite right.''

''You mean a voice can be changed to disguise the identity of the speaker?''

''Sure. It has to be done by an expert, someone knowledgeable about tapes and digital sound. But using a computer, it can be done. In fact, it's possible to create an entirely new voice in place of the original.''

''Incredible! If that was done, is there any way to recreate the original voice?''

''That would be very difficult. Perhaps impossible. It would really depend on how sophisticated the technician was who processed the voice. But with luck, it might be done.''

"Where do we start?"

"With a few basics. Or you won't understand the rest." Vanucci reached for a pencil and a white pad. "Sound is caused when objects vibrate. The motion in one direction squeezes molecules of air together. When the object vibrates in the opposite direction—think of a tuning fork going back and forth—it makes more room for the air molecules. That pattern is passed along in the air like ripples in a pond when you toss in a stone. The pattern repeating itself is called a sound wave. You with me so far?"

"Yes."

"Okay, you can't see sound, but you can draw a picture of the sound wave like this." He took the pad and drew a line that looked like a mountain range with a series of rounded peaks and valleys. "That," Vanucci said, "is a sine wave. Your ear would hear it as an even tone, like the one made by the tuning fork."

Danner took his jacket off and hooked it over the back of his chair. "Go on," he said.

"But sounds are different. A canary doesn't sound like a foghorn. That's because objects vibrate at different speeds, or frequencies. Frequency or pitch simply means how frequently, or often, something vibrates in one second. Look at this wave I just drew. There are ten peaks. If a sound wave does that in one second, it has a frequency of ten. In other words, ten cycles per second. Only now we usually say ten hertz, after Heinrich Rudolph Hertz, the nineteenth-century German physicist."

Danner nodded. "And the higher the frequency, the higher the pitch of the sound?"

"You've got it," Vanucci said. "Right now I'm talking to you at around ninety or a hundred hertz. The voice on that tape is about double that. The typical woman's voice has a higher pitch than a man's, in the range of two hundred hertz and above. The adult human can hear from about fifteen to fifteen thousand hertz. Above that you're into ultrasonics."

"Dog whistles," Danner said.

"Right. But our ears also hear sound as loud or soft, not just as high or low. And loudness is measured in decibels. Our conversation right now is about sixty decibels. A jackhammer in the street is about one hundred. Anything over one hundred thirty is painful to the ear. The degree of loudness is what we call amplitude. If you go back to the sine wave I drew, the height of the mountain peak is the amplitude of that sound. Obviously sound can vary both in frequency and amplitude. In plain English, it can be high or low, loud or soft.''

"You missed your calling. You should be a professor.''

Vanucci grinned. "I like what I do, thanks. Okay, what we're dealing with here''—he tapped the Sony—"is sound that has been recorded on magnetic tape. Whoever made that tape spoke into a microphone that converted sound energy into electrical energy. He captured that sound on tape. How? With a recording head, which is nothing but an electromagnet. It creates a magnetic field that varies with the incoming electrical signal.'' Vanucci paused and lit a cigarette. "The tape in that cassette is made of polyester with a thin coating of iron oxide. The tape is really a bunch of magnetic particles that jump around and rearrange themselves when they pass through the magnetic field. That's how sound is recorded. When the tape is played back, the process is reversed, and the magnetized tape produces an electrical current or voltage that can be amplified and converted back into sound energy.''

Danner grunted. "You're getting a little over my head. But I think I follow you.''

Vanucci snapped a cable into the output of the tape recorder and plugged the other end into a metal box about four inches high and twelve inches long that had a few knobs on the front. "This little gadget is called an analog-to-digital converter. It takes the analog sound, which is what we hear with our ears, and converts it to a series of numbers.''

"That's digital sound,'' Danner said.

"That's the process used, yes,'' Vanucci said. "What happens is that the A-to-D converter assigns a number to each bit of voltage as it comes out of the tape recorder. The voltage drops or increases with changes in loudness of the voice.''

"In other words, with changes in amplitude,'' Danner offered.

"You're getting pretty good at this,'' Vanucci said. "That's right. And the numbers assigned will be high or low, reflecting whether the voice at a given instant is loud or soft. The higher the number, the louder the voice.''

"How many numbers does it assign?" Danner asked.

"Well, an A-to-D converter is really an integrated circuit, a chip that can sample the voltage at a very fast rate. This particular one is an eight-bit converter, which means it has room for eight digits, or eight ones and zeros that can be arranged in binary form to represent any decimal number from zero to two hundred fifty-five."

"So the converter is really like a camera taking a picture of the voltage and assigning numbers to it?"

"That's not a bad analogy." He adjusted a knob on the front of the box. "And I'm going to tell it to assign numbers, or sample the voltage, at the rate of ten thousand times per second."

Danner nodded. He wondered how the voice, once taken apart and scrambled, could ever be reconstructed.

Vanucci put his cigarette down in the ashtray. "The cable running from the output of the A-to-D converter is plugged into this computer," he said, indicating the terminal sitting next to the converter. "The numbers will be stored in the computer." He pushed the "play" button on the tape recorder and waited.

"And you think this is what was done to the tape after the message was recorded?" Danner asked.

"My guess is it was," Vanucci replied. "We'll soon know." He turned off the Sony. "There. You've only got a minute of speech on that tape. Now it's all in the computer, in the form of six hundred thousand numbers."

Vanucci sat down at the keyboard of the computer terminal. "Now remember, the numbers we have are measurements of amplitude—loudness. If the voice was processed, they did it by changing around the frequencies."

"But how can you tell the frequencies? All you have now is a string of numbers."

"We have to convert the data from the time domain to the frequency domain. There are two ways to look at sound. You can look at amplitude and time, which is what we have now. Or—it's rather like turning a kaleidoscope—we can forget about time and do a spectrum analysis. Just look at loudness and frequencies."

Vanucci stubbed out his cigarette in the ashtray and continued. "The way we do that is by a complex mathematical process called a direct Fourier transformation. But the computer will do it for us.''

Vanucci punched in some instructions on the keyboard. In a moment, a bar graph appeared on the screen. ''Okay, what you're looking at now is a snapshot of the sound twenty thousandth of a second in duration.'' He hit a key. ''Here's the next frame.''

''Do you see anything?'' Danner asked.

''Not yet. We'll keep going.''

The computer was flashing a series of graphs on the screen. Vanucci watched them intently. ''Wait a minute,'' he said. ''Look at that.'' He pointed to the lines. ''We've come to the part where she's begun to stutter. I can tell because the spectrums are repeating.''

''Well, you'd expect that, wouldn't you?'' Danner asked.

''Yes, but look, I'll go back three frames.'' He pushed a key on the computer. ''Now here you see the beginning of the word 'p-p-p-particular.' These first three frames would be the first 'p' sound. The next three frames would be the second 'p.' '' He ran them for Danner.

''They look the same.''

''That's just the point. The three frames for the first interval are identical to the three frames for the second interval. It might sound that way to your ear when someone stutters, as though they are repeating the sound exactly. But in actual speech that's impossible.''

''There would be some slight variations?''

''Yes.'' Vanucci was excited. ''You see what it means. The stutter was created by a computer. It was inserted into the speech pattern.''

Danner stared at the screen. ''My God!''

Vanucci rolled back to the first letter p and instructed the computer: SET DATA TO ZERO LEVEL. ''What I'm doing is telling the computer to reduce all the sample magnitudes to zero for that range of time. I'm going to tell it to do that whenever there's an exact repetition of the spectrum.'' He punched some more keys. ''The result should be to remove the stutter.''

He rearranged the connections between the computer terminal and tape recorder, hooking them up to a new component.

''This little box is a D-to-A converter,'' he said. ''It will get us back again from digital sound to analog.''

In a moment, he played the tape over. This time, the voice sounded the same, but the stutter was gone.

Danner listened carefully. ''There's something haunting about that voice. But I still don't know who she is.''

''That's because the voice was processed. The pitch frequencies and the formant frequencies were manipulated and transposed to create a new voice.''

''Then how can you restore the original?''

''There may be traces of the original vocal tract. It's hard to remove them all. I may be able to find a pattern of alteration. And we can use trial and error. But the computer can't tell us, 'Yes, this is the right voice.' In the end, we won't be able to tell when we've hit on the original voice—unless you recognize it.''

''Because the computer can go on constructing voices indefinitely?''

''Pretty much. You see, there's a tremendous variety in people's voices. To begin with, your voice really has two parts. There isn't that much difference between your vocal cords and mine. In a typical male voice, the vocal cords open and close perhaps one hundred twenty times a second. But what makes our voices distinct are the differences in our vocal tract. Above the glottis, sound passes through your throat, mouth, and nose, and each of those parts resonates at a different frequency. Those are called the formant frequencies. They're what makes each of us sound different when we talk.''

Danner was disappointed. ''Then you're really searching for a needle in a haystack.''

''Let me play around with the numbers a little.'' Vanucci cycled back to the first frame on the computer. ''Suppose we reduce the high frequencies about eighty hertz and the lower frequencies about a hundred. Then we'll transpose down some of the formants. Like this. And see what we get.'' He was absorbed in thought, entering a lot of numbers on the keyboard, muttering about harmonics and integers.

Vanucci lit another cigarette, took a long drag, and exhaled the smoke. ''All right,'' he said. ''Let's try this.''

''This is your friend again,'' the voice repeated.

"Hey, wait a minute," Danner said. "That's a man's voice. Pete, that's it!"

Vanucci's streetwise features had formed into a wide grin. "I suspected it from the beginning," he said.

"Sonofabitch," Danner said. "Instead of a woman with a stutter, the voice is really a man who speaks normally."

"Whoever altered it kicked up the pitch and formant frequencies so that instead of a voice in the ninety to one hundred hertz range you had one up around two hundred hertz. It was that easy to change it from a man to a woman."

"The voice," Danner said. "It's almost familiar now. But there's still something wrong."

"We'll work with the formants," Vanucci said. "Like a composite photo that a police artist draws. Only we'll draw it in sound. You tell me how to change it."

"When he says 'Propaganda Due,'" Danner said. "Try making the voice a little richer. More bass."

"Okay, done." Vanucci played it again.

"Keep going. Let me hear the whole thing." Danner listened again. "All right," he said quickly, "the part where he says, 'The operational objective . . . of the new lodge.' Increase the amplitude on the second syllable of 'objective.' Give the speech pattern more emphasis."

Vanucci entered some more numbers and played the phrase over.

"Jesus, Pete. Play the whole tape again."

Vannuci cycled back to the beginning and played the tape over.

"What's the matter?" Vanucci asked. "You look like you were just run over by a Mack truck."

Danner sat back, the color drained from his face. He spoke softly, "Record the whole thing for me, will you?"

Vanucci obliged. "You know who it is, huh?"

"Yes," Danner said grimly. "I know."

Vanucci handed him the new cassette. Danner gathered it up along with the original. He shook hands with Vanucci. "Thanks, Pete."

"You'll get my bill."

Danner walked down the dingy stairs, turned into Spring Street, and followed it to West Broadway. He headed north up to Washington Square. It was chilly out, but he needed to think. He sat down on one of the park benches and watched a group of kids playing. Several mothers went by pushing strollers with toddlers bundled up in snow suits against the cold. He did not understand. It was baffling, and frightening, like being lost in a forest. What he had learned in the last half hour had turned all of his assumptions upside down. He thought of the woman with the stutter who didn't exist. But mostly he thought of the man who did. The man whose voice was on the tape.

CHAPTER
TWENTY-THREE

Deep in the valley below Grindelwald the skiers were crowding onto the platform of the cable car station. It was late in the afternoon, and they were anxious to get in one or two more runs down the Männlichen before it became too dark.

Above them towered the Eiger, silent and massive, a solid wall of snow and ice reaching almost straight up into the clear Alpine sky. From the valley, the tiny gondolas, hanging from their moving steel cable, climbed 6.2 kilometers in thirty minutes to a height of 7,317 feet. It was the longest uninterrupted cable car ride in Europe, a fact of particular interest to two of the men caught in the crush of skiers, who had chosen it for that reason.

The taller of the two stood poised on the metal grate, ready to board the bright red gondola that was swinging rapidly toward him. He wore a blue nylon Roffe parka and ski pants, photogray goggles, and a red wool cap that did not quite cover all of his white hair.

The 220 cable cars in the $11 million system were designed to move 900 people an hour to the top of the Männlichen at a speed of 840 feet per minute. Each car stopped on the platform for only thirty seconds. The empty cabin that was approaching jolted to a halt and the automatic doors flew open. The tall man slapped his skis in the metal containers on the side of the gondola and stepped quickly on board, carrying his poles.

His companion did the same with his skis and scrambled in after him. The cabin was small, but designed to hold four peo-

ple. A young French couple tried to move toward the gondola
to take the two empty places. They found their way blocked by
a pair of big, tough-looking blond men who stood watching the
car until the doors slammed shut and it had rocked off the platform with a rapid burst of speed. The young Frenchman started
to protest, but something in the faces of the two men made him
stop. He shrugged and told his girlfriend they would take the
next one.

Aboard the gondola, the two passengers sat facing each other
on the yellow slatted seats. Their knees touched in the cramped,
swaying cabin. The shorter man was dressed in bright yellow
and wore mirrored goggles that concealed his eyes. He was
stocky, but had the powerful build of a peasant. Beneath his ski
clothes, his arms and chest muscles were well developed by the
weights that he lifted each day despite the demanding nature of
his job. His features were thick, but intelligent, and his dark,
curly hair was graying in patches.

Aleksandr Sergeyevich Pavlov, sixty, chairman of the Committee for State Security of the Soviet Union, broke into a broad
smile, showing several gold teeth that caught the glint of the
late afternoon sun through the glass walls of the cabin.

"Perhaps an unusual meeting place," he said in heavily accented English, "but extremely private, and best of all, free of
our respective bodyguards."

"It was good of you to meet me on neutral ground," Brooks
Jordan said, returning the Russian's smile.

Pavlov wrinkled his brow and looked down at the deep snow
below. "It is a long way to the ground," the KGB chief corrected him, with a sweep of his hairy hand. "But we can pre-
sume the Swiss air is also neutral." He burst into laughter at his
own joke.

Jordan joined in. "You are looking well, Aleksandr Sergeyevich, and enjoying life, I see."

"At our age, we have no choice. It is required that we enjoy
ourselves." The Russian laughed again.

"You have a point," Jordan agreed. "Time passes without
regard to politics. How many years has it been?"

The Russian pursed his lips and thought for a moment.
"Since Berlin? Thirty, I would guess. Your hair was not white
in those days."

"And you were thinner. And much more serious."

The gondola was swaying in the wind more than 100 feet above the snow. It hung by a J-shaped metal bar from the single strand of cable overhead. The scene that stretched before them was spectacular: in a great arc to the south were the five snow-covered giants of the Bernese Oberland, the Wetterhorn, the Schreckhorn, the Eiger, with the snow following the contours of its scooped-out north face, the Mönch, and finally the Jungfrau, at 13,642 feet the tallest of all. The gondola with its two passengers seemed frail by comparison.

Yet these were no ordinary two men. Between them, they controlled secret power undreamed of by the greatest conquerors and rulers of the past. And like those predecessors, they wanted more.

At sixty, Brooks Jordan lived for power. He was totally absorbed by its pursuit and exercise. He was a man made for Washington, which was in a real sense a company town. Politics was the business of Washington, and power its product. Yet he had paid a price; there were hidden costs in his cold gray eyes. His wife, Felicity, who was much younger than he, spent a lot of her time at the Chevy Chase Club, playing tennis, she claimed. But her real hobby was having affairs. It was the one realm where Jordan's power was useless. When Felicity said her backhand needed work, Jordan knew, it meant she had lured yet another tennis instructor to bed. The CIA director was amazed at how many tennis instructors Washington seemed to have. It wasn't her backhand that she was working on, he would tell himself bitterly, it was her foreplay.

Within the agency, as anywhere, survival was the first necessity of power. One could not wield power out of office. In that respect, Brooks Jordan's uncertain future in the Forbes administration had an almost exact parallel in the shaky position of Aleksandr Pavlov within the walls of the Kremlin. Like Jordan, the Russian had been born in 1924, the year that Lenin died. He was one of eight children, the son of an illiterate flour mill worker. He was educated at the Kemerovo Technological Institute, in the coal-mining country of western Siberia. But like so many Soviet leaders, he built his early career in the Ukraine. He joined the Komsomol, and the party, and eventually became deputy chief of the youth organization. He rose through the party ranks, and by the 1950s, he had been selected by the KGB for special training and brought to Moscow.

In 1954, after his training had been completed, the KGB's First Chief Directorate posted him to Berlin, where he had some minor brushes with a young CIA agent named Brooks Jordan. After Berlin, he worked at the Moscow Center for a time; then he was sent to New Delhi, then Paris, and London, plums where he distinguished himself in agent spotting, recruitment, and operations. By the mid-seventies he was back in Moscow as a senior KGB official, where he displayed a special talent for protecting his flanks and advancing through the hierarchy at Dzerzhinsky Square. He briefly headed the KGB's Third Department, responsible for the United Kingdom and Scandinavia. Soon after, he was promoted to direct Department A, the branch that handled covert action and deception, which the Soviets preferred to call "active measures." The department was roughly equivalent to the Directorate of Operations in Langley. His record as chief of covert activities was outstanding, and he did not neglect his political ties to the Central Committee. In time, he was promoted to the top job, Chief of the KGB. Such promotions from within the ranks were rare, but not unprecedented.

When Yuri V. Kalin became general secretary of the Communist Party and leader of the Soviet Union, he inherited Pavlov as head of the secret police. By that time, Pavlov was too entrenched to be easily dismissed, but the relationship was an uneasy one. In much the same way, Lansing Forbes had decided to keep Brooks Jordan on at CIA after his own election as president.

Pavlov took a pack of Belomorkanals from his pocket and extracted one. Jordan saw that it was a *papirosy*, the kind in a long paper tube favored by the Russians. The KGB chief twisted the tube, to make more of a filter, and lit the cigarette. "I have followed your career with great interest since our encounter in Berlin," he said. "You have survived. We Russians respect that." He corrected himself. "No, we understand it."

"You have also done extremely well, Aleks," Jordan replied.

The Russian nodded his assent. "My position has greatly improved in recent months," he said. "With your help."

"Good. I'm glad to hear it."

The strong smell of the *papirosy* filled the cabin. Pavlov held it from underneath, Russian style, with his thumb and third finger. He took short, quick puffs. "Within the Politburo, I have been able to claim credit for disrupting your operations," he said. "Kalin has the impression that we have the CIA on the run." The Russian broke into a broad smile.

Jordan's eyes were expressionless but alert behind the gray goggles. "And now it's time for you to keep your end of the bargain," he said.

"I am prepared to do so, my friend," the Russian replied. He reached inside his parka and removed a white envelope from the pocket. "The drawings for the SS-18, Mod 4. We have 308 of them. But you know that, from your satellites."

"Yes," Jordan said. "We know." He took the envelope and put it in his pocket without opening it. "Perhaps this will help to ensure that they are never fired."

The Russian gazed out to his left at the north face of Eiger, where so many men had died trying to climb to the top. "The world has become too dangerous a place to entrust to the political leaders," he said.

Jordan nodded his agreement.

"And why should there not be discreet cooperation between our two agencies?" Pavlov asked. "After all, it is not as though we are breaking new ground. In 1962, we traded Francis Gary Powers for Rudolf Abel. There have been other trades."

"We've cooperated in outer space as well," Jordan observed.

"Yes. In seventy-five, our spaceship Soyuz 19 joined your Apollo 18 and our cosmonauts and yours ate dinner together in space. What we are doing now is merely an extension of what has gone before."

"The benefits will be enormous," Jordan said. "Not only for our countries, but for us."

Pavlov broke into a huge grin. "With Forbes, in your case."

"Yes." As both men knew, the secrets Jordan was receiving from Pavlov would solidify his position with the president. Jordan was aware that Vice President Brock and Richard Janney, the White House chief of staff, had been using the blown operations to attempt to discredit him with the president. It was a risk that Jordan had faced from the start. The documents now in his pocket would demolish the arguments of Brock and Janney. They would more than outweigh any temporary damage that might have been done to him by the blown operations.

"We all have our presidents," Pavlov said, a note of sympathy in his voice. "They seldom understand our work." Jordan nodded. "They are not professionals."

"Edgar Hoover," the Russian said. "He was the only one who knew how to handle your presidents."

"You're right. I didn't like the man personally. He hated the agency, as you know. But the power he had—the control he exercised over the country!"

The KGB chief stubbed out his cigarette in the ashtray on his right. "I have always admired the way he blackmailed Kennedy," he said.

"It was remarkable," Jordan reminisced. "Here the president was getting ready to fire Hoover—he was much too old for the Kennedys—so he merely drops by the White House for lunch and lets the president know that the FBI has learned all about his trysts with a woman that Kennedy was sharing with a Mafia chief. *Our* Mafia chief, by the way, the one we were using to try to poison Castro." Jordan laughed.

"You and I will become more powerful than our presidents," Pavlov boasted, "because we are sharing each other's secrets. When we meet next, I may be able to make available the plans of our most closely guarded weapon. The charged particle beam."

Jordan leaned forward. His gray eyes flickered. The Soviets were far ahead of the United States in research and development of the beam, which could, if perfected, destroy an incoming missile much more efficiently than a laser or any other known weapon. Pavlov's offer was staggering. It was more than the CIA chief had expected. "You would do this?" he asked.

Pavlov nodded. "Perhaps. I might reveal how our physicists at the testing facility at Semipalatinsk have solved the problem of curvature."

The major difficulty in the development of the beam, Jordan knew, was to find a way to prevent it from curving in the earth's magnetic field. The solution had baffled U.S. scientists.

"But you wish to bargain," Jordan said.

"It is in our nature to bargain," Pavlov replied. "I can provide the documents if certain conditions are met."

"What conditions?"

Pavlov hesitated for a second, then spoke. "If the CIA will assassinate Yuri Kalin."

Outside, golden shafts of light from the setting sun were striking the tops of the Eiger and the Jungfrau, leaving dark, cold shadows on the eastern faces of the jagged peaks. The stark white snow below them had begun to turn to shades of blue and gray. Inside the cabin there was no sound, except for the wind, and the throbbing, crunching noise of the cable moving steadily overhead toward the next steel tower.

Jordan cleared his throat. Pavlov could not see his eyes through the ski goggles. If he could have, they would have revealed nothing. Jordan spoke at last, breaking the Alpine silence. "Your price is too high."

"What I have to offer is worth it. Not only the beam. A continuous flow of the innermost secrets of my government into your computers at Langley. Information you can never obtain by other means. Information that will make you the most important man within the American government."

The CIA director stared out at the Jungfraujoch, the great snow-covered cradle lying between the peaks of the Mönch and the Jungfrau. "If Kalin is a problem," he said finally, "why can't the KGB terminate him?"

Pavlov grinned, showing the gold in his teeth again. "There is no one I could trust," he said. "Would you find it easy to persuade one of your Special Operations people—yes, we know that is the name of the unit now—to assassinate President Forbes?"

"It would be difficult," Jordan admitted.

"Kalin's people are all over," Pavlov said. "Even inside the KGB. Rybakov, the head of the First Chief Directorate, is loyal to him. There are others. Mazurov, Bukovsky. Many. Too many. But you, an outside agency, could do it."

"There are limits, Aleksandr Sergeyevich. Even for us."

Pavlov flushed. "The man is unstable. I will tell you something you do not know. A few weeks ago, in Chistopol Prison, in the Tatar Autonomous Republic, six men and two women were executed in the snow. Shot by a firing squad, buried in unmarked graves nearby, outside the prison walls. Do you know who they were? They were Kalin's personal chef, a man named Polyakov, and the rest of the kitchen staff in the Kremlin.''

''What had they done?''

''Nothing. Kalin has decided that some of the people around him are trying to poison him.''

''And you're not?''

''No. They were completely innocent. The man is mad. A danger to our country and to yours.''

Jordan nodded. ''Our psychiatrists have been watching his behavior very closely. It's extremely disturbing. But you have your own objectives, certainly.''

Pavlov shrugged. ''With Kalin gone, I can consolidate my power and that of the KGB. We can return to collective leadership in the Politburo. Our countries can look forward to a long period of stability.''

Although Aleksandr Pavlov did not know it, the operation he was proposing as the gondola swayed toward the top of the Männlichen was not an impossible idea to Brooks Jordan. Three months earlier, the CIA director had been summoned to the Oval Office by President Forbes, a seventy-two-year-old industrialist who had been appointed to the Senate by the governor of California, later elected to the seat, and then elected president in a conservative swing by the electorate. Only a few months after his election, Forbes, in a televised speech from the Oval Office, had accused Kalin of directly supporting and fomenting international terrorism.

Later, Forbes had signed a pact that made the United States a formal military ally of mainland China. The two countries now shared missile-monitoring bases in western China to keep watch on Soviet ICBM tests. Kalin had moved more troops to the Soviet-Chinese border, and Chairman Huang Li-teng, the Chinese leader, regarded Yuri Kalin as his greatest enemy.

If only Kalin were removed, the president had ruminated to Jordan in their private meeting in the White House, it would remove a major threat to world peace. The president had read the CIA reports on Kalin's mental condition, and they were more and more disturbing. National security was directly involved, since Kalin had nuclear power at his fingertips.

The departure of Kalin, Forbes had pointed out, would also ease the pressure on Chairman Huang. If the United States could somehow assist in that removal, it would solidify our ties with China, enhance our own security, and eliminate a major foe.

What the president did not mention was that at a summit meeting in Geneva the previous year, Kalin had publicly denounced Forbes at the opening session in front of the television cameras. He pronounced him qualified only to manufacture shoes. He had then spit on the floor and walked out of the meeting. His parting remark, roughly translated from the Russian, was to the effect that Forbes was not even fit to kiss his ass. The world was shocked, and the press had a field day, trumpeting headlines like: "Soviet Leader Humiliates Forbes, Spits and Splits."

At no point in the Oval Office meeting did the president actually suggest to Jordan in so many words that Kalin be assassinated. His language was always carefully ambiguous, but he talked circuitously about how his burdens would be eased if Kalin were out of the picture.

Jordan thought he understood, just as eight centuries earlier the aides in the court of Henry II thought they understood when the king asked: "Will no one rid me of this turbulent priest?" Now Kalin was Thomas à Becket. But Jordan had declined to journey to Canterbury.

The CIA director had replied that there were studies being undertaken by the agency, contingency plans, on how to incapacitate the entire leadership of the Soviet Union if necessary, studies involving biological and ultrasonic weapons, nerve gas, and lasers. But no specific plan to target the Soviet president. The conversation had ended on this inconclusive note.

Jordan had not acted, since he had received no clear instruction from the president. Now the head of the KGB was bluntly asking him to do what the president had only hinted at.

It was true that Kalin's behavior had become alarmingly erratic, even aside from Pavlov's story about the kitchen staff. Dr. Quimby's latest analysis—which was supported by the full membership of the CIA's Board of Psychiatrists—concluded that Kalin was a borderline psychotic and megalomaniac. The BOP assessment could not be lightly dismissed. And what was the responsibility of the agency for world peace? Eliminating Kalin might save the world. Jordan realized that the lives of millions of people could depend on the decision he reached in this fragile gondola swinging above the Swiss Alps in the fading twilight of an early December afternoon.

There were risks either way, that was the difficulty. Both agencies had engaged in assassination, of course. But it was a dangerous tool. So many things could go wrong. A failed attempt might trigger a war. Then lives would be lost, not saved. The CIA director hesitated, feeling impaled, unable to choose, frozen by the enormous pressure weighing upon him.

Pavlov leaned forward and gripped Jordan's arm. "My friend," he said, "let me tell you something. Every autumn, when the time is right, I go with my family to the birch woods near Moscow to hunt for the wild mushroom. My little girls collect the *svinushkas*, or little pigs, the tiny brown ones that are so plentiful and tasty. Myself, I search for the little foxes, the *lisichki*, or the *zelyonkas*. Above all, I hope for a *borovik*, the big, fat white ones."

Jordan nodded. "I know it is a popular sport in your country."

"More than a sport, a passion!" Pavlov exclaimed. "But not without danger. For among the edible mushrooms, sometimes looking exactly like them, are the *poganki*, the poisonous ones." Pavlov paused for effect. "Just so is Kalin. He is a *poganki*, a poisonous growth in our midst. He must be uprooted, destroyed. You, my friend Brooks, you have the means."

Jordan gazed out to his left, where the Lutschine had carved a deep gorge between the Männlichen and the Schynige Platte as it meandered past Schwendi and Gsteigwiler on its way to the Brienzersee. In a sense, he knew, the president had already authorized what Pavlov proposed. The risks were enormous. On the other hand, Kalin alive might be a greater risk. And Pavlov was a fount of secret knowledge about the Soviets, an intelligence source without precedent or parallel.

After a long silence, Jordan turned back to the KGB chief.

"Not only the beam weapon, you said. The flow of secret information will continue."

Pavlov broke out into a smile. "*Da.* I have promised it."

"And, after Kalin is neutralized," Jordan continued, "I will expect you to use your influence to end the pressure on the Chinese border."

"Your conditions are reasonable," the KGB chief said. "And accepted."

"All right," Jordan said. "It will be done."

"I suggest that we call it Operation Valki," Pavlov said. "For the city in the Ukraine where Yuri Vladimirovich was born."

"Very well, then. Operation Valki."

The Russian reached inside his parka and to Jordan's surprise, produced a small flask and two shot glasses. He poured the vodka and handed one of the glasses to Jordan. "Stolichnaya," he said. "One hundred proof. *Do dna!*"

Jordan raised his glass in turn and clinked it against the Russian's. "To Operation Valki," he said.

There was time for only one drink. The gondola was almost at the top now, and it began to rock as it moved into the covered station and settled on the metal grate of the platform. The doors sprang open and Pavlov jumped out first. They recovered their skis from the side of the cabin and pushed through the turnstile.

Outside, there was just enough light left for a final run down the mountain. There were only a few diehard skiers still on the Männlichen. Jordan stepped into the bindings of his Rossignol Stratos, planted his poles, and pushed off, schussing down the trail toward Grindelwald. Pavlov headed in exactly the opposite direction, skiing toward Wengen in the deep valley more than 3,000 feet below. Jordan assumed that Pavlov's people were waiting for him there.

Jordan was halfway down the mountain before the irony struck him. Speeding down the slope to Wengen, Pavlov, the KGB chief, was heading west. With a grim smile, Jordan realized that he, in turn, was moving east.

CHAPTER
TWENTY-FOUR

As soon as he returned to headquarters from New York, Danner called the director's office and asked for an appointment. He was told that Jordan was away but was expected back the following morning. The earliest that Danner could be scheduled was 11:00 A.M. He said that would be fine.

He telephoned Julie on his Red System phone and reached a secretary who said she was still out of the country. Her trip seemed to have stretched beyond three weeks. He was achingly disappointed at the news and longed to see her.

He dialed Imagery and got Sam Green, who invited him to come over for dinner that night. Sam said he would stop by the International Safeway in McLean, a favorite supermarket of CIA employees, and pick up a steak.

With the cassette safely tucked in the inside pocket of his jacket, Danner left the agency early. He knew what he had to do now. Only Jordan could help him; until he saw the director, he could not reveal his secret to anyone else. He must avoid Dixon Hadley, who might ask questions, and the best place to be was anywhere but headquarters. He drove south along the George Washington Parkway in the rain that had started falling early in the day and showed no sign of letting up.

On impulse, he turned around at Memorial Bridge and drove back up the highway to the first overlook, where he pulled off and parked. He sat for a long time, thinking about his meeting the next morning with Brooks Jordan. His plan would work. It had to. Carrie's safety hinged on it. The rain was running down

the windshield in rivulets. Far to his right, he could see the
Washington Monument through the rain and mist. After a while
he started up, drove aimlessly for a time, then headed south
again on the parkway. Across the Potomac, the dark spires of
Georgetown University pierced the slate gray sky. Below him,
the river looked cold and uninviting.

He drove home. At the apartment, he made a cup of coffee,
and spent what was left of the afternoon reading. Dinner that
night at Sam's was pleasant enough. Sam was curious about
how things had gone in Zürich but knew him well enough to ask
no questions. Danner did not volunteer anything about the
house on the lake. That night, however, he dreamed he was
being pursued by an enormous Doberman with sharp fangs and
huge, yellow eyes.

The director glanced at his watch, as if to remind Danner that
he was a busy man whose time was limited. They sat in the
apricot-colored armchairs in the corner, across from Jordan's
desk. Danner had his back to the window, and the director sat
on his right. They were alone, as Danner had requested.

Jordan looked unruffled, every white hair in place. Apparently he had no inkling of what was coming. If he wondered
why Danner had asked to see him alone, without Dixon Hadley, he did not ask.

There were no preliminaries. "I've done what you wanted,"
Danner said.

Behind the rimless glasses, the gray eyes betrayed nothing.
"You've found the mole." It was more of a statement than a
question.

"Yes."

Jordan, his face expressionless, asked, "And his identity?"

"You know that." Danner's voice was flat, without tri-
umph.

The director allowed himself to look puzzled. "I'm afraid
not."

Danner patted his breast pocket. "I have one of the tapes.
The voice has been reconstructed."

The director did not reply. He got up and walked over to the
window. The blinds were open and he gazed out at the barren
trees and the frozen ground, with its ragged patches of snow.

"Hadley was right," he said at last. "You are a remarkable man."

Danner was silent, waiting for the director to continue. Jordan left the window, walked back around the armchair, and sat down. He looked directly at Danner. "What you have accomplished is extraordinary. But you're wrong in your basic premise."

"I don't think so."

The director leaned forward. "There is no mole," he said. "The whole scenario is an agency operation. Run and controlled by me."

Danner shook his head. "That's an ingenious defense. But it won't stand up."

The director sighed, as though he were a schoolmaster with a slow pupil. "What you've stumbled into, or I should say penetrated, is the biggest counterintelligence operation in the agency's history. I am personally running the most valuable double agent we've ever had."

Danner did not try to conceal his skepticism. "Who?"

Jordan hesitated, but realized he could not stop now. Danner would have to be taken into his confidence, up to a point. "Aleksandr Sergeyevich Pavlov," he said. "The head of the KGB."

Danner was stunned. He felt as he had in Caracas the night three hired toughs slammed him against a brick wall.

"We're getting incredibly sensitive material from him," Jordan went on. "It's going directly to the president, EYES ONLY CATEGORY ONE ZEBRA. Locked dispatch case and four armed guards to get it across the river." With some satisfaction, he added, "Even Janney isn't cleared to read it."

For the first time, a note of doubt crept into Danner's voice. "But you've deliberately blown your own operations. You betrayed them to the Group. I have the proof here, on tape."

Jordan smiled. "Of course I had to give Pavlov something," he said smoothly. "One always does."

Danner felt his hands growing cold. The conversation was not going at all the way he had planned. "You've been trading in agency secrets."

"As director, I have that authority. None of the operations was vital. A third-rate defector in Tokyo. A few names in

London. And if you're thinking of Vienna, frankly, the Czech traffic is not that important to us. The Soviets don't tell them anything."

"What about MS/SKYLARK? He was shot."

"Not by us. In any event, Stein was expendable."

Danner remained unconvinced. Jordan might be telling the truth, up to a point. Perhaps he really had sacrificed the agency's covert operations to the larger goal of clandestine collection. But if so, he had crossed an invisible line; he had gone too far. Perhaps it was not Pavlov who was the double agent, but Jordan. How could loyalties be measured in such a complex web?

And Danner sensed that Jordan was telling him only a part of the story. There must be a great deal more going on, hidden motivations and nerve endings branching off in a hundred directions. "If there's no mole," he said, "why was I brought in?"

Jordan smiled again. "Dixon Hadley saw our operations going bad. He picked up traces of the old boys in each instance. Naturally, he assumed there was a mole. He insisted on bringing you in."

"Why did you agree to it?"

"I had to go along, or Dixon would have been suspicious. I admit I never thought you'd get this far. I owe you an apology. I really do. I underestimated you."

Danner weighed Jordan's words. The man was either the most brilliant masterspy in the CIA's history or a traitor. He didn't know which. He wasn't sure that Jordan knew, either. "Then it was you who told the Soviets about me."

"No," Jordan replied. "I may have mentioned your presence to the old boys. They were bound to find out anyhow, sooner or later. They could have tipped the Russians."

Danner erupted. "What the hell do you mean, could have? You know goddamn fucking well they did. You're the reason they grabbed Carrie. You're responsible!"

Jordan shook his head. "The Soviets acted on their own. I learned of it from Hadley, just as you did. The car we traced in Vienna."

Danner did not know whether the director was lying. But it

didn't really matter. "I want her back, Brooks. You're going to get her back for me."

The director licked his lips nervously. "I don't know if I can."

"You don't have a choice. You've betrayed agency operations to the KGB, operations you're sworn to protect. Your explanation won't wash. You're in trouble." He paused. "But I'm prepared to offer you a way out."

"I don't accept your premise. Not for a moment. But go ahead and spell out your terms. I'm curious enough to want to hear them."

"The deal is simple enough. My silence in exchange for my daughter."

The director drummed his fingers on the edge of his armchair. Finally he smiled. "That was your plan all along, wasn't it? You're the only one who knows the identity of the mole, to use your term. Whoever it turned out to be, you would have gone to him and offered the same deal. Am I right?"

"Yes."

"So you never planned to reveal the name to Dixon?"

"No."

"Hadley didn't see that, did he?"

"No."

"You've not told him whose voice is on the tape?"

"Not yet."

"What will you say when he asks?"

"If Carrie is returned unharmed, I'll tell him that it was a dry creek. That the voice couldn't be identified."

"And in the meantime?"

"In the meantime, I'll tell him the lab is still working on the tape. Trying to reconstruct the voice."

The director was silent for a long moment. Then he said, "Everything I told you is true. I've doubled Aleks Pavlov. The take is incredible. There have been certain costs. But to protect the operation, I'll accept your terms."

To protect your ass is more like it, Danner thought. "All right," he said. "How soon can you get her back?"

"It will take a little time," Jordan replied cautiously. "Not long. But there are certain matters pending that have to be brought to a conclusion. Then I can approach them."

"Each day is a long time," Danner said. "You'll have to move fast. I'll be waiting."

Jordan nodded. "I understand." He took his glasses off, polished them with a tissue, and put them back on, carefully. "I know you're surprised by what I've told you," he said. "But ours is not an ordinary profession. We construct mirror images, illusions. We deal in layers of truth, not in absolutes."

Danner nodded. "The old boys," he said. "They never realized what was going on, did they?"

"Of course not. They thought someone on the inside was trying to help them regain power. That was hardly my purpose, since I would have been the first to go."

Danner realized that the maze he had been traveling through was not what it had appeared to be. Brooks Jordan had turned it inside out. The director had betrayed his own operations to establish the trust of the head of the KGB. The old boys, for all of their expertise, had been used as cutouts, unwitting pawns in the director's larger game.

Jordan smiled, as if he read Danner's thoughts. "They were penetrated from the start, of course."

"Who did you have? Braswell?"

"Oh, we needn't get into that. I had three sources, actually. Old boys who couldn't stop being covert operators, even in retirement. They've reported to me on the Group's plans from the beginning."

"Lloyd never knew he was being used?"

"Never. When I learned of their plans to disrupt our operations, I decided to make it easy for them and send the anonymous tapes. The sort of clandestine touch that I thought would appeal to them."

Danner was not really surprised. "It's all a game with you, isn't it? National security, all the high-sounding foreign policy objectives, they're all justifications for the game, aren't they? The secret game."

Jordan shrugged. "Have you found anything else? The game is all there is."

"Secrecy is the end of intelligence," Danner said. "Not the means. It's taken me a very long time to understand that."

"Secrecy and power," Jordan corrected him.

"But the agency exists for its secrecy," Danner said. "The power flows from the secrecy."

Jordan nodded. "A fine distinction, perhaps, but I would accept it."

"Espionage is like the games we play as children," Danner said. "With secret hideaways, or a secret club. The club was not necessarily better than anywhere else, but it excluded the other kids. That's what defined it, made it important. The nonmembers."

The director laughed. "Just so."

"And all of us in the agency revel in our secret world. We are like humanoids, moving unrecognized among the rest of the population. We look just like our neighbors, like anyone else, but each morning we get up and disappear into a secret world. That's our reward, isn't it?"

"And our burden," Jordan said unctuously.

"Victory over the Soviets isn't our goal," Danner said. "Playing the game is enough."

"Neither side can achieve a victory," Jordan said. "And if we did, there would be no need for a CIA." He shook his head. "No, victory is the last thing we want."

"So, in the end," Danner said slowly, in the manner of a man to whom a truth has been gradually revealed, "moles don't really matter, do they?"

"No," said Jordan. "Not really."

Danner's tone changed. "But they matter a great deal to people on the outside."

Jordan understood his meaning. "There's no need for threats. I'll talk to Pavlov about your daughter." He paused. "We seem to see eye to eye. Why don't you consider staying on with us? I can arrange a high-level position for you. Deputy DDO to start."

Danner arose. "No," he said. "I've done my job. Now you do yours. Tell your Soviet friends I want my daughter back unharmed. As soon as I have her back, I'll be moving on. In the meantime"—he took the tape out of his pocket and displayed it to Jordan—"I'll hold onto this." He put the cassette back inside his jacket pocket.

As he walked down the corridor toward the elevators, he thought of the last time he saw Carrie, in the Montreal airport with the ice cream cone that had started to drip down the side. He wondered if he would ever see her again.

CHAPTER
TWENTY-FIVE

It was almost a week later when the telephone rang in Danner's apartment as he was having a second cup of coffee at breakfast. Dixon Hadley was on the line, and he sounded agitated. "Don't go in this morning," he said.

"What's up?"

"I need to talk to you. Drive into Washington and I'll meet you at the zoo."

"The zoo's a big place," Danner said. "Where?"

Hadley thought for a moment. "By the sea lions," he said.

"All right."

Hadley was waiting for him at the railing, pretending to study the sea lions in their pool, when Danner came down the stairs from the bear dens. He remembered having taken Carrie there years before, when she was very small. Mark, the giant Kodiak bear, had been her favorite. She could sometimes get him to imitate her as she rolled her hands in front of her chest. "Roll hands, Mark," she would urge him. "Roll hands." If he did it, she would throw him a carrot as a reward.

"Hello, Dixon. Pretty fucking cold spot you picked for our *treff*." He needled the DDO by using the Russian word for a clandestine meeting.

"But secure. We can talk freely here."

The wind came up, rippling the sea lion pool and sending dead leaves skittering along the paved walk. There were very few people in the zoo, and no one in sight. The snow had melted but there were wet patches and a lot of brown mud underfoot. Danner shivered, despite the heavy car coat he was wearing. "Yes, secure. Unless you've wired the sea lions."

Hadley didn't smile. "Anything new from New York?" he asked.

"No," Danner lied. "They're still working on the tape."

Hadley nodded. "I assumed as much." He pulled up his coat collar against the cold. "That's not why I asked you here. There's something else."

A fat sea lion hoisted himself out of the water with difficulty and waddled up onto a rock. He had white whiskers and reminded Danner of Graham Hovey, his English professor at Dartmouth.

"I'm worried," Hadley said.

Danner looked around. There was something missing. Then he remembered. There used to be a man selling fish from a battered ice cream cart. A dime a fish. Carrie loved to throw them into the water. He could still remember the expression of utter delight on her face as she watched the sea lions scramble for their snack. But the man and his cart had disappeared years ago. "What are you worried about?" he asked.

"Special Operations. There's something going on. I've picked up traces, but I can't figure out what it is."

Danner shifted his feet to keep warm. "What kind of traces?"

"SO is secretly training an agent as a clown."

"A what?" Danner wondered if the agency was getting even more bizarre.

"A clown. A circus clown."

"Why in hell would they do that?"

The deputy director shook his head. "I don't know. I haven't been able to find out."

"Where are they doing it?" Danner asked.

Hadley surveyed the sea lion, who was stretching on the rock, trying to soak up the pale sunshine. "That's just it. I don't know where it's going on or why."

"And the target?"

The deputy director shook his head. "I'm afraid I don't know that either. Or the name of the agent."

"How'd you learn about it?"

Hadley hesitated. Danner could see him weighing whether to

say more. "Jellison," the DDO replied at last. "He was brought in by SO to whistle a call. On another matter entirely. But while he was there, he overheard something about a clown."

"And he told you?"

"Yes. He thought it sufficiently unusual to report it to me."

"So Jellison works for you. A spy among spies. I hadn't realized."

Hadley smiled. "Roger has excellent hearing. Most blind people do. He also has a superior memory. Since he gets called in by almost every division in the Clandestine Services, he's in a position to hear a great deal. Over the years, he's been quite useful."

A gust of wind sent the leaves swirling around the two men. Danner shrugged. "Why tell me about it?"

"You're on a hold button at the moment. Waiting to hear from New York. I thought you might have a go at this in the meantime."

"It's not in my contract."

"Then do it as a favor to me." Hadley looked at him anxiously.

"It's that important?"

"I think so. You develop an instinct in this job. There are little signs floating around in the air. A lot of meetings on the seventh floor this week. And Jordan's been over to the White House twice."

At his confrontation with Jordan, Danner had sensed that the director was not telling him everything. He was intrigued by Hadley's information. What was it Jordan had said? There were "certain matters" pending that had to be brought to a conclusion before he could approach the Soviets. Intuitively, he felt that Carrie's safety might be involved. He realized something else; that even as he was repelled by the game, he was attracted to it.

"All right," Danner said. "I'll see what I can find out."

Hadley looked relieved. "Very good of you," he said. "Very good indeed."

They headed up the muddy path together toward Connecticut Avenue. As they left, the fat sea lion was joined on the rock by his mate, and the two of them began to bark. Danner wondered if they were remembering the man with the battered ice cream cart who used to sell the fish.

Danner called Sam Green from a pay phone in a gas station and they arranged to meet for lunch at J.R.'s Stockyards, a steak and hamburger pub in Tyson's Corner. Sam spent most of the lunch talking about his new girlfriend, a secretary in Central Reference. "She's a great piece of ass," Sam announced with satisfaction as he attacked a slab of rare roast beef.

"What happened to Liza Minelli?"

"Oh, Cheryl." Sam rolled his eyes. "Turns out she doesn't play unless she's bombed. And when she drinks, she's weird. So that was that."

Back in his office after lunch, Danner called *The Washington Post* and asked for Eric Benson in the Metro Section. His father Kit, an old agency hand, had stopped to chat in the cafeteria several weeks earlier and mentioned that his son was just starting out as a reporter. He was covering liquor store holdups in Northeast, but had hopes of one day making the national staff.

Benson was out, but called him back within the hour.

"Eric? This is Bill Danner. I'm an old friend of your dad's."

"Out at the pickle factory?"

Danner laughed. "That's right. Listen, I was hoping you could do me a small favor. I'd like you to check your library and have them pull any feature stories on retired clowns in the Washington area. Seems to me from time to time I've seen something about old circus hands gone to pasture."

"No problem. Sounds more interesting than the story I spent my morning on."

"What was that?" Danner asked.

"Playground vandals. The mayor has promised to crack down again."

Half an hour later, Benson called back. "There wasn't much in the clips," he said. "One story from 1950 about a retired clown, but the guy's probably dead by now. And a 1980 interview with Pops Henkel, a member of the Washington Clown Alley. It says he lives up near Frederick, and he's in his seventies."

"Thanks, Eric."

"You gonna run away and join the circus?"

"Maybe."

Danner checked with information and got a telephone listing for an Otto Henkel in Woodsboro. He wormed the address out of the operator. He started to call, then put down the phone. It would be better to go in person. He took the Beltway to 270 and headed north for Frederick. From there he cut east and north again through the Maryland farm country to the banks of Israel Creek.

The house looked almost abandoned. It hadn't been painted in years, and the screen door was punched out. There was a rusted, disabled Ford sitting in the front yard, next to a pile of old tires. Danner parked, got out, and picked his way through the mud to the front door. A dog started barking.

"Be quiet, Lulu." The old man who came slowly to the door was grinning, his square, weatherbeaten face crinkling with pleasure at his unexpected visitor. Danner noticed he was unusually muscular for an old man. But clowns, he remembered, had to be good acrobats.

"She gets excited," the old man said. "When she sees chickens or people. You're not a chicken, are you?" The man broke into uproarious laughter, enjoying his own joke. "She can dance, you know. Dance for the gentleman, Lulu."

The dog, a black-and-white short-haired mutt, got up on its hind legs and began prancing.

"That's pretty good," Danner said.

"She hears the music. In her head. Sometimes I play records for her." The old man smiled.

"Mr. Henkel?" Danner asked. "Otto Henkel?"

"Pops. Most people call me Pops. That was my professional name, you know."

"I know. That's why I've come to see you."

The old man peered at Danner carefully. "You don't look like circus folks," he said.

"I'm not," Danner said.

"Come in anyway," Henkel said. "It's too cold to stand outside." He led the way back into a dimly lit room and offered Danner a seat in a bedraggled stuffed chair. Henkel sat down opposite him on a couch that had once been green. The room was overheated from a wood stove that was going full blast in the corner. The dog followed them in and hopped up on the couch next to Henkel, regarding Danner intently.

"I wanted to talk to you about clowns," Danner said.

Henkel shrugged. "Sure. Maybe first you would like a beer?" Danner could hear traces of what he assumed was a German accent.

"Thanks," said Danner. "I'd like one."

The old man got up and shuffled out into the kitchen, returning with two cans of Pabst. He handed one to Danner.

"Prosit!" Henkel said, lifting the can and taking a drink.

Danner returned the toast. "When did you retire?" he asked.

Henkel wiped his mouth with the back of a gnarled hand. "Many years now. Many. But I was good, you know. I worked with Kelly, Adler, Lou Jacobs, Griebling. I had a funny act. I had a very little dog who would jump up into my back pocket, with just his head out. Then I was looking all over for him, but I never could find him. I worked the hippodrome track, and the center ring, always under canvas." He paused and took a drink of his beer. "Always under canvas," he repeated. "I never worked indoors, in a building, like they do now." Pops Henkel clearly disapproved of the fact that the big top was largely gone.

"How do you learn to become a clown?" Danner asked.

The old man looked at Danner through suddenly narrowed eyes. "You're too old," he said. "To be a first-of-May joey, you have to be young. Eighteen, nineteen, maybe a little older. But not a man your age."

Danner smiled. "No, it's not for me," he said. "It's my son. He has his heart set on joining the circus."

Henkel shook his head. "It's no life for a boy," he said. "Riding the trains, sleeping in a little cubbyhole, eating bad food. Do your show, make them laugh, and then on to tomorrow's town. Surrounded by midgets, and freaks, and Hungarian acrobats, and elephant shit. Did you even smell fresh elephant shit, Mr. Danner?"

"Sure. I've been to the circus."

Henkel looked at him. "The boy. He really wants to be a clown?"

"Has his heart set on it."

The old man sighed. "Then I suppose you won't be able to stop him."

"That's what I figure. So I want him to get the best training. Where did you learn how?"

Henkel grinned, the leathery face lighting up like a candle. "In Germany," he said. "I started with a little rinkydink mud circus near Altenstadt, sweeping up, carrying water for the animals. I watched, I learned. I came here, before the war, in the thirties. I was offered a job by the Cole Brothers. Twelve years with them, and then I was hired away by Ringling Brothers, Barnum & Bailey. When they folded up the canvas, I left and later I went with Circus Vargas. I stayed with them until I retired."

Danner nodded. "Is that how my boy should start? Get himself a job doing anything, just to be with a circus?"

Henkel shook his head. "No, no. Today is different, everything is different. Now he can go to school to learn."

Danner took a sip of his beer, hiding his eagerness. "Where?" he asked.

"Different places," Henkel said. "Maybe Clown College."

"There's a college for clowns?"

"Sure. The Ringlings run it. At their winter quarters in Florida. The Big Apple Circus in New York, they train clowns, too. And the Alvarez Brothers, they're Mexicans, they run a fine clown school in the Florida Keys. There's a lot of places he can go."

Danner stood up. "I've taken too much of your time," he said. "Thanks for the beer."

"Come again," said Henkel. "Me and Lulu, we don't get too many visitors." The dog, hearing her name, picked up her ears and wagged her tail furiously.

The old clown walked with Danner to the front door, and they shook hands. As Danner picked his way through the mud to his car, Henkel shouted after him. "Tell the boy you saw me," he said. "Tell him you talked to Otto Henkel."

Danner found Jellison in his little office on the third floor. He was listening to Bach's Brandenburg Concerti on his stereo. The akita was snuggled against his feet.

"Who is it?" Jellison asked.

"It's me, Roger. Bill Danner."

"Oh, hello." He waved his visitor to a chair and turned down the volume on the music a little.

Danner studied the blind man. He wore dark glasses beneath his thatch of gray hair, so it was normally very hard to tell his mood or expression. Even so, Danner could see that Jellison was unhappy. He usually had a friendly smile, but he wasn't wearing it this morning.

"What's the trouble, Roger? You look all gloom and doom."

"With good reason."

"Why? What's up?"

Jellison shook his head. "My days may be numbered here. It's the phone company. They're putting in ESS."

"What do you mean?"

"Electronic Switching Systems. They've already installed them in on about half the exchanges in the Washington area. We may be next."

"Makes your job tougher?"

"Very. The ESS recognizes the phone company's beeps and rejects foreign tones. It's going to eliminate most of the blue boxes. And unless my whistling is absolutely perfect, it won't go through."

Danner looked sympathetic. "That doesn't sound good. But the agency will still need sterile calls. Maybe the OTS wizards can come up with something."

"If they do," Jellison said, "they won't need me."

"You've got a problem. But you've been around long enough to have a pretty good retirement."

"It isn't that. I'll miss the contact with people. I like it here."

"It's a damn shame," Danner said. "You're a valuable man. I didn't know until yesterday how valuable."

Jellison smiled. "Hadley told me you might be coming by."

"Yes. I wondered if you could go over it with me."

"About the clown?"

Danner nodded, then caught himself. "Yes," he said.

Jellison shrugged. "There isn't much I can add. I was called in by SO to make a call. Belanger, their deputy, wanted to talk to someone in Hong Kong. He got tied up, and his secretary put me in his outer office to wait. While I was sitting there, a couple of young hot shots from the SO support staff were shooting the breeze. One of them said something about training a clown, and the other one laughed. It sounded pretty unusual, so I told Hadley.''

"They were talking about it right in front of you?"

"People forget that even though I can't see, I can hear. It happens all the time."

"And that's all they said?"

"Yes. I think he said the training had just started. That's all there was to it. Then I went in and whistled up Hong Kong for Belanger. After I got the connection, I handed him the phone and left.''

Danner arose. "Well, thanks, Roger. I hope things work out for you."

"You and me both," Jellison replied. He waved in the direction of Danner's voice. "Nice seeing you."

Danner returned to his office and pulled out a telephone book. He remembered having read somewhere that Ringling Brothers had its corporate headquarters in Washington. He flipped through, found a listing out on New Mexico Avenue, and dialed the number.

A woman answered. "I'm interested in your Clown College," Danner said. "Can you tell me where it's located?"

"Venice, Florida," the woman said. "But classes ended a month ago. Would you like me to send you an application for next year?"

"I'll let you know," Danner said.

Next, he dialed information and got the number of the Big Apple Circus in Manhattan. He called their headquarters and talked to a woman in the director's office. She was very pleasant, but explained that students enrolled for the fall clown classes had been accepted the previous spring.

He thanked her and dialed 305, the area code for the Florida Keys. The operator found a listing for Alvarez Clown Alley on Big Pine Key. He placed the call and got a secretary who put him on a hold button. While he was on the hold button, they played calliope music. Danner couldn't help smiling. He ordinarily didn't like people who played music when he was on a hold button, but this was different.

The secretary came back on. "Sorry to keep you waiting," she said apologetically. "It was the costumer in Miami. Can I help you?"

"I'm interested in enrolling in your clown school," Danner explained.

"Classes started a week ago," she said. "So you'd miss too much if you came now. But there'll be another session in January."

Danner thanked her and hung up. He called Nancy Baker in the secretarial pool. "I want to fly to Key West tomorrow," he told her. "Get me a round-trip ticket and leave the return date open. I'll need a car at the airport."

"You get to go to the neatest places," she said. "Do you need an assistant?"

"Not this trip," Danner said. "Maybe next time."

He looked in the agency telephone directory and dialed Norm Appelman, the CIA's liaison man with the Federal Aviation Administration. The agency had people in charge of contacts with most other units of the federal government, not only the obvious ones like the FBI and NSA, but any agency that had data bases and information that might be of use to CIA. Through its liaison network the CIA could plug in, sometimes unofficially and informally, to a vast web of data in government files.

The phone was answered on the third ring. "Appelman," the voice said.

"Norm? Bill Danner. Can you get me a list of all passengers who've flown from Washington to Key West in the past month?"

"I guess so. But it may take a while."

"Why?"

"Well, the information exists, all right. The airlines have to keep passenger lists for two months. Most of them store the data in their computers for six months or a year."

"Then what's the problem?"

"Even when there's an official request like this, the airlines are slow getting the names over to FAA. And FAA is fussy about giving them to us. They always want something in writing that states the reason for the requirement."

"Tell them we're on the trail of an international terrorist group that's planning to divert Florida flights to Cuba. That should speed things up."

"Are you?" Appelman sounded alarmed.

"Would I lie to you?" Danner asked.

"I guess not," Appelman replied uncertainly. "When do you need the list?"

"This afternoon."

Danner could hear Appelman suck in his breath. In the federal government, a request for anything to be done the same day was almost unprecedented, unless the president wanted it.

"You've got to be kidding," Appelman said.

"It's up to the FAA," Danner answered nonchalantly. "If the airlines all want to be landing in Havana, they can wait until next week to deliver the list."

"I'll talk to Buzz Conway," Appelman said. "Maybe he can expedite it."

"Thanks, Norm." Danner hung up. He dialed Dixon Hadley, got Melinda, and asked to speak to the deputy director.

"Dixon? I'm going to Florida tomorrow."

"You've found something?"

"I think I know where the training's going on. There's a clown school on Big Pine Key."

"All right," Hadley said. "But be careful. SO protects the integrity of its own operations."

"I'm not surprised."

"They're fully responsible for their operational security. And they're good at it." Hadley sounded worried.

"I read you. But this is only the training phase. The agent, whoever he is, isn't operational yet."

"Even so."

"All right." Danner hung up.

Nancy came in with the airline tickets. She was young, blond, and had nice hips. She would probably have made an enjoyable companion for a weekend in Florida at that. He watched her walk out the door and sighed, wishing Julie were back.

Late that afternoon Appelman arrived with the list. He was a serious, round-faced young man who wore glasses and a perpetually worried expression. "Here it is," he said. "Seventeen hundred names. I really had to scare Conway to get it so fast."

"You're a good man, Norm. I really appreciate it."

Appelman basked in the praise. "I just wanted you to know it wasn't easy," he said.

"Sit down," Danner invited him." Our work is just beginning."

"What do you mean?"

"How many copies did FAA send over?"

"Two. I kept one and gave you one."

"Okay, I want you to Xerox two copies of your list. Get one over to IRS and one over to Social Security. Have them run the names through their computers."

Appelman frowned. "They won't do it. Because of the Privacy Act. It's almost impossible to get anything from either of them any more."

"You're the liaison for both agencies, right?"

"Sure. That's why I know they won't play."

"Go in back channel if you have to. Tell them there's no privacy problem. We don't want anything from their files sent over to us. Nothing."

Appelman looked puzzled. "Then what do you want?"

"Simply that they indicate the names of anyone on the list they can't identify."

"You mean anyone who didn't file an income tax return or doesn't have a Social Security number?"

"You've got it. Anyone who *isn't* in their files."

Appelman nodded slowly. "It's a very unusual request," he said. "But I don't really see why they should object. I can get them going on it tomorrow, I guess."

"Terrific. I'll be out of town, but I'll call you for the names. There shouldn't be very many."

Appelman got up to leave.

"There's one other little thing," Danner said.

"Yes?"

"Since I'll be out of town, I thought maybe you would do me a favor?"

Appelman appeared even more worried than usual. "If I can," he said cautiously.

"I was wondering if you could take your copy of the list down to Personnel and have them check it. Just to see if any name on the list matches that of any agency employee."

Appelman looked like a man who had stepped into quicksand and could not find a tree branch to grab onto. "I can do it," he said. "But, my God, does that mean the terrorists have someone here? Inside the agency?"

Danner wore a grave expression. "Norm, for your own personal safety, after you get the information I need, I'd advise you to forget that we ever talked."

"We haven't," Appelman said, bug-eyed. "Ever." He stood hesitantly for a moment. Then he opened the door and fled.

CHAPTER
TWENTY-SIX

The phone booth at Key West International Airport was hot and stuffy. It had a fan but the switch was broken. Danner was glad he hadn't worn a tie.

He fished a telephone credit card from his wallet. On the second try he got through to Appelman at headquarters, who sounded only slightly less alarmed than he had the previous afternoon.

"Any luck?" Danner asked.

"Some," Appelman replied. "I've got four names for you. One from Personnel that matches a name on the passenger lists. And three who don't have Social Security numbers. They're not in the IRS computer, either."

"Good work. Go ahead and give them to me."

"I'll start with the name from Personnel. It's Osmond J. Funkhauser." He spelled it. "We have someone by that name in the Covert Procurement Branch. His extension is 6024."

"Must be the same one," Danner said. "There can't be too many people named Osmond J. Funkhauser." He made a note of the name, although he could not imagine that SO would recruit a purchasing agent for operational purposes. Or if it did, that he would fly under his true name. Still, it was worth checking. Stranger things had happened in the agency.

"The other three names," Appelman continued, "are Juan Perez Escobar and Hector Diaz Fernandez, both of Bogota, and Dominique Cobb of New York City."

Danner wrote them down. "And no other names turned up?"

"Nope. That's it."

"Okay, thanks, Norm." Danner hung up, dialed area 703, and then Funkhauser's direct line at headquarters. Covert Procurement was a logistical support branch for the Directorate of Operations. They used "sterility codes," separate from the usual purchasing codes, to buy everything from ballpoint pens to automobiles, or fine crystal for the safe houses. Whenever something was needed for an operation that could not be traceable to the agency, Covert Procurement handled it. There was, Danner knew, plenty of room for hanky-panky, because the sterility codes could also be used to hide illegal purchases.

Funkhauser's intelligence assistant answered the call. "Mr. Funkhauser just stepped away from his desk," she said. But when Danner insisted it was important, the IA volunteered to go find him. After a moment, he came on the line.

"Mr. Funkhauser? This is Bill Danner in the DDO's office. Routine audit, nothing to worry about. I'd just like to know the purpose of your trip to Florida last month."

There was a long pause and then Funkhauser, his voice shaky, replied. "Oh my God. I knew this would happen. I knew it. And I'm only six months short of my twenty years." He sobbed, unable to continue.

"Take it easy," Danner said.

"It was the Kitcraft Corporation," Funkhauser went on. "The people we get some of our office supplies from. Mostly spiral notebooks, white pads, gum erasers, and rubber bands. I've dealt with them for years. They have a company yacht and invited me down for a fishing trip in the Florida Keys."

"Where'd you go?"

"Key Marathon and Largo. We also went over to Bimini, but only for one day, I swear."

"Bimini is British. That means you were in foreign waters. That could be serious."

"My God, I've never done anything like this before," Funkhauser wailed. "I knew this would happen. I'm the kind of person who never does anything wrong—I never even run a red light—and the minute I do, I get caught. I knew it."

"Technically, I should report this to the Inspector General," Danner said. He was grinning in the phone booth. "But I'm a fisherman myself. If you're that close to retirement, I guess I can let it go, this time. But don't ever do it again.''

Hope and relief flooded Funkhauser's voice. ''Never,'' he promised. ''Thank you, Mr. Danner, bless you. If you ever need anything, just call me. My first name is Osmond.''

''I know,'' said Danner. He hung up, laughing, and opened the door to the phone booth to get some air. He stepped out for a moment, removed his jacket, folded it up, and put it on top of his overnight bag.

Then he called Danny Keeler at the Drug Enforcement Administration in Washington. He had worked with Keeler on a couple of cases years ago, when DEA was known by a succession of other initials.

''Bill?'' Keeler's booming voice almost took his ear off. Danner wished he could sit down. He wondered whatever happened to phone booths with seats. ''I thought you'd gone to Canada,'' Keeler said. ''Years ago.''

''Just back on TDY,'' Danner explained. ''What do you have on a Juan Perez Escobar and a Hector Diaz Fernandez?''

''The Colombian coke queens.'' Keeler laughed. ''You're moving in pretty fast company. They're big dealers. I mean big. And they're lovers. Clever as hell, too. We haven't been able to bust them.''

''Where do they operate?''

''Out of Bogota and Miami. They have mansions in Colombia and on Star Island, in Biscayne Bay. And a fleet of boats. It's the usual pattern. Most of their stuff is grown in Peru and Bolivia and processed in Colombia. Then they move it into the States, flying in to little airstrips in South Florida. But some of it comes by boat to the Keys. There's a million little inlets and coves where they can land at night. And the coke is forty thousand dollars a pound wholesale and ten times that on the street.''

''We're in the wrong business.''

''Yeah. I'll say this for them. Their coke is the highest quality.'' Keeler laughed again. ''Well, you know, fags have good taste. It's a class operation.''

''Okay, thanks, Danny.'' Danner left the phone booth, took out a handkerchief and mopped his brow. Funkhauser, Perez, and Diaz. That left Dominique Cobb.

He found the car rental counter and had to wait on line for about ten minutes before he reached a clerk. She was Cuban, very pretty, with olive skin, dark hair, and flashing eyes. He signed the rental agreement and she handed him the keys. "Enjoy your stay," she said, giving him a big smile.

He checked his watch. It was late in the morning as he drove north on U.S. Highway 1, past Boca Chica Key, Halfmoon, Sugarloaf, Pirates Cove, Summerland, and Ramrod. Whoever named the islands, Danner thought, had a sense of romance. He might even enjoy the trip, he thought, if he didn't get wiped out by a geriatric driver coming at him on one of the narrow causeways.

Traffic was fairly heavy; it took Danner an hour to drive the thirty miles north from the airport to Big Pine Key, one of the larger islands in the string that stretched south and west of Miami and the Everglades to within ninety miles of Cuba.

The town of Big Pine was not exactly a metropolis: it consisted of a couple of convenience stores, a restaurant, and a single motel called the Tradewinds. He parked in the driveway and went into the lobby. At the front desk, a lisping room clerk seemed to have a lot of trouble finding his reservation. Finally he came up with it. "Sorry to keep you waiting," he said, smiling too much and handing Danner the key. "Front please."

A swarthy, shifty-looking bellman materialized, took the bag, and led Danner to the room. To his surprise, it turned out to be pleasant, overlooking the water, not the highway.

Danner tipped the bellman, locked the door, and peeled off his sweaty clothes. He jumped in the shower and washed away the airport phone booth. Then he got out, dried off, and put on some clean sports clothes.

Feeling better, he walked back to the lobby and dropped his oversized key off at the desk. The room clerk was still smiling.

"Do you have a Dominique Cobb registered?" Danner asked.

"Yes, indeed," the clerk said. "She's been with us for some time. I believe she's one of the students over at the clown school. We have several of them staying with us."

Danner asked how to get to the school.

"Just cross the highway and turn onto the blacktop. Drive inland as far as you can, past the trailer camps, and turn right toward Doctors Point. You'll come to a canal. It'll be about the fourth house on your left, a big white villa with a red-tile roof.''

''Thanks.''

The clerk kept smiling. ''Not at all.''

Danner got in the car and followed the directions. The land was flat and scrubby, with patches of sand and mangrove swamps off to his left. He passed several trailer camps and turned right. There were rows of retirement houses along the canal, so that residents could keep their powerboats moored by their front doors.

He pulled up in front of a large Spanish-style house on the water with a red-tile roof. There was no sign on the building, but it was the only place that matched the motel clerk's description.

Danner walked up the driveway and tried the front door. It was open and he stepped inside. Several students, some in clown costume, were lounging around in the large front hall. Most of them looked to be in their twenties. One or two gave him a curious glance, but no one challenged him.

There were classrooms on either side of the hallway, and groups of students were wandering in to one of them from the garden at the rear of the house. Apparently a class was about to begin. Danner slipped in with the last of the stragglers.

He found himself in a large room in which several long tables had been set up with small mirrors spaced at three-foot intervals. About three dozen students sat at the tables. Danner took a seat near the rear.

In a moment, a fat man dressed in blue jeans and a white T-shirt did a forward somersault into the room and landed gracefully on his feet. ''Ta-da,'' he said with a flourish of his arms. The class applauded.

Danner asked the student on his right which of the brothers it was.

''Chico,'' she whispered. ''Pepe is the short one. He's not here yet.''

Danner stuck out his hand. ''Bill Morrissey of *The Miami Herald*,'' he said. ''I'm doing a feature on the school.''

Chico Alvarez was a big, dark-skinned man of about fifty, with a jet-black mustache. He smiled at the students, displaying a lot of white teeth. "This afternoon we start off again with makeup class. The first two tables will do *auguste*, the rest of you whiteface. Pay attention and let's try to do better than yesterday."

Danner wondered why the brothers had set up their school for clowns in such an out-of-the-way place. Probably, he thought, because the rent was low and the good weather allowed them to work out of doors most of the year.

Alvarez was walking among the students, watching. "*Cuidado!* Don't get the greasepaint into your ears," he said. "Just a little on the outside. And always keep your eyes closed when you powder."

The girl Danner had spoken to carefully wiped away portions of the greasepaint on her cheeks, on the end of her nose, and in two lines coming straight up from her eyebrows.

"Why are you taking the stuff off?" Danner asked. "You just put it on."

"You have to remove it in the places where you're going to put on the colors," she said. "I want red on my cheeks. If I put it on over the white, it will turn pink."

She picked up a white cotton sock filled with baby powder and patted down her face, keeping her eyes tightly closed. Then from a bottle, she poured a little olive oil into the palm of her hand. She mixed in some red greasepaint and rubbed it around. "The oil dilutes it and makes it a little easier to work with," she said.

With her fingers she painted her cheeks and the end of her nose red, then filled in the lines radiating from her eyebrows in blue. She powdered after applying each color. Using a matchstick, she drew black eyebrows and made a face at Danner.

"Not bad," he said. "Pretty good, in fact."

The *auguste* clowns were painting on mouths with grotesque lower lips, some reaching down to the bottom of their chins. All but a few were putting on red noses—hollowed-out plastic balls attached with an elastic band that went around the back of the head. Danner watched the students, wondering which one might be Dominique Cobb.

Chico intervened here and there, advising the students when he thought they were doing something wrong. "Follow the nat-

246 *David Wise*

ural geography of your face," he instructed them. "Take advantage of the lines you already have."

In a few minutes, they were done. Each of the students had on a different clown face.

"Now you look like clowns," Chico said. "But it's only the beginning. If you're going to succeed in the circus, you need more than greasepaint. You have to develop a clown personality and *be* that person. You can't just go out in a clown face and a costume and wave your arms and think people are going to laugh. They won't. Clowns need individuality, and they need gags, of course. This morning we're going to work on gags again."

As he spoke, a wiry, muscular man about half his size came quietly into the room and sat down on a stool in the front of the room. Pepe Alvarez moved like a very good acrobat. He had a highly mobile face that constantly changed expression. Danner imagined he could be very funny.

"Okay," Pepe said to the class. "Let's start by reviewing what we've learned so far. What are the three basic kinds of clown gags?"

A skinny youth sitting in front of Danner raised his hand. "Ring gags and stop gags."

"Pretty good," Chico said. "One and one makes three. You're going to be a terrific juggler, Larry."

The class guffawed, and Danner imagined that the young clown was blushing under his pink greasepaint.

"Walkarounds," Larry blurted out. "That's the third kind."

The class applauded. Chico was clapping on his stool like a seal and Danner joined in the laughter.

"Ring gags are called ring gags," Pepe said, "because they take place in the ring. They're the classic set gags that clowns have used for years like the wrong tooth gag. The clown dentist has a pair of oversized pliers and pulls out a huge foam rubber tooth from the patient, who then howls that it's the wrong one. Or the sausage machine, where a dog is dropped into a meat grinder and a string of sausages comes out the other end. Now, this morning I want to try the scrubwoman and the thieves again. I wasn't satisfied with it yesterday."

Several students groaned.

"Okay," Pepe sang out. "Thieves to the front." A blond

woman in whiteface, wearing a derby, got up and went to the front of the room, joined by Larry.

"Scrubwoman," Pepe ordered.

A dark-haired, heavyset youth made up as an *auguste* came forward. Chico handed him a mop and a red wig, which he put on. He gave the blond clown a bundle of dowel sticks painted red and wrapped in wire with a long fuse hanging down. "The dynamite," he said. "This chair will be the safe."

"Okay," Chico yelled, "start the ring gag."

The scrubwoman started swabbing the floor with exaggerated gestures. The two thieves stole in and made for the safe. The Chaplinesque woman with the derby played the safecracker. She was good. She put her ear to the tumblers, spun an imaginary dial, and listened. She shook her head; no luck. She motioned for the dynamite.

Larry brought the bundle of sticks over and placed it next to the safe. Then he lit a match on his rear end, and with an elaborate gesture, lit the fuse. The thieves stole back out of the way.

"C'mon," Pepe said. "Look scared. There's going to be a big bang, right? One of you put your hands in your ears. That's it, Larry. You'll make a clown yet. You, Dominique, cover your eyes."

Danner started at the name. Cobb was the woman in the derby! The charlady, mopping closer to the safe, spotted the dynamite, looked around, and seeing the thieves, assumed that they had left it by mistake. She picked up the dynamite with the sputtering fuse and threw it at the thieves. Larry caught it. Dominique motioned frantically to him to get rid of it. Larry tossed it back to the scrubwoman. The dynamite went back and forth a few times. Finally the thieves put it down by the safe again and ran.

"Policeman, get ready!" Pepe shouted. A girl wearing a Keystone Cop helmet edged up from the back of the room.

"Boom!" Pepe shouted. "The safe has just exploded, and the smoke is coming out. Cue, policeman."

The Keystone Cop rushed to the front, blowing her whistle and pulling out an imaginary gun. She chased the thieves around the room.

"Now, remember," Chico said as the chase went on full tilt, "the blowoff of this gag is when the policeman—I should say policewoman—fires her gun. If this were a real performance, someone would be standing in the wings ready to fire a blank in a shotgun. The minute you thieves hear the shotgun blast, you would push the button on your ass pads.''

The class giggled. "Don't laugh. The ass pads are metal and they protect your rear end from getting burned. When you push the button, the charge from the battery will ignite the thimbleful of black gunpowder attached to the pad. The smoke will pour out as though you were both nailed in the butt with one shot. Go!''

The cop took aim and fired. "Boom!" the class shouted in unison. Dominique and Larry reacted as though they had just been shot in the tail; everybody laughed, Pepe and Chico included.

"Very nice," Chico said. "Everyone's timing was much better. Remember, the best teacher is the audience. You do something and it falls flat, you learn. There's nothing worse than people sitting there with stone faces.''

Pepe looked at his watch. "Okay, everybody," he said. "Let's take a break. Five minutes.''

About half the students piled out of the classroom, heading for the garden, but others stayed behind, talking in small groups. Several, including the woman in the derby, remained at the tables, working on their makeup.

Danner moved to one side, where he could get a better look at the woman called Dominique. She was not wearing a wig, but her face was covered with thick greasepaint and she had on a big red nose. Her hair was the wrong color, but there could be no doubt.

Quietly, he slipped into the empty chair next to her. She turned and stared at him, her clown face forming a mask of fear and surprise.

Danner smiled. "Hello, Julie.''

CHAPTER
TWENTY-SEVEN

Julie could only stare at him, her green eyes wide. She sat there wordlessly in her greasepaint and costume, like a mime.

"We can't talk here," she said finally. "Come outside."

He followed her into the garden. They walked over to the edge of the water, well away from the other students, who were smoking and chatting.

"What are you doing here?" she said, her voice low and intense.

"We heard that SO was training a clown. Hadley asked me to look into it."

"My God. Nobody is supposed to know I'm here. I don't know what to do."

"I'd like to kiss you," Danner said quietly. "But your nose is in the way."

It broke the tension. Julie started to laugh, and then they both laughed.

The students were drifting back toward the house. "We'll talk later," she said. "I have to go back in now."

He followed her into the classroom and took his seat at the back again.

Chico continued the lecture on gags. "Okay," he said. "The clown car is another famous ring gag. We'll be practicing with that later in the semester. The clown car is a real car, with an engine, but the insides have been taken out so the passenger compartment is just a shell. That's how so many clowns can fit in."

The girl who had played the cop raised her hand. "What's the best way to think up a ring gag?" she asked. "In other words, how can we develop our own material?"

"The way we usually do it is to start with the blowoff and work backwards," Chico replied. "For example, maybe you want to have a big clown shrink into a little clown. So you decide to use a washing machine. You have a midget clown hide in the machine when you roll it out into the ring. Then maybe you have two women clowns getting into a fight. They throw buckets of water at each other and slap each other around noisily. Then one woman throws the other into the machine and turns it on. After a minute, you open up the washing machine and out pops the midget."

The class laughed. "Why is it funny?" Larry asked.

"Surprise," Pepe replied. "Most clown gags are built on three things: surprise, public embarrassment—somebody dropping their pants always gets a laugh—and deflation; throw a snowball at a man in a top hat, or have a dignified matron take a pratfall on a banana peel."

Chico interrupted: "A lot of gags, like the midget in the washing machine, involve transformation. For example, instead of the midget popping out, you could have the woman come out through the wringer absolutely flat. The clown stays inside the washing machine, of course, and we use a plywood prop painted to look like the clown. Or the old Turkish bath gag, where a big clown is steamed into a midget. The dog that turns into sausages is a transformation gag, too."

Pepe explained the difference between other kinds of clown gags. "A stop gag is performed on the hippodrome track," he said. "It takes about thirty seconds. Then the clown moves on and stops in front of another section and repeats it."

"A walkaround is a sight gag," he continued. "And just like it sounds, the clown doesn't stop, he keeps walking around the track. You might have a flower in one hand and a big fake onion in the other. When you eat the onion and breathe on the flower, it falls over. One of my favorites is the old water-spraying suit. The clown looks like he's been shot full of holes. He drinks a cup of water, and it sprays out of his body like he's a Swiss cheese."

Hardly pausing for breath, Pepe launched into a discussion of the history of clowning. He talked about mimes in ancient Greece, court jesters and buffoons, and harlequins who worked with mountebanks, the medicine men of the Middle Ages.

"You've all heard of Grock, the great Swiss clown. And the three Fratellini brothers, who were the toast of Paris in the 1920s."

"What about Soviet clowns?" a student asked. "Aren't some of them pretty good?"

"Oh, yes," Pepe answered. "Russia has a strong tradition of mimes and troubadours, the *skomorokhi*. And Russia has produced some famous clowns in our own century. One of them, Vitaly Lazarenko, led marches on stilts during the Revolution."

"What about Popov?" another student asked.

"The greatest of the Soviet Clowns," Pepe said. "A fantastic juggler and slack-wire artist. His most famous gag is the fireball. He's a doctor and he peers down the throat of a drunk, using a match to see better. All of a sudden—whoosh, out comes the fireball from the patient's throat. It's a great blow-off."

It was late afternoon by the time classes were dismissed. Julie excused herself and went to the dressing rooms to take off her makeup.

Danner waited for her in the car. They drove out to the point and parked by the water.

Julie touched his hand. "I'm glad to see you," she said.

"You were gone too long. I missed you."

She brushed her hair back. "I felt the same way. But you've put me in a very tight spot by coming here. If I say anything, I may be placing you in jeopardy."

"Why?"

"The SO security hoods are wild men. Cowboys. I can't predict what they might do."

Danner shrugged. "Then don't say anything."

"If I don't report you, I'm endangering the operation."

It was late in the day and a lot of powerboats were heading into the canal, Danner noticed. People who retired to Big Pine Key seemed to spend all of their time fishing.

"I don't know how you found out," Julie added. "I don't expect you to tell me. But by the rules I should inform SO we've been damaged.'' She bit her lip. "Except I can't, dammit.''

"I'm sorry. I didn't know it was you. Not until I saw you in class this afternoon.''

She was silent, staring straight ahead at the water.

"Why clown school?'' he asked gently. "What's going on?''

"I don't know yet. I won't be briefed on the operation until the training is over.''

"Oh.''

She looked at him. "You sound as though you don't believe me.''

"I think I believe you.'' It would be normal procedure on a high-security operation to train an agent before revealing the mission.

"Then what's the problem?''

Danner exhaled. "I didn't want to get into this. You said I held back when we made love. I guess the reason is that I haven't trusted you completely.''

"But why?'' She searched his face.

"Partly because you work for SO, and so did Rossi. But mostly because of Vienna.''

"What about Vienna? I don't understand.''

"That night in your apartment. You knew I was going to Vienna. You talked about what a beautiful city it was. Your favorite.''

"But you *said* you were going there.''

"I didn't. I never mentioned Vienna.''

"You must have.''

"No. I'm sure.''

She avoided his eyes. "Let's get some air,'' she said.

They got out of the car. The sun was setting over the Gulf of Mexico, turning the palm trees gold. They walked along by the water's edge.

Julie stopped and faced him. "All right,'' she said. "I made a mistake. A slip. We knew where you were going.''

Danner tried to control the anger he felt. "Jesus Christ,'' he said. "Even you.''

"You don't understand.'' She touched his arm. "SO has been tracking you from the beginning. But there was nothing wrong with it. The director asked us to. I suppose he was checking up to make sure you did your job. I saw the traffic.''

"And our meeting, the matchbook, our love for each other, was all of that because the director asked you to?''

"For God sakes, Bill.'' Her eyes flashed. "Of course not. How could you even think that?'' She put her arms around him and burrowed her head into his shoulder. He hesitated, then put his hand on her cheek.

She looked up and there were tears rolling down her face.

"I'm sorry,'' he said. "It's the damn agency. It's even created suspicion between us. I'm sorry.'' He shook his head.

"You mustn't blame everything on the agency. You've been doing that number for twenty years. First you blamed the agency for Lisa, then for the divorce, then for Carrie's kidnapping, now for our problems.''

"And with good reason.''

"The agency isn't evil, it's the world we're trying to cope with. Blame human beings, blame Adam and Eve for God's sake, but don't blame the agency.''

Danner laughed. "I'm not holding the agency responsible for original sin. But we've corrupted the ideals we were set up to defend. Like a serpent eating its tail. You're loyal to them. I know better. Believe me, you won't find salvation in the agency.''

"I'm not seeking salvation. I'm just trying to do my job.''

"So am I.''

"And have you?'' Her voice was challenging.

"What do you mean?''

"Have you found the mole? That's why you were brought back, isn't it?''

It was Danner's turn for silence.

"You see?'' Julie said. "I'm not the only one who isn't telling everything. You do the same.''

"All right. You've got a point. I can't talk about the mole. But I was asked to find the agent being trained as a clown. And to find out why. I've done half of that. I found you, but I don't know why you're being trained. You don't either, you say. Okay, I believe you.''

She kissed him on the cheek. "That's a start.''

"I'll be going back to Langley in the morning. But Julie—" He broke off.

"Yes?"

"Through all this agency shit and double dealing, and the secrecy and concealment that we're surrounded by, drowning in, we have to find something we can hold onto and believe in. To keep from going under. I thought once that could be each other. And maybe it still could. I'm not saying it is, but maybe it could."

They held on to each other for a long time, saying nothing. And finally Julie looked up at him, and they sought each other's eyes, and she said, "Yes, maybe it could."

It was dark by the time they got back to the motel. Danner parked and suggested they have dinner at the little restaurant across the highway. They walked toward the lobby entrance.

"I want to freshen up for a while," Julie said. "How about a drink in my room before dinner, in, say, half an hour?"

"I'll be there."

Danner went back to his room, stripped off his clothes, and got in the shower. The flow was powerful and the water felt good on his back and shoulders.

He dried off, got dressed, and went up to Julie's room. She opened the door and he went in. She looked lovely. She was wearing a navy blue skirt and a white silk blouse that accentuated her deep tan.

"I'll make the drinks," Danner offered. "What will it be?"

Julie thought a moment. "Vodka and tonic," she said.

Danner smiled. "That's what you were drinking the first time we met." He paused. "You look sensational."

"Thank you." She came over and kissed him lightly on the lips.

"I'm glad we talked," she said. She smoothed the lapel on his jacket. It was a small gesture but it bespoke their intimacy. "I love you," she said.

"And I love you." He put his arms around her and kissed her.

"But love," Julie said. "It isn't just reaching out to someone to keep from drowning."

"Then what is it?"

"Love is caring about the other person, caring about what happens to them, whether they're happy and fulfilled. Not because of how that affects you, because it does, but for the sake of the other person."

Danner thought about it. "I care about you that way," he said. "And that's why I wish you didn't work for the agency."

"It's my choice. You did, after all, for twenty years."

"I know. And the truth is that part of me is still drawn to it, even now. I never faced that before. It's seductive. That's why you should get out. Before it's too late." He took some ice for the glasses from the bucket and busied himself making the drinks.

While he did, Julie wandered out on the balcony. It was sparsely furnished, with two outdoor chairs and a little table between them. He brought the drinks. She was standing at the railing in the moonlight, and the tropical breeze caught her hair, ruffling it gently.

"Are you counting the stars?" he asked.

She turned, took both drinks from his hands, and set them on the table. Then she put her arms around him and gave him a kiss that neither of them wanted to end.

When it did, he took her hand, and they walked back into the room. They embraced again and he began unbuttoning her blouse slowly. Dinner could wait.

CHAPTER
TWENTY-EIGHT

Standing in line to get through the badge machine in the lobby, Danner found himself right behind Sandy Berens.

She flashed him a smile. "Where'd you get that beautiful tan?"

"Bermuda," he lied. "I took some leave."

"Julie's still off in Abu Dhabi, I guess, getting sand in her shoes. She doesn't answer her phone at home or at her office."

"Yeah. It's getting to be a long trip. How's everything in Imagery?"

"The usual. Sam's very upbeat these days. He's got a new girlfriend, in Central Reference."

"I know."

They checked through and rode the elevator together. Danner got off at the fifth floor and went to his office. He checked the inhouse telephone directory and dialed Violet Lemley in Personnel.

"This is William Danner," he said when she came on the line. "Code 3941. Level one clearance. Verification for access, extension 6161, the DDO."

"Yes, sir."

"I want to see your file on Julie Nichols. N-i-c-h-o-l-s. She works in SO." Danner gave her his room number and she promised to have the file sent up.

Next, he dialed Melinda and asked to see Dixon Hadley. She gave him an appointment for 11:00 A.M. He went downstairs for a cup of coffee and ran into Kit Benson. Danner asked how Eric was getting along at the *Post*.

"Okay," Benson said. "But some days he thinks he'll never write about anything but sewage treatment plants. He gets discouraged."

"I called him the other day," Danner said. "He checked something for me. He's a nice kid."

"Yeah." Benson shook his head resignedly. "But I never figured any son of mine would work for a newspaper. He wants to be an investigative reporter, so he can expose things. And me in the business of keeping secrets for twenty-five years."

"Maybe that's why he did it."

"I never thought of that," Benson said, rubbing his chin. "You know, you might be right."

Danner finished his coffee and went back up to the office. He pulled a picture of Carrie from his wallet and looked at it. Then he stared out the window for a long time.

A knock on the door interrupted his thoughts. It was the messenger from Personnel. He signed for the envelope, sat down and opened it.

The file was in a brown manila folder, with metal clips on the top, so that the pages flipped up. It was in reverse chronological order, with the most recent entries uppermost.

He felt uncomfortable, knowing he was violating her deepest privacy. But there was no alternative. He began at the beginning at the back of the file. The first document was a basic biographical sheet. Julie Lanier Nichols had been born on May 6, 1956, in Philadelphia, the daughter of Sinclair and Katherine Nichols. Because Sinclair Nichols was a foreign service officer, she had lived abroad with her parents in a series of posts, including France, Austria, Italy, Belgium, and—here Danner was startled—the Soviet Union. Julie had never mentioned that she had lived there.

He read on. There was a Potential Recruitment Report from Professor Alison Bently of Bryn Mawr College, dated March 1976, suggesting that Miss Nichols, because of her fluency in several foreign languages, her international background, and her father's government service, would be an excellent candidate for agency recruitment. The PRR was stamped "Approved" by Personnel. It was followed by a second report from

Bentley stating that Nichols had been recruited in the spring of
her senior year.

The file contained the usual lengthy application form that
Julie had filled out, an extensive background check by the Office of Security, and the results of a polygraph test that had been
administered when she was accepted for employment. The subject, according to the polygraph report, drank alcohol in moder-
ation, had never used hard drugs, and had engaged in sexual
intercourse with four different men while an undergraduate at
Bryn Mawr. Danner was surprised to find himself feeling jealous; he supposed the number was actually low for a Bryn Mawr
student.

There was a copy of the secrecy agreement Julie had signed
when she joined the CIA in 1977, in which she promised never
to reveal classified information that she had learned in the
course of her employment. The file showed that after her JOT
training, she had been assigned to the Central Cover Staff of the
Directorate of Operations. The following year, the polygraph
test had been readministered, with no negative results. The periodic evaluation reports from her supervisors all gave her high
ratings.

Under languages, she was listed as fluent in English, French,
German, Italian, and Russian. Danner checked back to the first
document in the file. Sinclair Nichols had been posted to
Moscow as second secretary of the American Embassy from
1962 to 1964 when Julie would have been six to eight years
old—an ideal time to learn a language.

One other item caught Danner's eye. During her weeks at
ISOLATION base, the agency's code name for The Farm, Julie
had distinguished herself on the rifle range. Most trainees at
Camp Peary were content to be rated as a Marksman. In the box
that evaluated her ability with firearms, Julie Nichols was listed
as a Sharpshooter.

He checked his watch. It was time for his meeting with Hadley. He found the DDO ministering to Socrates, leaning over
the birdcage with an eye dropper. "Vitamins," he explained.
"For his water dish."

"How's he been?" Danner asked, hoping that perhaps some
rare macaw affliction might have struck.

"Not too well," the deputy director replied gravely. "He's

been off his feed. I give him parrot mix—you know, sunflower seed, peanuts, hot peppers, all ground up together. But he's been very picky of late. Hardly touches the stuff. I'm hoping some extra vitamins will help."

"Can't hurt," Danner said. "Might pep him up a little."

Hadley waved him to a chair. "Well," he asked, "did you find him?"

"Her."

Hadley looked surprised. "Who is she?"

"Julie Nichols. I know her. She's living in Big Pine Key at the Tradewinds Motel under the name of Dominique Cobb. And she's enrolled as a student at the clown school."

"What's she learning?"

"Makeup, gags, slaps and falls, acrobatics, unicycling, you name it. They're teaching her whatever she needs to know to be a professional circus clown."

"Aaarwk!" Socrates screeched. "Need to know!"

"But what can the objective be?" Hadley asked.

"She wouldn't say. My guess is it's to provide access to the target."

"She'll tell SO you found her, I suppose. That will complicate matters."

"I don't think she will. I told you, I know her."

"I see." Hadley cleared his throat. "Did she say anything at all about the operation?"

"Nothing. She claimed she hadn't been briefed yet. But I read her personnel file this morning. I learned two things I didn't know. She's fluent in Russian and she's a sharpshooter."

"So the target is in the Soviet Union."

"Yes. The Russians are big on circuses, you know. You remember their famous clown, Popov? And I think they have bears that do remarkable things, like roller-skate and ride motorcycles."

"Motorcycles? They have bears that ride motorcycles?" Hadley looked distressed.

"I've heard they do. And dancing cows."

Hadley shook his head. "It's just one more example of an area where we've relaxed and become soft and flabby while they've pulled ahead of us."

"I don't suppose it really matters. I mean it's not like it involved national security, or anything."

The DDO got up and began pacing the room. "No, but it's symptomatic. And the target. Do you have any clues about the target?"

"I'm working on it. I suppose what we should do next is to access the SO computer somehow. We've got to know the details of the operation."

"That will be very difficult. There are only a few terminals and they're all kept in an extremely high-security area, as is the computer itself. The SO computer system is completely separate from ours."

"I know that. But do I have your permission to talk to Roudebush in Lockpicking?"

Hadley hesitated. "Well, I don't see why not," he said after a moment. "Provided that you don't tell him what you really have in mind."

"All right," Danner said, getting up to go. "I hope the vitamins help."

The deputy director looked at him suspiciously. "It's good of you to care."

Danner returned to his office and found a free terminal for the DDO computer across the hall in Near Eastern Operations. He logged on and asked the computer to tell him what foreign government officials had circus interests or backgrounds.

After a few moments he got back three readouts. Ian Blackwood, the Minister of Defense of New Zealand, had once been a circus acrobat. Esmeralda Gonzales Ortega, the wife of the president of Bolivia, was an ex-trapeze artist who had been quite successful in Europe two decades earlier. And Yuri Vladimirovich Kalin, general secretary of the Communist Party, president of the Soviet Union, had a daughter, Galina, who was married to a star of the Moscow Circus. Kalin, the computer added, was himself a circus buff who attended performances whenever his duties permitted.

Everything fit now. Julie spoke Russian, she was a crack shot, and her target was Yuri Kalin. Her mission was to kill him at the circus. He felt numb at the enormity of the plot, and trapped by the dilemmas it posed for him.

He loved Julie; he could not change that. Yet if she succeeded, he would never get his daughter back. He knew that instinctively. And Julie herself would not get out of Moscow alive; he was sure of it. She was expendable. Like Max Stein.

Jordan had ordered the operation. He alone controlled SO. Now it was clear what Jordan had meant by "certain matters" to be resolved.

Danner quickly returned to his office and dialed the Soviet Russia Division. He waited for Peter Ostrovsky, an old SR hand whom he knew, to come on the line.

"Peter? Bill Danner." He tried to keep his voice from betraying the urgency he felt. "I need to know the performance dates of the Moscow Circus."

"Which one? They have two, you know."

"I didn't know."

"There's the old circus, or *stariy cirk*, at—just a minute and I'll check it for you." Danner heard some pages turning. "At 13 Tsvetnoi Boulevard. It's very small and traditional, and a little down at the heels. The big, glamorous one is the new circus, or *novyi cirk*, out in the Lenin Hills area, near the university. Here it is, at 17 Prospekt Vernadskogo. It's in a very snazzy modern arena."

"And the dates?"

"Well, this time of year both troupes are in Moscow, not on tour. They perform some afternoons at three and almost every night, normally at seven o'clock."

"Thanks, Peter. You certainly have everything at your fingertips."

"Well, normally I wouldn't. But it's funny the way things run in cycles."

"How do you mean?"

"Well, the reason I'm up on all this is that only about a week ago I was asked for the same information. By somebody in SO."

The first thing that struck one about Roudebush was that he was extraordinarily fat. His stomach rolled over his belt and his jowls and double chin almost hid his collar. He kept a box of chocolates on his desk and helped himself frequently during the day. He had long ago given up trying to be anything but fat. He was also the best lockpicker in CIA, a man whose pudgy fingers could perform miracles with pin tumblers, wafer discs, and combination locks. Roudebush's idea of a good joke was to leave a chocolate, or sometimes even a bottle of champagne, inside a friend's safe to which he did not have the combination.

He sat now in his office, hands clasped across his belly like a silent Buddha, blinking at Danner through his thick spectacles. It was Roudebush who had provided the key to the skylight on Wellington Lloyd's roof, and Danner began by thanking him.

"I knew it would work okay," Roudebush replied in a gravelly voice, "once you showed us the picture. Still, I'm glad to hear it. Chocolate?" He offered the box to Danner. "These are great. Some have cherry syrup inside and some have coconut and almonds."

Danner took one. It was caramel and stuck to his teeth.

"Good, huh?" Roudebush asked.

"Delicious," Danner replied. "But let me tell you why I'm here. I have a requirement to get through a high-security lock, almost certainly pin tumbler. I can try it with picks, but I wondered if you had something more sophisticated."

"Why don't you take one of our people along with you?" Roudebush asked. "Let us handle it."

"Can't," Danner said.

Roudebush took off his glasses and polished them with the end of his tie. His hair looked like his barber had used a sugar bowl to cut it. The effect was to make him look even fatter, because it exposed the folds of flesh on the back of his neck.

He inspected his glasses, holding them up against the lights in the ceiling. Satisfied, he put them back on. "We do have something you could use," he said. "You could send them a Valentine." He grinned at Danner's bewildered expression.

"What do you mean?" Danner asked.

"Valentine is a gadget we have that's practically foolproof. But you have to have access to the target twice."

"I can do that."

Roudebush got up and moved, surprisingly nimbly, to a wall safe. He spun the dial, and removed a device with a thin metal rod on one end and wires leading to what looked like a meter or dial.

"The little rod vibrates electronically when you push this button," Roudebush said. "You insert the rod in the keyhole and the vibrations can read the length of the tumblers. That's translated into numbers that will show up on your LED dial, here. Just write the numbers down as you get the digital read-out, give them to us, and we'll machine the key. The numbers will tell us how deep to make the cuts to bring the pins up to the shear line, so that the plug will turn and the lock will open.''

Roudebush packed the device into a small leather case and handed it over. ''Thanks,'' Danner said. ''I'll be back with the readout as soon as I can access the target.''

''I hope it's a pretty girl's apartment,'' Roudebush said with a leer. ''I always like to think we send Valentine to a pretty girl.''

He put out a fat hand and Danner forced himself to shake it. He returned to his office and dropped off Valentine. Then he went downstairs to Data Processing and asked to see Tom Sandifer.

In a moment Sandifer came out and escorted him back to his small office. He was a young man in his late twenties, with a dark beard and mustache and a self-assured manner.

Sandifer stuck out his hand with a friendly grin. ''Dixon Hadley's office said to give you whatever you needed. What's up?''

''I have to penetrate a high-security computer and get into the data base. I need you to tell me how.''

Sandifer whistled. ''That's going to be tough. Where is it located?''

Danner hesitated. ''In the United States. For operational reasons, that's about all I can tell you.''

''Well, let me start by asking what you know about the system. What's the PCZ like?''

Danner looked at him blankly.

''Physical Control Zone. In other words, how well is it protected?''

''It's well guarded, and in a secure installation''—Danner saw no reason to tell Sandifer he meant the building they were sitting in—''but I can gain access to a terminal.''

''Good. For two reasons. If they rely on their physical security, there are less likely to be too many protective measures built into the system itself. The less access, the less need for software controls." He stroked his beard. "Do you know anything about their authentication system?"

He remembered Julie explaining the SO computer to him on the Monument grounds. "I know a password I can use to log on. It belongs to someone else."

Sandifer smiled broadly. "Excellent. Then you can go in piggyback, masquerading with someone else's user ID. The problem is that there will be multi-levels of security. The minute you seek access to specific files, the computer will ask you for another password. Probably for several, the deeper you go into the data base."

"That's where I need your help."

Sandifer thought for a moment. "In a dedicated system like that, the main frame computer will probably be locked up tight as a drum and equipped with TEMPEST. That's a security system approved by NSA. It means that the computer is protected against electronic emanations that could be picked up by a hostile service."

Danner thought of the catering trucks circling the agency and nodded.

"I suppose there's no way you could gain access to the Data Base Administrator's password?"

"No."

"Too bad. The DBA can see everything in the system, of course. He has unrestricted access."

"Wouldn't that be nice." Danner grinned.

"Still, if you can get access to a terminal and log on, as you say you can, you're halfway there. There are a lot of methods for penetrating a computer," Sandifer added, adopting a professorial air. "Browsing, for example. If you know file names, you can sometimes browse through them and look for what you want."

Danner shook his head. "I don't know the file names," he said. "It's one of the things I'm looking for. A particular file."

"Another way we call scavenging. When a user deletes material from his file, it isn't erased. It's still in the memory. You can create a direct access file, tell the computer to retrieve an item near the end of the new file, and it will print out everything above it, including the old material. The problem is you're only getting the discards, scraps. And you'd almost have to be the next user, before the discarded stuff gets overwritten.''

"No good for my purposes," Danner said. "I need full text, and I can't be sure of next-use access. In fact, it's unlikely. ''

"We could try a NAK attack," Sandifer said doubtfully. "You interrupt a demand for a password, for example, and sometimes the computer can be spoofed into leapfrogging over the security barriers and putting you in the file you want. But the system you describe probably wouldn't have that vulnerability.''

"Where does that leave us?'' Danner asked.

"With only one recourse. We'll have to use brute force. Attack the CPU with a program that will try thousands of possible passwords until it hits on the right one.''

"Won't that take a lot of time?''

"Yes. That's the disadvantage. But you don't have much choice.''

"The program will try every possible combination of the letters of the alphabet?''

"Not unless you're willing to spend your golden years at the keyboard. NSA is set up to do that, using monster computers like Cray-1. We're going to use a microcomputer.''

"So you have to find shortcuts.''

"Right. First of all, you may log on with an alphanumeric password that combines letters and numbers. But after that, most passwords are simple English words. Because people have to remember them. Our own computers are programmed to take long, complex passwords. And what do people use? 'Boxcar' or 'Puppy.' We see it all the time.''

"So the microcomputer will try all possible combinations of something short, say five letters?''

Sandifer shook his head. "No." He punched out some numbers on a pocket calculator. "You see, even with five letters, if you had the micro try every possible permutation, you would have to do twenty-six to the fifth power, or 11,881,376 tries. That's how many times five letters of the alphabet could be used to make different passwords.''

"But they wouldn't all be real words.''

"That's the point. So we don't have to try them all. It gets worse as you go up the scale. With a six-letter password, you'd have to try 308,915,776 permutations, twenty-six times as many. And with a password that used all twenty-six letters of the alphabet, there is no way in English to express the number of permutations." He punched out some more numbers. "It would be a number greater than six followed by thirty-six zeros. To give you some idea, a trillion has only twelve zeros."

"So what's the solution?"

"A dictionary. Most computers have them now. You know, you run a dictionary to see if there are any misspelled words in a manuscript, for example. We can use the same principle here."

"I think I understand. How would it work?"

"Most dictionaries are eighty or a hundred thousand words. We don't have to go that high. The vocabulary of an educated adult might be, oh, thirty thousand words. Nobody knows for sure. But to find a password, we don't have to try every permutation. We can program the micro to search for the combinations of letters that have meaning. In short, words."

Danner nodded.

Sandifer continued. "I assume you want something small and portable. We'll fit you out with an Epson HX-20 with a disc drive. It's a Japanese micro, eight by eleven inches, so you can easily put it in an attaché case. It has a processing chip, a couple of memory chips, a display, and a keyboard. That's all you need."

"You'll write the program?"

"Oh sure." He thought a moment. "I think we'll set it up with the words ordered sequentially according to frequency. We'll add in a thousand of the most commonly used proper nouns. A total of thirty thousand words. If you had to run the whole program, it might take an hour. But there's at least a fifty percent chance you'll hit on the right password in half that time."

Danner arose. "Thanks a million. I really appreciate it."

"No problem. Come back tomorrow about this time and I'll have your Epson, with the program all ready to roll on a floppy disc." He shook hands. "Oh, and good luck."

Danner returned to his office. At six o'clock he went down to the cafeteria and had dinner—overdone roast beef and mashed potatoes with a lot of brown gravy. The mixed vegetables proved to be mostly lima beans. Danner wondered whether the KGB secretly ran the agency's cafeteria.

He dropped by the DDO employees' lounge and watched the evening news on television. President Forbes was defending his economic program against attack in Congress. He called on the American people to give him more time to correct the mistakes of the past.

Around nine o'clock, he wandered back up to the fifth floor and returned to his office. The building was mostly empty now, except for the watch officers in the ops center and a few employees working late. Down in the pit, the workmen would be methodically destroying the day's take of classified waste. Guards in their blue uniforms patrolled the corridors, but Danner did not run into any on the way back to his office.

He waited at his desk impatiently as the hours ticked by. Shortly after midnight, he took the Valentine and walked down to the A corridor. He went up the stairwell to the sixth floor and stepped out into the hall. There was no one in sight.

He made his way to a door marked "Special Operations— Restricted Area." In smaller letters, a sign warned: "Personnel Without SO Clearance Are Forbidden to Proceed Beyond This Point."

Danner looked in both directions. There was no guard in sight, but he would have to work quickly. Taking the device from its case, he inserted the thin metal rod into the keyway of the lock and pushed a button. He could feel the rod vibrating inside the lock. A series of red numbers were flashing on the dial and he wrote them down. He removed the rod, put Valentine back in its case, and started for the stairwell. A guard, a tall, alert-looking black man, rounded the corner and headed toward him. "Good evening, sir," the guard said as he drew abreast. "May I see your badge?"

Danner looked sheepish. "After twenty years, I still forget." He grinned, dug into his pocket for the badge, and handed it to the guard.

The man inspected it carefully, making sure Danner's face matched the photograph. "Thank you, sir," he said, handing the badge back. "Please remember to display it."

"Sorry about that," Danner said. He continued walking, to the elevators this time. When he reached his office, he sat down for a moment. His heart was pounding. He looked at his hands. They were steady, but the palms were sweating. The people in Lockpicking, he decided, earned their money.

CHAPTER
TWENTY-NINE

The SO offices were darkened and deserted. Danner closed the door softly behind him. Roudebush had cut the key himself during the afternoon, and it worked smoothly on the first try.

He looked at his watch. It was 1:00 A.M. He figured he would have five hours, maximum, before some of the Special Operations early shift reported in.

He took off his jacket and laid it along the bottom of the door so that no light would show in the corridor. Even so, he used a pencil flashlight to orient himself. He moved down a darkened inner corridor past a row of silent offices. Halfway along, on the left, the beam of his flashlight picked up what he was looking for.

The computer terminal stood in a room about twenty feet square with no windows. He stepped inside, closed the door, and turned on the light switch. He was bathed in a bright fluorescent glow from the ceiling fixtures. He blinked a moment as his eyes adjusted, then looked around. Aside from the terminal, which rested on a stand of white formica, there was nothing much in the room—a small walnut conference table with some blue chairs around it, and a single file cabinet.

Sitting down at the terminal, he snapped open his attaché case, took out the microcomputer, and put it aside for the moment. He switched on the terminal of the SO computer.

On the cathode ray tube the words PLEASE LOG ON appeared in orange letters against a black background.

He typed in: LOG ON.

The computer responded: ENTER USER ID.

NICHOLS, he replied.

The computer answered: ENTER PASSWORD.

He entered 8L6D4Z, Julie's alphanumeric password.

As far as the computer was concerned, Danner was Julie Nichols, an authorized user. The terminal hummed obediently and flashed the word COMMAND.

Danner took a deep breath and typed in: LIST DIRECTORY. He was asking the computer to tell him what categories of files were stored in its data base.

The computer responded:

USERS
OPERATIONS
RESEARCH
COVER
WEAPONS
POISONS AND DRUGS
SUPPORT

So far so good. But he had not really encountered the computer's security safeguards yet. He decided to try browsing through the user files, if possible. He might be able to pick up traces of the operation that way.

RETRIEVE USERS, he typed in.

Somewhere nearby, in the complex of Special Operations offices, the main frame computer was on line in a locked room. It knew that an authorized user had given it an unauthorized command. On the screen the words INVALID COMMAND appeared.

Danner thought for a moment. He assumed that Brooks Jordan, as director, had access to anything in the SO computer, even if he seldom if ever used it. He tried a long shot and typed in: RETRIEVE ACCESS DIRECTORY JORDAN.

ENTER PASSWORD, the computer came back.

Danner was stumped. But it was not unexpected. The SO computer had multi-levels of security, as Sandifer had warned. It was a little like driving down a street in an unfamiliar neighborhood. You could see all the houses, but you could not get into one without a key.

He did not know Jordan's password. But he remembered

what Sandifer had told him. People often used familiar words
as passwords, so that they were easy to remember. He typed in:
COVERT.

The computer came back with INVALID PASSWORD.

He tried once more, offering LANGLEY. The computer rejected it again. He shrugged and entered DIRECTOR. INVALID
PASSWORD, the computer replied, TERMINAL DISCONNECTED.

Three strikes and you're out, Danner said to himself. At least
there were no alarm bells ringing. *None that you can hear,* he
thought.

It felt warm in the room, and Danner rolled up his shirtsleeves. He would try another path into the data base. He
logged on again and repeated the same steps through the point
where the computer had listed its directory of files. Then, instead of demanding the list of users and Jordan's access file, he
entered: LIST FIELDS OPERATIONS.

The computer had been willing to list operations as one of its
files. Perhaps it would also tell him the subheadings under that
entry.

The CRT printed out:

    CATEGORY
    CODEWORD
    START DATE
    BUDGET
    OP OBJECTIVE
    DESCRIPTION

Danner smiled. The night was young. He entered: LIST CATE-
GORY.

The computer obeyed, answering with:

    HOMETOWN
    STRANGER
    BOTH

Just as Julie had told him on the Monument grounds, the
computer broke down operations into domestic and foreign. RE-
TRIEVE CATEGORY STRANGER, Danner typed in.

FOUND, the computer replied.

LIST CODEWORD, Danner commanded.

The computer began to spew out a list of code names of foreign operations—

CODEWORDS (STRANGER):
BANJO
REDEYE
MANTIS
VALKI
CLOVER

Danner stared at the screen. One of those operations must be Julie's. But which one? REDEYE might have something to do with the Soviet Union. But so could VALKI, which sounded foreign. On the other hand, code names often gave no hint of the nature of the operation they protected. He might as well try them in order. He typed in, RETRIEVE CODEWORD BANJO.

FOUND, the computer responded.

Danner, tense now, typed in: LIST OP OBJECTIVE.

ENTER PASSWORD, the computer demanded.

Danner reached behind the terminal and unplugged the RS232C twenty-five pin connector. He took a Y adaptor out of his attaché case. To it he connected the leads running from the main frame computer, the SO terminal, and the Epson. The microprocessor and the regular terminal were now interfaced and wired to the main frame.

Danner moved over to the keyboard of the micro and as Sandifer had instructed typed in three words: RUN BRUTE FORCE. Like David and Goliath, the tiny micro was now literally attacking the much bigger main frame computer. The thousands of circuits on the silicon chip inside the Epson were systematically searching the 30,000-word dictionary for the correct password. The words it tried were not echoing on the terminals. All Danner could see on both screens was INVALID PASSWORD, constantly flashing.

Each time the micro tried three wrong passwords, the terminal disconnected, but Sandifer, anticipating that, had programmed it to log on again, cycle back to the same point, and try the next three words. All of this was taking place in milliseconds.

Still, it was a time-consuming process. Danner looked at his watch. It was after 2:00 A.M. According to Sandifer, the microcomputer could search the entire dictionary in about an hour. But it might hit on the correct password sooner.

Danner sat back and tried to relax, keeping one eye on the screen of the micro. As soon as he hit on the password, the computer would list the operational objective. Once he read that, he would know if it was the file he was looking for. But he would have to try each one to tell.

His watch said 2:34 when the password PICNIC came up on the screen of both terminals. The BRUTE FORCE program had worked. PICNIC was the key to BANJO. The words appeared quickly:

> OPERATIONS STRANGER BANJO OP OBJECTIVE: OPERATION
> BANJO IS DESIGNED TO WEAKEN THE REGIME OF CUBAN
> PREMIER FIDEL CASTRO BY RELEASING DISEASE-BEARING
> MOSQUITOES IN SELECTED AREAS OF ISLAND.

One down. Using the micro as a terminal, Danner typed in: RETRIEVE CODEWORD REDEYE.

FOUND, the computer replied.

LIST OP OBJECTIVE, Danner commanded.

ENTER PASSWORD, the computer countered.

Danner typed in: RUN BRUTE FORCE. Once again the micro attacked the larger computer, systematically searching the dictionary for the password. Danner checked his watch. Three hours left. He had to be out before 6:00 A.M. After that there would be no margin of safety.

It was almost 3:45 A.M. before the password ZULU flashed on both screens. The computer responded:

> OPERATIONS STRANGER REDEYE OP OBJECTIVE: OPERA-
> TION REDEYE IS DESIGNED TO CHANNEL COVERT FINAN-
> CIAL SUPPORT TO ELEMENTS OF THE LABOR PARTY IN
> AUSTRALIA IN ORDER TO ASSURE SECURITY OF CIA/NSA
> BASE AT ALICE SPRINGS.

Special Operations cast its net wide, Danner thought. But it wasn't what he wanted. He typed in: RETRIEVE CODEWORD MANTIS.

FOUND, the computer replied.

LIST OP OBJECTIVE, Danner ordered.

ENTER PASSWORD, the computer responded.

RUN BRUTE FORCE, Danner came back. He watched as IN-VALID PASSWORD flashed repeatedly on the screens. Watched and waited. This time the search was faster. It was 4:15 when the password OXBOW appeared.

The computer obeyed:

> OPERATIONS STRANGER MANTIS OP OBJECTIVE: OPERA-TION MANTIS IS AN UMBRELLA OPERATION DESIGNED TO DESTABILIZE UNFRIENDLY GOVERNMENTS IN CENTRAL AMERICA BY COVERT FUNDING OF OPPONENTS IN POLITI-CAL PARTIES, LABOR UNIONS, BUSINESS, AND THE NEWS MEDIA.

Danner cursed his luck. He was learning everything except what he wanted. RETRIEVE CODEWORD VALKI, he ordered.

FOUND, the computer responded.

LIST OP OBJECTIVE, Danner ordered.

ENTER PASSWORD, the computer answered.

RUN BRUTE FORCE, Danner typed. It was 5:10 A.M. before the micro came up with CRYSTAL, the correct password.

The computer complied:

> OPERATIONS STRANGER VALKI OP OBJECTIVE: OPERATION VALKI IS DESIGNED TO BRING ABOUT A CHANGE IN THE LEADERSHIP OF THE SOVIET UNION THROUGH THE NEU-TRALIZATION OF YURI V. KALIN.

Danner literally felt his hair stand on end. This was it! Quickly, he typed in: DUMP VALKI. If it worked, he would get the full text of the operation now.

Both terminals responded. Danner moved over to read it on the larger screen:

> OPERATIONS CATEGORY STRANGER VALKI. START DATE 12/4. BUDGET: OPEN. OP OBJECTIVE: OPERATION VALKI IS

DESIGNED TO BRING ABOUT A CHANGE IN THE LEADER-
SHIP OF THE SOVIET UNION THROUGH THE NEUTRALIZA-
TION OF YURI V. KALIN. DESCRIPTION: IN ORDER TO AC-
COMPLISH THE OPERATIONAL OBJECTIVE OF VALKI A
TARGET ACCESS STUDY UNDERTAKEN BY SO PLANNING
GROUP/D UNDER THE DIRECTION OF THE DDSO HAS DE-
TERMINED THAT HIGH SECURITY SURROUNDING TARGET
AT ALL TIMES NECESSITATES APPROACH DURING PUBLIC
APPEARANCE. PLANNING GROUP/D BASED ON INFORMA-
TION OBTAINED FROM SR DIVISION IN PRETEXT QUERY
HAS DETERMINED THAT KALIN IS CIRCUS BUFF WHO REG-
ULARLY ATTENDS MOSCOW NEW CIRCUS AFTERNOON
PERFORMANCE ON THIRD WEDNESDAY OF EACH MONTH.
DIRECTOR SO AND DDSO HAVE APPROVED APPROACH TO
TARGET AT MOSCOW CIRCUS 12/19.

"Jesus." Danner spoke aloud in the empty room. The nine-
teenth was less than a week away. He read on.

SPECIAL OPERATIONS OFFICER J. NICHOLS HAS BEEN SE-
LECTED FOR THIS PRIORITY ONE ASSIGNMENT. NICHOLS
UNDER THE OPERATIONAL PSEUDONYM DOMINIQUE COBB
CURRENTLY UNDERGOING CLOWN TRAINING AT ALVAREZ
CLOWN ALLEY BIG PINE KEY FLORIDA. SCHOOL IS UNWIT-
TING AS TO HER TRUE IDENTITY AND MISSION. OPLAN FOR
HER INSERTION INTO SOVUNION FOLLOWS: J. NICHOLS
WILL ENTER SOVUNION WITH TOURIST VISA VIA HELSINKI
UNDER PSEUDONYM SISTER MARY WALSH ART HISTORIAN
CATHOLIC UNIVERSITY. STATED PURPOSE OF HER TRIP
WILL BE TO STUDY RUSSIAN RELIGIOUS PAINTINGS AND
ICONS IN MOSCOW MUSEUMS AND CATHEDRALS. UNIVER-
SITY IS UNWITTING. NICHOLS WILL WEAR PLAIN CLOTHES
RATHER THAN NUN'S HABIT TO AVOID ATTRACTING AT-
TENTION AND ALSO BECAUSE OFFICIAL SOVGOVERNMENT
POLICY DISCOURAGES CLERICS FROM WEARING GARB
WHILE VISITING SOVUNION.

The screen was scrolling rapidly. Danner looked at his watch
nervously. It was getting late.

ONCE IN MOSCOW NICHOLS WILL SHED IDENT SISTER
MARY WALSH. UNDER THE PSEUDONYM LUDMILLA PET-
ROVA SHE WILL BE INSERTED AS CLOWN IN MOSCOW CIR-
CUS WITH COOPERATION OPPOSITION SERVICE. TROUPE
WILL BE TOLD SHE HAS BEEN PROMOTED FROM LENIN-
GRAD CIRCUS. NICHOLS IS FLUENT IN RUSSIAN. NICHOLS
WILL HAVE NO CONTACT WITH AMEMBASSY OR MOSCOW
STATION WHICH IS UNWITTING.

OPLAN CALLS FOR NICHOLS AS PETROVA TO APPROACH
TARGET DURING PERFORMANCE AT NEW CIRCUS 17 PROS-
PEKT VERNADSKOGO ABOVE MENTIONED DATE AT 3:42
P.M. MOSCOW TIME (7:42 A.M. EST). CLOWNS MAKE EN-
TRANCE IN CLOWN CAR 3:30 P.M. NICHOLS/PETROVA
WILL PLAY ROLE OF GUNSLINGING AMERICAN COWBOY
CLOWN IN WESTERN SALOON. AS OTHER CLOWNS AT-
TEMPT TO APPROACH BAR SHE WILL DISPATCH THEM
WITH BLANK-FIRING BLUNDERBUSS PROP. AS LAST
CLOWN FALLS SHE WILL SWITCH TO A TOKAREV 7.62MM
AUTOMATIC LOADED WITH REAL BULLETS AND PROVIDED
BY OPPOSITION SERVICE. OPLAN CALLS FOR NICHOLS/
PETROVA TO FIRE THIS WEAPON AT TARGET AND ESCAPE
IN CONFUSION IN CLOWN CAR WHICH SHE WILL DRIVE
FROM ARENA THROUGH UNLOCKED GATE INTO N.
KOPERNIKA STREET BEHIND PERFORMERS' ENTRANCE
WHERE CAR AND DRIVER PROVIDED BY OPPOSITION SER-
VICE WILL BE WAITING AT CURB.

CAR WILL RETURN NICHOLS TO HER HOTEL. SHE WILL
CHANGE INTO CIVILIAN CLOTHES EN ROUTE AND AT
HOTEL RESUME IDENT SISTER MARY WALSH. NICHOLS/
WALSH WILL LEAVE MOSCOW IMMEDIATELY ABOARD SAS
FLIGHT 731 DEPARTING MOSCOW FOR STOCKHOLM 6:45
P.M. IF AIRPORT CLOSED DUE TO SUCCESSFUL TERMINA-
TION OF TARGET NICHOLS/WALSH WILL DEPART NEXT
AVAILABLE FLIGHT.

OPERATION VALKI IS PRIORITY ONE AND WILL BE
CARRIED OUT ENTIRELY BY SPECIAL OPERATIONS PERSON-
NEL. NO DDO PERSONNEL ARE CLEARED FOR ACCESS
VALKI. OTS IDENTIFICATION DIVISION WILL PROVIDE
PASSPORT FOR SISTER MARY WALSH ON ROUTINE BASIS
WITH NO ACCESS TO OPLAN OR OP OBJECTIVE. BECAUSE

OF EXTREMELY SENSITIVE NATURE OF THIS OPERATION
ALL SO PERSONNEL CLEARED TO PRIORITY ONE LEVEL
WILL EXERCISE UTMOST CAUTION IN HANDLING VALKI
MATERIAL.
APPROVED, DCI, DSO, 12/5.

Danner checked his watch. It was 5:47 A.M. He logged off
and the computer answered him:
TERMINAL DISCONNECTED. USED 1800 SECONDS CPU SIX CON-
NECT HOURS 12/14.
He turned off the microprocessor, unplugged the connections
on the adaptor, and reconnected the RS232C twenty-five pin
connector to the dumb terminal, which he then switched off. He
put the Epson back in the attaché case. It had done its job well.
He looked around to make sure the room was clean.
He picked up the microprocessor, turned off the lights, and
opened the door. The offices were still dark, but it would be
daylight soon.
Danner felt his way along toward the front door, not daring to
use his pencil flashlight now. He picked his jacket up off the
floor and put it on. He took a deep breath, then opened the
door.
Two cleaning ladies were mopping the corridor. They paid
no attention to him. He closed the door behind him and strode
down the hall as though he belonged there.
He returned to his office a floor below but did not turn on the
lights. He flopped into his chair and leaned back exhausted.
After a few moments, he pulled up the blinds and sat down
again, watching the dawn come up. He needed time to think.
He was chilled by what he had read and knew that he would
have to try to stop it. Operation Valki carried with it the risk of
a nuclear war. With both sides poised to annihilate the other in
minutes, it was insane for an intelligence service to liquidate a
Soviet or American president, no matter what the rationale.
Once again he thought through the compelling personal reasons to act. Julie was risking her life, probably in the mistaken
belief that the operation had been ordered by the president. She
didn't understand; that was not how the game was played. No
matter how the operation had come into being, Lansing Forbes
would preserve his plausible denial. He would be able to say he

had never ordered the assassination. He would even issue a statement deploring the violent act of a deranged, lone assassin and expressing his sympathy to the Soviet people. The escape route had probably been included in the plan for Julie's benefit; she would never make it back. Danner felt sick.

The winter sky was turning pink in the east, shading, even as he watched, to blood red. Above all, he knew he would have to act for Carrie's sake. Once Kalin was dead, Aleks Pavlov would in all probability become the new leader of the Soviet Union. And when he did, he would have no further need to intrigue with Brooks Jordan. Or to send Carrie home.

Perhaps Jordan didn't see that, but Danner did. The pale winter sun had risen over the barren trees, bringing the light of the new day. He went over to the window and lowered the blinds. He returned to his desk, sat down heavily, and felt the stubble on his chin. He longed for a cup of coffee but was too weary to go downstairs.

He leaned back in his chair and shut his eyes. He stayed that way for two hours. He shook himself awake at 8:30 and dialed Melinda.

"It's Danner," he said. "Let me speak to Dixon. It's urgent."

Hadley came on the line immediately. "Yes, Bill?"

Danner's voice was tired. "It's worse than you think," he said. "And we don't have very much time."

CHAPTER
THIRTY

Austrian Airlines Flight 601 from Vienna to Moscow had less than a dozen passengers. Danner was seated toward the rear of the plane. He was deeply absorbed in a catalogue, clamped inside a black binder, that had pictures of pipes and flues.

In Danner's pocket was a U.S. passport and a Soviet visa, both made out in the name of Richard Culver. In his visa application, Richard Culver stated that he was a representative of a heating supply company in Indiana that was seeking to expand its markets into the Soviet Union.

His dark hair was now crew cut and dyed brown; all traces of gray had been removed. He had on a pair of glasses in a black frame that to a casual observer appeared to have thick lenses, but which did not, in fact, affect the wearer's vision. In his wallet were business and credit cards and an Indiana driver's license in the name of Richard Culver, a card attesting to his membership in the Kiwanis Club of Indianapolis, and a color snapshot of a woman sitting in front of a fireplace with a teen-aged boy and girl. The back of the snapshot was inscribed: "Love, Jennifer, Susan, and Jack."

The pilot announced on the intercom that the aircraft was over Soviet territory and that it was forbidden to take photographs. The flight attendant served a light lunch. Danner ate mechanically, engrossed in his heating supply catalogue.

He was actually thinking back over his battle with Dixon Hadley. The DDO had agreed that Operation Valki must be stopped at all costs. It had been more difficult persuading Had-

ley to send him in alone. At first, the deputy director had
wanted to use Moscow station. Danner had argued persuasively
that the station's loyalties would be divided. Jordan had ordered
the operation, Hadley was countermanding it. Total chaos
would result if the station were brought in. He had to do it
alone.

There was another reason that Danner did not mention. He
trusted no one now, not even Hadley.

The seat-belt sign flashed on and the jet swung into its final
approach to Moscow's Sheremetyevo Airport. It was after 4:00
P.M., Moscow time, when they touched down in the rain. The
gloomy December sky was rapidly growing darker. Danner advanced his watch as the plane taxied toward the terminal, passing several Aeroflot jets parked along the tarmac. The Russian
aircraft were white, with blue stripes down the length of the
cabins and red flags on the tails.

They stopped at a long, bright red, enclosed ramp and the
passengers debarked. Inside the terminal, the first thing Danner
noticed were the armed, uniformed militiamen. They seemed to
be everywhere. Most of them appeared to be young, rawboned
recruits from the provinces, serious and unsmiling.

With the other arriving passengers, Danner lined up to go
through passport control. Two grim-faced officers sat behind
the thick glass in the booth. They wore green uniforms and
green shirts, and the tops of their peaked caps were the color of
billiard cloth. Arriving passengers awaited their turn, then
slipped their passports and visas through a narrow opening at
the bottom of the glass.

The guards took about five minutes to examine each set of
travel documents, so that it seemed to take forever to reach the
booth. Danner noticed that a long, narrow mirror had been
mounted at an angle opposite the window, behind and above
the passengers. Unknown to the travelers, the officers in the
booth could see their hands. An unduly nervous passenger, or
one who made a sudden move to conceal something, would be
detected.

Danner got to the window at last and shoved his passport and
visa through. The young guard on the left examined the pictures
on both documents and studied Danner for a long time, comparing his face to the photographs. Danner kept his hands at his

sides. He wasn't worried. The visa was real, routinely issued to an American businessman by the Soviet Embassy in Washington. The passport was fake, but because it was typed on a real blank provided by the State Department to the CIA it was indistinguishable from any other U.S. passport.

The guard tore off one half of the visa and kept it. He slid the other half and the passport back under the window.

Danner moved on, claimed his bag from a conveyor belt, and lined up to go through security. It was similar to security at any other airport, except that it was for *incoming* passengers. He stepped through the metal detector and it beeped. The guard brusquely motioned to him to empty his pockets. He took out the coins, placed them in a dish, and satisfied the machine.

He retrieved his bag and prepared to go through customs. Two blue-uniformed officials sat behind a high yellow counter that housed a bank of huge, built-in X-ray machines. The machines said "Phillips" on their sides. He chose the official he thought looked slightly friendlier and placed his bag on the scale in front of him. The X-ray device closed over it. Danner held his breath. The radio inside his suitcase was the one piece of equipment that might get him in trouble, because of what it concealed. He had not asked the State Department to pouch it in. State had smuggled in weapons for the agency in a lot of places in the past, but they were becoming increasingly fussy about using the diplomatic pouch for that purpose. Danner waited tensely. But the official, who must have seen the radio on his screen, did not ask to examine it. The machine slid open again and Danner picked up his bag.

In another few steps he passed through the roped-off, restricted area into the main terminal. There was a change window to the left, and he bought $100 in rubles. He turned and walked straight ahead on the slick, brownish-black marble floor past a bank of futuristic-looking pay phones in round, plastic bubbles. It was a long walk to the taxis.

He took the first one in line and the driver, a young, blond man who spoke a few words of English, took his bag and put it in the trunk. "Hotel National," Danner said. He got in and they started up. It was very cold out and completely dark now. The rain was sluicing off the windshield in sheets. Danner could see little as the cab barreled south on Leningradskoye shosse. He noticed a number of army trucks on the road, mostly heading in the opposite direction, out of the capital.

Landing in Moscow was a little like stepping into a military encampment, Danner decided. Troops and guns were as much a part of the landscape as in a banana republic. Only here they wore fur hats and never smiled.

The driver, who said his name was Volodya, groped beneath the dashboard and came up with a battered paper bag. He put it on the seat next to him, reached in, and produced a jar of caviar with a blue metal top. *"Ikra,"* he said. "You like to buy for dollars? I make good price, much better than the *beriozka.*"

"No thanks," Danner said.

"You don't like caviar?" Volodya sounded incredulous. "Then maybe you like change money. I give you four rubles for a dollar." He held up four fingers. It was more than five times the official rate.

"Nyet," Danner said. "No thanks." Volodya could turn around and sell his dollars for almost twice what he was offering. But he might also be a low-level agent for the KGB. The last thing Richard Culver, heating supplier, needed was to get hauled in on a currency rap before he even made it to his hotel.

They were getting closer to the city. The taxi swung onto Leningradskiy prospekt, and Volodya pointed out the Dinamo Stadium on the left. "You like soccer?" he asked.

"Yes," Danner said. "My kids play every weekend in Indianapolis."

"You are Greek?" Volodya seemed surprised.

"No, American. Indianapolis is a city in our Midwest, about where Omsk would be in the Soviet Union."

"You are visiting Omsk?" Volodya was impressed. "It is very far. Very far, Omsk."

Danner gave up, and sat back. In a few moments, they were at the National. He paid the driver, collected his bag, and went inside.

The eighty-year-old hotel, where Lenin had lived for a time, was directly across the street from the Kremlin and Red Square. The girl at the desk handed him a little card on which she wrote his room number, 413, and circled a number 6. "That is your room, that is your floor."

"They don't match."

"That is because the lobby is on the first floor and the dining halls on the second floor. The rooms begin on the third floor."

He picked up his bag and squeezed into one of the two tiny elevators that faced each other on either side of the small lobby. He rode up with two Arab businessmen and a fat woman and her male companion who looked as though they might be visiting Rumanian party officials. He got off at six, the top floor, picked up his key from an ancient *babushka*, and found his room.

It was huge, with high ceilings, and on the front of the hotel. There were two enormous French windows and a tiny balcony outside. He turned off the lights and opened the curtains.

The view was spectacular. Directly in front of him, two huge red stars atop the towers of the Kremlin glowed brightly against the black winter sky. Just to the left of the towers he could see Lenin's tomb in Red Square, beneath the high brick walls of the Kremlin. The rain had stopped, and a light snow was falling over Moscow.

He opened the French windows and stepped out onto the balcony in the biting cold. He felt exhilarated, an enemy agent standing at the very center of Soviet power. Somewhere in the same city, Julie was preparing to alter the shape and nature of that power, only two days from now. Unless he could stop her. A few blocks to his left, out of his line of sight, Aleksandr Pavlov was probably in his office on Dzerzhinsky Square attending to the final details of Operation Valki. Off to his right, an unsuspecting Yuri V. Kalin, leader of the Soviet Union, would be getting ready for bed in his apartment on Kutuzovsky prospekt. Perhaps even Carrie was somewhere in Moscow.

The snow was coming down harder now, settling on his hair and shoulders. He remembered a story he had heard long ago, although he did not know if it was true. Stalin was meeting in the Kremlin with his military advisers. The Germans were at the gates of Moscow and the situation looked hopeless. Stalin went to the window and looked out for a long time. Snow had begun to fall. Then he turned, and said: "Gentlemen, our problem is solved. General Winter has arrived."

Danner shivered on the balcony. He stepped back in the darkened room, slammed the French windows shut, and shook the snow off his suit. The odds against him were overwhelming. Unlike Stalin, he could not expect help from the elements.

In the morning, Danner went down to the second floor and had a breakfast of ham and eggs, toast, and coffee. The food was good but it took forever to come. Afterward, he went outside and bought four copies of *Pravda* at a news kiosk near the hotel. Then he went back up to the room and spent some time acting like Richard Culver. He had with him the name of Nicolai Tolichev, an official of the Ministry of Foreign Trade.

He was not able to reach Tolichev but finally talked with an assistant, a Miss Kisalova. "You cannot meet with Mr. Tolichev," she said. "This is not possible."

Danner sounded disappointed. "I've come all the way from Indianapolis, Indiana, to meet with Mr. Tolichev. I was told he was the right official to see."

"Is not possible."

"But why?"

"He is, um, very busy, Mr. Tolichev. He cannot see you. It is not possible."

"Well, is there someone else I can see?"

"Yes, certainly."

Danner tried to sound relieved. "Wonderful. Who can I see?"

"I don't know."

"Miss Kisalova, you say I cannot see Mr. Tolichev."

"It is not possible."

"But you say I can see someone else."

"*Da.*"

"Then, can you tell me how I can see someone else if I don't know his name?"

"You must find out the proper official."

"How do I do that?"

Miss Kisalova was beginning to lose patience. "There is no one at the Ministry of Foreign Trade who can see you. You must call the Ministry of Light Industry."

"Who shall I ask for there?"

"I don't know. You are speaking to the Ministry of Foreign Trade."

"Well, can you at least tell me who is the head of the Ministry of Light Industry?"

"Certainly. Comrade Tarasov. But he will not speak to you. He is the minister."

"Thank you very much."

Miss Kisalova did not reply. She had hung up.

Danner suppressed a strong desire to laugh. He knew he better not. The hotel room, like all hotel rooms in Moscow in which foreigners were put, was undoubtedly bugged. Peter Ostrovsky in the Soviet Russia division had told him that there was a closet on every floor of the Hotel National jammed with wiretap equipment and manned by a live KGB agent at all times.

Danner called the Ministry of Light Industry and asked for Minister Tarasov. He was transferred around to five different extensions and then cut off. He called again and finally reached a low-level official in the division of heating and energy supplies, one Viktor S. Chudin. Chudin gave him an appointment for Thursday at 11:00 A.M.

"I can see you for fifteen minutes," he said. "Not more."

"Could you make it half an hour?" Danner pressed.

"It is not possible. Perhaps you should try the Ministry of Foreign Trade."

"No, no," Danner said quickly. "I'll see you on Thursday."

Grinning, Danner hung up. It occurred to him that the bureaucracy in Washington could take lessons from the bureaucracy in Moscow. But the timing of the appointment was perfect. This was Tuesday. The final act of Operation Valkir was to take place tomorrow, Wednesday. He now had an official reason for waiting around Moscow.

He picked up the telephone again, dialed the American Embassy, and asked for the commercial attaché. He got a secretary, identified himself as Richard Culver, and explained that he was an American in Moscow on business. "I think I'm getting a runaround from the Russians, ma'am," he told the secretary. "I'd like to come in and see if I can get any help from the embassy. They do business here different from back home."

"Certainly, sir," she said. "If you'll come to the embassy,

I'm sure that someone will see you. We're at 19–23 Tchaikovsky Street.''

Danner went over to the armoire and removed a Pan American flight bag. He crumpled and stuffed in the copies of *Pravda* so that it looked full, put the bag over his shoulder, and went down to the lobby. In front of the hotel, he hailed a taxi.

"Amerikanskoye posol'stvo," he told the driver. The taxi moved along Prospekt Marxa past the Kremlin, then swung into Kalinina prospekt. They passed the huge Dom Knigi bookstore and turned right into Tchaikovsky Street, which formed part of the city's outer ring. The driver executed a wild U-turn and pulled up in front of the embassy.

Danner paid him and got out. The embassy was an ancient orange-yellow building of nine stories with two seven-story wings on either side of the central portion. Danner thought it looked like an old apartment house in the Bronx. Two militiamen in thick gray double-breasted coats and bluish fur hats guarded the archway that served as the main entrance. He had no trouble getting past them once he produced his American passport. There was no gate. It occurred to Danner that the Soviet Union was probably the only place in the world where the U.S. Embassy did not need a gate to protect it. In a police state, no one would dare to attack it unless ordered.

In the archway, he went through a small door on the left and found himself in a narrow hall that was badly in need of paint. There was no guard to stop him. He made his way past a series of administrative offices, and found the elevator. A sign instructed visitors to go to the ninth floor.

When he got off, he found himself in a small reception area. A uniformed Marine guard, blond and crew cut, sat behind a high counter. "My name's Culver," Danner told him. "I'd like to see the commercial attaché. I called a little while ago."

The young Marine checked the embassy telephone directory. "That would be in the economic section, sir. Mr. Merrill. I'll see if he's in, sir." He dialed an extension, spoke briefly to someone, and smiled at Danner. "He'll be out in just a moment, Mr. Culver, sir."

"Thanks." Danner sat down on a dowdy beige vinyl sofa. The whole embassy was shabby-looking. Danner wondered whether the Russians wanted it that way, or whether the State

Department ran a low-budget operation in Moscow, figuring that few Americans ever saw the place.

"They're building a new embassy just behind this one, sir, closer to the river," the Marine guard said, as if he had read Danner's thoughts. "The Seabees have been working hard. It's coming along."

In a moment, a gray-haired, handsome man of about forty-five strode into the reception area. "Mr. Culver? Charley Merrill. My secretary says you've been learning about the bureaucracy in Moscow. Come on back and let's see if we can be of any help."

"I surely do appreciate it," Danner said as they walked down the hallway. "I did get one appointment with a Russian, but it means I have to wait around all week to see the fellow."

Merrill led the way into an office, and then into a conference room that looked as though it had been built inside another room, with double walls. They sat down at a table, which was empty except for two packages wrapped in brown paper and sealed with string and tape.

"We can talk here," Merrill said. "The walls are metal-lined and the room is swept twice a day. Your trip in okay?"

"No problems," Danner said.

"The packages arrived by pouch this morning from Helsinki," Merrill said. "They're right here."

"Good." Danner unzipped the airline bag and took out the crumpled copies of *Pravda*. In their place, he put the larger of the two parcels. It just fitted into the bag. He stuck the smaller parcel, which was about six by eight inches, in the pocket of his raincoat.

"We got a Top Secret RYBAT from headquarters saying you were coming," Merrill said, "but that Moscow station was to have no contact, except for our meeting this morning. It was signed by the DDO himself."

Danner nodded.

"Whatever it is, it must be pretty important," Merrill probed.

"I guess so." Danner got up.

Merrill cleared his throat. "Well, I'll escort you out. Good luck." He extended his hand. Danner shook it, picked up the bag, and put the strap over his shoulder.

By the elevator, Merrill said, "Sorry we couldn't be of more help, Mr. Culver. But you know there's really not a lot the embassy can do in these situations."

"Well, thanks much for seeing me, anyway," Danner said. "It feels real nice to have a little bit of the USA under my feet."

Merrill smiled. "I know what you mean. By the way, we have a snack bar downstairs called Uncle Sam's. Any American is welcome there after six P.M. We even serve pizza."

"Mighty nice of you," Danner said. "I might just drop by for some real food."

Outside the embassy, Danner hailed a taxi and had him drive to the Alexander Gardens. He strolled along the paths beneath the Kremlin walls and sat down on one of the yellow benches. He looked around. There did not seem to be anyone following him.

People streamed by, Slavic-looking men in dark leather jackets and wool caps, an occasional self-important bureaucrat in a greatcoat and fur hat carrying an inevitable briefcase, and mothers with small children in brightly colored snowsuits. Even in the garden, the acrid smell of Russian cigarettes hung in the air.

It started to drizzle. He got up, strolled along past a couple of news kiosks and a snack bar, and came to the tomb of the Unknown Soldier, where militiamen stood at rigid attention by the eternal flame. As he watched, a bride and groom timidly approached the tomb. The man wore an awkwardly fitting dark blue suit and the woman was holding up her long white dress to keep it from dragging on the ground. She bent over and put down a bouquet of flowers by the flame. Two other couples were waiting their turn in the light rain.

Danner turned the corner into Red Square and walked across the rough cobblestones toward St. Basil's Cathedral, with its striped onion domes and brick mosaic. Before reaching the cathedral, he turned left into Kuybysheva Street and ducked in the entrance to the GUM, Moscow's largest department store. In the crush of people pushing through the double doors he was shouldered and buffeted by stocky peasant women. When he got inside, he felt like he'd made a first down.

The store was very old, with vast skylights and walls painted sickly green. It was built on three levels, with narrow catwalks spanning a center court. The third floor seemed to be off-limits to all but GUM executives. The first two floors were swirling with people, women mostly, but a fair percentage of men.

He fought his way to the second floor, where word had obviously passed that a shipment of boots had arrived. Three hundred people were crammed into a room in front of the boot counter; Danner estimated it would take four hours before those in the rear would have any hope of reaching the counter. Even as he watched, another swirl of people moved toward a counter selling pots and pans; by some mysterious method the shoppers, like swarming bees, had learned that desirable merchandise was being sold. After a few minutes in the GUM, Danner got into the rhythm of shopping in the Soviet Union. One went to the GUM not to buy a particular item, which might well be out, but to see what was being offered today and get in line in the hope of buying it.

Men were lining up in the fur hat department as he pushed by. It was pretty clear that the shoppers at the end of the line had no precise idea what kind of hats were being sold up front. They were queuing up on the theory that if there was a line, something good must have come in.

Important party officials, Danner knew, did not have to go through the exhausting gymnastics of the GUM. They had their own special stores, hidden from view and well stocked with high-quality goods, including some from the West. Foreign visitors, too, could avoid lining up in the GUM or other ordinary stores. For them, Western goods, expensive cameras, perfumes, clothing, and jewelry, as well as the best Soviet items—vodka and caviar—could be purchased for hard currency at any one of a half dozen *beriozkas*, or dollar stores, around Moscow. But the secret stores, as well as the *beriozkas*, were denied to the ordinary workers streaming by him in the GUM.

Danner snaked his way from one department to another, losing himself among the crowds, until he reached a little stand-up snack bar at the far end of the store on the second floor. He went in and ordered a ham sandwich and a glass of hot tea. He ate quickly, keeping an eye on the door and glancing down into the street occasionally. He could see no one watching him, but it would have taken Houdini to stay on his tail in the GUM. He finished his tea, went downstairs, and found an exit into the street.

He had been "dry cleaning" himself, as the KGB would have termed it. The technique called for mingling with crowds in a busy store, then leaving by a different exit. Done properly, it was an almost sure way of shaking surveillance in a congested urban area.

Outside, Danner walked a block and hailed a taxi. He told the driver to take him to the Yaroslavsky Station. In the station, he mingled with the crowds again. Men and women and what looked like whole families struggled under the weight of battered suitcases and cardboard boxes as they headed for the trains.

There were emotional embraces and tears for those coming and going. He found a checkroom in the corner of the station. A wrinkled crone took the airline bag and handed him a metal claim check, which he pocketed.

In the taxi on the way back to the hotel, he thought about the parcel now sitting in the checkroom of the Yaroslavsky Station. There was some risk leaving it there, but he could not take it to the hotel. It was unlikely that his room would be tossed—he was only one of many American businessmen who visited the Soviet Union every month—but if the parcel were found at the hotel and opened, he would be in trouble.

He thought of trying to find Julie, but rejected the idea. He would stick to his plan. The attempt against Kalin would take place on Wednesday afternoon, in less than twenty-four hours. Until then, he would have to be patient and live his cover.

He had the taxi drop him off in front of the Historical Museum. The double lines of people stretched across the Fiftieth Anniversary of the October Revolution Square into the Alexander Gardens, and back again into Red Square and Lenin's tomb. Lenin had been dead for sixty years, but still the people lined up, regardless of the weather, to visit the mausoleum.

Richard Culver was waiting around Moscow for his appointment at the Ministry of Light Industry so he would join the lines, like any visitor. He walked over to the militiamen standing behind the barriers near the Alexander Gardens and showed

his passport. They motioned him into the special line for foreigners.

Even the privileged line moved slowly, inching its way
across the rough cobblestones of Red Square. The tomb itself
was built of blocks of reddish-brown and black marble in the
shape of a ziggurat, tiered in successively smaller rectangles
like some 4,000-year-old temple to a Sumerian god. The upper
level served as a reviewing stand for the Kremlin leaders on
state occasions. Wreaths of flowers had been placed along the
front wall of the tomb; on either side of the doorway two soldiers in gray greatcoats, blue caps, yellow belts, and white
gloves stood motionless, facing each other, rifles at rest.

Inside, Danner went down a flight of steps, then up some
more steps to the right, and into the center of the mausoleum.
Lenin lay on a raised red bier, bathed in a blaze of very bright,
white spotlights. The rest of the room was completely dark, to
increase the dramatic contrast. His right hand was clenched, his
left hand open, a balding little man with a reddish beard and
hair, the face chalky white.

The waxen figure under the floodlights was the supreme icon
of the Soviet state. There was no time to study the body more
closely; the guards kept the crowd moving silently around the
bier and out the door. Once outside again, Danner was routed
along a path that ran behind the tomb and directly beneath the
Kremlin wall. In the grass strip between the wall and a line of
fir trees, other Soviet heroes were buried—among them Stalin,
Brezhnev, and John Reed. Danner noticed that Stalin's grave
and a statue of the Soviet dictator occupied a prominent spot
right behind Lenin's tomb. Nikita Khrushchev, the man who
denounced Stalin's crimes, was buried in Moscow but not here,
in the place of honor.

Danner walked across Red Square to St. Basil's and went inside. He spent the rest of the day as Richard Culver might,
sightseeing, visiting art galleries and museums, and just walking around Moscow. He returned to the hotel late in the afternoon and made a reservation for dinner at the Uzbekistan.

The restaurant was crowded when Danner arrived, but he
was given a good table in a room where a band was alternating
fast Russian tunes with American rock music. In front of the
bandstand a dozen Russian couples were dancing, moving

faster and faster as the music speeded up near the end of each song. To Danner's right a large table of foreigners were enjoying themselves noisily. They were drinking a lot.

A heavyset man in a blue blazer got up from the table and lumbered over in his direction, almost crashing into a waiter. "Bill," the man bellowed. "Bill Danner. I can't believe it!"

Neither could Danner. The words sent a chill down his spine. It was every spy's nightmare—to be working under a pseudonym and recognized in some unlikely setting by an old acquaintance. But it sometimes happened, and it was happening now.

The fat man was at his table. "Don't you remember me? Eddie Swenson from White River Junction. We were in Miss Blaney's class together in the eighth grade. The glasses had me fooled for a minute. But it's you all right. How the hell are ya? Jesus, imagine running into you in Moscow."

Danner shook the man's pudgy hand. "I'm sorry to disappoint you, Mr. Swenson. My name's Richard Culver. I'm from Indianapolis. I've never lived in White River Junction, wherever that is. But I'm might glad to make your acquaintance."

Swenson blinked in confusion, then turned pink. "Sorry, " he mumbled, backing off. "I must have made a mistake." He shook his head. "I would have sworn you were Bill Danner."

He retreated back to his table, as Danner smiled politely. Fat Eddie Swenson. He remembered being in a snowball fight with him too many years ago. Fat Eddie had turned and run, and all the other kids pelted him with snowballs on his ass. It made such a good target.

Danner could only pray that nobody had heard Swenson call out his name. He signaled the waiter for his check, paid, and got out of the restaurant as fast as he could. He hailed a cab in Neglinnaya Street and took it back to the National. It had started to snow again, and there were not many people on the streets.

It was almost midnight when he got back to his room. He opened the curtains and stared out again at the red stars glowing atop the Nikolskaya and Spasskaya towers. Inside the Kremlin walls he could see the floodlit red flag flying atop the green dome of the Council of Ministers Building. He wondered whether Kalin was working late in his office on the third floor.

The general secretary of the Communist Party of the USSR
and chairman of the Presidium of the Supreme Soviet would
have no way of knowing that the American looking out of his
hotel window only two blocks away had come to save his life.
Or that if he failed, fifteen hours and forty-two minutes from
now, Yuri Vladimirovich Kalin would be dead.

CHAPTER
THIRTY-ONE

Danner was up early and had breakfast brought to his room. He drank two cups of black coffee. Still not fully awake, he opened the doors to the balcony to let in the cold winter air for a few moments.

He looked down into Red Square. There was no unusual activity. The double line of people waiting to visit Lenin's tomb was already forming. It was an ordinary day in Moscow.

He felt good, and not really nervous, except for a little tightness in his stomach muscles. He lay down on the Oriental rug in the center of the room and did some calisthenics to loosen up.

After that, pacing the room, he reviewed the plan of Operation Valki in his mind once more. He had memorized the details he had acquired from the SO computer, but he wanted to be sure he had not forgotten anything. He checked his watch. It was time to begin getting ready.

He took the parcel from the pocket of his raincoat, carefully cut the string, and unfolded the brown wrapping paper. The clown costume inside was made of lightweight nylon and had been prepared by the Physical Disguises branch of OTS. It consisted of yellow pants that came to just below the knees, a loose-fitting red-and-purple-striped shirt, and a latex mask of a smiling clown face with a red nose.

He took the radio from the night table, released a small lever on the back, and slid the inside of the case out. He brought it over to the desk by the window, where the light was better. Using the screwdriver on his pocket knife, he removed the six screws that held the thin lead lining together; it fell apart, revealing the Taser.

The battery-powered electronic stun gun was not much bigger than two packs of cigarettes and looked like an ordinary camping flashlight. But it could fire two small barbed darts up to a range of fifteen feet. Very thin wires that remained attached to the darts sent a low-amperage electrical pulse of 50,000 volts into the target. The first jolt from the Taser would knock down a 250-pound man. The target could be kept immobilized by pressing the trigger and sending continuing pulses of electricity along the wires for a few seconds. The Taser worked by causing involuntary muscle contractions, but it left no harmful aftereffects.

Danner got dressed, but not in the business suit that Richard Culver had worn. Instead, he put on a pair of dark, heavy slacks, a T-shirt, and over that, a blue sweatshirt with two large side pockets. He slipped the Taser into the right-hand pocket and put his wallet and the metal claim check in the left pocket. After that, he put on the clown costume.

The striped shirt was loose enough to conceal the bulge made by the stun gun. He stood in front of the full-length mirror and tried on the mask. Richard Culver, businessman, had been transformed into a grinning clown.

He took off the mask, put on his black raincoat, and buttoned it. It completely hid his costume. He rolled the mask up into a ball and shoved it in the pocket of his raincoat.

He checked the room and realized he had not put the radio back together. He replaced the screws in the inner shell that had held the Taser, and slid it back into the case.

Everything else looked normal. He left Richard Culver's passport and thick glasses on the night table; he would not be needing them any more. The clothes, shaving kit, and suitcase would be left behind, a present for the KGB. He would not be returning to the room.

He glanced at his watch: 1:30 P.M. Time to go. He walked down the hall, dropped his key off with the old woman at the desk, and took the elevator downstairs. He walked up Prospekt Marxa as far as the Lenin Library and spotted a taxi with the small green light on the dash that meant it was empty.

He hailed it, got in, and told the driver to take him to the *novyi cirk*.

"*Prospekt Vernadskogo*," the driver said, nodding. He took off, threading his way rapidly through the traffic and driving southwest, away from the center of the city. Soon they were barreling along the Komsomolskiy prospekt and past the Central Stadium in Luzhniki. They crossed the Moscow River on the Metro Bridge. It was an unusual structure. Cars used the top level of the bridge; the lower level, enclosed in glass on two sides, was the Leninskiye Gory Metro stop.

Once across the river, they were in the Lenin Hills. Danner looked back and could see the city behind him. Off to his right were the towers of Moscow University. "*Vernadskogo*," the driver said, gesturing and indicating that they were close to their destination. In another few moments he pulled over and pointed across the street. "*Novyi cirk*," he said. Danner paid the fare and got out.

He crossed the boulevard and joined the crowds streaming toward the arena. There it was: the Moscow Circus. He was suddenly aware of the excitement and tension rising within him. The circus building was round and attractively modern, with a domed metal roof and glass walls. It was set back from the street on a broad, paved plaza in which squares of grass alternated with concrete.

He walked as far as the entrance but did not go in. Through the glass walls, he could see buffet areas where people were already buying food and drink, and the coat rooms.

He continued around the arena. At the rear, he came to the square, two-story administration building made of rough-cut stone. There were steps nearby leading to the lower level of the plaza. He walked down them and came out on N. Kopernika Street. There was no sign of the driver, but it was still early.

The quiet residential street ran parallel to Prospekt Vernadskogo but was much narrower. There were blocks of orange-colored apartment buildings on the opposite side. From his vantage point, Danner could see that the first floor of the stone administration building was connected to the circus arena on the ground level. The performers' entrance was set back about twenty-five feet from the street. He walked past the entrance. There were driveways on either side of the building, wide enough for trucks to bring in the animals. Lightweight, aluminum gates closed off the driveways; the gates had an unusual sunburst design and were obviously meant more for show than for security. He noted with alarm, however, that both gates were locked, although only with small padlocks. According to the op plan, the gates were to have been left open.

It was 2:30 P.M. and performers and workmen were streaming into the back entrance. He got out his wallet and removed the laminated pass that the OTS Identification Section had prepared for him. It had his photograph in color. The cyrillic lettering identified him as Mikhail N. Osipov, an employee of the *novyi cirk*. He hoped it would work.

Inside the drab lobby, he was surprised and relieved to see that there were no armed guards, only performers and employees hurrying to and fro. Framed photographs of acrobats and other circus artists decorated the walls. The people who had entered just ahead of him were moving to the left, where a thirty-foot-wide concrete ramp led down to the floor of the arena. An ancient gray-haired woman sat behind an old wooden desk at the head of the ramp, eyeing those who streamed past. A few of the employees flashed their ID cards at her, but most didn't bother. Danner held his card casually in his hand but made no effort to display it.

At the bottom of the ramp, he stepped into a scene of noisy confusion. To his left was a labyrinth of dressing rooms and offices. On the right, the animals were lined up in their cages—bears, leopards, monkeys, and behind them, several elephants in a large holding pen. Scantily clad women in miniskirts, some a little beefy but many quite attractive, were lining up for the opening production number. A group of muscular acrobats was practicing on mats in a corner, and a blond woman wearing almost nothing strolled by with a python draped around her shoulders and thighs.

There wasn't much time. Danner ducked down a corridor until he found an empty dressing room. He went in, removed the clown mask from his pocket, and took off his raincoat, hanging it on a hook behind the door. He checked his costume in the mirror and decided it looked good. He put on the clown face, which attached behind his head with an elastic band, and cautiously stepped out again.

It was five minutes before 3:00 P.M. Walking back toward the ramp, Danner heard the band strike up as the audience broke into loud applause. That would be Kalin, arriving for his ringside seat.

Danner mingled with a group of performers lined up along the main runway leading into the arena. Precisely at 3:00 P.M., the curtain opened and the orchestra struck up a fast Russian folk tune. The miniskirted dancers pranced down the runway. Standing in the shadows along the side of the runway, Danner got a good look into the arena.

In the style of Soviet and European circuses, there was only a single ring, with the seats slanting steeply upward like a modern version of a Greek amphitheater. There were four runways leading into the ring, but the one in which Danner stood was the widest. The audience entered their seats from two higher levels near the top of the arena.

Danner scanned the crowd. Then he saw him: Yuri Kalin, grinning and gesturing to his blond daughter on his right, sat directly across from the main runway, in Row 1 of Section E. Two men in dark raincoats flanked the Soviet leader and his daughter, and two more plainclothes types occupied the seats directly behind them. Other than that, there appeared to be no security. Danner was amazed. In a similar setting, an American president would be protected by swarms of Secret Service agents, at least some of whom would be stationed backstage.

The dancing girls, who reminded Danner of something out of the Copacabana circa 1948, made their exit, and a whip-cracking animal trainer, a blond, bare-chested man, entered from the middle runway with a leopard act. At its climax, one of the leopards jumped up on a horse and rode it around the ring. The audience clapped rhythmically to show its approval.

Danner checked his watch: 3:10 P.M. He felt tense but calm. His timing would have to be perfect; there was no room for error. He touched the Taser in his pocket. A female aerialist in red tights was climbing up a rope to the very top of the domed ceiling as the house lights were dimmed. Cleverly placed spotlights formed six shadows of her body on the ceiling as she went through her routine. She worked without a net and it was a long way down.

The lights came back on, and the pace picked up. An elephant lumbered down the main runway, past Danner, and stood on one foot in the center of the ring. Two monkeys dressed as little girls cavorted into the arena, carrying a flowerpot between them on a yoke. Another monkey rode in circles on a pony, then suddenly dropped his pants, provoking squeals of laughter from both Kalin and the children in the audience.

The nearly naked lady with the python came out and performed a very sinuous, sexy dance in a single spotlight. She was followed by a tall, gangly young man who appeared with a suitcase full of trained cats. One of them navigated across a parallel bar while hanging upside down by its paws.

Then, with a great fanfare from the orchestra, the performing bears came tumbling in, dressed as musicians. With their trainer conducting, the bears began to play the accordion, cymbals, balalaika, and tambourine. Kalin led the rhythmic clapping again.

A bear on roller skates glided by Danner into the ring, followed by another on a bicycle. At the climax, two bears came roaring into the ring driving motorcycles. The lights were dimmed and the bears turned on the lights on their motorcycles, to the delight of the audience. Danner looked at his watch. It was 3:30, time for the clowns.

They made their entrance from the opposite side, in a yellow car with flowers painted all over it. The car came roaring into the arena, tooting its horn, and screeched to a stop in the center of the ring. Out tumbled about ten clowns, including two who climbed through the sun roof. The audience laughed and cheered.

Danner tried to pick Julie out of the melee. He couldn't at first, but then his heart leaped as he saw her, dressed in a Russian version of an American cowboy costume. She wore oversized shoes and carried a blunderbuss. The Soviets had mixed up the Wild West with the Pilgrims, Danner thought.

With an exaggerated gunslinger's strut, she flapped over to the bar that the prop men had set up in the ring and ordered a drink. The clown bartender, a young man with red freckles pasted on his face, poured her a beer in a huge glass in which the head rose up about a foot and overflowed.

Feigning anger, Julie pointed her blunderbuss at the bartender. He ducked behind the bar, emerging gingerly a moment later with a fireplace bellows that he used to blow the foam off the heroic-sized beer. Kalin and the rest of the audience howled at the gag.

A rival clown in a cowboy hat and spurs bellied up to the bar in macho style and drew his six-shooter. Julie shouted and pointed up to the ceiling. When the cowboy, distracted, looked up, she shot him with the blunderbuss. The blank cartridge in the gun made a loud bang and a cloud of smoke poured from the muzzle.

One by one the other clowns challenged Julie to a shootout, but she mowed each down in turn. Pudkov, the dwarf clown, was the last challenger left. As he approached the bar, twirling a six-shooter, Danner began moving down the runway into the arena.

Julie had dropped the blunderbuss and drawn the Tokarev from the holster on her belt. She was standing no more than thirty feet from Kalin, and there was no one in the line of sight.

Danner broke into a run, reaching for the Taser as he did. The dwarf was coming from Julie's right, but ignoring him, she turned slightly and took deliberate aim at Kalin. Danner, in a crouch, approaching at full tilt from Julie's left, fired the Taser.

Julie never saw him coming. The darts caught her in the thigh, and she fell hard, dropping the gun. Danner picked her up, carried her to the clown car, and put her in. Pudkov tried to stop him, but Danner kicked the dwarf, who fell over backwards howling. The audience, confused at first, started to laugh, thinking it was all part of the act. Out of the corner of his eye, Danner saw Kalin's bodyguards hustling him up the aisle toward the exits.

The orchestra struck up a brassy tune as Danner turned on the ignition. The car responded and shot forward out of the ring toward the main runway. No one tried to stop him. At the end of the runway, Danner turned right, heading toward the locked gate on the south side. He hit the gate at thirty miles an hour, and it flew open. Danner kept going along the driveway, straight into N. Kopernika Street. There was a black Volga waiting at the curb, engine running, just where it was supposed to be. Julie, unhurt but disoriented, was sitting up groggily as Danner brought the car to a sudden stop and tore off his mask.

She stared at him. "You?"

There was no time to reply. He jumped out of the car, grabbed her, and pulled her to her feet as half a dozen tough-looking acrobats and jugglers came running down the driveway after them. Julie got in the back seat of the Volga and Danner tumbled in beside her.

The driver, a thin-faced, dark-haired man of about thirty, turned and looked at Danner questioningly.

"Tell him there's been a change of plan," Danner said tersely. "I'm coming along for the ride."

Julie exchanged a few quick words in Russian with the KGB man, who shrugged and hit the gas pedal. Two of the acrobats were almost at the car as it began moving, and one of them, a dark, squat, and muscular man, managed to jump up on the hood. He started to pound on the windshield. Then he thought the better of it and rolled off unhurt as the car picked up speed.

The driver turned left, toward the university, and wheeled back onto Prospekt Vernadskogo, heading for the river.

"Why did you do it?" Julie demanded. "Valki wasn't just our operation. The president ordered it."

"Did Jordan say that?"

"Not directly. But they never would have sent me in otherwise."

Danner looked at her. "Your faith is charming. But it doesn't work that way." The car swerved to avoid a truck. "I had a lot of reasons. There's no time to explain them now." He was ripping off his clown costume.

"I have to change into my dress," Julie said. She took off her costume, stripping down to her bra and panties. The driver was eyeing her in his rear-view mirror.

"Tell him to watch the road," Danner snapped. "He'll rack us up."

Julie wriggled into her dress. "There," she said. "The floor show is over."

"We can't go to your hotel," Danner said.

"Why not? That's where he's supposed to take us. I turn back into a nun and get out tonight on an SAS flight."

"Not any more. The KGB is looking for you now. Pavlov will have to tell Kalin he has a dragnet out all over Moscow."

The driver was crossing the Metro Bridge at a fast clip, leaving the Lenin Hills behind. But instead of going straight ahead

on Komsomolskiy prospekt, he suddenly swerved left, into
Luzhniki. He pulled up on a deserted service lane near the Central Stadium.

Before Julie could question him, the driver slipped from behind the wheel and came around to the side of the Volga. He
held a Makarov 9mm automatic with a silencer on it and he was
pointing it through the closed window straight at Danner. With
a slight movement of the gun, he motioned them out of the car.

Danner opened the door fast, catching the driver in the groin
and knocking him off balance. He vaulted out of the car and
decked the man with a hard right to the jaw. The driver fell and
the gun went skittering along the pavement. The KGB man
wasn't moving.

Danner jumped in the driver's seat and Julie moved up beside
him. He took off swiftly, heading back to the boulevard. But
instead of staying on it, he turned right and crossed the river
again at the Andreyevskiy Bridge. "They won't expect us to
come this way," Danner said. "We'll take Leninskiy prospekt
and circle the city on the outer ring."

"The driver," Julie said after a moment. "He was outside
the whole time. He had no way of knowing I didn't shoot Kalin.
He was going to kill us."

"They never planned to let you out of Moscow alive," Danner said. "If you had succeeded, the KGB had to kill you. The
Soviets would never allow an assassination to go unpunished. It
might be seen as the supreme act of revolt against their system.
You were expendable, all along."

"And Jordan knew that?"

Danner shrugged. "I don't know. He could have guessed."

Julie brushed her hair back with her hands. Danner gave her a
handkerchief. "Better get off as much of your clown face as
you can."

She worked on the greasepaint while he maneuvered through
traffic to the outer ring that skirted Moscow to the east. "Where
are we heading?" she asked.

"To the Yaroslavsky Station. I have to pick up a package
there. And we'll get rid of the car."

From the ring, Danner swung right onto Krasnoprudnaya
Street and drove past a cluster of three railroad stations. Danner

pointed to the buildings. "That's the last glimpse of Moscow for the prisoners exiled to Siberia."

Julie shuddered. "Where do they send them?"

"To Sovetskaya Gavan', a transit prison in Primorskiy Kray, the Far Eastern Maritime Province. From there, some of them are shipped to Magadan, on the northern rim of the Sea of Okhotsk. It's totally remote. There are no roads, and no way to get out. A lot of them are put to work mining gold in the Kolyma Valley. So many intellectuals have been sent to Magadan that it's called the university of the north."

Julie looked at him. "And us. Are we going to get out?"

His eyes met hers. "I don't know. We're going to try."

He turned into a side street beyond the stations and parked. "It's best that we split up for a while," Danner said. "Start walking back toward the ring. I'll duck into the Yaroslavsky Station. I won't be long. I'll catch up with you around the Hotel Leningradskaya."

"All right." She touched his hand for a moment, then turned and began walking. He watched her go with a tenderness that seemed incongruous in the midst of their danger, but no less real. He waited a few minutes, then started in the same direction. The station was crowded, for which Danner was grateful. In his sweatshirt and dark pants, and without his thick glasses, he did not look at all like Richard Culver, the American businessman. There was a line at the checkroom. When he finally reached the counter, he fished in his pocket for the metal disc. The woman attendant took it, and after what seemed an interminable wait, came shuffling back with the flight bag containing his package.

A dark-haired man in a leather jacket and a snap-brim hat stood watching the line intently from about fifteen feet away, but made no move toward him. Danner assumed he was a plainsclothesman routinely assigned to the station. Trying to act naturally, Danner sauntered out the front exit and turned right.

He walked along Krasnoprudnaya as fast as he dared, between the Leningrad Station on his right and the Kazan Station on his left. He crossed the street and saw Julie walking slowly about a block past the hotel. He hurried to catch up with her.

She looked enormously relieved to see him. She slipped her

hand under his arm and fell into step, holding on tightly. "I thought something might have happened to you," she said.

"There was a line," he explained. "I'm okay." He looked around for a taxi, spotted one, and flagged it down. "The Kremlin," he told the driver. "The Troitskaya Gate."

Julie gave him a questioning look but said nothing. The driver was chattering away in Russian. Danner caught the word *"dzhinsy."*

"He wants to know if we have any blue jeans to sell," Julie explained.

"Tell him we're getting a big shipment next week," Danner said, "but we're sold out today."

They were at the Kremlin. Even Danner was struck by its size close up. The fortress of the czars was massive, a mile and a half around, with walls twenty feet thick and sixty-five feet high. He paid the driver off and they went across the bridge and through the gate.

"Troitskaya," Julie said. "This was the entrance Napoleon used."

"Let's hope we're luckier."

They walked straight ahead toward the yellow-and-white Council of Ministers Building, joining the flow of tourists. The armed militiamen kept the crowds on the sidewalk, across the wide, cobblestoned plaza from the government buildings. Danner looked at his watch as they moved along in the crush of visitors. "There's a British Airways flight out of Moscow two hours from now," he said quietly. "We're going to be on it."

"They'll be watching the airport," Julie said.

"I know. Trust me."

He led the way toward the river, past the Ivan the Great Belltower. A busload of Italian tourists had assembled on the steps of the Cathedral of the Annunciation. At the wooden doors the tour leader, a large woman with a brassy voice, was arguing in Italian with a Russian custodial official. The tour leader pointed to a string of about fifty paper tickets she was holding. *"Biglietti per tutti,"* she was saying, with a sweep of her hand toward her charges.

Finally the Russian, a woman in a blue smock with a wrinkled face, shrugged and opened the doors. The Italians surged forward, and Danner and Julie fell in with them. *"Andiamo,"* Danner said. *"Che bella chiesa."*

"Bellissima," Julie agreed.

They followed the tour group into the iconostasis. "The Blagoveshchensky Sobor," Julie whispered. "I remember visiting here as a child. We're in the private chapel of the czars."

One entire wall of the small chapel was filled with icons and murals, an astonishing overwhelming display of artistic riches. "The Cathedral of the Annunciation was built in the fifteenth century and destroyed in 1547 during the reign of Ivan the Terrible," the guide was saying in Italian. "The magnificent icons you see before you were painted by Theophanes the Greek, by Andrei Rublev, and by Prokhor of Gorodets. The floor on which you are standing is made of polished tiles of agate jasper."

Danner nodded to Julie and they slipped away from the group toward the back of the cathedral, where they found the restrooms. There was no one around. Danner discarded the flight bag, untied the parcel, and handed Julie some dark clothes and a white blouse. "Go inside and change," he said. "I'll be doing the same."

She emerged five minutes later in the blouse, navy blue skirt, and blazer of a British Airways flight attendant. She had tied a red, white, and blue silk scarf around her neck and wore a dark blue cloche with a downswept brim.

Danner was waiting for her, smiling broadly, in the dark blue, gold-braided uniform and crushed cap of a pilot.

"You look terrific," Julie said. "Who are we?"

"Stewardess Flora Begg, of Chippenham, Wiltshire," he said, "and Senior Captain Alan Fraser of Plaxtol, Kent." He handed her a British passport and a laminated ID card. Both contained her photograph in color, and her new name. The card had red stripes running diagonally across a white background and proclaimed in bold letters: "Flying Staff British Airways."

"Who did these?" she asked.

"Hadley arranged the passports through our liaison with MI six. The OTS Identification Section provided the cards. The uniforms were pouched in." He looked at his watch. "We're members of the crew of Flight number seven eleven, leaving Moscow for London two hours from now."

"What about the real crew?"

"They're expecting us. MI six has alerted them."

They left the cathedral together and turned right, past the Grand Kremlin Palace, once the home of the czars and now the meeting place for the Supreme Soviet. They walked along the river side of the Kremlin, heading for the Borovitsky Gate.

They were approaching the gate when Danner grabbed Julie's arm and said quietly, "We're going to turn toward the embankment, stop there a minute, and then stroll back the way we came." Julie saw them at the same instant, four men in civilian clothes who had blocked off the exit through the Borovitsky Tower. They were stopping people and asking to see their identity papers.

Danner pointed across the river as though he were explaining the sights of Moscow to Julie. Then they turned and headed back through Cathedral Square. They walked in a circle until they were close to the Troitskaya Gate, where they had entered. It was blocked as well.

"They've sealed off the Kremlin," Danner said. "We're trapped."

"We've got our passports and our British Airways IDs," Julie said. "We could try to get through."

Danner shook his head. "No. I don't like it. We wait."

They turned and walked back into the center of the Kremlin, where dozens of tourists were gathered around the huge Czar Cannon, taking photographs. They were mingling with the crowd, feigning interest in the cannon, when a woman with a Kodak camera approached.

"Pardon me, Captain," she said in an accent that immediately identified her as American. "Would you mind taking a picture of my husband and me standing in front of the cannon? I wanted to get one with both of us."

"Not at all," Danner said affably. "Just push this button here?" He glanced up at the man waiting expectantly by the cannon and froze. It was Eddie Swenson.

His old classmate did not recognize Danner underneath all the gold braid. His wife joined him. Beaming, they posed for the snapshot and thanked Danner, who smiled and strolled off with Julie.

The encounter had given him an idea. A large, cream-colored bus was parked nearby. Danner recognized it as the Moscow city tour, which left from behind his hotel.

The tour guide was nowhere to be seen. Danner and Julie got on and took seats near the rear. They waited, and in about ten minutes, other passengers began climbing aboard.

Among them were Fat Eddie and his wife, who, seeing the British Airways crew members, turned and waved from their seats near the front. When the bus was full, the tour guide and the driver climbed aboard. The guide, a middle-aged woman with a schoolteacher's manner, picked up her microphone as the bus started to roll.

"Moscow was founded in the year eleven forty-seven," she said in accented but good English. "The first walls of the Kremlin were built in eleven fifty-six, the present walls in fourteen ninety-two. The Ivan the Great Belltower on your right is the tallest in the Kremlin. The Czar Cannon, which some of you have been admiring, is the largest gun in the world. It was cast in bronze in fifteen eighty-six, is five point three four meters long, and weighs forty tons. The gun has never been fired."

The bus was easing toward the motor exit from the Kremlin at the Spasskaya Gate. Julie squeezed Danner's arm. A wooden barrier and armed, uniformed guards barred the way. To the side of the barrier, a black Chaika was parked with its motor running. One of the guards motioned the bus to stop.

While Danner and Julie watched, a short, stocky man in a dark suit got out of the limousine. "My God," Danner said in a low voice. "It's Pavlov."

The KGB chief boarded the bus, followed by a thin-faced younger man. Danner felt his hands grow cold. It was the driver. Julie recognized him at at the same instant.

"We've had it," Danner said.

Pavlov and the driver walked slowly down the aisle, scanning the faces of the passengers. They stopped when they came to Danner and Julie. Pavlov was smoking a *papirosy*.

Danner saw the younger man nod.

"I regret the delay," Pavlov said politely. "May I see your identity papers?" Up close, Danner could see the KGB chief had a muscular, powerful build. The thick features were impassive.

They handed over their British documents. Pavlov studied them for a moment. "Captain Fraser, Miss Begg, would you be so kind as to step outside?"

There was nothing to do but obey. They were caught. Pavlov would not shoot them on the bus. Danner wondered if the basement cells of Lubianka would be next. He shuddered at the prospect.

Pavlov dismissed his aide and walked with them, away from the bus. The armed guards were close by, watching carefully. "Mr. Danner," he said, "I have several options. The most attractive would be to have you and Miss Nichols executed." Their breath was visible in the intense cold. Danner waited for Pavlov to continue.

"But," the KGB chief said, "the usual procedure would be to interrogate you first." He took a drag on his *papirosy* and smiled. "If so, what you say might be inconvenient for me."

Julie nodded but said nothing.

"I will therefore exercise my second option, and let you go." He handed them back their passports and identity cards. "I should warn you, however, that my generosity does not extend to my troops. Their orders are to find you. I cannot change those orders. You are, in short, on your own."

"The driver," Danner said.

"You should have killed him, Mr. Danner. Now we will have to remedy your oversight."

Pavlov escorted them back to the door of the bus. "I apologize for the inconvenience," he said. "Goodbye, Captain Fraser," he called out as they got aboard. "And Miss Begg. Have a safe journey home."

Danner and Julie edged back down the aisle to their seats. The soldiers pulled aside the barrier, and the bus started up through the gate. As it rolled into Red Square, Eddie Swenson turned to his wife.

"Did you hear that?" he asked excitedly.

"Hear what, dear?"

"That guy. The airline guy who took our picture. The Russian called him Captain Fraser. I recognize him now. He was at the restaurant last night. And he said his name was Culver. But I know him! His real name is Danner, I swear to you."

Eddie Swenson's wife smiled indulgently. "You've been seeing too many spy movies, dear."

Danner and Julie left the bus at its next stop, across the river from the Kremlin. Everyone got off. While the tour guide was busy pointing out the cathedrals and buildings on the embankment opposite, Danner and Julie drifted away and rounded the corner.

Julie leaned up against the wall of a building to recover. "I thought it was all over," she said.

"So did I." He glanced at his watch. "We've got some time to kill. We don't want to wait around the airport. It will be crawling with security." He flagged down a taxi and they got in.

"Dzerzhinsky Square," he told the driver.

"You must be crazy," she said to him quietly, so the driver could not hear. "That's KGB headquarters."

"It's the last place Pavlov's people will look for us," Danner said. "Under their noses."

She shook her head. "I hope you're right."

They got out at the corner of Prospekt Marxa and Dzerzhinsky Square, by a little flower stall. On the opposite side of the square stood KGB headquarters and Lubianka Prison, two seven-story buildings joined by a common facade. The bottom two stories of each of the buildings were gray, the top five stories orange. Danner pointed across the square to a modern gray structure. "That's the KGB's new building," he said. "They're expanding."

"It's still early to start for the airport," he added. "Come on." He led her downstairs through the underpass to Detsky Mir, Moscow's biggest toy store. They came up by the front entrance and were immediately caught in a crush of determined shoppers.

They let the crowd carry them along, then spun off to the right toward the doll counter. There were hundreds of dolls sitting on the shelves behind the long counter, but most of them looked alike. Even so, the customers, mainly women, were lined up three deep.

They pushed their way through the milling crowds on the

ground floor for a while, looking at toys and stuffed animals, and then Danner pointed to his watch. They battled their way out to the street again.

Danner hailed a cab on Prospekt Marxa. "Sheremetyevo," he told the driver.

He was a stocky, blond young man who lapsed into sullen silence when Danner made it clear they did not want to buy any caviar or rubles. It had started to rain, and Danner worried about the time. The wet roads would slow the traffic to the airport.

"As members of the flight crew," Julie asked quietly, "do we go through a special entrance at the airport?"

"No. We go through regular customs, passport control, and security. In the West, flight crews go to a special customs counter and a badge is enough to get them in and out of most airports. But here, you have to go through the whole drill like any other passenger."

"But we have no visas," Julie said. "They'll know something's wrong."

Danner shook his head. "No. It's the one concession they make. The flight crews have permanent visas on file, since they go in and out so often. We'll just have to show our passports and the ID cards."

"Suppose they check the visa file. They'll realize we don't exist."

Danner smiled. "But we do. Flora Begg and Alan Fraser are real employees of British Airways. They sometimes fly the Moscow run. Their visas are on file with the Soviets."

"The photographs on the visas," Julie said. "They won't match ours."

"That could be a problem," Danner admitted. "But the names of Begg and Fraser were chosen because they're approximately the same physical types as we are. In our uniforms, we should pass muster. Besides, they don't often check the visa file. Usually you just show your passport and flash the plastic."

They were at the airport. Danner paid the driver and they walked into the terminal. Three men stood just inside the door, looking over the arriving passengers. Two wore dark blue raincoats and the third had on a heavy gray overcoat. All three wore snap-brim hats that were too small for them.

"KGB," Danner said when they were out of earshot. "You can always spot them by the dark coats and the tight fedoras that sit up on top of their heads."

They walked through the long terminal on the slippery marble floor, past the Intourist desk, the information desk, and a flight of stairs that led up to a bar and restaurant. "Just keep smiling," Danner said, out of the corner of his mouth. "You're a stewardess."

"Flight attendant," she insisted. "Stewardess is sexist."

"The British still say stewardess. Don't blow it now by using the wrong title."

"All right," she whispered. "Stewardess. But why aren't *you* smiling? Pilots smile, too."

"No, they don't. They look macho, and serious. Like Marlboro man."

"Pilots *smile*," she hissed.

They were approaching the customs barrier and the restricted area. There was an opening at the center of the barrier, and they fell in behind a group of passengers. On either side of the opening, more plainclothesmen were scanning the faces of the departing travelers. Danner prayed they would not look too hard at the British Airways pilot and the smiling stewardess.

They showed their passports and cards and got through the first barrier. Their documents were examined briefly by the customs officials sitting behind the bank of yellow Phillips X-ray machines. A severe-looking woman behind the counter asked, "Do you have anything to declare, Captain Fraser?"

Mustering his best British accent, Danner replied, "No. We just did a bit of window shopping this time, I'm afraid."

"I tried to get him to buy me an absolutely super mink hat," Julie said, smiling and taking his arm, "but he wouldn't."

"Very well," the woman said without cracking a smile, "you may pass through."

The real test still lay ahead, Danner knew. Passport control. Passengers were checking their bags onto a conveyor belt. Danner and Julie walked past the baggage counter and turned right toward the glass booth. "There's an overhead mirror," Danner warned. "They'll be watching your hands. Try not to show any nervousness."

Julie took a deep breath. There were two more men in dark

coats and small hats standing near passport control. Danner went first. The uniformed border guards behind the glass looked even younger than the ones who had checked his passport on the way in four days before.

The guard on the right examined the passport carefully and studied Danner's face, comparing it to the picture. Then he handed the passport to his companion, who went through the identical process. The ID card received the same scrutiny. After about five minutes, both documents were returned through the little opening at the bottom of the glass. Danner was motioned along, but he hung back to stay near Julie.

She shoved her passport and card through the window. The young militiaman inspected the passport, turned to the color photograph, and eyed Julie. He handed it to the other guard, who looked slightly older and equally grim. He studied the photograph and Julie's face.

"Get the visa file, Sergei," Julie heard him say in Russian to his companion.

The younger guard swiveled in his chair and dug through a stack of papers behind him. "Why are they taking special precautions today?" he grumbled. "It makes more work for us, that's all."

The older guard shrugged. *"Ya ne znayu,"* he said. "I don't know. I heard there was some trouble at the *novyi cirk*. They are looking for a girl."

"Who knows? Maybe it's this one."

"If you catch her, Sergei, maybe they will give you a medal."

The younger guard shot a glance at his companion and said quietly, "Better they should give me a transfer back to Krasnoyarsk. Then I could see my family again. Here it is," he said, removing a paper from the stack. "Flora Begg. Age twenty-eight, British subject, stewardess authorized to work Flight seven eleven."

"Her height, age, and hair color are about right," the older guard said. *"Devochka nichevo.* She's not bad, Sergei. Would you like to get her in bed, eh?"

Sergei studied the visa photograph and compared it to the passport picture, looked at Julie, and back again at the visa.

"She doesn't look the same," he said doubtfully. "Her hair is longer in the visa picture."

Julie, pretending she understood nothing but that she had guessed the drift of the conversation, ran her fingers through her hair and smiled at the younger guard. "I've had it cut, love, since that was taken."

Danner looked at his watch. "They're taking a bloody long time tonight aren't they? We're going to be late taking off."

The young guard contemplated Julie for another minute while Danner said a silent prayer. Then the guard slowly closed the passport and pushed it and the card back through the window. Julie, breathing easier, gathered them up.

They walked toward the gate. "What was all that about?" Danner asked.

"There are extra security precautions today. That's why he checked the visa file." She smiled, keeping up the front. "And they're looking for me."

They came to another barrier, a door frame that was a metal detector. They walked through without setting off the buzzer. But a guard with a powerful hand-held detector frisked their entire bodies. Around Danner's right pants pocket, he got some beeps.

Danner dug in and came up with some coins. The guard confiscated them. "No rubles may leave the country," he said.

At the gate, the final barrier, passengers were showing their boarding passes. Danner and Julie flashed their British Airways cards. An armed militiaman was watching them.

They walked up the closed ramp into the plane, a Boeing seven thirty-seven. The senior steward, a thin blond man, greeted them with a smile. "Captain Fraser, Miss Begg, good to have you aboard." They took seats near the rear of the cabin.

There were a few Russian passengers aboard the plane, so Julie and Danner said very little to each other. Danner stared out the window at the huge red letters atop the terminal, watching the rain coming down on the tarmac. Julie closed her eyes and put her head back.

In a few moments the jet surged down the runway and they were airborne. Julie reached over, took his hand, and smiled. "Thank God," she said.

"Don't celebrate yet. Until we're out of Soviet airspace, the plane can be recalled."

A shadow of alarm crossed her face. "How long will that be?"

"Well, it's almost sixteen hundred miles to London and the flight takes a little over four hours." He took the route map from the seat pocket in front of him and studied it. "I'd say more than a third of the trip is over Soviet territory. So, about an hour and a half."

"I think I need a drink."

"So do I."

Danner buzzed for the steward. He asked for a Scotch and Julie ordered a gin and tonic.

The steward hesitated. "Since you're both off-duty," he said with a smile. He brought the drinks back.

Danner drummed his fingers on the arm of his seat and looked out into the blackness. "Cheer up," Julie said. "We're going to make it."

"Viktor S. Chudin will be annoyed."

"Who's he?"

An official of the Ministry of Light Industry. I have an appointment with him at eleven tomorrow." He touched his glass to her. "It looks like I won't be able to keep it."

Julie laughed. "To missing your appointment." She raised her glass.

They were both beginning to unwind when the captain came back and stood in the aisle by their seats. His expression was grave.

"Captain Fraser, Miss Begg, I'm very sorry to have to tell you this. But the Soviets have recalled Flight number seven eleven to Moscow."

The younger passport guard, Danner thought. He had finally put it together and notified the tower.

"What are you going to do?" Julie asked quietly.

"Well, the rules require us to turn around and fly directly back to Sheremetyevo. We don't want to jeopardize our landing rights. And, of course, if we refuse they could scramble their MiGs and try to force us to go back."

"Where are we?" Danner asked.

"Over Latvia. We're well past Riga, but still about thirty

miles inside Soviet territory.'' The pilot glanced at his watch. ''Our airspeed is five hundred sixty miles per hour, or more than nine miles a minute. Even as we talk, we're getting closer to the border. Technically, we should turn back. But if we never received the message—well, that's another story then, isn't it?''

Julie smiled. ''Thank you, Captain,'' she said. ''Thank you very much.''

Danner looked through the window of the cabin. There was a break in the clouds and a bright moon shining on the water far below them. The gods had been kind. They were over the Baltic Sea.

CHAPTER
THIRTY-TWO

By the flickering firelight, Brooks Jordan's face was half visible, half obscured in shadow. He sat in his chair by the hearth, sipping his brandy occasionally, listening, but saying little.

Danner had insisted on meeting the director at his house in Spring Valley, in a setting where Jordan would draw no advantage from the trappings of office. Outside, the winter night was cold and crisp and the capital was covered with fresh snow.

"You should not have meddled," Jordan said finally. "The president ordered the operation."

Danner rattled the ice cubes around in his drink. "I doubt you can prove that," he said.

"He didn't put it in writing, if that's what you mean." Jordan got up, took a poker, and pushed the front log closer to the one behind it. "They never do."

"Targeting Kalin was too damn dangerous. You put the world at risk."

Jordan's eyebrows arched. "Kalin alive may be the greater risk."

"Maybe. But up to now, the superpowers have stopped short of killing each other's leaders."

"We haven't had to face the same situation up to now. Kalin is unstable. His finger's on the button. According to Quimby—"

Danner cut him off. "Bullshit. I don't think that's why you did it at all. I think you cut a deal with Pavlov."

Jordan sighed. "Perhaps if you sat in my chair, you might

have a different perspective. Like so many people, you long for an orderly world. It isn't like that. The world is an uncivilized place.''

''Yes, but our only chance for survival is to pretend it's civilized,'' Danner said. ''There have to be limits. Rules of the game. Even for the agency.''

''Of course there have to be rules,'' Jordan replied. ''But the normal rules don't apply to us. That's why we were set up. We were created to break the rules.''

''Not when millions of lives are at stake. Valki could have triggered a nuclear war.''

The director shrugged. ''It doesn't matter now. It's over.''

''I want to be sure of that. The terms I offered you at our last meeting still stand: my silence for my daughter. But I want Carrie back safely within forty-eight hours. No delays, no excuses.''

''I don't know whether the Soviets will return your daughter now. Pavlov may be rather cross with you.''

''Forty-eight hours,'' Danner repeated. ''Tell him.''

Jordan stared into the fire. ''And if I fail?''

''Either Carrie is freed or I go public with the whole fucking story. The old boys, the tapes, Wellington Lloyd, the Moscow Circus. Everything.''

Jordan coughed slightly. ''I wouldn't do that.''

''There's something more. I want your personal guarantee that there will be no more trading secrets with the KGB. I'm ready to talk to the Senate Intelligence Committee and the television networks. If I do, you and Pavlov will both be finished. He'll be shot. You may end up in prison.''

The director glowered at him, his face contorted with anger in the firelight.

''And in case you should get any other ideas, I have the tape with your voice on it, and the full text of Operation Valki on a floppy disc. Both in a safe place. They'll be made public if anything happens to me.''

Jordan seemed to sag into his chair. He ran his fingers through his snow white hair in an uncharacteristic, nervous gesture. ''All right,'' he said in a hoarse whisper. ''I agree.''

Danner arose. ''The game will go on,'' he said. ''But by the old rules. The old rules were safer.''

Jordan didn't reply. He stared into the flames. Then, in a sudden movement, he hurled his brandy snifter into the fireplace, shattering the crystal into a thousand tiny fragments.

Twelve hours later, the telephone rang in Danner's apartment. He groped for the receiver by the bedside.

The voice was heavily accented. Slavic, Danner guessed. "You must go to California today," the man said. "Be on the beach at Carpinteria at sunset. At precisely that time, begin walking south. Come alone."

This was it. Danner called United and was able to get a seat on the midday flight to Los Angeles. He peeled off his pajamas and stepped in the shower. He let it run cold to jolt himself awake.

He put on his terry cloth robe, made some toast and coffee, and ate quickly. Still in his robe, he packed an overnight bag with a couple of shirts, a travel kit, and an extra suit.

He thought of calling Francesca, but there was no point in getting her hopes up. And the voice had said come alone. He didn't want his ex-wife, Detective Radley Walker, and the Santa Barbara *News-Press* showing up on the beach.

He dialed Sam Green and caught him before he left for the agency.

"Sam? Bill. Take a walk at ten o'clock. I'll meet you by the north parking lot."

"Hey. Real spy stuff. Okay."

Sam was waiting for him, bundled up against the cold, when Danner drove into the north lot a few minutes after ten. He parked and got out. They tramped through the snow together over what, in the summertime, was a lawn.

"I don't have a lot of time to explain," Danner said. "I'm on my way to the airport. I want you to have this key. If anything happens to me, call Andy, my head guide. He'll tell you the number of a safe deposit box, and the name of the bank. There are certain materials in there. See that they get to the Senate Intelligence Committee."

"Jesus," Sam said.

Danner handed him the key. "Hang onto it, old buddy."

"Take care of yourself," Sam replied. "I'd rather not have to use it."

They walked back to the car in silence and Danner got behind the wheel. With a wave to Sam, he drove out the gate and across the barren winter landscape to Dulles.

He checked in, got his boarding pass, and found a window seat near the rear of the jet. He was too keyed up to read and passed most of the time half-watching the movie. The flight landed on time. LAX was crowded as usual, and it was after 3:00 P.M. by the time he had rented a car. He drove north up the coast on Route 1.

The traffic thinned out a bit after he passed Malibu. There were patches of fog on the coastal highway, but in between, the view of the Pacific from the craggy cliffs was spectacular. He pushed on beyond Point Mugu, took the Rice Avenue cutoff to avoid Oxnard, and barreled along past the cabbage fields on Highway 101.

Soon he was in Ventura, where the road ran along the ocean again. The fog had dissipated now and he could see the channel islands. He glanced at his watch. He would be in plenty of time.

At Carpinteria, he swung onto the Casitas Pass exit and zigzagged slowly through the quiet back streets toward the water. He didn't want to be early. A little before 5:00 P.M., he pulled into the parking lot behind the beach.

It was deserted, and getting chilly. The wide, white sand beach stretched for almost a mile to the south. Off to his left, a road paralleling the beach led into the campgrounds. The sun was low over the Pacific and the seagulls were wheeling close to the waves, looking for supper.

He got out and walked over the dune. He stopped for a moment at the gnarled eucalpytus, with its astonishingly thick branches, that had been Carrie's favorite climbing tree. He touched the trunk and was surprised to find tears welling up in his eyes.

He caught himself and shook off his emotions. It was not the time for that. He could be walking into a trap, he knew. The KGB might take its revenge, even here on a California beach at sunset. For that matter, Brooks Jordan had ample reason to want him out of the way.

The sky was pink but already there were dark shadows on the dunes as the sun slipped into the water. He looked out toward

the islands and wondered if they would be bringing her by boat.
At 5:05 P.M., he began walking south along the deserted beach.
There was no one in sight; only the sounds of the wind and the
gentle surf lapping against the shore broke the stillness.

Suddenly, the harsh report of a car engine starting up echoed
across the dunes. To his left, along the treeline, he could see a
camper moving slowly down the road until it went beyond him
and disappeared from view.

He walked for perhaps ten minutes in the fading light, working his way steadily south along the shore. It was then that he
saw a tiny speck moving along the beach toward him. In the
half light he could not tell whether it was a child or an adult.

He broke into a run and realized in a moment that it was a
child. His child. Carrie.

She saw him now and they were running toward each other,
both laughing and crying, and then she was in his arms and they
were hugging each other, the tears streaming down their faces.

"Carrie," he said softly, over and over again. "Carrie, darling. Are you all right?"

She didn't speak, but she was clinging to him, holding on
tight. "Yes," she said at last. "I'm all right. They didn't hurt
me. Oh, Daddy."

Gently, he brushed her tears away with his hand. "Thank
God," he said. "Thank God."

She looked up at him and smiled. "I want a chocolate
milkshake."

"Ten. Well, not all at once. One to start." He was laughing
through his tears.

"And a double cheeseburger. With everything."

"Deal."

They began walking back up the beach toward the car.
"Who were they?" she asked. "Why did they do it?"

"I'll try to explain. Not now. There'll be time, later."

"Is Mom all right?"

"Yes, she's fine."

"And Mr. O'Malley?"

"He's great. Andy's taking good care of him."

They walked on and he reached into his pocket and took
something out of an envelope. It was brittle and dried out, and
he kneeled down at the edge of the sea to wet it in the salt water.

"What's that?" Carrie asked.

He answered by reaching over and gently putting the maple bud on her nose. She laughed, remembering. "I know now. That day on the river. You said it would bring you luck."

He put his arm around her shoulder and drew her close. "It did."

CHAPTER
THIRTY-THREE

Francesca was so happy to have Carrie back that she did not cross-examine or blame Danner. Her daughter was safe, and home again; for the moment that was all that mattered.

Danner took care of telephoning Detective Walker. "She's back," he told him. "Turned out the whole time she was staying with her aunt in Milwaukee."

"It's usually that way, sir," Walker said. "Like I tried to tell you. But I'm glad everything turned out okay."

"So are we. Thanks for all your help."

Danner checked into a motel on Cabrillo and spent several days in Santa Barbara visiting Carrie. The doctors said she had come through her ordeal remarkably well. Aside from some loss of weight—Carrie complained that her captors fed her a boring diet of soups and bologna sandwiches—they found no physical damage. But Carrie was having some trouble sleeping at night, and occasional anxiety. The psychologist who talked with her warned Danner and Francesca that it might be many months before the effects of her experience could be fully evaluated.

Danner tried to make their time together as relaxed and pleasant as possible, free of any pressures. They visited familiar places. They went horseback riding and hiking together in the Santa Ynez. He took her to the 1129 Restaurant on State Street, and they sat out in the garden under the palm trees and ate shrimp and avocado salads.

For dessert they went to Baskin-Robbins in Coast Village and bought chocolate milkshakes. They drove down to Butterfly Beach and sat on the rocks drinking the shakes and looking out at the islands.

Carrie pointed to her left, down the beach. "Do you remember the big pine tree that used to be right there against the dune? It was really good for climbing. It had huge branches, and on the hot days in the summer the dogs used to love to sit under it because it had so much shade."

"I remember." Danner said. "What happened to it?"

"A couple of years ago there was this storm, and it tore the roots out. The tree fell over and died. I really miss it. The dogs do, too."

"You miss a lot of things when they're gone."

Carrie was silent for a moment. A shadow crossed her face. "The people who kidnapped me, why did they do it? For money?"

"No. They were Russians. They wanted to stop me from doing something.

"Did they?"

"No. But I tried to work things out so they would let you go."

Carrie had reached the bottom of the milkshake. She was sucking on the straw and making a slurping noise to get the last bit. "That was so excellent," she said. They got up and tossed the cups in a trash barrel on the beach.

Suddenly she tapped Danner on the shoulder. "Tag. You're it!" And she was gone, racing down the beach. Danner sprinted after her and finally caught up. He was breathing hard, and they were both laughing.

They collapsed on the beach to catch their breath. Carrie became serious. She picked up a fistful of sand and let it stream slowly between her fingers. "Are you through being a spy again?"

"Yes."

"What will you do now?"

Danner had been thinking about that during their days together in the hills. "Go home, I guess. Go back to the river."

She smiled. "I'll come and see you and Mr. O'Malley in

June, like always. We'll go fishing and *this* time, you better not go away.''

Danner gave her a hug. ''I promise.''

The huge red, blue, and black Calder mobile was slowly rotating over their heads in the light and airy East Wing of the National Gallery. The sun was streaming through the glass walls and the skylight. They stood at the balcony railing, looking up at the Calder.

''He was only in this room once,'' Julie said. ''To measure the space. He died before they installed it.''

Danner nodded. ''People think it's powered by a motor. But it isn't. It's perfectly balanced, and the movement of the air is what makes it turn. They say at night when a guard walks by, it will start up.''

They stayed there together for a long time, watching the bright shapes turn in the sunlight. Then they walked up the steps to the Terrace Café overlooking the Mall and got a window table. They each ordered a glass of white wine.

When the waiter had gone, Julie said, ''You're sure, then? You're leaving.''

Danner shrugged. ''My work is over.''

''I'll miss you.''

He hesitated. ''I've been thinking,'' he said.

''About what?''

''Everything. While I was untangling the whole mess at the agency, I found out some things about myself.''

''Such as?''

''I've begun to care about life again. And about you. I've discovered a lot of feelings I didn't know I had.''

''So maybe it was for the best that you came back to Langley for a while.''

The waitress put their drinks on the table. Danner took a sip of his wine. ''I don't know. I've led a very warped existence. Almost twenty years in the agency is bound to make you different from other people. It's so far removed from ordinary experience, how could it be otherwise?''

''I guess it can't. It's part of what happens to us.''

''When I quit in seventy-seven, I realize now I was running

away from life. Hiding in the woods." He smiled at her. "It doesn't work."

"You've changed. You really have."

"Yes." He touched her hand. "Julie. Will you come with me?"

They looked at each other, and he could see tears in her green eyes. And love. She shook her head. "Don't ask me to choose," she said. "Please."

"I am asking."

She looked out at the snow on the Mall for a long moment before she answered. "I belong here," she said.

"I know I'm a lot older."

"It isn't that. My work is here. I want to continue my career. At the agency."

"Even though we love each other?"

She nodded. There were tears in her eyes again.

They were silent. "All right," he said. "Thanks for the dance."

She tried to smile through her tears. "Thanks for coming to the party."

Andy was waiting at the airport in Fredericton. The guide broke into a big grin when he spotted him getting off the Air Canada flight. "Welcome back, Mr. Danner."

"Good to be back," Danner said. He shook the guide's callused hand. They drove north through the snow-covered countryside in Andy's beat-up Chevrolet. The guide didn't say much; it was not his way.

Danner got his first look at the river at Boiestown. It was frozen solid, but in another eight weeks the ice would start to melt. And far upstream, in the cold waters of the spawning grounds, the first salmon would begin to hatch. He was glad to be home.

They drove through Doaktown and Blissfield, crossed the river at Blackville, and swung south on Route 118 to camp. He got a hug from Mrs. Anderson, the cook and one from Johnny who was beside himself at seeing Danner again. They sat around the kitchen table and broke out a bottle of Scotch. Just as Danner raised his glass to toast them all, Mr. O'Malley jumped up on his lap. The cat seemed to know him, and rubbed the side of his face against Danner's hand. He'd have to send a full report to Carrie.

"There's salmon in the salt barrel," Mrs. Anderson said. "I'll grill some for you tonight, if you'd like."

"I would," Danner replied. "And I'd like everyone to stay for dinner, if you can." They did, and afterwards, by a roaring fire in the living room, they brought him up to date on the gossip and happenings along the river.

There was a lot of work to do to get the camp ready for the first guests in the spring; and in the weeks that followed, Danner and the guides were kept busy. More snow came and once the temperature dipped to 30 below. But Danner enjoyed getting outdoors, and he threw himself into his work. He tried not to think much about Julie.

In April, spring came to the Miramichi, and life changed. Geese were honking overhead each day, returning home from their winter journeys. The sun warmed the river and the ice finally broke with a great roar. Pale green leaves appeared on the white pine, the maples, and the poplars. The bank beavers were busy, and there were deer, rabbits, and bear in the woods. And when the ice had cleared, at night Danner could hear the shad splashing and jumping their way upriver.

The young alevin were almost ready to hatch now, and in mid-April the season would open for the early fish, the dark salmon that had spent the winter under the ice and were on their way back to sea. Then, in May, the Atlantic salmon would begin their run, entering the river near Chatham. The fiddleheads would bloom along the riverbanks, and Cookie would boil them for the salmon dinners. The gorbys would chatter by day, and the whippoorwills would own the night. And Danner would get out on the river again.

On a morning late in April, he arose early to fish the home pool. It was a clear, sunny day. Winter was finally gone, and there was the smell of spring in the light breeze from the northwest. He was wearing his waders, standing near shore and casting with a white Butterfly, when he heard the drone of an airplane in the distance.

He looked up and was surprised to see it was a seaplane, following the river from the south. The aircraft turned, headed into the wind, and landed in front of the camp. It taxied over toward Danner. He wondered if it was a guest. They sometimes arrived by air but he was not expecting anyone for two more days.

The plane was only thirty feet away now, and the pilot cut the engines. An attractive woman dressed in blue jeans and a bright red sweater stepped out on the pontoon.

"Mr. Danner," she called.

"Miss Nichols?"

"I was wondering if you could use an extra hand at your fishing camp?"

Danner looked doubtful. "What kind of experience do you have?"

"Well, I used to work for the government. But I quit. There was someone I missed too much."

The seaplane was drifting close to shore. Julie was only a few feet away now. She was smiling broadly.

"If you quit your job," Danner asked, "what are you doing now?"

"Now much," she confessed. "I guess you could say I'm an unemployed clown."

Danner thought about that for a moment. "Well," he said finally, "in a way, so am I. I guess I'll take a chance."

He waded over and lifted her off the pontoon. And then, carrying her in his arms, he came ashore.

THE #1 THRILLER OF THE YEAR!

THE DELPHI BETRAYAL

LEWIS PERDUE

From the depths of a small, windowless room in the bowels of the White House...orchestrated by the finest minds and most powerful political forces of our time...spearheaded by a vast consortium of the world's richest multinational corporations—an awesome conspiracy that would create economic chaos and bring the entire universe to its knees.

A riveting international thriller
in the tradition of Robert Ludlum and Ken Follett.

☐ 41-728-4 **THE DELPHI BETRAYAL** $2.95